It's All Academic
David Fleming

iUniverse, Inc.
New York   Bloomington

It's All Academic

Copyright © 2010 David Fleming

iUniverse books may be ordered through booksellers or by contacting:

iUniverse
1663 Liberty Drive
Bloomington, IN 47403
www.iuniverse.com
1-800-Authors (1-800-288-4677)

ISBN: 978-1-4502-5695-7 (pbk)
ISBN: 978-1-4502-5696-4 (cloth)
ISBN: 978-1-4502-5697-1 (ebk)

Printed in the United States of America

Library of Congress Control Number: 2010913491

iUniverse rev. date: 9/22/2010

Contents

Part One: Orientation

Chapter One

Michael Hartley's dead body turned up at the same time I turned up for my first day at Boan University. I, of course, didn't know that at the time, but only found out when Bil Berninski interrupted the President's Cabinet meeting later that morning. Little did I know at the time how the specter of Hartley would haunt my tenure at Boan.

I barely had time to dump my box of personal belongings: my Duquesne and Ohio State diplomas, my recognition rewards from Farrington College, my pictures of Natalie and Alyssa, all the various knick-knacks gathered through the years that had made my office at Farrington resemble some over-stocked stall at any number of craft and antique malls across the country. I had told Natalie that my office at Boan would not end up that way, but in the month leading up to my first day, the box had not been cleaned out before I dropped it off at my office in the Boan Administration Building.

I dumped the box on the corner of my massive mahogany desk at 7:15 AM, and pulled from the top one item: a trio of pictures of my family connected in one large frame. In one picture from the previous spring, Natalie and Alyssa are hugging each other under the crabapple tree at our old property. The tree's amazing pink colors frame their beauty wonderfully. Next to that, there is a picture of the two of them sitting on a blanket by the fire pit behind our current house. The night sky behind them is similar to the pink of the crabapple tree. Natalie is laughing at something Alyssa has said, while Alyssa's own expression is of one deep in thought. And, then, in the third picture, Alyssa is playfully smacking her mother with a stuffed Boan Sturgeon. You can read on the stuffed fish, "You can come to Boan, You can graduate from Boan, but you're Boan Forever." Natalie thought it tacky when I brought the stuffed sturgeon home for Alyssa after my interviews, but I was enamored by it. The trio of pictures was set on the desk's best vantage point: "The past, the present and the future," I whispered to myself, grabbing my notebook and pen.

I dashed across campus to Butler Hall, where President's Cabinet was to begin promptly at 7:30. Earlier that morning, kissing Natalie good morning, I had told her that the 7:30 Monday morning Cabinet meetings would kill me.

"What's the big deal?" Natalie asked while peeling and sectioning grapefruit. "You almost always get to the office before 8:00."

I was fidgeting with my tie, bothered by the length. No matter how many times I had worn ties during the fifteen years of my professional life, I still often left too much dangling. It was one of those little things that could drive me crazy. "That first half hour, though, is my time. I like sorting through the weekend e-mails, prioritizing my tasks for the day, skimming the *Chronicle's* headlines."

"Uh-huh." Natalie was paying more attention to breakfast than to my answer.

"What is the President's Cabinet, Daddy?" Alyssa was reading a book, twirling her long black hair with her fingers, at the breakfast table. No matter how many times we told her not to read at the breakfast table, she still did. I was a bit of a hypocrite to chastise her for reading at the table. I did the same thing growing up. My daughter had definitely inherited from me a lot more than dark brown eyes, a crooked nose, and a tendency to walk pigeon-toed.

"It's when the president's direct reports meet to discuss high level decisions for the university."

"Uh-huh." A book dominated my daughter's attention. It was hard to criticize her there.

Truth be told, anxiety gripped my stomach. Unwilling to admit it openly to my family, I worried that I had ascended to a provost position too quickly. Advancement had been easy at Farrington, where the culture evolved alongside of me. However, Boan represented new territory. I had spent two and a half packed days of interviews with Boan leadership. Boan's president, Bob Berrian, was an intense man known for pushing his people hard, but rewarding them when they succeeded. In contrast, Farrington's provost, Neil Jensen, was laid back, who, while enjoyable to work for, could have provided me greater direction and acknowledgement. As a result, I approached my first day at Boan feeling a combination of excitement and intimidation. Would my instincts guide me through the unexpected? I would hopefully find out soon enough, getting my trial by fire at a President's Cabinet meeting.

Walking the short distance to Butler Hall, I wondered what would be on the agenda. During the interviews a number of interesting strategic ideas had emerged: expanding the College of Arts and Sciences; starting a football program; instituting a professor emeritus program; developing partnerships with regional high schools; increasing scholarships. The last few weeks, in the transition between Farrington dean and Boan provost, I bounced back and forth between surges of excitement and deep feelings of dread regarding my potential success.

I bounded up the stone steps of Butler Hall and through the heavy wooden doors, instantly reminded of a church entrance. In the hallway, Hank Turing, the CFO, tried to balance a cup of coffee, bagel, knife and container of cream cheese. "Hey, Hank, can I help you?"

"Oh, hey, Mark. Welcome. Helluva way to start a job, eh, with a five-hour cabinet meeting?" He continued to try to balance his breakfast. Had he not heard my offer, or was he simply ignoring it?

"Five hours! You're kidding me, right?" My right hand went out to support the dangling cream cheese container, but Hank remained oblivious to my attempt to help.

"No. The intent is to work hard to 12:00, then do lunch together and discuss more topics informally." Hank moved toward the door of the meeting room, and I had no idea how he planned to pull the door open as he balanced his breakfast and his notebook crammed full of papers. His full head of dark, black hair was blown across his head, giving him a little boy look.

"Hmm. Wish someone had told me this at the interviews. It might have changed my decision. Here, let me help with that door." As with Butler's outer doors, the inner doors were heavy oak.

Hank chortled and tried to pull the door handle with his pinky finger. I simply jumped in front of him and grabbed the door. "Uh, thanks," Hank muttered as he walked into the room.

So far, no one else had arrived. Three tables had been moved to form a U-shape in the center of the room. There was little else, a chalkboard, tables shoved to the side, and no windows. Gazing around the barren room, I realized I needed to find coffee.

"Is there no coffee brought to this meeting?"

"Usually." Hank didn't offer explanation as to why he had brought his own coffee.

"So, where did you get your coffee and bagel?"

"Back at the commons area." Hank waved his arm in such a way that he could have been referring to at least three of the cardinal directions. I decided to stick my head out Butler Hall to try and recognize the commons. It had served as one of dozens of buildings for wining, dining, probing and prodding candidates during the interview process. I glanced at my watch: 7:23. Was there time to grab coffee and get back? Probably not.

"Be right back," I muttered to Hank, who had settled into a corner seat at the U-shape table.

Opening the heavy door to look out of Butler Hall, I saw President Berrian walking with Caroline Cruz and Veronica Miller toward Butler Hall. So much for getting to the commons.

"Mark!" bellowed Bob Berrian as he came to the foot of the steps to Butler's main door. "Welcome! Welcome! So glad to have you starting with us today."

"Thanks, Bob. I have one important question if you want me to be productive at all at this unfortunate hour. Where's the coffee?"

"Haven't they brought any?" asked Veronica, Bob's administrative assistant. "Dang, those girls can never get it to us by 7:30."

"I suspect it's pretty hectic in the kitchen in the mornings," responded Caroline sharply. "After all, they have to take care of the students in the dorms." The nicely shaped, sharply dressed Cruz served as the Executive Vice President for Student Services, who during my interview sessions responded in cutting and quick ways. At both interviews in which she participated, she sat apart from everyone else. Was that her choice or others'? "I'm constantly telling Bob that we must put students first," she commented directly to me.

"What the hell is an idea like that?" laughed Berrian as he crossed through the door I held open for him. His black pinstripe suit was freshly tailored—no wrinkles or crinkles or rumples. Immediately, my suit pants didn't seem up to snuff, already looking pathetic from the fifteen-minute drive to the office. Berrian's blond hair was also perfectly coiffed, and the aroma of a men's cologne lingered strongly for several seconds after he had entered Butler Hall. He truly looked intimidating, standing over six feet, four inches tall in an impeccably tailored suit.

Veronica nodded her thanks as she entered Butler Hall, and Caroline Cruz, who delayed on the steps for several seconds, finally crossed through and allowed me to re-enter the building.

"Anyway, don't worry about it, Mark. The coffee will get here!" Berrian moved quickly toward the meeting room. I clearly had to abandon the hope of coffee until the "girls" brought some.

"Who the hell we missing?" barked President Berrian as he settled down at the head of the U, Hank to his right.

"Uh, Shue and Woo, sir," said Veronica, settling directly to the president's left, bustling about to set up her laptop.

"Shue and Woo? That sounds like a combination pest control business and dating service," I chuckled.

My new boss laughed. 'That joke isn't that funny,' I thought.

"That's a funny one, Carter. Chalk one up to the new guy. Shue's going to have some stiff competition."

"What kind of competition, Mr. President?" asked Howard Shue, appearing in the doorway. "I do believe a call to human resources is required to report your reference to *stiff*." Instantly, my self-consciousness regarding my attire faded away. Shue's suit represented the exact opposite of Berrian's. Berrian's was conservative in its black pinstripe; Shue's cream. Berrian's was accompanied by a tasteful tie that likely cost him three figures; Shue's tie was adorned with the Nike logo. Berrian's was neatly pressed and still didn't look like he had ever been in it; Shue's was wrinkled and showed wear in the elbows. Rumors had it that Berrian and Shue were thick as thieves, but comparing them now, I wondered how that could possibly be true. Howard's mismatch went all the way to his physical being: overweight, maybe five and a half feet tall, balding brown hair that barely covered from the top of his forehead to the top of his ears.

"Speaking of HR, we're still waiting for Mr. Woo, aren't we?" Berrian looked at his watch. "7:33. I say we start anyway. Veronica, you have agendas to pass out?"

"Yes, Bob." She started handing sheets of paper down the table. Veronica's hands, despite her age—she had been at Boan for over twenty-five years—were remarkably wrinkle free and sported a slightly outrageous bright red fingernail polish. Her lips barely had the hint of a red lipstick that accentuated her angular face and short brown hair nicely.

Two places remained for me to sit, both at the ends of the U. Howard had slid in next to Hank, while Caroline took her place next to Veronica. I decided to stay on the other side of the U from Caroline. I took my jacket off and hung it on the chair behind me. Berrian had taken his off, but Howard and Hank had not.

The agenda had not been sent out ahead of time. I kept waiting for it the previous week. Everyone at Farrington College had been religious about getting agendas out a week ahead of time. Sometimes that drove me crazy, but no surprise agenda items showed up at a meeting. I wasn't sure, yet, what to make of the lack of advanced agenda at Boan.

"O.k., here's what we got. Enrollment update from Howard. House of Cards Scholarship night, Howard. Endowment Perpetuity, Howard. Sexual Harassment policy, Victor. You can bring up your stiff joke then, Howard." Berrian laughed at his own joke so hard that he actually ended up coughing for a couple of seconds. I looked longingly at the door, hoping for the mythical girls with the coffee.

Berrian charged on reading the agenda: "Spirit Week, Caroline. Library renovation update, Hank. Debit cards, Caroline and Hank. Cabinet retreat, me. Average Class Size, Caroline. College of Education Naming, Howard. Textbook buyback policy, Caroline. Hiring Update, Victor. Bowling Team Incident in Gray Dorm, Caroline. Carter Initiation, all."

Wow, there I was at the end of a fourteen-item agenda. I don't know what scared me more: The length of the agenda (at Farrington, we knew that anything more than a six-item agenda would result in a meeting of over three hours; Hank had already acknowledged this morning that we would meet for five hours); the thought of an initiation (whatever the hell that meant); or that my initiation would come at the end of this certain-to-be-exhausting meeting. No one had told me that provosts should pass endurance tests.

"Well, if you ask me, Bob, my initiation must be surviving a fourteen-item, five-hour agenda!" Perhaps the joke was inappropriate especially for day one, but frank and good-natured honesty had been the foundation of my reputation as Dean of Arts and Sciences at Farrington.

Bob, Veronica and Howard laughed quite loudly at my quip; Hank and Caroline barely cracked a smile.

"Anything we should add to the agenda?" asked Berrian. No one's eyes lifted from the spot on the table directly in front of them. "Nope? Then, how's enrollment, Howard?"

"We're above on actual, behind on stretch, right about on target for goal." Howard shuffled a thick stack of papers, a series of spreadsheets with maybe thirty or forty lines of tiny print each page, around in front of him. "I think we're doing pretty well for this time of year," Howard added.

"What do you mean this time of year?" asked Hank. "It's late summer. If we don't hit fall stretch goals in the next six days, we're going to fall behind, no matter how damn good the actual is."

"Well, stretch is tricky to predict."

"Try."

"Try what, Hank?"

"Try to predict. You say we're behind on stretch. By how much? What is the ripple effect of that non-stretching?" Hank took a huge bite out of his bagel. My grapefruit and yogurt certainly wouldn't hold me long. I looked back at the door. 'Where the hell is that coffee?'

Howard leaned back in his chair and looked at the president, as if he was the judge in a trial who would over-rule Hank's objection. Berrian simply smiled and nodded to Howard to continue.

Howard sighed. "O.k., I'll try to make this as simple as possible." He ruffled through his pages of spreadsheets again. "First, let's remove all the new admissions reps. That's anyone who has started in the last six weeks. They have not been here long enough yet to impact their stretch goals. Second, take the...."

"Hold on, Howard. How many reps are 'new' as you've just defined it?" Caroline snarled.

"That would be, uh, hold on a minute." Howard had one of the sheets from his pile up close to his glasses as he tried to read the tiny font. "I believe that is five new reps."

"Does each have the same stretch goals?" Caroline asked.

"No, certainly not," responded Howard. "For instance, Carla Hoopsnaggle is the new nursing admissions rep. Her stretch goal is twice what the others are, as frankly all we have to do is scrawl 'nursing degrees' on a napkin and leave it on the street to get a ton of applicants. Similarly, Wayne Wellington has a higher stretch goal for applicants in the education graduate program. Jeez, teaching jobs are disappearing every day, and you still get a bunch of yahoos who want to get a teaching degree. And then there's poor Emma Firth, who has to drum up fine arts students. Her stretch goal might as well be double her actual goal, which might as well mean that she has to start two whole students."

"Sorry I'm late," whispered Victor Woo as he sprinted into the room. He stopped and looked suspiciously at me, and then cautiously took a seat next to Caroline. 'I evidently have taken his seat,' I figured, 'and he's not happy sitting next to Cruz. Tough! That's what he gets for being late.'

"Victor!" said Berrian sharply. "What's kept you?"

"Oh, a minor crisis at the Bursar's Office. A student called our office to complain about Brad Knight and there's no one over there, yet, except for me."

"Christ! Knight," grumbled Hank. "What the hell did he do this time?"

"Typical Brad. The student complained that she couldn't pay cash for her fall classes and Brad told her that people only used cash for cocaine and hookers."

Howard and Veronica laughed. I stifled a smile. No one else must have found it funny.

Victor was noticeably the youngest member of the President's Cabinet (he looked barely thirty, although apparently he would soon turn forty). He wore a robin's egg blue polo shirt with the Boan seal on it and a pair of Dockers. For the second time this morning, I took comfort in my appearance. Victor's informality suggested that he was more a fish out of water here than Howard. Despite Howard's slovenly appearance, he still matched the group by at least attempting to dress in business attire.

"I assume Knight'll be leaving the building soon?" asked Berrian.

"I'll take care of it as soon as I leave this meeting, sir." Had I really just heard of a termination tossed off as casually as a lunch order?

"Well, that gives him a few more days," giggled Howard. This time Veronica laughed loudly. I carefully watched Berrian, trying to read his reactions.

"O.k., keep us posted, Victor. Now, where were we?"

"Mr. Shue was telling us about the infamous stretch goals, sir," said Hank.

"Yes, that's right, Hank. Thanks for the direction. Anyway, not all the newbies have the same stretch goals, but I've taken an average 'reduction' for them that comes to ninety-six fewer new students for stretch goals, but that still means we're only about ten fewer students from regular goals, and yet twenty-eight more students for actual goals." Howard smugly leaned back in his chair.

I've been told that a good CFO is a pit bull. Hank must have been the alpha of the litter. "O.k., but what does that mean about the other fourteen members of your fine admissions team, Howard? Where exactly are they for the stretch, the goal, and the actual?"

"Do you really want the breakdown on each one, Hank?"

"Maybe just hit a few highlights."

Howard picked up his stack of papers and waved them wildly at Hank. "It's kind of hard to do highlights from all these reports." The color in Howard's beet-red face had drained.

"Now, now, kids. Settle down," said Berrian. "What exactly do you want to know, Hank?"

Hank shifted in his seat and took a drink of his coffee. For the third time, I looked lovingly toward the door, only to be disappointed by its immense closure. "All I know is that we always get these updates and they are so general. And then when it comes time to work on our budget, the situation is never as cheery as Mr. Shue seems to suggest. I'd like to get a head start on the 'WTF' moment this year."

"May I ask a question?" I interjected, raising my hand timidly in the air. 8:02: did I want to dip my foot in the icy waters yet?

Everyone looked at me. No one said anything. I felt a lump forming in my throat.

"Well, go ahead, Carter!" Berrian seemed exasperated by my interjection, yet at no time by the merry-go-round discussion consuming this meeting.

"Why is this all so complex? Why a distinction among goals, actual goals and stretch goals? Does all that really matter?"

Hank stared at me in amazement. "Of course it does. The entire university budget is based on the budget goals, but we want to promote a culture of high achievement, so all enrollment representatives get a stretch goal for enrolling students—you know, something to shoot for."

"So, why not reduce the discussion to just those two goals? Why add the 'actual goals'?" I could feel a headache slowly building.

"Actual goals reflect necessary adjustments made throughout the year, Mr. Provost."

"Necessary for what, Mr. CFO?" I asked, determined to hold my ground now that I had staked a claim on it.

"To adjust for changes! Jeez!"

"Come on, Hank, cut the new guy some slack. Explain it more. Maybe I'll finally get it," said Caroline with a steely look.

Hank sighed. "If we have a poor fall, then we adjust for winter. If we have a good winter, we adjust for spring. And so forth."

I nervously played with the stubble on my face. "At this point, though, aren't we in a new cycle with the upcoming fall semester?"

"Not at all, Mark. We have already adjusted from a poor summer enrollment that will cut into the fall enrollment."

Caroline must have clearly understood that I still wasn't getting it. "Don't kill yourself over this, Mark. Most of us are confused; some of us simply descend into the madness quicker than others."

I decided to give up. "O.k., how about a suggestion, then?"

"My, oh, my, Mark is going to be quite the addition to our team, isn't he?" said Berrian, without clearly indicating whether he was being sarcastic or not.

"Do we get those reports that you are holding, Howard?"

Howard looked aghast. "These?"

"Yes, those. I figure it would help all of us to see those reports, perhaps in anticipation of this meeting, so that we can be more educated in our questions." Hopefully the last bit of that statement had not been picked up by Hank, but did register with Howard.

"No. Once a quarter when we meet with the board, then I send out a one-pager like this to all of cabinet ahead of time—so we can all be on the same page when the board asks us questions."

"I think you could do both. Get us copies of those for the weekly meetings, and copies of the board updates for the quarterly meeting. That would make it all the more likely that we would be on the same page." I looked down to see my pen had come apart. I must have nervously been playing with it and had pulled the pen apart. I quickly started first aid on it.

Howard looked to Berrian again for help. "Well, if that's what you want, Bob?"

"I see them at our one-on-ones every week, but I could see why the others might want them. Veronica, make a note. Starting next week, Howard gets enrollment reports to the team in advance. How much time do you need, Howard?"

Howard's face again drained of color. "There's not much logic in getting them prepared much sooner than Friday. How about Friday morning? Does that give *everyone* time?" he asked, looking only at me.

"I like that," said Caroline. She flashed a smile both enchanting and frightening. I felt a little flush of sexual attraction and my skin curling at the same time. 'Do I want to be on the same side as her?' I wondered. She *had* just supported me in my first blind attempt to get involved. Nevertheless, with her bright blue eyes and long black hair, she had the potential to be a real vamp. It made me wonder if she developed the tough exterior to combat the potential sexual attraction many men (and, for all I knew, women) might have for her.

"Can we get back to an explanation of actual vs. stretch vs. goal?" Hank had gotten up and leaned against one of the walls. The green on the wall he leaned against was a slightly lighter shade than the green on the other walls. How peculiar? With no windows in the room, sunlight had not bleached that wall.

Howard sighed. Before he could respond, we heard a knock on the door.

"Come in," said Berrian.

At the door stood a short, stocky man in a security uniform. His face was pockmarked, and his blond goatee probably contained more hairs than the top of his head. Shuffling like a character from a Dickens' novel, he entered the room.

"Excuse me, sir, but we have an incident."

"An incident? What is it?" Berrian had risen out of his seat.

"We called the police, and they are already over at Muswell Hall." The man stared at a spot behind the president, avoiding eye contact at all costs.

"Damn it, Berninksi. What the hell happened?"

"Dean Hartley was attacked, sir. It appears he's dead."

"What!" All of us, except Caroline, immediately rose from our seats.

"One of his students found him lying on the floor of his office. There's quite a bit of blood." Berninski hopped back and forth on each foot.

I had, of course, met Dean Michael Hartley during the interviews. A big man with a ruddy complexion, he talked in a big booming voice in an attempt to convince via volume rather than by content. The entire hour spent with Hartley consisted of nothing but clichés. I remember telling Natalie afterwards that the most irritating cliché had been "throwing ideas against the wall to see what sticks." He had thrown that weak idea out five times during my interview with him.

Hartley is, or now **was**, the Dean of the College of Education. My perception was that his faculty generally accepted him, but that may not have been the case outside of his own college. Several red flags had come up during my interviews, leading me to already identify him as a subject of conversation with Berrian during my first one-on-one.

"And the police are already here? How long ago did this occur, Berninski?" Berrian asked the question of the quivering man, but he was looking at Victor, who shook himself. Actually, everyone but Caroline shook a little bit. The president's displeasure filled the room.

"Sometime before 7:30, sir. The student made a call from the Muswell emergency phone about 7:35."

"What fucking time is it now? 8:09! Why the hell did it take so long to notify me?" Berrian's eyes narrowed and conveyed a deep anger that thankfully wasn't directed at me, but had been spread between Berninski and Woo.

"I wasn't sure what to do. I tried to call Jones, but he didn't answer his phone or his page."

"Uh, Garrett Jones would have been at Central High School this morning, sir." Victor composed himself enough to interject. "He went there to talk to students about our public safety program. He's always been successful at bringing students in for that program."

"Is that actual or stretch students?" asked Hank.

"Shut the hell up, Hank," bellowed Berrian. "And it still took you a half hour to come here?"

"Well, when I couldn't get Jones, sir, I called the police. You have to understand, there's a lot of blood and the student was screaming and crying and attracting a lot of attention. I just wanted to get a policeman here as quickly as possible. In fact, there are two of them over at Muswell right now. I figured I would take you to them."

Berrian ran his hands through his hair while he thought for a moment. Meanwhile, behind Berninski, a girl pushed a cart that hopefully had coffee. 'Could it really be?' I thought.

"Alright, Woo, come with me." Berrian grabbed his suit jacket to put it on. "Let's go over to Muswell. Everybody else hang here for the time being. Caroline, why don't you cover your items until I get back? I think most of those don't require my presence." Berrian grabbed Victor Woo's arm and started pulling him to the door.

"Uh, sir, I don't think that's a good idea." Caroline's face was as stone. "Your input, support and decisions are required for all of my items. Perhaps we should adjourn the meeting for another time."

"Don't be ridiculous. We got too much to cover, and once I figure out why our own boneheads didn't respond via chain of command, I'm sure the police will be able to handle the investigation." Both Woo's and Berninski's heads hung low with the president's reference to 'bonehead.'

After they had left the room, Howard let out a deep breath. "We're all boanheads at heart," he quipped. "It's our namesake." Boan University had been founded by Christopher Boan, one of Indiana's greatest sons.

I headed to the table where the girl continued to set up the coffee. She acted completely oblivious to the entire conversation she had walked in upon.

"Hi," I said, taking a cup. "I could use the coffee, especially with this turn of events."

She barely looked at me, reminding me of the slaves who for years served their masters without "listening" to anything being said around them. She looked to be about sixteen.

"Give me a minute to hit the head," said Howard racing to the door. Caroline and Hank looked at him with a healthy dose of scorn.

Veronica had worked her way to the coffee table and next to me. "Well, welcome, Mark. What an inauspicious beginning." While still shaking, she had taken the group's standard flippant attitude in her comments.

"So, do we really think Berrian will want to resume this meeting when he gets back?" I asked.

Caroline chortled. "Oh, yeah. Bob's a stickler for staying on task. Last year, we had a power outage for two hours and he kept us in a meeting. Had us move to a classroom upstairs where there are windows."

"Yeah, but the death of a dean is much greater than a power outage. Between helping out with the investigation and spinning all the PR, we need to be out on the front lines."

"We'll see," pronounced Caroline with no hint of a smile. "Very few of us liked Hartley, anyway."

"Caroline! Show respect for the dead," Veronica cried.

"I don't mean that to sound mean," Caroline responded, although I was at a loss to find any other way to interpret what she had said. "I'm just being matter of fact. Michael had pissed off so many people that the list of suspects could be long, and there are probably more people who will rejoice at his passing than will mourn it. At least here at Boan."

I stared in my coffee, not sure how to proceed. Not even 8:30 on my first day and I feared I'd already entered the twilight zone.

"Now, now, Caroline. Veronica is right. Let's keep our heads on straight about this." Hank had moved to the coffee table to refill the cup he had brought in.

"Looks like you might start right off with a dean search, Mark. Lucky you!" Caroline's thin lips still refused to crack into a smile.

"Caroline!" Veronica had wrapped her arms around herself in an attempt to warm herself up. It certainly wasn't from the temperature.

No one said anything for a few minutes as we all got lost in our thoughts. I thought more about my one meeting with Hartley and my natural immediate dislike of the guy. One runs across people like Hartley in academia all the time: deans and full professors so full of themselves that no one else can measure up to them in their own eyes. Contentious, arrogant, brash, loyal only to themselves. Uncomfortably, I felt relief knowing I wouldn't have to deal with Hartley as a direct report. I had been fortunate at Farrington to put together a team of chairs who did not represent traditional academics, putting egos and degrees aside for the betterment of our team. Fate had given me a head start on putting together that kind of team here at Boan. I wondered how quickly the news would get out to the rest of the university, especially the rest of my direct reports.

Finally, Howard came in wiping his hands on his pants. 'Aha, that helps explain the foulness of that suit.' "So, what now?" he asked.

"I guess we'll do some of my items from the agenda," Caroline had sat back down and put on a pair of thin glasses to look more carefully at the agenda in front of her. Why hadn't she donned them earlier when we all reviewed the agenda together? Was this a sign of how she only cared about what directly involved her?

"We could discuss Spirit Week. I'm not sure there's anything there that demands Bob's attention at this moment."

"Wait a minute! What about enrollment?" snarled Hank. "I still want answers from Howard."

Howard glanced at Caroline, but said nothing. Veronica's typing on her laptop provided the only noise in the room. "I tell you what, Hank. Let's allow Howard to get us the weekly report for the next meeting, and then when we have all that information in front of us, we can let Howard walk us through it. Can that work?" posed Caroline.

"Sure," mumbled Hank and Howard.

"Good. Then, onward to Spirit Week."

I had to laugh. "You have got to be kidding me. We've got a dead dean on campus and we're just going to go ahead and discuss Spirit Week! That's insane."

"It's four weeks away, Mark," said Caroline rolling her eyes. "Hartley's death will be old news by then. Life goes on and we have to give the student body a healthy social life."

"As opposed to someone giving Hartley's body an unhealthy social life," cracked Howard.

My mouth surely hung open. I got up to refill my coffee cup, if for no other reason than to cover my facial reactions. I couldn't wait to call Natalie to talk about this ominous beginning.

"Mark, we really want academics to push Spirit Week and to involve students from the academic perspective. In the past, we've had little support from faculty for the events, and it's frustrating to hold a 'dunk-the-mascot' event when only about twenty-five students show up."

"Ah, I love the dunk-the-mascot event," said Howard. "Seeing that sturgeon flounder in the water, trying to catch his breath. What a sight."

"That's very good, Howard," I responded, already disgusted with myself for being able to plunge back into business so quickly since our interruption.

"Don't praise him," grumbled Hank. "He uses that 'sturgeon flounder' line every year."

"I see no reason to abandon good material."

"Maybe you should start with good material." Hank apparently loved to rise to the challenge that was Howard.

"Can we stay focused, gentlemen?" snapped Caroline. "So, anyway, Mark, in the past the faculty have openly challenged us about letting students out of classes for these events during Spirit Week. We would appreciate you encouraging them to let students have time to participate in the events."

I could smell something fishy, even without using a bad fish joke like Howard's. "Uh, o.k., when do the events occur?"

"Between 11:00 and 1:00 every day of Spirit Week."

"Hmm?" I paused. "And is it safe to assume you pick those times because it's when the most students are actually on campus?"

"Oh, yes, all of the classes are full between 11 and 1."

"So, you want my faculty to give up any number of class sessions for these events." It was not a question.

"Yes."

I looked around the room to see if anybody would jump in with a comment similar to what I was ready to say. Veronica's look suggested she empathized, but no one else's did.

I chose my words carefully. 'Don't want to get off on the wrong foot,' I thought, then immediately countered that with, 'Jeez, a dean has probably just been murdered. What is the right freaking foot to get off on?'

"How many contact hours do the students typically lose from the course if they are excused from the classroom for these activities?"

"Oh, anywhere from one contact hour to three or four hours, depending upon how often the class meets."

I leaned across the table to make my point more emphatically. "Well, I think I can understand the faculty's potential resentment of giving up the functional role of a university for these other activities. Don't get me wrong,

I know and I'm sure most of the faculty know, that a well-rounded student is most likely to graduate, but course material is supposed to be covered."

"Oh, come on, Mark. Everybody knows that most students skip at least one or two classes a semester anyway. This 'every contact hour needs to be met' sacred cow is a load of hooey," said Howard. I couldn't tell if he was joking, goading me, or simply supporting Caroline.

"And that's relevant how?" I could feel my blood pressure rising. In eleven years at Farrington, I had never raised my voice in a meeting, but I wouldn't last eleven hours at Boan without doing that.

"Couldn't they do extra credit assignments? When Bill O'Reilly came here to speak two years ago, most of the faculty encouraged students to go hear him and then gave them assignments as extra credit or even required."

"O'Reilly spoke here?" I nearly choked on my coffee. "I can only imagine the assignments faculty came up with. I'm used to a fairly liberal faculty, so did the faculty skewer O'Reilly?"

"No, not really. Many of them thought it was cool that a TV star came to speak." Caroline had shifted in her chair, revealing a bit of calf between the slit of her business skirt. For the second time, I was struck by contrasting feelings of attraction and repulsion.

"I tell you what," I said, recognizing the political suicide of squashing this idea on the first morning of my first day here. "Let me talk to the deans...."

"All but one," joked the ghoulish Howard.

I glared at him and marched on. "Let me talk to the deans and get the pulse of this issue with the faculty. Can I get back to you on this?"

Caroline hesitated. "Sure," she said drawing out the word into two syllables. "I mean, Spirit Week goes on whether the faculty support the events or not. I just don't want to get chewed out by Berrian for having such minimal student participation."

I ignored the comment. "Great. I'll try to get you an answer by the end of the week."

"Excellent," responded Caroline with a touch of sarcasm in her voice. "Meanwhile, Mr. Turing, as usual we have under-budgeted for Spirit Week. I begged for $6000 last spring to properly fund the week, but we slashed the budget to $900 right before July first. Any ideas on how I can move some money into there so that we can have more than a clown from a kid's party?"

Hank laughed. "Hell, you can have that for free. Just put some makeup on Howard."

We all laughed loudly, even Howard. Hank came back to Caroline's request. "Give Aaron a call. Tell him what you need and he'll move the money into that account."

"Super," replied Caroline with even more sarcasm than when she told me 'excellent.' "That'll do it for Spirit Week."

I reluctantly raised my hand. "Can the new guy ask another question? I'm just trying to learn the ropes around here."

"Shoot," said Caroline.

"Explain to me how the budget works then. If Caroline had to cut that budget right before the fiscal year, and then with one brief plea to the CFO at a meeting to have the money reinstated, she gets it, then explain to me why you prepared the budget back in the spring."

"Be careful, Mark," warned Howard. "You are getting into budget actuals, budget goals and budget stretch numbers."

Hank glared first at Howard, then back at me. Caroline kept her head down and Veronica stared at her laptop. "Adjustments have to be made, Mark. But, don't get any ideas. Aaron Cartwright watches over the budget closely. He'll make sure everything is on the up and up."

I hesitated. Was this another battle to choose on the first morning? Despite the continually developing headache, I decided to go in showing arms, as opposed to simply retreating. "I understand, Hank. But, at Farrington we spent a long time planning for the budget, accurately capturing our needs for the budget, and then carefully tracking every expense throughout the year. This *sounds,* and, trust me, I've only heard one brief statement, like all the work can be easily overlooked as we move money around. Are you able to keep track?"

"Of course." Hank must have decided to cut me a break, because he then smiled and went on. "Don't worry; it will make sense to you after you meet with Aaron. Have you set up a meeting with him, yet?"

Was he being serious? "Uh, no. After all, I'm now into my ..." I glanced at my watch, it was 8:53. "First ninety minutes at Boan, and all of them have been spent in this meeting."

"Death by meetings, eh, Mark?"

"Howard!" shrieked Veronica. "Stop it with the death jokes."

"Well, these meetings can be murder, Veronica."

"Alright, let's move on. What should we cover next on the agenda?" asked Caroline.

"How about the textbook buyback policy?" suggested Veronica.

"Sounds good. I think we need to tighten this policy up," recommended Caroline, rifling through a stack of papers. "If you'll remember," she continued, pausing as she searched for a specific piece of paper. "Now where did I put that sheet?"

Hank had gotten out of his chair to throw the trash from his breakfast away. Howard checked his BlackBerry. I looked at Veronica, who merely smiled. I realized I needed to start thinking who I would name as interim Dean of Education. 'Assuming Hartley really is dead.'

"Ah, here it is," exclaimed Caroline, holding a yellowed piece of paper above her head like a day trader on Wall Street. "The policy for textbook buyback. This thing has been the same since I arrived here four years ago, but every year we have students complain that they can only get the maximum refund for their books within the first ten days of classes, although we allow for pro-rated refunds on classes throughout most of the semester. There's a legitimate argument for creating a similar refund period and process for texts as the one that occurs for the classes themselves."

"Caroline, we go over this every year. We're at the mercy of the book companies, who will only accept books back during a small window of time." Hank still stood near the garbage can, which forced Caroline to twist to have to look directly behind her.

"At some point we have to take a stand with the book companies, though, Hank."

"Well, as long as Carter's faculty change textbooks every year we're screwed at having any leverage on this thing."

"Gee, it didn't take long for them to be my faculty, Hank," I said, smiling. "I know at Farrington we often had to change textbooks simply because editions changed."

Hank had moved back to his chair. "I don't know, Mark. I have the feeling that many faculty change on a whim. I could be wrong, though."

"I think Hank's right, Mark. I think many of our changes come directly from the faculty decisions." Caroline had turned back to face the full table, and smoothed her blue skirt as she did so. "Anyway, that's not actually the issue, per se, here. Every year on our student satisfaction surveys we get creamed on the scores for textbooks and the bookstore."

"What's the nature of their complaints?" I asked, sure I knew the answer.

"They cost too much. The bookstore won't give them a full refund when they return them. They never used their textbooks. That's one for you, Mark."

"Ah, I see. Farrington had pretty much given up competing with Amazon. com and had created a system where the bookstore worked in collaboration with Amazon.com as needed. Would we do anything like that here?"

Hank snorted. "Amazon.com sells their books so much more cheaply than us that I can't imagine having any kind of partnership with them." I worried that my presence so far was only annoying Hank.

"Well, how much do we mark up books, then?" I asked.

Howard's attention was drawn away from his BlackBerry. "I hear the students don't mark them up at all. That's why there's the claim that they never open them."

"Ha, ha, Howard. Really, Hank, how much?"

"About 40%."

"Holy crap!" I pushed my seat back. "That's outrageous."

"It's in alignment with what other bookstores do. There is profit to be made in books."

"Jeez, at Farrington, our mark-up was about 15%, and I thought that unconscionable." I peered in my cup trying to decide whether to get more coffee or not.

"Well, we're no hoity-toity institution like Farrington, Mark," Hank joked.

"Hmm. I don't know." I looked around the table. Veronica was typing fast and furious on the laptop. They couldn't be notes at the moment; perhaps she was responding to e-mail. Howard was back on his BlackBerry thumbing some response to somebody. Caroline had her head back, eyes closed, rubbing her temples.

"You o.k., Caroline?" I asked.

"Uh, yeah. Look it's about fifteen after nine. I say we table this item until the whole group is back, and let's take a quick break. I am getting a massive headache. Maybe one of us can find out when Bob and Victor will get back."

Everyone grunted agreement with Caroline's recommendation, and Howard left the room in a flash. I got up, stretched my arms to the ceiling, and stifled a yawn.

"Be careful, there, Mark," said Caroline. "You need to be in tip-top shape to survive these marathon meetings." She also headed to the door, so I jumped in front of her to hold the door open.

"I have a headache, too. Is yours typical of your reaction to these meetings?"

"No. I'm sure it came about because of the interruption and Bob's ignorant suggestion to keep running the meeting while he is gone."

I laughed uncomfortably because she gave me no clue as to whether she was trying to be funny or not. 'Get into no poker games with Caroline.' "I am glad that I'm not the only one who found it odd that he wanted to continue the meeting while a murder investigation started up."

"Oh, the murder. Jeez, that's nothing. I expected him to stay, tell security to keep us posted, and then plow on." As I watched her walk away, steely resolve down to her high heels, I realized she would be a fascinating colleague.

Chapter Two

Given that the break was only a few minutes, sunlight beckoned more urgently than the restroom. Opening the heavy exterior doors of Butler Hall, I stepped in to blinding sunlight, immediately turning my head toward the building to shield my eyes from the sun's intensity.

When my eyes had recovered, I turned back around and surveyed the campus. Off to the left, two police cruisers were parked on the grass near Muswell Hall, near where Hartley's body must lay. A small group of gawkers standing by a tree about twenty-five yards from the cruisers were being pushed back by two officers. One person appeared to need restraints. Elsewhere around the square, people pointed and gesticulated wildly.

I longed to stay outside and inhale the fresh air for longer than a couple of minutes, but more meeting called. Not far, next to a small amphitheater with a class in session, I found the men's restroom. Inside, Howard stood over a urinal, left hand leaning against the wall as if to hold himself up.

"You're not tired are you, Howard?" I asked.

"Maybe a little. Let me ask you, Mark: are you into fantasy baseball?"

"Not anymore. I tried it in graduate school but never got into it. Why? Are you?"

"Yep. I was up late last night watching that Red Sox/White Sox game on ESPN. Extra innings. I had two pitchers get toasted in that game. They may have cost me first place."

My bladder relinquished its contents as I stood over the urinal. No sound at all came from Howard's. "Uh, sorry to hear that," I murmured. The last thing I wanted to do was stand at the urinal and discuss real baseball statistics used in an unreal world.

"Meanwhile, Bobby boy has Verlander who gave him a complete game shutout yesterday. That will be enough to push him back into first place."

"I assume that when you say 'Bobby boy,' you mean Berrian?"

"Of course." Howard made it sound like I didn't realize the sky was blue.

"Hmm?" I started to zip up and considered for a quick moment skipping the washing of my hands and thus not having to continue this discussion. However, hygiene won the day, and the discussion did not improve.

"The son-of-a-bitch beat me in fantasy football this year, is killing me in Mafia Wars, and has beaten me fourteen straight times at ping-pong."

"Ping-pong! Mafia Wars! Jesus Christ, Howard, maybe you should not get involved in any games with the president." Hands dripping, I twisted away from the sink so that my tie didn't fall into the mess a public washroom quickly becomes. A dreaded air dryer was the only option for a towel. That meant more time in the restroom, but at least the noise might drown him out. Waving my hands underneath, it came on and I held my hands underneath.

Howard moved closer to me, supposedly skipping the hand-washing part completely. "That's a funny one, Mark. No, the president won't allow you not to participate. He'll be twisting your arm left and right for all sorts of competitions. It will start with Friday afternoon basketball."

"Basketball," I said, turning my hands over. "That does sound like fun. How many people play?"

"About eight to twelve, depending upon the turnout."

"Anybody any good?"

"Heck, no. We're all pretty bad, but that doesn't stop a lot of competition and side bets from going on."

"Side bets?"

"Yeah, like the losing team has to buy the winning team breakfast, or has to bring snacks and beverages the next Friday."

"How often does Berrian's team lose?"

"Oh, rarely. And I do my best to make sure I'm on it every time."

"Interesting, Howard. Anyway, we should probably head back to the meeting." I held the restroom door open for him. A young man, in all probability a student, ducked out of the amphitheater and raced into the restroom before I could let the door go.

The door to the amphitheater slowly closed behind him, and I could hear a deep male voice booming, "regulation is the adversary of supply side economics." Peeking through the now closed door, I saw an instructor in a Hawaiian shirt pacing on a stage with about fifteen students spread throughout the auditorium.

"Howard," I called, racing to catch up to him before he got to our meeting room. He stopped and turned toward me.

"I'm surprised there's a class in there. I thought classes didn't start until next week."

"Oh, that would be one of our accelerated honors courses. We run those all year round. They have their own schedule." I nodded my head in understanding. 'Acceleration' permeates many conversations in higher education. How can students complete their degrees more quickly? Prevailing solutions include either shortening the length of a semester or the length of the entire degree program. Both solutions have generated much debate.

Howard started to move toward the meeting room. I grabbed his shoulder to stop him.

"I remember some discussion about accelerated classes at the interview, but I don't remember an association with honors students. I think I would have remembered because at the time I was concerned about the notion that the accelerated classes would be open to all students."

Howard picked at some lint on his pants. "Well, we actually have four different accelerated programs that we run, so it could have been any of them that you heard about at the interview."

"Four! This is on top of the regular fifteen-week semesters?"

"And don't forget online."

"Yeah, I know. I took a long look at the online delivery system in preparation for the interview. I guess I just don't remember much information shared with me about all of these accelerated deliveries."

"Well, all four of them are the brainchild of Berrian from last year. He challenged us to create more opportunities for students to complete their degrees in the quickest amount of time." I had let go of Howard's shoulder, and he now held the door for me.

"Hmm?" I mumbled, walking past him into the room. Veronica, Hank and Caroline were already in their seats waiting for us to resume. "Howard's been telling me about the accelerated programs," I announced, in an effort to bring them into the conversation.

"Ah, yes. 'Whatever your need, we can provide the speed' campaign," cackled Caroline.

"I'd like to understand a little more about them, but given our agenda, I'm not sure this is the best time to ask questions about them."

"Actually, that discussion would fit with my agenda item on average class size, but we need Bob here for that one." Caroline's frustration plainly showed through her clipped speech.

"Let me guess. All these ways of taking classes is hurting your ability to get critical mass in any specific class. As a result you are cancelling classes because of low enrollment." I figured it didn't take a genius to see that unintended consequence.

"That's what we've unfortunately discovered," grumbled Hank.

"But we're giving students what they want," countered Howard.

"And the president," said Caroline tapping her pen on the table.

"Well, if you don't mind, can you quickly characterize the kinds of accelerated programs for me?" I asked.

"There's basic accelerated: seven weeks of classes within the fifteen-week semesters. There's blended accelerated, which are five-week courses within the fifteen-week semesters, and which utilize online. There's the honors accelerated, which are four-week courses that run on their own schedule and are only for honors students, and then there is the accelerated for professionals, which goes on its own four week schedule and is available only to working adults, who also get credit for prior learning." Caroline continued to tap her pen sharply on the table as she enumerated these.

"Jeez," I muttered under my breath, while agitatedly writing notes. I regretted not finding aspirin during the break. "What a nightmare! How does the registrar keep up with all these different calendars?"

"Hard to say," laughed Howard. "Mitch had to take a leave because of a nervous breakdown."

I looked around the room to see if anybody was laughing with him. No one was. "You're not kidding, are you?"

"No, he's not," said Veronica. "We're not sure when he's coming back. That's an item I have to remember to assign Victor for next week's meeting: registrar coverage."

I made a few notes on my agenda to remind me to find documentation on these deliveries, and to ask Berrian why these hadn't been discussed with me during the interview process. Meanwhile, the room had grown silent again.

"So, do you think you can cover anything for average class size, Caroline, or do I note that it has been tabled for another meeting?" asked Veronica.

"Table it," snapped Hank.

"Despite our need, we go at turtle speed," mocked Howard. "What about this bowling team incident, Caroline? I think we all could use a good laugh right now."

"Judicial Affairs is all over it, so this is just informational for all of us." Caroline again looked through her pile of papers to find what she wanted to reference. "Seven members of the bowling team who live in Gray Hall got a little drunk Friday night."

"Bowlers drunk? What is this world coming to?" joked Howard. He had completely removed his tie and shoved it into his jacket pocket.

"And it seems that about 1:30 AM, they decided to practice in the hallways." Caroline plowed on, ignoring Howard. "However, they had no pins available, so they barged into one of the fine arts student's room and 'borrowed' ten puppets to use as pins ..."

"Puppets? What the hell?" Hank had pushed his chair back from the table to lean it against the wall.

"Yep, apparently, the kid's thesis was going to be a puppet show rendition of *The Iceman Cometh*."

Unable to control myself, I started laughing hysterically. Caroline shot daggered looks at me, but I couldn't help myself. "Wait, wait," I interrupted, struggling to speak through my laughter. "Does that actually mean we would have Pearl the puppet prostitute?"

"That would bring a whole new meaning to a 'woody,'" said Howard.

"I thought the whole point of a prostitute is sex without all the strings attached." Hank had joined in the fun.

Even Veronica struggled to control her laughter.

"Oh, shut up and grow up, you guys. Can I finish describing the incident?"

"I don't think you need to," I said, fighting again to speak through laughter. "I think we can all see how this is going to turn out: 'The bowling ball cometh.'" Veronica howled in appreciation.

Caroline sighed. "Yes, the bowling team apparently set up ten puppets in the hallway and proceeded to bowl, until the distraught student called security."

"Well, you have to admit that's the kind of anarchy that never actually occurred in Harry Hope's saloon."

"Hey, there's our Hickey, now," interrupted Howard looking at the door. Indeed the president had returned, with a woman I didn't know and Victor Woo in tow.

"Huh?" Berrian looked at Howard suspiciously.

"Better our Hickey than our Godot," I responded.

"Godot? Oh, some literary reference. So disappointed I missed it. Everyone, this is Detective Marsh. She's been one of the officers at the Hartley scene. She asked if she could come over and ask us a few questions." Berrian went to his seat at the head of the U. Victor slipped around Detective Marsh quietly, and took his seat at the end.

"What exactly happened, Detective Marsh?" I asked.

"It appears that someone bludgeoned Mr. Hartley with one of his awards." Marsh glanced around for a place to sit. Caroline pulled a chair from the jumble of desks and chairs near the one wall and pushed it towards Marsh. "Thank you," said Marsh, an attractive short-haired blonde who stood about five feet three inches tall. 'She's no Columbo,' I thought, 'a little more on the Cagney side. Or was Lacey the blonde?'

"We're guessing that it happened early this morning, probably around 7:00. We think the student who found him may have arrived at the office within fifteen or twenty minutes of his death. What time did you all get here?"

"I got here right about 7:30, detective," answered Howard. "In fact, I came straight from my car to this meeting, as I do every Monday morning."

"And you are?" Marsh had pulled out a notebook. From my vantage point, I could see that many pages were already full. Were all of those observations about Hartley's murder?

"Howard Shue, ma'am."

"And what's your role, here, Mr., or is it Dr., Shue?"

"Mister is fine, detective. I oversee all of admissions and development."

"Development?" Marsh clearly looked puzzled.

"You know, the fund-raising piece."

"Oh, o.k. Thanks." Marsh looked a little skeptical about Howard's response. His slovenly presentation and laid-back nature were certainly contrary to any admissions or development vice president I had ever known. However, something must work, as Boan enrollment had gone up in the more than two years he'd been in the role, and the annual campaigns for fund-raising also exceeded goals.

"And, did you see anything suspicious, Mr. Shue, either in the square or down at Muswell Hall?"

"Well, I didn't go through the square. From my parking spot, I had a quick dash to the side of Butler Hall, and I came in through that door. Never actually went into the square, detective."

Marsh nodded, jotted something in her notebook, and then turned to look at me. "How about you, sir? Who are you?"

"I'm Mark Carter. I'm the provost, also known as the chief academic officer. This is actually my first day." That sounded really stupid to say.

"Huh," said Marsh smiling. "Dean Hartley reported to you, then, wouldn't he?"

"Well, uh, if alive, yes."

"Hartley reports to a higher authority now, Carter. Or, maybe a lower authority?" Howard pointed to the floor.

Marsh smiled uneasily at Howard, then turned to Berrian. "President Berrian, who has been the interim provost up until today?"

"That would have been Jennifer Riley, detective. Dr. Riley is the dean of our business college." Berrian casually leaned back in his chair, as if he had been interrupted by a stranger lost on campus.

"O.k., after this, I would like to go talk to her. Where can I find her?"

"I can help you with that," volunteered Veronica. "I'll look up her schedule while you're talking."

"So, Mr....," Marsh hesitated, while going back over her notes, "Carter, or is it Dr. Carter?"

"It is doctor, detective, but I'm not big on titles."

"Great. So, when did you get on campus?"

"I probably got parked a little after 7:00 AM. I know I dumped my box of stuff in my office around 7:15 so that I could get over here to Butler Hall in time for this meeting."

"Where's your office?"

"Administration Building. It's where all of our offices are." I looked at my colleagues for visual confirmation of this fact.

"Actually, mine isn't there," said Victor. "I'm in the basement of Dred Hall."

Marsh smiled. "You university types and your building names. Dred Hall!"

Berrian's casualness abruptly disappeared as he noticeably took offense. "It's named after one of our greatest benefactors, detective. Samuel and Imogene Dred have been supporters of this university for over fifty years. Perhaps you have heard of "I.D. Clothing'? Samuel named that after his wife's initials."

"Uh-huh," replied Marsh, who then turned back to me. "So, what direction is the Administration Building?" she asked.

"Uh. I think it's, uh, ..." I looked around the room panicking. I had absolutely no bearings.

"It's that way, detective," said Caroline pointing behind my head, exasperation distinctly showing in her voice. "South of where we are right now."

"O.k." Marsh paused and looked at her notes. "You would have been walking directly toward the murder scene, Dr. Carter. Do you recollect seeing anything, especially down by Muswell Hall?"

Closing my eyes, I tried to remember if I had seen anything. I couldn't recall observing anything. Jeez, how lousy of a potential eyewitness could I be? "Nothing, detective. I'm sorry, but I remember seeing nothing. If I'd had some coffee, I might have been more alert."

Marsh gave an uneasy smile. "O.k., I have already talked with Mr. Woo here. Ma'am, how about you?"

Caroline stood up and over the sitting detective. "I am Dr. Caroline Cruz, Executive Vice President for Student Services. I got here about 7:10. I stopped in the president's office after checking into my office quickly, and then walked over with him and Ms. Miller." Caroline nodded toward Veronica, who gave Detective Marsh a sheepish "that's me" grin.

"I was aware of nothing abnormal on the walk over here, but then again Bob and I were in a pretty deep conversation about something."

"What were you talking about?"

While I didn't think it was possible, the question appeared to make Caroline more peeved than she had been, "Why does it matter, detective?"

"Just wondering. That's all. One never knows what might be important."

"It's o.k., Caroline. Go back into your cage." Berrian's disparagement of Caroline in front of the detective surprised me, and reminded me to always be cautious around him. "We were discussing our bowling team, Detective Marsh. It appears that there had been an unfortunate incident in a dorm this weekend involving our bowling team and a fine arts student's project." Berrian, like Caroline, had also stood up and had moved to lean against the wall behind Hank and Howard.

"Bowling! Wow, who would've known that a university would have a bowling team?" Marsh rolled her pen across her notepad and chuckled.

"If the murder weapon had been a bowling ball, you would be onto something, wouldn't you, detective?"

"Howard!" shrieked Veronica. "Stop being so ghoulish."

"That's o.k., Ms...." Detective Marsh looked for the name on her notepad. "... Ms. Miller. As you may know, cops can develop an unfortunately ghoulish sense of humor in situations like this, so I'm used to it. I should ask, though, would there be any connection between the incident and Dean Hartley?"

"I can't see why, detective," responded Victor. "Sure, some members of the team are in the College of Education, but the incident was just a stupid prank by kids who had imbibed too much. We hadn't even gotten around to processing them through our judicial affairs department. Even then, any sanctions and punishments come from the university and not the specific college. Education, in this case."

"Hmm?" Marsh continued to scrawl notes into her notebook. Turning back to Caroline, she continued her questioning. "Both you and the president confirm seeing nothing out of the ordinary. How about you, Ms. Miller? Were you paying more attention to your surroundings or to the bowling team story?"

Veronica laughed. "Kind of both. I was listening, but since I wasn't directly involved in the conversation, I was looking around some. I seem to remember a group of students leaving Hope Residence Hall at about the same time we walked across the square, but I don't remember which way they headed."

"Hope? Where's Hope?"

"Anywhere but here, detective," cracked Howard.

"You're quite the comedian, aren't you, Mr. Shue?" challenged Marsh.

"Sorry. I just can't pass on obvious lines."

"He's not lying, Detective Marsh. Howard is the king of all medio ...cre comedy." Berrian slapped Howard on his shoulder.

"Ah, very good, Mr. President." Howard tried to slap him back, but Berrian ducked out of the way.

"Nevertheless, could someone tell me where Hope Hall is?"

"Hope *Residence* Hall," said Caroline, dragging out the key adjective, "is directly east of us, right now, meaning it's northeast of the Administration Building, and a little southeast of Butler Hall."

"Thanks. So back to you, Ms. Miller. You are ... ?" asked Marsh.

"I'm his assistant," Veronica answered, pointing at Berrian.

"And did I get yet what time you got to campus today?"

"No, not yet. I arrived a little after 7:00. I got here and immediately went in to Bob's office to confirm the agenda and run copies. That's a pretty standard Monday morning for me."

"And do all of you park in the same lot?"

"Yes, we do, detective," replied Berrian. "It is a lot directly behind the Administration Building. A small lot reserved only for those of us in that building."

"Does that mean the lot doesn't have a view of the square out here, and thus no view of Muswell Hall?"

"That would be correct."

"Thank you, President Berrian. That just leaves you, sir." Marsh pointed her black pen at Hank.

"Hank Turing. I'm the CFO. I did get here about 7:10 or 7:15. I actually didn't go directly to my office but hustled over to the commons to get a bagel and a coffee."

"The commons? That's the large modern building next to Muswell Hall? Where the police cruisers are parked?"

"I don't know where your people parked, officer, but, yes, I am referring to the modern building to the east of Muswell Hall."

"That means you might have passed by Muswell Hall close to the time of the murder. Did you notice anything? See anything? Hear anything?"

"Not that I can remember, and I've been spending my time while you went around the table thinking. On my way to the commons I stayed on the sidewalk on the far east of the square, so at that point I never got that close to Muswell. Outside of passing a few stray students, I don't remember seeing anybody."

"How about when you got to the commons?"

"Well, as usual, service kind of sucked. The one girl in there was trying to take some breakfast orders from a couple of students ahead of me. Nervous about being late, I kept looking at my watch and after getting the girl's attention I left three dollars by her register. Then, I headed out." We watched Hank pretty intensely. At least the summary of his morning was somewhat interesting.

"And did you walk in front of Muswell Hall?" asked Marsh.

"No, I was in a hurry, so I took the diagonal across the square to get to this meeting. I wasn't aware of seeing anybody until I saw Mark here at the door. I was trying to balance my food and drink and kept my eyes down."

"That is true, detective. I can vouch for his shaky hold on one bagel and one coffee." I got a slight smile from Howard for my response.

"O.k." said Marsh, busy writing down more notes in her notebook. For several minutes, no one said anything, and we could hear the scraping of Marsh's pen on her notebook and the belabored breathing of Victor Woo. A murder on campus must be an HR guy's worst nightmare.

"Will that be all, detective?" asked Berrian. "I would like …" He looked at his watch, and I glanced at mine—it was 10:25. "I would like," he repeated, "to resume my meeting if that would be possible."

"Almost, sir," she responded. She placed her pen down on her pad. "The only other question I have concerns possible motives. In situations like this, it is typical of people who know someone who just got murdered to think only the positive and not want to reflect on negatives such as reasons why someone might want to kill the person, but we need your help in giving us some potential leads." She paused. "Can any of you think of anyone who might have had a grudge against or a reason to kill Dean Hartley?"

"Christ, detective. It might be easier if you asked us to give you a list of people who didn't have a grudge against Hartley." Caroline pulled no punches.

"Caroline," gasped Veronica.

"Oh, hush, Veronica. We all know this. Let's start with the fact that he was a conniving, lying son-of-a-bitch. Heck, three or four faculty that I know of said that Hartley supported their tenure and then were furious to find that he rejected their tenure when the votes came up. Or, how about Kiana King? She was fit to be tied after Michael gave her no credit for the partnership with the Wayne Technical Center. Or, how about …?"

"Hold on, Dr. Cruz. Can you slow down a minute?" Detective Marsh had picked up her pen and was feverishly writing again. "First, who is this Ms. King? Or, is it Doctor King?"

"No 'doctor'. She is the dean of our allied health college." Berrian looked sternly at Caroline, while responding to Marsh. Since her head stayed down as she wrote, I had no idea if she could see the glance he exchanged with Caroline.

"Ah, and what about this partnership?"

Berrian paused for a couple of seconds while he stared down Caroline. To her credit, she did not look away from him. That steely resolve in Caroline reminded me of the age-old line, 'Keep your friends close, but keep your enemies closer.'

"I assume what Dr. Cruz is referring to, detective, is an articulation agreement we had in January with the Wayne vo-tech center that involved actually all of our colleges. For whatever reason, Michael got to be the point person for all the press releases. I don't exactly remember why he got center stage, but the other deans created some backlash, although Ms. King raised the biggest stink."

"How so, President Berrian?"

Berrian sighed and leaned back in his chair. "Well, at an all-faculty meeting in March, and I'm not exactly sure how it got started, a bit of a shouting match between Hartley and King took place in front of the entire faculty."

"Were there any verbal threats?"

"I don't really remember. Perhaps Dr. Riley could confirm for you?"

"Who's Dr. Riley?"

The president sighed, as if dealing with an eight-year old. "We told you. The dean of the College of Business, but more importantly the interim provost at the time."

I couldn't help but interject. "Was there an incident written up for HR, Victor?" I asked.

Victor looked at me with fear in his eyes, clearly not on solid ground here. It's never good when the head of human resources knows he's feeling a lot of heat.

"I, uh, well, I don't believe anything formal was ever written up," Victor stammered. "I know some of my staff did interviews with Michael, Kiana and Jennifer, but I don't think any of them thought the incident merited documentation."

"Hmm?" I shrugged my shoulders, but made a note on my pad to talk to King and Riley about the incident. I cared little about the specifics, but more about the effect on the faculty. I had learned while a dean at Farrington just how much damage could occur when sparring transpired in front of faculty. Heck, that incident caused our whole science division to petition to be split off from the arts and sciences and be moved to the College of Health. Luckily, I had been able to prevent that from happening, much to the chagrin of my colleague, the health dean, who dreamt of additional revenue streams with science.

"O.k.," said Marsh. "Now, how about these faculty? What can you tell me about those faculty who lost their tenure because apparently Dean Hartley did not support them?"

Now Caroline hesitated. "I probably spoke out of turn, there, detective. Frankly, this is the kind of juicy rumor-mongering that goes on around here. Again, I would think that maybe Dean Riley could help you, although several go so far back that you might want to talk to our retired provost, John Palmer."

"Hah. You might as well add John Palmer to your list of suspects, detective," spoke Hank, jumping in.

Marsh sighed. "Dr. Cruz wasn't kidding, then, was she, when she said there'd be lots of candidates for motive. Why would the retired provost have a motive to kill Hartley?"

Hank glanced at Berrian, perhaps wishing he hadn't jumped in so quickly. Berrian, though, was looking at his watch, and may have tuned us out. His checking of a timepiece affected me like a yawn. I glanced at my watch: only 10:37. "Well, rumor has it that Hartley was having an affair with Palmer's wife. In fact, the story goes that Palmer 'retired' early because his wife demanded it when Palmer discovered the affair. She claimed he had been negligent at home by working so many hours at his job."

"No, you don't say," joked Howard, looking up from his BlackBerry. "People work too many hours here? Never!"

"Shut up, Howard," declared Berrian. "Do you ever give that wit of yours a rest?"

Marsh continued to scribble on her note pad. "O.k., so I have Dean King, John Palmer, some faculty that I'll have to track down via either Palmer or Dr. Riley. Oh, by the way, does Palmer still live in the area?"

"Yes," answered Howard. "He lives near me on Cattail Lake— about a half hour away."

"Uh, thanks," said Marsh, scribbling the information down. "Now, who else might have a motive?"

All of a sudden we were quiet. The looks from the president clearly suggested that we should offer no more suggestions.

"How about students? What was his relationship with students?"

After several seconds, Victor surprisingly spoke up. "Well, as a dean, he would have been the one to often have to bear bad news to students. Graduation requirements not fulfilled. Grades that wouldn't be overturned. That kind of stuff."

"Did Dean Hartley have a secretary who might have kept track of students who met with Hartley?"

"The deans share an administrative assistant, Cicely Irons. Each one of them probably works differently with Cicely. Check with her."

"I'll do that. We'll probably want to see Dean Hartley's e-mail. Will we have any problem getting that?"

Hank looked to Berrian for guidance. With a slight nod of the head from him, Hank responded. "We should be able to do that, detective. Alan Yost is my CIO. He can help you out."

"Detective, I think we may have done all we can to help you right now. Why don't you talk to these other people and allow me to continue with my meeting? I can assume you are done for now." The last statement was just that, and not a question, coming from Berrian.

Marsh stuck her pen back in the pen holder on her notebook pad and pushed her seat away from the end of the table. "I suppose so. We know where to find you."

"And, detective, I trust that you will be able to convince the media to keep this as low key as possible. The university needs to protect its image, of course."

"Well, **President** Berrian." Marsh enunciated Berrian's title with all the emphasis available to her. "I can't guarantee anything. You will have the press swarming you, so some of that will be how you can handle it. From our end, it doesn't help us to let the media get out of control either. Mostly, we'll just have to see how the investigation proceeds." Marsh smiled for several seconds. "In the meantime, expect me to get back in touch."

"Detective," said Veronica, getting up as Marsh turned to the door. She had a piece of paper in her hand. "Here are some of the names, office numbers and phone numbers of a few of the people we discussed here today. In a couple of cases, I noted their schedules for today, also."

"Thank you, Ms. Miller, very much!"

"Well, that was interesting," announced Berrian, after Marsh had left, getting up to get some coffee. "Let's hope like hell they can solve it quickly and that it's not one of our people responsible." Bob poured himself some coffee, then suspiciously sniffed at his cup.

"How can it not be one of our people, Bob?" asked Caroline. "Student, faculty member, administrator, we're all Boan."

"Don't be so hasty. It could have been a family member, a friend, a non-University vendetta. One's got to stay optimistic about these things." Berrian had taken off his jacket again, hanging it over the chair. "Anyway, you heard pretty much the basics there from Marsh. Victor and I have contacted the communications department and they'll be working with the media. Later this afternoon, after this meeting is over, I'll give a prepared statement that they are working on right now."

"Is it best to wait until later this afternoon, sir?" Caroline asked the question on my mind.

"Bully! Of course, it is. If I go running to the media right now, it looks like we're trying to cover something up. Makes much more sense to let the police get a better handle on this, so that I can know what to respond to. For now, if anyone wants a statement from leadership, they'll be told that we are in an all-day meeting and will respond when we are done. So, what did you get accomplished? It's 10:50. You've been meeting for three and a half hours almost. What's crossed off the agenda?"

There was a lengthy pause as we all pretended to review our agenda and notes. 'He can't think we accomplished that much given the interruptions and the distractions.' Nevertheless, I wasn't going to be the one to point that out. Howard would surely be the one.

Veronica scrolled on her laptop, reviewing the notes. "Enrollment: basically good, per Howard. Request to have weekly actual, goal and stretch reports sent to members of cabinet. Howard to produce every Friday. Spirit Week: Mark to discuss with deans the possibility of allowing more students to miss class to participate. Caroline to call Aaron Cartwright to move more money into the budget. Textbook buyback policy..." Veronica hesitated. "Well, help me out, gang. I have a few notes here, but no action steps."

"We decided to table the discussion until Bob and Victor returned," said Caroline.

Howard sat straight up in his seat. "Holy cow, they're back."

"Ha, Ha. Howard. Let's put that off until next week then," responded Berrian.

Veronica typed for a few seconds on her laptop, obviously catching this for her records, and then started scrolling with her index finger again. "Average class size: well, that's right, it's been tabled also. Also, a request by Mark to discuss accelerated more."

"Why for?" inquired Berrian.

"Oh, it doesn't necessarily have to be as part of cabinet, Bob. I was merely asking some questions, and I actually have a note to discuss in a future one-on-one. I think it just got mixed into the minutes because it is related to average class size."

"That's right," said Veronica. "Sorry about that." She smiled, hit probably her delete key, and then proceeded with the review of the meeting so far. "Is that tabled for next meeting, or do we come back to that today?"

"Next meeting!" exploded the president with a surprisingly unexpected intensity.

Veronica continued as if the explosion was nothing new, which it probably wasn't for her. "After that, we discussed the bowling team incident, but got interrupted by you and Detective Marsh. I believe, however, that Caroline was merely informing the leadership team, and there is nothing else for it. Is that correct, Caroline?"

"Yes, V." I was surprised to hear Caroline use a nickname for anyone at the table, although if it would be anyone, Veronica made the most sense. No professional threat there.

"Excellent. Good progress. Thank you, Caroline, for leading."

Caroline nodded, lips pursed tightly.

How could he be pleased with the progress? By my count, we still had nine more agenda items and only a couple of more hours. Maybe the meeting would move more quickly now that the president was back and in control.

"Go back to the beginning, Veronica. What would be the next item on the agenda not covered?" asked Berrian, wiping away some crumbs, probably from Hank's bagel, on the table in front of him.

"That would be 'House of Cards Scholarship Night' and Howard."

"Ah, yes, the gambling blow-out for raising money!" stated Howard. "The publicity on this has been pathetic, to put it mildly, and we're now less than a month from the event."

"Didn't I see something in the *Hooks, Lines and Sinkers* last month?" asked Victor.

"I don't remember. However, it doesn't cost us anything to promote this in the student newspaper and our students are hardly the high rollers we want for the event. Can't we get something into the local papers in the surrounding area?" Howard played with a loose thread on his shirt sleeve.

"Good lord, we need to find an EVP for Communications and Relations," sighed the president. He scrolled down his agenda with his finger. "I hope to god you have an update on that under 'Hiring Update', Victor."

"Yes, sir, I do. Kraft and Selbst have two candidates coming to campus first week of September." Kraft and Selbst was the search firm that worked with me to get the provost position. Tina Noone, the liaison for Kraft and Selbst, evidently exerted a lot of influence with Berrian when it came to the provost search. I could only assume the same for this EVP search.

"I hope to god these two are better than that idiot they brought to campus last month. What was his name?" Berrian chewed on the end of his pencil.

"Wesley Calvin, sir," offered Victor weakly.

"Oh, god, yes. I kept wanting to call him Wes Craven. What a freaking nightmare? I hope you told Kraft/Selbst that we expected better results."

"I did, sir. Still, I caution you about talking to them directly. That's what happened before." Victor kept his eyes down while speaking.

"You've made your point, Victor. However, I don't think any of us are unhappy that Mark is with us."

I smiled uneasily. How should I take that exchange? Victor had confirmed my suspicion that Noone had incredible power with the president.

"Anyway, think positively everyone. Veronica, make a note that I will talk to communications about more publicity. How many people have RSVP'd, Howard?"

"About twenty-four people, sir. The usual culprits: board members, retired faculty, and a couple of jocks."

"Which jocks?" asked Hank, suddenly coming to life.

"Uh, I'm pretty sure Sherman Head and Larry Garth have confirmed."

I knew of Sherman Head. Everyone knew of Sherman Head: Boan's most famous alum. An outstanding basketball star at Boan, he went onto the NBA to have a spectacular career, used his fame to leverage several key business deals, including his endorsement of computers used in probably 75% of the secondary schools in the Midwest. He was a reputed multi-millionaire now, and everything he touched, including executive production of mediocre movies, made him more and more money. A devoted Boan alumnus, he came to several basketball games every year, and participated in any number of fund-raising events, such as this "casino" scholarship night.

However, I had no clue about Garth.

"Uh, who's Garth?" I had to ask.

"Larry Garth was a star member of our soccer team about ten years ago. He's done pretty well in the European League, and played on the last two U.S. World Cup teams." Hank looked at me with obvious surprise that I hadn't heard of Garth.

Apparently I continued to lower Hank's estimation of me. "Oh, I don't pay that much attention to the World Cup."

"Well, we better get more than twenty-four people. I'll light a fire with communications. Meanwhile, what's my role again?" Berrian inquired.

"You're the kick-off speech. Then, we'd like to have you do the opening deal."

"Excuse me," I interrupted. "Opening deal? Is this like the opening pitch?"

"Of course," replied Howard.

Caroline had a partial smirk on her face, but otherwise I was alone in my mirth.

Berrian clapped his hands. "Anything else, Howard?"

"No, sir."

"Then, how about endowment perpetuity?"

Howard ruffled through his notes. "Well, as most of you know, since the principal remains intact, endowments typically can go on for basically forever. The question is what to do if the name associated with the gift brings about an inappropriate association that hinders the university's reputation. We now need to consider the case of Peter Taylor."

"As in Taylor Field House?" I asked.

"The one and only. I don't know if you saw this story, Mark, but when Taylor passed away last spring, there was some speculation that he had once been a member of the Nazi party."

Berrian shook his head. "That was ugly."

"The press had their usual field day, didn't they?" chimed Hank.

"Yeah, well two weekends ago, there was a Sunday four-page spread in *The Chicago Sun-Times* on Taylor's so-called Nazi associations. Very little direct evidence, if you ask me, and spotty journalism at its worst." Howard nearly spat out the last phrase.

"So, do we look into pulling his name from the field house?" asked Berrian.

"What else can we do?" said a forlorn Victor.

"It's our first test of the perpetuity clause since we adopted it two years ago. I think we need to be careful in how we react," offered Hank.

"Does anybody know if we've received any flak about it?" asked Berrian. "Is the *Hooks, Lines and Sinkers* interested in digging up this non-story?"

"I wouldn't worry, sir," declared Caroline. "Most of today's students don't even know the field house is named after a ninety-year old man who had a soft spot for the institution where his son got his degree. For all they know, students think we named it after Lawrence Taylor."

I laughed, seeing Caroline for the first time participating in the friendly joking that formed a significant part of the weekly meetings. "Or, maybe Elizabeth Taylor," I added.

A few people chuckled. "Or, Taylor Hicks." All of us erupted at Howard's joke.

"Anyway," Howard went on, after letting the laughter die down a little, "there's not a whole lot of press right now, but we should have a plan. My recommendation would be that we take a resolution to the board to drop the Taylor name."

"Wait a second, Howard," I exclaimed. "Everyone at this table seems to think that a) the story is mostly hogwash, and b) that no-one has even made the association yet. Why do we have to do anything right now?"

"You need to get ahead of these things, Mark," offered Berrian. "We have a board meeting on October 1, so we need to be prepared, because in the six weeks or so between now and then, the story could get worse, and the connection with the field house could be made an issue by alumni, or some reporter trying to make a name for himself, or even a board member."

At the next break I definitely needed to find aspirin. "It still seems kind of rotten. Anyone talk to the family? I'm assuming there's family left?" I asked.

"One daughter and her family. The son died in the Vietnam War, and Taylor's wife passed away years ago."

"I would think the daughter deserves some conversation about this." I felt ready to dig in my heels.

"Too premature, Mark," countered Berrian. "Whenever we talk to her, we need to already know what we want to do."

A knock on the door interrupted us. "Come in," boomed the president.

The same frail girl who had brought us coffee earlier in the morning was now most likely wheeling in our lunches. Either that or shoes for all of us, because the boxes easily could have come from the local Foot Locker.

Berrian sighed at the interruption. "Looks like lunch is here. It's only 11:40. Let's just plow on until around noon, then we'll break into them. Now, anything else on this Taylor issue?" While the president paused, the girl struggled to move a heavy ice bucket of soft drinks onto the table alongside the wall. Then, she started to clear the coffee. I was disappointed to not see a fresh batch of coffee with lunch.

"I guess not. So, Howard, why don't you draft language for the board meeting about the Taylor name?"

"I still think we're being a bit heartless," I responded.

"Oh, I'm sorry. I thought I had already allowed the topic to have one last pass around the table." Again, Berrian's mood had turned on what seemed a minor comment. I was rapidly learning how my new boss's focus could shift dramatically from supportive to challenging.

"You're right, Bob. My bad." I vowed not to open my mouth again until I was putting lunch in it.

"Let's get this other naming issue out of the way, Howard. What about the College of Education Naming agenda item?"

"This will be a little awkward given the turn of the events with Dean Hartley this morning. Mike and I were working on a couple of key alumni to endow the College of Education and to bear their name. Michael wanted us to pursue the afore-mentioned Sherman Head despite many objections."

"To start, that idiot Head was an Arts and Sciences major. Why would he want his name on the College of Education?" snapped Caroline.

"I think because Porterhouse's name is already on the College of Arts and Sciences," replied Hank.

"And he can't have a stake to that College," spoke Howard.

"The pun master is at it again," groaned Berrian.

"Then, let him have the College of Education." Victor said. "I assume he has that kind of money to throw around."

Hank chuckled. "Heck, yes. It would be a small drop in the bucket for him."

"So, what's the problem?" demanded Berrian.

"He was hardly a great student while here, Bob," spoke up Caroline. "He graduated with a 2.2 in General Studies. The faculty has always had some difficulty with him being such a visible figure in anything but the sporting arena. When some of them heard that Michael pushed for Sherman Head's name on the college, many complained."

"Maybe we should call Detective Marsh back for additional motives," chimed Howard.

"Money talks, bullshit faculty can walk," sniped Berrian.

"Wow, Bob," I said, breaking my vow of silence, "tell us what you really think! Kidding aside, though, has something like that ever been an issue before with an alum who wants to give a huge gift?"

"Most of our alumni made their money as a result of their hard work at Boan, not from their athletic abilities, so this is new territory for us." All of a sudden, Victor had become chatty.

"I still think we tell the faculty that we appreciate their opinion, but we go where the money is." Berrian pushed back his chair as if to indicate the discussion was over. "Let's grab some boxes and move on with a working lunch."

I prayed that my disappointment in not having free time to enjoy lunch didn't show. I stayed in my seat to let the others get their first choices.

"I've got an idea," announced Hank, as he grabbed a Coke and waited for Howard to pick through the boxes. "Let's kill two birds with one stone; as soon as we pull Taylor's name off the field house, let's offer it to Head."

"Heckuva idea, Hank," declared Berrian, checking his BlackBerry. "Give me a minute to check a call and we'll get back to work over lunch."

I slumped and laid my head on the table.

Chapter Three

It didn't take me long to become completely disconnected from the meeting over lunch. As soon as I started biting into my ham and Swiss sandwich, a wave of sleepiness swept over me.

I drifted off to arbitrary thoughts not connected in any way to the meeting: the thought of Michael Hartley, a man I had barely met, dead; Alyssa in a white, flowery dress that she had worn to her cousin's wedding early in the summer, an image so sweet and beautiful that I reveled in it for quite a long time; the dead fox Alyssa and I had found on our property on just our second day in the house, his eye glazed over and yet haunting; the good-bye party thrown by my staff at Farrington back in May, replete with DVDs and books and compact discs, all titles I coveted (my staff certainly knew me well); the box of personal items still sitting on my desk in my yet-to-be-used office; Natalie's smile when I told her I had accepted the position at Boan and that we would be moving to only about an hour away from her sister; my father's haggard face when I had last seen him, a face weary with untold stories from when I had previously seen him four years earlier; the bottle of Bass ale waiting for me when I got home ... if I got home.

Caroline awakened me out of my trance by snapping her fingers in my direction. "What are your thoughts, Mark?" she asked.

"Uh, sorry," I stammered. "I was distracted for a second. What's the question?" I asked.

Caroline sighed. "Should the renovation of the library be postponed until next summer?"

I flushed with embarrassment to have missed, I assumed, the background for this question. Clearing my throat to buy some time, I glanced at the agenda. If we had been staying on topic, I had completely missed everything on sexual harassment. At this point, better to show my ignorance than fake an answer.

"You need to excuse me. I think lunch knocked me out a bit. Can you back up and give me the particulars again?" I looked at Berrian and shrugged my shoulders.

"It's simple, Mark," said Hank, requiring me to turn from addressing Caroline to looking at him. "The plan for the library renovation was to have it start this fall, but our latest survey of students says that the archives and the study areas, which would have to be shut down for several months, will be needed. That's why Caroline has recommended waiting until next summer."

"It sounds like a good plan to me. Needless to say, I haven't even talked with, uh," I struggled to remember the head librarian's name, "um, Carla about that."

"Do you mean Charlotte?" asked Victor.

"Uh, yes, Charlotte." 'Duh,' I thought. 'Charlotte Webb. How could I forget that name, especially for a librarian?' "Anyway, if we know it will disrupt students, then obviously we put it off."

"We're always disrupting students, you know. We still have over 60% of them around during the summer." Disorientation still swarmed over me: was Hank taking issue with me or with Caroline?

"If we can minimize the disruptions, then our student satisfaction results are better," challenged Caroline.

I rubbed my eyes. "Anyway, unless I missed something else, I would agree with Caroline's suggestion."

"Alright, let's take a quick break," said the president. "Maybe Mark can get back in the game. It is 12:45 right now, so come back at 1:00."

As Howard raced by me, I approached the president. "I'm sorry, Bob. I'm not used to meetings running longer than two or three hours, tops. It was part of the Farrington culture to keep meetings brief. Give me time, I'll adjust."

"I hope so," joked Berrian, although whether a half joke or a full joke was unclear. He followed Caroline out the door. Somehow, Hank and Veronica had already left the room also.

Victor stood over his chair, checking his BlackBerry. "I zoned out there, Victor. Anything I missed about sexual harassment?"

"Don't do it."

I laughed nervously. "Thanks for the tip."

"That's what she said," cracked Howard coming back into the room. He must hover, waiting for his opportunity to spring a joke.

Victor rolled his eyes at Howard, and then turned to look at me. "Basically, our lawyers tightened the policy. There was an incident, well, with Hartley, last year that caused us to want to make some things tougher and clearer.

Since you didn't know the previous language, it's not that important. The new language is in that memo I shoved over to you."

I looked down to see a two-page memo from Victor on Boan letterhead. It could be read later.

Victor had stopped checking his BlackBerry and headed to the door; Howard resumed checking his BlackBerry. I pulled my boring old Verizon phone out of my pocket and noted no messages. Just as I liked it.

"Either of you have any aspirin?" I asked, rubbing my head.

"Always carry it," said Victor, pulling a small bottle out of his pocket, and handing me two of them.

Finding a water fountain, I took the aspirin and ducked into the restroom again. Leaning over the urinal, this time wonderfully alone, I reviewed the morning's meeting so far. I tried to recall my various comments and the effects they had on my colleagues. I had certainly participated more than I would have predicted. Outside of the interruption by Detective Marsh, we had covered a lot of the agenda items. Maybe there was hope, with four or five agenda items left, that we could be done by 2:00 and I could get settled in my office. However, washing my hands, I counted off the agenda items discussed but not particularly settled: enrollment, spirit week, at least one if not both of the silly naming issues. What had we accomplished? The only resolution that came to my mind was that the library renovation had been put off. I needed to make a note to alert Charlotte Webb. I wondered if she would spin back a response: "terrific."

I hustled back into the meeting room right before Veronica, who had come in from outside. We were the last to return. Howard, Victor and Berrian checked, what a surprise, their BlackBerries, Hank looked at a newspaper he must have found somewhere, and Caroline tried to get all the empty lunch boxes piled into the undersized trash can.

"Garrett Jones just texted me, sir," said Victor, breaking the silence. "He's back on campus. He says that most of the police and other related personnel are gone, with the exception of Marsh and Klinger, who continue to interview people on campus."

Berrian did not look up from his BlackBerry. "Tell Jones that I want him and you to meet with me right after this meeting," he barked. "I want a complete debriefing of how security handled this mess."

"What time should I tell him is the end of this meeting?"

I watched with rapt attention, hoping to hear an hour somewhere this side of nightfall.

Berrian glanced from his BlackBerry to his watch. "Oh, who really knows? Just tell him you'll call him when we're ready. We can go back to my office for that meeting."

Victor quietly sighed; Caroline and I, closest to him, had to have been the only ones to hear. One could sympathize for poor Victor more and more as the day went on.

"Alrighty, then. We continue," said Berrian as we all settled back into our seats. "Debit cards. Caroline and Hank, the floor is yours."

Hank pulled out of his pile of materials some stapled handouts. Even from the other end of the table, I could recognize thick packets of materials. So much for moving quickly through the rest of the agenda. Hank started to show his own impatience with the shaking of restless legs.

"As everyone knows, except Mark, we've been looking into a system that can give students ID/debit cards that can serve all their purposes for money exchange: tuition, bookstore, meal plans, parking, copying, athletic events, you name it. Typically, these cards are called 'One Cards,' because they are the one card that can serve almost every need for students. Even faculty and staff would get these, so we can also run our incidental charges through the card."

As Hank talked, I skimmed the eleven pages in the packet, relieved to see that all but the first two pages provided examples of other schools' cards. I saw an Oklahoma *Sooner OneCard,* a *UNC One Card* for North Carolina, the U Conn *Husky One Card,* the Miami Dade College *MDC One Card,* the Sacramento State *Sac State OneCard,* the University of Colorado *Buff OneCard,* the Troy University *Trojan OneCard,* the Clemson University *Tiger 1 Card,* and the College of Southern Idaho *CSI Eagle OneCard.* All of these must have been connected to Higher One, the bank discussed on the first two pages of Hank's handout. The naming of these cards lacked originality, although the Buff OneCard and the Trojan OneCard sounded like a bad combination in a dark bar after a few drinks.

"Now, we pretty much know after the presentation at the July cabinet meeting that we want to go with Higher One." Hank had been storming on while I had absent-mindedly flipped through the pages. "They clearly are the major players in this field, and have the majority of the contracts across the country."

"Is that a good thing or a bad thing, Hank?" asked the president. "I don't want to be in the same ranks as the College of Southern Idaho or Miami Dade College," he sneered. I wasn't the only one skimming the handouts while Hank talked—another reason to force all university administrators to teach a class. A good teacher learns early in a career not to pass out handouts while trying to make important points. Inevitably, the teacher loses the students' attention. A glance at my colleagues confirmed that all were looking at various pages in the packet.

"That's something we could discuss, sir, but at the July meeting you requested that we commit to Higher One and get this thing wrapped up."

"I seriously doubt that's something I would have said."

"I believe so, sir." Hank looked desperately to the rest of us for guidance. "Caroline, do you remember that? You and I are pursuing this together."

"You forget that I was in Hawaii during that meeting," smiled Caroline wickedly. An element of ruthlessness certainly infuses these meetings.

"Oh, yeah. Anyway, Bob, we can go back and talk about the other companies, but I'm pretty sure you said to go with Higher One and move quickly." Hank had begun to sweat.

"I didn't say that, Hank. But that's o.k. It's like with my wife, sometimes I say one thing and she hears something else."

I shuddered at Berrian's patronizing comment. Acting as cautious peacemaker, I said, "perhaps the minutes can confirm."

Veronica shook her head at me. "I'll dig them up now, but they may not offer much."

Shocked, I started to open my mouth to say something, but Veronica distinctly mouthed to me, "don't go there." I looked over at the president, who was slapping Hank on the back.

"It's o.k., Hank. If that's what you and Caroline recommend, then by all means, we'll do it. I still expect the Boan card to be individualized and unique to us."

"What nifty name shall we give it, sir?" asked Howard, rousing himself from a semi-comatose state. "There are some good names here: the Trojan One Card, The Tiger 1 Card (I wonder if this means that Tiger Woods has the Tiger 2 Card), and my favorite for the meal plan, the Husky One Card."

Caroline glared at Howard. "We've already set up a contest for the students to name the card, Howard. The winner will get $200 donated directly to his or her account once the cards are set up." Caroline pointed at the second page at the handout. "You can see that proposal at the bottom of page two, where the dark, thick line is."

"I like the SturgOneCard," mocked Howard. "Can I submit names? I won't take the $200."

"Oh, shut up, Howard," grumbled Caroline.

"I could see the One Boan Card. Available to anyone with a spine!" I joined the fray. Howard's silly interjections during the meeting were addictive and contagious. Veronica snickered.

Howard refused to step aside. "How about the Boan University Sturgeon One Card, or more succinctly the BUS OneCard? We could see if the city could allow our students to get a bus pass through it."

"That's not a bad idea, Howard," pronounced Berrian.

"It isn't?" questioned Howard and I in unison. "You do realize, sir," Howard said, "that I sometimes use humor in stressful situations."

"What the heck is so stressful now, Howard? It's not like a ping-pong match. Besides, sometimes out of silliness comes a good idea. Hank, can you look into that with the City Transit Authority?"

Hank looked at Caroline, who took the bullet for him. "I can look into that, Bob. After all, I'm the one that negotiated getting the campus on a different route."

"Recognize, however, Bob," continued Hank, "that this will add additional cost, which we will have to pass on to the students. One of the things we need to decide is what will be the services allowed for students on this card."

"I can help with that, Hank," said Caroline. "Obviously, we want to be able to electronically transfer tuition, financial aid, refunds, fines, all that stuff up front. I think that's a given, right?" She looked uneasily toward Berrian, but the president nodded his head slightly.

"Great," Caroline went on, "then we could use it as a basic student ID that will work for the library, the athletic events, the bookstore, the meal plans, parking, access in and out of residence halls, maybe all university buildings, campus ATM's, and so forth. There are a lot of options."

"Don't forget, Bob," jumped in Hank, "that we also want to consider using this for faculty and staff, so that all of us would have these capabilities. **And,** we could include payroll."

"Can everybody use them off campus, like at Mario's Pizzeria or even the McDonalds out on Jefferson Street?" asked Berrian.

"Absolutely, it can work just like a debit/credit card."

"Do parents have the ability to put money directly into their children's accounts?" I inquired.

"You bet," said Caroline.

"And what's the cost to us?" asked Berrian.

"That depends, to some degree, on the number of services the card provides. Interestingly, the more standard services, the cheaper the cost is to us. Of course, something like a City Bus pass is not standard and will almost certainly cost more." Hank raised his voice slightly to make the latter point.

"Then forget that stupid idea."

"Excellent point, Bob," said Howard. "I get worried when you start taking me too seriously."

"I doubt that could ever happen, Howard."

"In addition," continued Hank, raising his voice this time to cut through the old boy networking of the Howard and Bob show, "the cost depends upon the number of people who use it. If we decide to add faculty and staff, well, then, that adds a lot more users, which actually decreases overall costs."

"Don't forget, also," interrupted Caroline, "that we will have other costs associated with this. Card readers for buildings, if we go that route, for the parking lots, for the copiers across the campus, and so forth. I think that's where we still haven't anticipated costs."

"Yost is looking into that, Bob."

"Anything else, Hank and Caroline?"

"I think that's it for now, Bob," responded Hank, after giving Caroline a couple of seconds to say anything. "I'll bring the costs to a cabinet meeting in the near future."

"Keep me posted on that naming thing, Caroline," said Howard. "I'm starting to like the simple Boan Sturgeon One Card, or the BS One Card. What do you all think?"

"Oh, shut up, Howard," snapped Caroline.

Howard feigned being hurt. "That has to be the fourth or fifth time this meeting, Mr. President, that someone has told me to shut up. I'm quite wounded."

"You're right, Howard. Being told to shut up five times in a meeting is unacceptable. So, Howard?"

"Yes, sir."

"Shut up! There, now you are at an even half a dozen."

Howard feigned even more shock and resentment, Veronica gave a half laugh, but for the most part, the natives had become restless and unresponsive. I fought to keep my eyes open. The room felt incredibly hot. I looked around the room for a thermostat, but saw nothing. Meanwhile, Berrian charged ahead.

"O.k., cabinet retreat. We put off the usual July retreat until Mark had started, so we need to get back to planning one. We need to identify a potential date, a location, and a topic. Veronica, you want to start with possible dates?"

"Sure, Bob. In keeping with past practice, we're looking at Thursday and Friday possibilities. That way, if anyone wants to take advantage of the location, they can stay over for the weekend. As I looked through the fall schedule, I had to eliminate dates that Bob couldn't do, dates with important Boan events that some or all of you couldn't miss and any potential holidays. With that I see two possibilities: October 12 and 13, or November 2 and 3."

My colleagues scrolled through their BlackBerries to review their calendars. Not having that on my Verizon phone, I leaned back in my chair, closed my eyes and tried to think of any conflicts at home. Nothing came to my mind. It took all my effort to reopen my eyes. While the group prattled on about the possible dates, I doodled on my notepad.

I refocused myself upon hearing Berrian declare, "I think we have October 12 and 13 as the dates, then."

"Friday, October 13, with this bunch," chuckled Howard. "That's scarier than Jason Voorhees any day."

"Next, location! Where should we have it?" posed the president.

"Surely Crystal Lake is not booked?" I offered.

"Huh?" said Caroline.

"Don't worry, Caroline. Mark's got more Howard in him than we knew. Crystal Lake was the setting for the *Friday the 13*th movies." Berrian did crack a smile in offering his explanation.

"I have checked some of the places we've used in the past," announced Veronica, putting us back on task. "There's the Waterbird Lakeside Inn near the Dunes. They generally have availability in the fall."

"Ugh," groaned Berrian. "I hated that place. It was packed and full of kids when we went there. I don't think we should go there again."

Even though I knew better, I found myself drifting off again. My notes scrawled on the agenda were illegible at times. I vainly tried to remember what word I had written next to "textbook buyback policy" on the agenda. I really needed to work on my attention span.

I was fully extracted from my stupor by the ever-present rumble of a Berrian point. "Veronica," he snapped, "let's shoot for Chicago. Keep us posted."

"Next, agenda!"

"Here you are, sir," said Howard, passing his meeting agenda to the president. Even from my seat, I could see little written on it. This contrasted greatly with mine, already filled with notes, doodles, and an ornate "help me" scrawled along the bottom. 'When had I written that?' I wondered.

"Jesus. What a smart ass. The agenda for the retreat!" Berrian crumpled up Howard's agenda and aimed a perfect shot at the trash basket in the corner. Unfortunately, since the basket was full of our lunch boxes, it bounced to the side of the trash and landed under the table where our empty soft drink cans stood, waiting for, what I assumed was, recycling.

Howard shrugged his shoulders and got up to retrieve the wad of paper. I got up to stretch and to force myself to be more attentive.

Victor raised his hand. "Yes, Victor."

"Perhaps we should review the strategic plan and provide updates."

Hank and Howard groaned virtually simultaneously. "Victor," spoke Hank, "we update that damn thing two or three times a year. How many times do I have to hear a GAP report?"

"Say what?" I asked.

"That's the 'Graduation Advancement Plan,' Mark. Advisors are supposed to track their work with all students about keeping them on a four-year graduation plan." Caroline jotted something down on her agenda while responding to me.

"It's part of our retention metrics, Mark," continued Berrian.

"Yeah, we hammer it home every year, and yet despite minimal advances in the percentage of plans completed," offered Hank, "our retention numbers go all over the place: one year we went up 9% in retention, the next down 4.5%, despite the stupid GAP numbers being slightly higher."

"So, despite the GAP, there was a GAP in student success, eh?" I quipped.

Caroline smiled. "Yeah, something like that."

"The year retention went down 4.5% I charged Caroline and the provost, meaning you, now, to take over the retention committee and find out why students are leaving." Berrian had popped a second mint or lifesaver into his mouth.

I noted that "retention" was already written on my agenda as something to clarify from Bob at my first one on one. When had I written that down?

"Provost Palmer and I continued to find data that showed that students left because of inability to complete their degrees, usually in the form of hidden pre-requisites, or canceled classes, or curriculum changes. So, we keep trying to use the GAP as an indicator of student completion of graduation requirements, but the numbers don't yet validate it. It's been frustrating for me, although Palmer typically blew it off." Caroline's clipped speech returned when mentioning my predecessor.

"Why's that?" I asked.

"He harped on the idea that the greatest indicator of student success was whether students were first generation college students in their families."

"Ah, so he thought success was in the genes."

"Then, the GAP should be ..."

"Damn it, Howard. Don't even go there. We can all see that jeans joke coming from a mile away." Berrian's mood continued to swing from moment to moment. "Besides we've gotten a little away from the discussion at hand. Do we review the strategic plan at the retreat?"

"Because we always did the retreat in July," suggested Veronica, "we naturally spent some of the time going over the new fiscal year's goals, so the strategic plan became a natural discussion point in July."

"Are you looking at the old agendas there?" Berrian asked Veronica, who was peering at her laptop.

"Yes. Last year, we discussed goal setting on Thursday morning, central services restructuring in the afternoon, athletic expansion Friday morning, and then leadership training that Friday afternoon. Remember, that's when we had Richard Branson come in to speak to us."

"Richard BRANSON!" I nearly jumped out of my chair. "That had to cost a pretty penny."

"About a $100,000," grumbled Hank.

"Holy crap," I whispered, cowering back down in my seat.

"That's right," said Berrian. "We have occasionally had speakers come to the retreat. That's another option."

I looked at my watch: 1:54. My back hurt, my butt hurt, my brain was mush, and I had just learned that we had spent $100,000 on a guest speaker. For a moment, I envied Michael Hartley.

"Other potential topics?" asked Berrian.

Howard jumped in. "I think we should discuss tuition control. We haven't done a good job at keeping tuition down in these tough economic times. We need to take a long, hard look at our projections for tuition for at least the next two or three years. I would even propose that we offer a tuition freeze or some other option for students, such as a cap on tuition if students take so many credit hours." Howard paused, apparently expecting Hank to contribute additional information. When he didn't, Howard continued. "The truth of the matter is my reps are getting killed on the front lines by our tuition. They say that with almost every student, they have to justify the tuition costs."

"That's the same everywhere, Howard," responded Berrian. "Our tuition increases are about the same percentage as IU's, Purdue's, Ball State's, Butler's, and so forth. We remain competitive in the state."

"Yes, but there is a reputation gap, Bob," said Howard.

"Oh, god, not gap again," joked Hank.

"Oh, cut him some slack, Hank. He needs an outlet." I grimaced at my own bad pun.

Howard offered a weak smile at me, but turned back to look at the president. "All kidding aside, Bob, so many potential students look at the cost to go to Boan, and then ask how we compare in terms of educational quality with the big schools in the state."

"That's a load of crap. Indiana doesn't necessarily have quality. There's no real evidence that their students as a group get a better education than ours."

"Whether there is evidence or not, Bob, this is a perception. And perception is reality to the person who holds it."

"Don't wax philosophical with me, Howard. We have to reduce the gap between perceptions and realities. And nobody make a gap joke." Berrian's eyes darted between me and Howard. As for me, I continued to struggle to stay engaged in the conversation. My limit had been reached for this meeting.

Victor raised his hand. Besides me, only Victor raised his or her hand when making a point. "Could I suggest, sir," Victor said, after Berrian acknowledged him with a slight nod of his blond head, "that we make the reputation/perception issue a main topic point at the retreat? This is something we've been hearing, both from Howard's staff and from surveys, for several years now."

Berrian sighed. "My university does not suffer from a reputation problem. If your staff thinks so, Howard, then perhaps we need to replace them all."

I could see Howard biting his lip, considering how to respond. To my surprise, Caroline came to his defense: "I don't know, Bob. Ever since Howard redefined his reps' roles and brought in his people, enrollment has gone up. So, they are obviously doing something right." When neither Berrian nor Howard responded, she resumed. "I agree with Victor that this could be a great overall subject for the retreat. I see lots of great angles. First off, given that Howard's staff says this, why are they still doing so well with enrollment numbers? We should look at that. The reputation may be a moot point if we are still able to convince enough students to come. Secondly, we could then have a presentation from Mark about the educational quality. You know, 'what has he seen in his first three months,' kind of presentation. Then, perhaps we could ask institutional research for some comparative data on how these other institutions define their educational quality. This could lead to great discussions about defining our niche, our marketing strategies, and who knows what else."

I was impressed by Caroline. For one thing, in a meeting apparently full of snippets of information and discussion, Caroline's offering stood out for its real merits. For the first time someone thought big picture, and I was immediately hopeful. We hadn't succumbed to pedantic quibbling over what bank should sponsor student debit cards, or about whether someone's name did or did not belong on one of our buildings. We had been given something to dig our teeth into, even if that digging wouldn't happen for three months. I felt rejuvenated.

Since no one else had said anything, I supported Caroline's suggestion. "This is a great idea, Caroline."

"I agree," Veronica declared, "even though my opinion is not important."

"Oh, hush," said Berrian in a slightly patronizing manner to Veronica, "it does too. How about the rest of you? Victor, I assume you like this as it is an offshoot of your initial suggestion?"

"Yes, I do."

"Howard?"

"Absolutely."

"Hank?"

"Uh, sure." Hank was hardly enthusiastic.

"What's wrong, grumpy?" asked Berrian.

"My ass just hurts from sitting in these lousy chairs for so long."

"Hey, facilities are your area. Order new chairs."

Hank offered a half smile and squirmed in his seat, apparently trying to find a better comfort level.

"O.k., so Howard and Caroline will start collecting information from the people who work with the students. Mark, you will work with the deans to identify how they see quality in their programs. Then, let's see…" Berrian reviewed some notes he had taken during Caroline's comments. "Oh, yeah, we need to have IR do some research for us."

"Tanya Tyler can do that, sir," responded Victor.

"Oh, yeah. She's that hot shot person we stole from IPFW, isn't she?"

"The one and only."

"Hmm? Maybe we should have her come to the retreat for at least one session."

"That would be a good idea, Bob," said Caroline. "And maybe Charlie Durant from Marketing?"

"Good idea."

Everyone remained quiet while we took some notes. I had to flip my agenda over to write "Educational Quality: Deans, IR, other?" Given a meaty topic, general thoughts formed in my mind about how to set up my piece of this. I added 'library and online' next to the word 'other' in my notes.

"So, that covers the retreat, right?" asked the president.

None of us said anything to the contrary, with only me nodding my head in affirmation.

"O.k., what next? We have to be getting close to the end of this agenda."

"Victor and hiring updates," said Veronica, who of all the members of this group appeared to be the least affected by the long meeting. Impressed, I made a mental note to ask how she managed that.

"Oh, yes, Victor, hiring updates. Where are we? How are we doing with the VP level searches and will we have faculty and other front line personnel in place by the first day of classes?"

Victor nervously shuffled through his handouts and pulled out copies of a spreadsheet. I reached across the table to grab mine and ones for Howard and Hank.

"We already talked about the EVP for Communications and Relations," said Victor, "and you can see it on the first line. Two candidates for campus interviews first week of September."

"And you've met these candidates, Victor?" asked the president.

"Yes, as has Howard who has been part of the search committee."

"And these are better candidates than the crap that came through last time?"

Victor looked to Howard to see if he would respond first. They held eye contact for a couple of seconds and then Howard, rolling up his sleeves, answered. "I think so, Bob. The woman has a long history of media relations at universities in Texas. The man has been the VP of Communications for a small college in Ohio. Neither one has everything we want, but both are good candidates."

"Hmm," muttered Berrian. "I'm still a little skeptical of Kraft and Selbst on this one." He paused for a moment, but when no one else added anything, he prodded Victor to continue. "O.k., what else?"

"The next three lines," continued Victor, "are the VP level searches currently going on. We're still looking for the VP of Facilities, and have just begun the VP of Training and Development and VP of Corporate Services searches."

"Corporate? That's an open position?" asked Berrian.

Howard sighed. "Yes, sir. It has been since Washington resigned."

"Does it have to be a VP position?"

"We discussed this, Bob, several weeks ago, and you supported it."

"I don't remember that. You sure?"

"Yes. At my one on one on July 9, followed by a quick update at the cabinet meeting on July 15." Howard checked his calendar via his BlackBerry.

"Hmm? You sure I didn't say that it was a possibility?"

"No, Bob. You blessed it." Howard certainly knew how to cover himself, even if he was a horrendous dresser.

"Fine. What else, Victor? How about advising and faculty? Are we fully staffed for those areas?"

"Advising is close. Caroline has one more entry level position she is trying to fill. Do you have any idea how far along you are, Caroline?"

"I don't know. I can text Jenny right now and ask her."

"Meanwhile, it's a little more complicated for faculty, Bob. For full-time faculty positions, we're short three nursing faculty and we're still looking for a full-timer in sculpture. Also, there are a large number of classes that have not had adjunct faculty assigned to them."

Berrian's fist slammed down on the table. "What the hell? Let's begin with the nursing. Those positions are always open. Why the hell can't we fill them?" Before even allowing Victor or someone else to respond, Berrian turned to me and pointed his finger at me: "I tell you, Mark, you need to work with Dean Linares. I'm getting tired of unfilled nursing positions."

"I'll make a note of that, Bob," I said, writing down NURSING FACULTY in all capital letters on the backside of my agenda.

"In defense of Linares, sir, these aren't the same open nursing positions. We did hire full-timers for the positions that had previously been open—there had actually only been two—but these three are open because of faculty resignations over the summer."

"What?" growled the president.

"Well, it seems that word got out about how much more we would pay the new nursing faculty, in order to entice them to come, than the current faculty. At least two of the three took exception to that, demanded immediate pay raises, and when we told them we couldn't do that right away, left us. As for the third, I believe she left us to have a baby."

"The only one credentialed to teach OB/GYN, I bet," chuckled Hank.

Victor smiled. "No, but that was one of the other two."

"Christ, what a nightmare. Still, look into this, Mark. We got those blue-hairs from the NLNAC coming in November, and this is the kind of thing they dinged us with last time. Lord, what I would give to not have a nursing program," sighed Berrian.

"And not have a university, probably, Bob," said Howard. "The nursing program still attracts a lot of students, many of whom we move into the other health classes."

"Yeah, yeah, I know. Give it a rest, Howard." Berrian leaned back in his chair and rubbed his eyes. "What other ones did you mention, Victor?"

"Sculpture and ..."

"Right! Freaking sculpture. Why the hell do we need a full-time faculty member in freaking sculpture?" A vein had appeared noticeably on the president's head.

"I'm not sure we do, Bob," said Victor. "This position had carried over last year with Palmer. He was adamant that fine arts needed one full-timer in each medium, and when Karen Neagle retired two years ago, we ended up with nobody in sculpture."

"Mark, look into that, too. Jesus."

"Will do, sir," I replied, adding SCULPTURE next to my notation about nursing.

"And then there are the un-contracted adjunct sir?" said Victor, checking off his last row on the spreadsheet in front of him. "If you look at that last line, sir, you'll see that forty-three sections don't have an adjunct assigned to them yet."

Berrian sighed. "Why not?"

"There's a different story for each one, sir. Adjunct come and go, and often leave us in the lurch a week before classes because they can make more money at another institution. Sometimes we've added classes because classes have filled. Sometimes the courses need credentialed adjunct that we can't find."

Berrian looked at me and sighed. "Mark, this is unacceptable. We should never be this close to classes and not have faculty assigned. You need to figure this out. If there's something Victor's group is not doing to help you, let him know. If your people are simply not getting it done, that is not acceptable."

"Uh, yes, sir," I responded, adding ADJUNCT next to SCULPTURE on my agenda backside. "I will point out that what Victor said is typical of the issues Farrington had also. No matter what, we always scrambled to fill a final few sections at the last minute every year."

"A few might be alright. Forty-three is appalling."

"Yes, sir." I looked to Victor to see if he had anything to add. His look suggested that he did not.

"Oh, Victor," spoke Howard in a sing-song voice.

"Yes, Howard," replied Victor, apparently ignorant of the tone of Howard's voice.

"Don't forget to add one dean of education to your list now."

"Really, Howard," gasped Veronica. "You're awful!"

"Thanks."

"Victor?" said Caroline, leaning over toward him. "Jenny confirms that final round interviews for that advising position are this Thursday."

Victor nodded confirmation and scrawled on his spreadsheet.

Suddenly, Berrian's mood changed from night to day. "Excellent. That brings us to the last item, which is Mark's initiation."

"I thought that was just it, sir," I half-heartedly joked.

"What was?"

"That last ten minutes. Or, maybe I should say that last ..." I looked at my watch: 3:03. "The last seven and one-half hours."

"No, the initiation is that you have to give us your immediate feedback on this meeting. What worked? What didn't work? What did you like? What didn't you like?"

I swept my eyes around the room, looking for signs of a joke. "You're kidding, right? Where's the guy who jumps out and says 'Candid Camera'?"

"No, really, Mark," said Berrian.

"He's not kidding, Mark. I had to do that when I started," revealed Caroline.

"How about the rest of you?" I asked.

"Oh, we were lucky, Mark. We preceded Bob in taking these positions," replied Howard.

Everyone sat silently, looking at me. Caroline glanced at her watch and I realized my answer would not be that important to them; getting the hell out of this room was important.

"Well, uh, gee, Bob, I'm pretty brain dead right now. Can that be the first thing at the next cabinet?"

"No. Tell us now." As I hesitated, Berrian tried to encourage me more. "This is important, Mark. We want to make sure we are working effectively as a team, so we need to know what connected with you and what didn't."

I hesitated one more time, bit the bullet, and jumped in. "I liked the sense of humor of everyone in this room, Howard's bad puns included. I think having that willingness to laugh at ourselves and each other is important." I paused again; while I could easily name a couple of things not to like, I didn't want to launch into them so quickly. Besides, outside of the ungodly length of the meeting, it hadn't been that bad, had it?

"In addition," I went on, "I like the diversity of topics here. I think I learned a lot about the breadth of things that we concern ourselves with. That's good for a first day. On the negative side, I think the meeting went on a tad too long." I stopped to gauge reactions. Caroline's seductive but mysterious smile had appeared, Bob's head angled down as he wrote, I assumed, my responses on his agenda, and Howard played with his BlackBerry. Hank, Veronica and Victor gave nothing away.

"Perhaps we could be a little tighter with agenda items. I don't want to say too much, but I am surprised by the number of items, and how some perhaps didn't merit this highest level of discussion." This time Veronica's warm smile accompanied the smile that hadn't left Caroline's face. No one else had changed in terms of their reactions.

"Finally," and I paused to articulate this in the best way possible, "what I want to reinforce for my part of these meetings, is that when I have an agenda item, I will make sure everyone gets copies of any relevant handouts well before the meeting. This is my commitment to you." I wasn't sure how many of my colleagues would turn this statement around to reflect what hadn't happened at this meeting. Reactions certainly hadn't changed from anything else I had just said.

I stopped and leaned back in my chair. For several seconds Berrian wrote, Veronica typed and everyone else waited.

Finally, the president looked up. "Is that it?" I nodded in affirmation. "Excellent. Meeting adjourned. Victor, call Jones and tell him to meet us at my office in 15 minutes."

And with that, he was gone. 'Who was that masked man?' I thought, tempted to quip it to the group, but people busied themselves by collecting possessions. "Thanks, all," I said, apropos of not particular gratitude, but just that it felt as if someone should say something at the end of this marathon session.

"See you, Mark," said Veronica as I left the room. No one else said anything. I raced to the Butler doors to gulp in whatever fresh air lay outside.

Chapter Four

Outside the air was heavy with humidity and the sky had turned overcast. A thunderstorm headed our way. It was still a welcome relief from the meeting room. I scrambled toward the Administration Building, only to hear "Hey, Dr. Carter. Welcome!"

A female figure approached me from the middle of the square. She wasn't close enough for me to make out her features, and I feared she would be someone I wouldn't recognize. As she got closer to me, I realized it was Henrietta Van Wyck, the faculty member who had chaired the provost search committee. Henry, as she preferred, was a short, slightly heavy-set woman, with long black hair, thick glasses, and a wonderful laugh. She had put me at ease in the provost interviews, simply by her personality.

"Hi, Henry. How's it going?"

"Not bad. I've been working on my human resource syllabus. I had some good ideas over the summer and finally came to my office today to incorporate them."

"Sounds good. When's your first day of class?"

"Next Monday. It's a Monday/Wednesday morning class."

I waved at Hank as he lumbered past me toward the Administration Building.

"Hi Mark. Hi Henry," said Hank, as he passed us.

"Hi Hank." Henry waited until he had gotten far enough away from us, then leaned toward me in a conspiratorial whisper. "So, you started right away with cabinet. Was it as weird as faculty think it is?"

I laughed. "You have to give me some context. Weird in what way? Weird in a *Blue Velvet* way? Or, something else?"

Henry responded with that deep heartfelt laugh I enjoyed during the interviews. "That's a good question. Hmm? Are you into Neil Young?"

"Absolutely. Even now that he is Neil Old."

Henry smiled, appropriately, but didn't laugh outright. "O.k., then I mean weird in a *Trans* kind of way. The faculty's perception is that cabinet meetings are so different from everything else related to leadership."

"I'm not sure I understand," I responded, looking at the sky to make sure the clouds weren't ready to pelt us with rain.

"I'm not sure I can explain it exactly. Boan's crafted a very public image of leadership. You know, *Harvest, Rust Never Sleeps, Comes a Time*. But, out of the limelight, leadership is doing stuff that we can't quite understand: *Trans*."

"Hmm? Maybe that's something I can't tell yet. What I can say is that it wasn't what I expected—which may not be a bad thing. Just different."

Henry smiled. "Oh well. I hope we're all wrong. Anyway, I want to get to my car before the rain starts," she said while looking to the sky. "See you later."

"You, too, Henry," I replied to her back as she shuffled away from me. I turned back toward the Administration Building and picked up my pace.

As I got in the building and turned down the hallway to my office, my administrative assistant, Shelley Ford, appeared. Extremely young, only a couple years out of one of Boan's own programs, Shelley had been promoted by Provost Palmer from a lower level position only two or three months before he abruptly resigned.

"Hi Shelley," I said, passing her in the narrow hallway.

"Afternoon, Dr. Carter. I'll be back at my desk in a couple secs."

"That's fine. I just got out of cabinet."

"Yeah, I know. When the first one of you gets back, the word gets spread quickly among the assistants."

I laughed. "I see. Is that so you all can get off of FaceBook and look busy?"

"Of course not." Shelley looked mortified by the suggestion.

"Just a joke, Shelley. So, who returned first?"

"I think Hank. I believe Leona told Melody who told me and so forth."

I smiled, not particularly caring for the specifics. "Anyway, back to the office to salvage at least an hour or so for the day."

In my office, I quickly shut my door and collapsed into my desk chair. It was now 3:20 and I wanted to go home. Since I had started early, Natalie knew to expect me around 5:00. Thankfully, I had only a ten-minute drive home. Skipping out early might be too tempting on days like this. However, after a few minutes of pulling all the paperwork from cabinet out and spreading relevant things around the desk, I took a deep breath and decided to get motivated for at least a little bit of measureable work.

I swung my chair around to turn on my computer, noticing next to it paperwork relating to technology policies that must have come from informational technology. On the second page I found my user name and default password, but I had already gone into the system last week and changed my password. I logged into the computer and sat back to wait for it to get fully ready. I looked around my office, admiring the mahogany desk and bookshelves. The office was gorgeous but certainly expensive to furnish. Out my window, I could see the parking lot. Howard walked toward a black sedan. Since I had to continue to wait for my computer, I figured Shelley could come in and help schedule my first week. I went and opened my door. Across from my office several of leadership's administrative assistants sat in a room converted into cubicles. I could see Shelley's back as her computer faced the window in the room. "Hey, Shelley, can you come in for a minute?"

"Sure, Dr. Carter," she said, grabbing a yellow pad of paper.

Back in the office, I motioned for her to sit down. She had thick red hair tied in a bun. The red hair was a bit of a shock against the sunflower-patterned dress that she wore. Still, she showed exuberance and excitement with her job. That attitude could be wonderfully contagious.

"Can you help me set up a schedule for this week? I need to see all the deans and would prefer to do it in brief one-on-ones. In fact, if you could, don't even call them one-on-ones. Maybe just 'initial meeting.' And if it's easier, I'm glad to meet at their offices. It will get me around the campus more."

Shelley busily wrote this down. "So, that's Riley, King, Fulbright, Linares, Steward and Hart ..." Shelley covered her open mouth with her hand as if she could prevent the name 'Michael Hartley' from escaping her mouth. "Oops, I guess not Dean Hartley?"

"No, in fact, schedule at least an hour with Dean Riley to help me figure that out. We might even need more time," I continued while looking at the to-do items from my cabinet agenda. "Perhaps, with her it could be a lunch meeting?"

Shelley nodded while she wrote. "By the way," I asked her, "have you heard more about Hartley?"

"No. I figured maybe you had."

"No. The detective came to cabinet for awhile, but we weren't told much." I pulled out a stress ball from my box of belongings and squeezed tightly.

"Rumor is a wrestler killed him."

"A wrestler," I exclaimed. "Good Lord, why a wrestler?"

"Someone said that a gay wrestler killed Hartley because he rejected his advances." Shelley put her hand up to her mouth again.

"O.k., Shelley, here is my first and, hopefully, only rule for working for me. College campuses are notorious for rumors: Professor X sleeping with Professor Y's wife kind of thing. I want you not to get caught up in that. It is unhealthy, almost always about stuff that isn't true, and can actually get in the way of productivity." Shelley looked devastated by my words. "It's o.k. I'm not blaming you, but at least the provost's office will do its best to remain above all of this."

"Yes, sir."

"And you don't have to call me, sir. You don't even have to call me Doctor Carter. Mark is fine."

"Yes, sir."

I smiled at Shelley's complete failure to see her gaffe. She did seem like a sweet girl. "So, anyway, you can probably try to schedule thirty-to-forty-five minute meetings with the other deans. Set me up with Charlotte Webb similarly. Also, could you schedule a brief meeting with the VP of Accounting? What's his name?" I fumbled through my cabinet materials trying to find where I had written it down.

"Aaron Cartwright?"

"Yes, him. I need a meeting with him, also. Again, I'm willing to meet at his office or somewhere else." I bounced the stress ball off my wall.

"No prob."

I looked through my notes from cabinet. A couple of other people, institutional research and marketing folk, should be scheduled for a meeting, but not this first week. I swung my chair around to face my computer and clicked on my calendar.

"Do you know if I have any appointments already set up?" I asked her, even though confirmation of that should show up on the screen at any second.

"Tomorrow is all day with HR, I believe. And then Melody sent an appointment to you about fifteen minutes ago to meet with Caroline."

"That was fast," I exclaimed with surprise. I racked my brain trying to think of any specific follow-up from cabinet that required meeting with Caroline. However, I couldn't think of any. I wasn't sure what to make of her setting an appointment this quickly. I chewed on the end of my pencil, deep in thought.

"Anything else, Dr., uh, I mean, Mark?" asked Shelley.

"That's probably it for now. Anything you'd like me to know?"

Shelley hesitated. "Well, I kind of hate bringing this up on your first day, but my husband is going to Florida the second week of September for a conference, and I'm really hoping to go. Dean Riley gave me tentative approval a few weeks ago, but obviously it's your call now."

"Don't sweat it. Save the sweat for Florida." Shelley didn't crack a smile. I shrugged. "Just send me an e-mail with the specific dates and I'll note it."

"Great. Thanks. If I don't see you before I leave, have a great evening." Shelley bounded out of her chair, leaving me to admire her energy.

For my last hour at work, I got organized, or at least as organized as I could, given my mental and physical exhaustion. Physical activity did wonders for my brain-dead body. I emptied my box, finding a place for almost everything brought from the Farrington office. I arranged several more pictures of Alyssa and Natalie around my desk and my computer. They both had been great about moving almost two hundred miles to a new city, meaning a new school for Alyssa, and a new job search for Natalie. So far, we all had been happy with the move. We all loved our house in a quaint old neighborhood and spent most of our evenings on the wrap-around porch. Alyssa had seen her new school and deemed it acceptable, and Natalie had made friends with several women in the neighborhood.

I scattered numerous mugs, hung the usual diplomas on the wall, and pinned curled-up *Far Side* cartoons above my computer. I took my to-do list from the cabinet meeting, struggled to read my hand-writing, quickly typed it up, ran off a copy, and left it sitting in the center of my desk. I clicked on my calendar, saw that I didn't have to be at HR until 9:00 and rejoiced knowing that I could have my more typical morning. After taking care of all these organizational details, I decided to head home. I packed up nothing.

Across the hall in the administrative assistant area, the lights were already out. As I walked down the hallway, I passed Hank's closed door. Through the door he could be heard yelling at someone on the phone. I thought about saying goodbye, but decided against it. As I walked to the car, a few people from a distance waved at me, but I wasn't close enough to identify them.

Sliding in the car, I immediately opened the glove compartment and rooted for The Smiths' *The Queen is Dead*. Finding it, I removed Dire Straits from the player, and popped in The Smiths. As I backed out of the parking spot, the song segued from the "take me back to dear old Blighty" opening to the title track, and I turned up the volume as Morrissey's voice filled the car.

At a stop light not far from campus, I sang along, "Oh, has the world changed or have I changed?" An elderly woman in a BMW gave me a disapproving look. 'My luck, she's a board member.' I turned the volume down, but as soon as the light changed and I could move again, the volume increased.

When I arrived home, the music still blaring, Natalie met me at the garage door. "That's a bit loud. Is that a sign of a good day or a bad day?" she asked a little pensively.

"Hmm? That's a good question. I don't really know. Could it be both? Or, better, neither."

Natalie gave me a kiss and a hug as I got out of the car. Her short, black hair smelled wonderful. "As long as it wasn't appreciably bad, I don't care. Usually, you play The Smiths when you have had a bad day."

"Is that really true?" I responded as we walked into the kitchen.

Natalie laughed. "Oh, yes. And, then, when I heard that a dean was killed today, I assumed a bad day."

Howard's morbid sense of humor was contagious even when we were miles apart. I couldn't stop myself. "The dean is dead, boys," I sang, "and it's so lonely on a limb."

"Mark!"

Even more than the black humor, I felt horrible that again Hartley's death got pushed so easily from my mind. "Oh, that's right. That's just part of a real interesting day. Let me get changed, and I'll grab a beer and we can talk on the porch." As I walked up the stairs, I yelled, "Where's Alyssa?"

"She's at the Fosters. I told her to be home by 6:30." The Fosters were a nice family of neighbors, with four girls, two older than Alyssa, one the same age, and one younger. We felt blessed that Alyssa fit in with them so well.

I changed into some shorts and a Monty Python t-shirt, and quickly raced back down the stairs. I peeked out the front door and saw Natalie already sitting in a rocking chair and a bottle of Bass sitting on the table next to my rocking chair. "Ah, a perfect setting," I said, settling down.

"So, how was your day?" I asked Natalie. She proceeded to discuss some decorating she had done to the family room downstairs. Even though interested, I had trouble paying attention. After a couple of minutes, she could clearly tell.

"Why don't you talk about your day? Then, after dinner I'll show you what I did in the family room."

"It's kind of hard to capture, Natalie," I started. "First off, cabinet took more than seven hours."

"You're kidding." Natalie shivered a bit and drank from her glass of wine.

"I'm also not sure what kind of impression I made."

"What do you mean?" Natalie's bare foot was stroking my shin.

"I wasn't shy about asking questions and pushing buttons. As a result, who knows how I fit in? I'm not sure the CFO has much faith in me; the head of student services frightens the hell out of me; the head of HR seems like a quivering wreck; the head of admissions is a wise-cracking slob; most of all Berrian's moods change by the minute."

Natalie laughed and kicked my shin. "Stop exaggerating!"

"No exaggeration, dear. And instead of being a good little boy and staying quiet in order to assess my situation, I wasted no time jumping into discussions and expressing concerns." Up the street I could see a dog barking at a cat up in a tree.

"Have you been having doubts, Mark?"

I looked at my wife in surprise. "Has it been that obvious?"

"Goodness, Mark, I've known you for fifteen years. I can read you like a cheap novel."

The dog was literally hurling himself at the tree; the cat had moved out onto a sturdy limb. "A cheap novel, eh? Am I that transparent?"

"Don't be silly." Her foot was back to rubbing my shin, causing me some distraction. "Despite all your successes, you have always fought self-doubt. When we dated, I was surprised by that, but after knowing you a little while, I came to recognize it."

Unsure of how to respond, I sipped at my beer and watched a neighbor drag the dog away from the tree.

"Why wouldn't you be successful at Boan, honey?"

I swayed the beer bottle in my hand. "My worries up until today had been that I had succeeded entirely within the crazy culture that is Farrington. I knew the peculiarities of the faculty and my colleagues and had learned how to interact with all of them. I'd assumed Boan would be entirely different, and that I would be the odd man out."

"And after today?"

I chuckled. "I guess I now see myself as the normal man in with all the odd ones."

Natalie sipped her wine. "Please, tell me more about your day."

I recreated as well as I could the highlights and the lowlights of the day. Like any good spouse, Natalie listened, nodded, and expressed support or disbelief as needed. In essence, what she said and how she reacted was not overly important. What was important was that she listened. Later, as I turned off my reading lamp to go to bed, I remembered the one thing she said during that lengthy monologue that captured my love for my wife.

I had been telling her of the bowling team incident and the fact that we had a fine arts' student doing a puppet show of *The Iceman Cometh*. With her perfect deadpan delivery, Natalie had countered, "It could have been worse. It could have been *A Long Day's Journey Into Night*. Oh, wait, that was your meeting."

"With that kind of wit," I had replied, "you'd fit in well with that meeting."

"Don't even wish that on your enemies, mister," she had joked, good-naturedly smacking me on my shoulder.

I slept well that night, dreaming of Natalie running cabinet, with Bob Berrian watching helplessly through a two-way mirror.

Part Two:
Welcome Week

Chapter Five

For the rest of the week, the Michael Hartley investigation resembled a highway in the distance. Most of the time, I found myself too consumed by the immediate noise and activity around me, but on peaceful occasions, the dull roar of the investigation could be picked up.

The all-day human resources training scheduled for Tuesday turned out, mercifully, to be just half a day. I was inundated with paperwork, handbooks, and cheap giveaways. The various incident forms, leave forms, injury reports, service requests and so forth could be found on our intranet, but for some reason, hard copies of everything got handed out. Walking back from Dred Hall to the Administration Building, I labored to balance a Boan coffee cup (proclaiming the Boan Values: "Act with Honor; Honor all Actions"), key ring, window decal, pen set, and letter opener on top of fifty or so pages of handouts. I passed several unknown people in the square, whose looks told me that they too had done this walk of shame: "Hi, look at me, I'm the new kid in class. My name is Mark. I just moved here from Ohio. And I'm just geeked to be going to Boan this year!"

Still, as I got to my office and dumped my pile of stuff, I was glad that HR finished with me before lunch. I now had plenty of time to look through a folder listing key provost projects left in my file cabinet by Jennifer Riley. I had forgotten about it until this morning, when I found it in the bottom drawer. It cataloged key concerns identified by John Palmer, with her additions.

I closed my office door and picked up the light file; three pages had been written (handwritten, at that) by Palmer, and then Riley had added three typed pages. Palmer had outlined twelve major academic concerns, Riley had added substantial comments on each of those twelve, and then added number thirteen. Both needed to be summarized into one document for myself. With both of their documents spread around my desk, I worked away at my computer, attempting to capture the basic concern and any specific actions or thoughts by either Riley or Palmer:

- Consistency in courses: Across colleges? Within colleges (education, especially!)? Within specific courses? Per specific faculty? Institutional research has developed a research plan reviewed by J. Riley on June 11.

- Research dollars: Drop in academic research dollars by more than half a million over last five years. What is going on? J. Palmer felt stonewalled in being able to investigate. J. Riley requested this on cabinet agenda three times. Apparently never covered in cabinet.

- Nursing shortage: Complaints between faculty and Dean Linares frequent. HR brought in at least five times by J. Palmer, by J. Riley twice. Pay issues. Workload issues. "Potential prima donna culture"—J. Riley.

- Online: Too many online courses being offered—J. Palmer. Resentment by some faculty. No standards? "Can of worms?"--J. Riley.

- Budget: All department budgets cut dramatically. Administrative staff cut. Lack of clarity on how budget is prepared—J. Riley.

- Adjunct quality: Not enough quality control measures for adjunct--J. Palmer. Differences in credentials by college. Business is only college with defined and publicized credential expectations – J. Riley. Allied health, potentially worst--J. Riley.

- Internships: Arts and sciences needs internships--J. Palmer. Education needs evidence of internship successes--J. Riley. Task Force formed 5/1.

- Recognition program: Faculty feel undervalued. No true recognition for academic accomplishments. Brought to cabinet, last J. Palmer meeting. Overindulgence of faculty?--J. Riley.

- Law School proposal: Brought to Provost Circle in November by J. Riley. Not supported by Provost Circle. Discussed with president at 1 on 1, May—J. Riley.

- Tuition Benefits: Proposal to cabinet for Boan to pay more when faculty pursue advanced degrees. HR to do more competitive analysis. No data as of August 1—J. Riley.

- Living/Learning Community: Faculty lead quit February. No volunteers to replace. Recommend to eliminate LLC taken to June retention committee. Not supported--J. Riley.

- Smartboards: Faculty believe classroom smartboards need replaced. Denied during budget cycle—J. Riley. Rift between faculty and IT developing—J. Riley.

- Enrollment in fine arts: Proposal to eliminate, cabinet 7/2—J. Riley. Postponement for new Provost.

I leaned back in my chair and let out a deep breath. "Pieces of cake!" I muttered. Still, from this list, initial meetings with the deans could be structured. That reminded me that education still needed an interim dean. I stepped out of my office and headed down the end of the hallway to Berrian's office. His door open, he was in. Veronica was not at her desk, so I stuck my head around the door frame and called out to the president.

"Hi, Mark," he said, barely turning his head from his computer.

"Quick question, Bob: I need to assign an interim dean for education. I will talk to Riley, but do you have any thoughts? Anyone you definitely don't want me to appoint?"

"Oh, that's right." Bob stared out his window. He pointed toward Hope Residence Hall. "Look, there's Detective Marsh right now. I wonder how the investigation is going. Hopefully, they identify who did it quickly and get this over with."

"I agree," I replied, although swift justice often doesn't equate to true justice. 'Take the time to get it right,' I thought. "Anyway, I only know of two education faculty off the top of my head: Christina Llewellyn and Dewayne Wilson. Otherwise, I'm really relying on you and Riley."

"Oh, Christ, not Christina! She talks too much and creeps me out. Can you imagine her in front of the press?" Christina did look masculine, but during my interview, she came across as very intelligent, even if a bit chatty. I was disappointed that Berrian had dismissed her so quickly.

Berrian pulled a bottle of cologne out of his desk and splashed some on his neck. "Excuse me, Mark, but I have to go meet a board member for lunch in a minute."

"I like Christina, but that's o.k. How about Wilson?"

"Who is he?"

"Tall black guy. Special Education. Like Christina, you had him on my search committee."

Berrian furrowed his brow and pursed his lips. "Not remembering him.

You'd think I would. Victor picked many of those search committee members. Anyway, talk to Riley, and then tell me who you recommend."

"Would it be worthwhile to ask one of the other deans to pick up education? It's nice sometimes to have several options."

"Who would that be?" He had begun to comb his hair to a mirror positioned discreetly behind a picture on his side desk.

"Maybe Riley again? She's proven she could handle the interim provost position."

"That could work. Anyone but Linares, o.k.?"

"Definitely. I'm not sure it makes sense to combine nursing with anything else, even short term," I said.

Berrian had leapt out of his chair, heading past me to the door. "Keep me posted. I don't want to keep Matilda waiting."

Walking back to my desk, I saw Shelley heading into her office. "Oh, hi, Mark. I just got back from lunch, but I'm glad I saw you. You probably haven't had time to check your calendar yet, but I got a number of your initial meetings set up. I believe Dr. Riley is lunch tomorrow, Dr. Fulbright is lunch on Thursday, and Dr. Stewart is lunch on Friday. All in the cafeteria."

"Wow! I'm going to get fat in this job," I declared, "as that's a lot of lunches."

"I told them all to meet you in the cafeteria, unless they hear differently. You can always do the salad bar. That's what I always choose over there." Shelley smiled and continued. "Meanwhile, Ms. King and Ms. Linares have yet to respond. Ms. Webb is sometime early Thursday morning, and Aaron Cartwright is tomorrow morning. You'll see the specific times on your calendar."

"Thank you, Shelley." I looked at my watch: 12:45. "I should probably grab lunch myself. You recommend the salad bar?"

"Oh, yes, it's all you can eat. And there are so many yummy salads. I can eat a lot and feel like I haven't wrecked my diet."

"Goodness, why does every fit woman think they need to diet? Shelley, you don't need to lose weight."

"Thank you, Dr. Carter," she responded flirtatiously, "but, my husband disagrees." Shelley whistled as she settled back at her desk. If I wasn't mistaken, she was whistling "Stand by Your Man." I watched her back for a second. Could innocent little Shelley be more world-wise than I had initially thought?

I decided to dash back into my office and quickly call Jennifer Riley about the interim dean position. It took me five minutes to figure out the directory function on the fancy phone system, then, as I tilted the chair back to relax while the phone rang, I saw a directory of phone numbers on the top of my pile from HR.

Riley answered on the fourth ring. "Jennifer," I said, "it's Mark Carter. How are you doing?"

"Mark! Fine, thank you. Welcome. I came by to see you yesterday but you were still in **Cabinet**." She said the word as if expressing it would bring unforeseen horrors on all whom she loved. I laughed.

"The way everybody says '**Cabinet**' around here, I expect horses to whinny in absolute torture, Jennifer."

Jennifer laughed also. "That's **Frau Riley, Doktor,**" she countered.

"Why do I have the feeling I'm going to start hearing the strains of violins?"

"Mmm. Mmm." Riley's monster groan was perfectly pitched, and I cackled.

"Look, Jennifer. I need to decide who is going to replace Hartley, but I don't know the players, so I thought you and I could maybe brainstorm. What do you think?"

"That will be tough. Tell you what, Mark. Have you grabbed lunch yet?"

"No, in fact, I will head to the cafeteria right after this conversation."

"I'll meet you there in ten minutes. We can discuss this and maybe cover a few other things that we would have talked about tomorrow. I'm assuming you can spare some time?" she asked.

"Actually, I can. My HR marathon session apparently was only a sprint."

Jennifer chuckled. "I figured as such. Victor keeps scheduling these full-day orientations for new employees, but for at least a year now, they have only been about half a day, and no one seems to have alerted Victor. Anyway, give me ten minutes."

Ten minutes later, I found Jennifer at a table in the far corner of the cafeteria. The cavernous room was mostly empty, although without a doubt in a week all the students would be back and it would be packed again. A couple of people at a table in the center of the room waved at our table as I set my notebook down before getting my food. I had no idea who they were.

"I hear the salad bar is the thing to go for," I said, as Jennifer arose to walk through the line with me.

"Oh, god, no! I abhor salad bars. The most unsanitary place in a cafeteria. You must have been talking to Shelley?"

"How'd you know?"

"Lucky guess. Don't forget, she served as my secretary the last six months or so."

I stopped by the pizza station as Jennifer broke away to a different section. I chose two pieces of vegetarian pizza, located the beverage station at the far end, and poured myself some iced tea. Next to the beverages, I found napkins and silverware. Jennifer still lingered by the hot meal service, so I paid and went back to my seat.

A few minutes later, Jennifer returned with a panini and chips. She took off her brown jacket and set it on the back of the chair behind her. She wore a sleeveless cream blouse revealing freckled arms. They matched the freckles on her face. With her elongated glasses, she looked quite the professional academic.

"So, we've established so far that we both like *Young Frankenstein.* That's a good sign."

Jennifer pushed her coffee cup toward me. "Ovaltine?"

I laughed loudly and slapped the table. "O.k., O.k., uncle! I know when I've been beaten."

I bit into my pizza, surprised by how cold it was. "Damn, that sure looked like a heat lamp."

"Ah, I should have warned you. More likely a lava lamp. Always go to the stations where they prepare the food right there for you. Especially during the summer months when there aren't many students around. A lot of food sits out during the summer."

"I should have known that. Oh, well, live and learn." I drank some of the iced tea, and stared out the window.

"So, what are you hearing about Hartley's death?" asked Jennifer.

"Nothing since yesterday. You?"

"I spent an hour yesterday with the spunky Detective Marsh. I think she's getting fed up with turning over rocks, only to find various disgusting vermin crawl out from under them." She took a healthy bite of her panini and a little mayonnaise dribbled off the corner of her mouth. She quickly swabbed at it with her napkin.

"I have a feeling Caroline Cruz started her on the rock-turning episode. What time did you talk to Marsh?"

"At some point in the mid afternoon. I don't really remember. I was working on some minutes from my advisory board meeting when she interrupted me. I never did get back to them."

I looked at my second piece of pizza with disinterest. Bad pizza made for a better diet plan than Shelley's. "Is there anybody in the college that Marsh might suspect? That would be a good way for me to whittle down the possible candidates for interim dean."

Jennifer grinned. "Oh, yeah. I think she's got her sights on three or four of them."

"Caroline had referenced that some of the faculty were upset with Hartley backing out of tenure support. Is that true?"

"Sadly so, Mark. I have to be honest with you; Hartley really did make a lot of enemies around here. I swear I spent most of my time as interim provost dealing with complaints against Hartley."

My iced tea finished, I looked out the window again. A couple of workmen sweated from exertion while dealing with a pipe dug up next to the building. "If that's the case, I guess I'm surprised you only had to spend an hour with Detective Marsh."

"Oh, I just gave her the highlights. I'm sure she'll come back."

"Related to that, what kind of fallout came from the public dispute between King and Hartley?"

"Are you referring to the time when she called him out at the all-faculty meeting about the articulation signing?"

I looked around the mostly empty room a little nervously. We could have delicate conversations here as well as anywhere. "Yes, that one."

Jennifer had picked up on my unease with our public conversation. "Don't worry, Mark. We're o.k. There's almost no-one else in here and no-one close to us." She still lowered her voice to more of a whisper. "The scene was ugly: Kiana screaming at Mike, who had that damn smirk constantly plastered on his face. Between you and me, though, I don't think she killed him over this."

"Don't worry. That's not why I asked. I am more concerned with public reactions. I've seen incidents like that become problems because they are public." I paused and looked at the workmen again. "Did anyone push on you or HR to address the situation?"

"Surprisingly, not, Mark. Don't get me wrong. I was angry at both of them, and HR came in to have discussions with both Mike and Kiana. The crazy thing is that no one in the faculty really cared."

"I find that hard to believe. These are faculty. Their sense of curiosity alone should have kept you hopping."

"You'll come to understand better, Mark, I think, when you really get to meet more of them. In many ways, King has always been seen as the crazy dean and Hartley as the jerk dean, so to everyone watching, the scene was probably something they had expected, or even already experienced once or twice before." My look must have suggested doubt, because Jennifer shrugged her shoulders.

"I thought of asking Kiana about it. Do you think I should?"

"I wouldn't go there. I don't think you'll gain much."

"Well, anyway," I said, changing the conversation. "None of this is an immediate concern. Who might be a good interim dean for the time being?"

Jennifer barely hesitated. "Christina Llewellyn. No one else."

I groaned. "Ugh. Anybody else?"

"Why? What's wrong with Chris?" Jennifer had finished her panini and picked at her last few potato chips.

"I threw her name out to Berrian. I don't think he thinks too highly of her."

"I'm sure he wouldn't. That's too bad, not only for Christina, but also for the university. The rest of the faculty are either too green or too angry."

"You're kidding me, right?"

"Heck, no. Most of the old-timers hated Hartley so much that they either became major pains-in-the-ass or disengaged completely. There are four or five relatively new ones that Mike hired as people retired. Christina was really the only faculty member, as far as I knew, who blew Mike off, but still did what she had to do."

"Am I right in thinking that Wilson is one of the new guys, then?"

"Dewayne? Yeah, why?"

"I tossed his name out to the president. He couldn't remember him."

"Not surprised there either. Dewayne served on your search committee, didn't he? Long-term there may be hope for Dewayne, but right now if you put him in that spot he would completely drown. So much he still has to learn. Heck, I've been doing this for years, and there's still stuff I don't know." Jennifer laughed loudly and I noticed that as she laughed I could see her gums. Why would I notice something like that in the middle of a great conversation?

"I agree. Let me throw out one more possibility, and feel free to tell me I'm nuts."

"Shoot."

"Would you be willing to take on education in the interim while we search?"

"You're nuts."

"Like I couldn't see that one coming." I watched Jennifer closely to try to discern her seriousness.

"Did you know that I had been the interim provost before we hired Palmer, and that before that I had served as the interim dean for business?" Jennifer played with a piece of paper on the table.

"No kidding? Did they not find a dean for business and you took it full-time?"

"Not quite. We hired this guy from Vanderbilt, J. Billings Gadfly. What a jerk! He lasted just over a year, got the college accredited, and then bolted to be president at some small college in Illinois. Last I heard he had left that position for a presidency at Seton Hall. And all this is within the last five years."

"Yowzah," I said, watching the workmen outside the window again. "Typical of many of the finer presidents in academia today, isn't it?"

Jennifer sneered. "They give us all a bad name."

"No doubt. But, look at you, you've been dean for almost five years. I guess I can't quite say you're always the bridesmaid."

"I look horrible in lavender taffeta."

"It wrinkles so easily."

We both laughed the kind of laughter that develops when you know you have found a good colleague. I would like working with Jennifer. My gut told me to ask her to be interim dean of education, but I knew it should wait until Berrian's approval. "All right. Give me a little time to check with Berrian. What I think I'm hearing is that you would be open to being the interim dean. Is that correct?"

"What the heck? I'd do it. It's about time somebody brought a little business to the college of education!"

"Touché!" I shouted, raising my empty iced tea glass to toast with Jennifer's empty coffee cup.

For the next forty-five minutes we addressed other issues on both of our minds. I asked her about the thirteen issues identified by Palmer and her, and she gave me more background on roadblocks, u-turns, and directions planned for each of those issues. She, in turn, asked me to think about some marketing of programs, grade point average requirements for courses, and a professor emeritus program. The discussion was easy, engaging and invigorating, and my outlook improved greatly. Near the end we engaged in a little bit of banter about my colleagues at the leadership level. I'll give Jennifer credit. Her comments were droll, but not mean-spirited, insightful, but not self-serving, pointed, but not over the line. Finally, close to 2:30, we left the cafeteria, the only patrons who had been in there for the last half hour.

As we stepped outside, Detective Marsh could be seen walking into Muswell Hall. "Oh, boy, the stench of murder is still upon us," I said.

"It could be worse," responded Jennifer.

"How?"

"Could be raining."

I looked up at the cloudless sky. After a couple of seconds, I got the joke. "Thanks, Eye-gor!"

When I got back to the office, I checked to see if Berrian was in, but he wasn't. I shot him a quick e-mail suggesting that I announce Jennifer Riley immediately as the interim dean, and that we ask Victor about how quickly we could post for Hartley's replacement. Each moment, I felt more and more ghoulish for looking past Hartley's death and moving forward.

The rest of the afternoon I spent with additional organization of my office and notes from the first two days. A number of things needed to be done as soon as possible, which meant by the middle of my second week. I had listed these on a sheet of paper so they could easily be checked off as accomplished. For instance, I wanted to walk through the halls during peak class times next week, when classes started, meeting students, faculty and staff. I desperately needed an updated course schedule. I looked to find Shelley across the hall, but she wasn't there. Someone else's administrative assistant sat in there, but I had no idea who she was. Caroline Cruz could get me the schedule. The impenetrable phone system almost sucked me in before I remembered my hard copy of the directory of extensions.

Caroline's extension kicked into a cold voice-mail after four rings: "You have reached Dr. Caroline Cruz, Executive Vice President for Student Services. Leave me a detailed message and phone number and I'll call you back as soon as I am able." Each word got clipped off in the way she spoke during cabinet. I left her a message to let me know where to get a course schedule. After I left the message, I remembered Shelley referencing an appointment with Caroline. Clicking on my calendar, I found it scheduled for first thing tomorrow morning. 'Probably could have waited until then.'

Additional matters needing attention in the next few days included a visit to the library to look around more, the composition of an initial e-mail of introduction to all of academics, and the creation of a one-on-one agenda for the president (an appointment that Veronica would apparently send me). My e-mail revealed nothing scheduled yet for this week or next. In addition, I needed to get online to find the academic calendar so that important dates got scheduled on my calendar; and I needed to set up my first staff meeting. Still feeling a bit energetic from my time with Jennifer Riley, I decided to tackle the most substantial of those tasks: writing an e-mail of introduction to all of academics.

I tinkered with that language for quite awhile, interrupted by a phone call from Natalie, who wanted to let me know that Alyssa had hit a neighborhood boy. Poor Natalie was horrified and I probably didn't help by asking whether the boy went down like a sack of potatoes. Several e-mails came in that I read and addressed, including one from my racquetball partner at Farrington, Frank Wirth, a good friend I would miss tremendously. As a faculty member in the technology department at Farrington, Frank had been a confidante I had relied upon throughout my career at Farrington. Since we held positions in different colleges, we rarely had conflicts of interest. It reminded me that as provost I would be hard pressed to find someone like that. Everyone, theoretically, could want something from me. "It's lonely at the top," I chuckled. Based upon my lunch with Jennifer, I hoped that perhaps she could fill that void.

I sent off the e-mail about 4:00 and checked to see if Berrian was back in his office. I could tell he was by the smell of the cologne before I poked my head through the doorway to his office.

"Hey, Bob, I sent you an e-mail about this, but I might as well ask while you're here. I'd like to name Riley as the interim dean for education. It sounds like no one else is up to the task. Jennifer's pretty good at this interim stuff."

"That's fine with me." Bob waved me off with his hand as he pored over a file on his desk.

"Great. I'll touch base with communications about getting a message together." Bob ignored me while he continued to read, so I headed back to my office, almost running into Shelley as she came out of her office.

"Oh, Mark. Just who I was looking for. I got Dean King on the phone. She's hoping to meet with you tomorrow early afternoon. What time do you think your lunch with Dean Riley will end tomorrow. I have you scheduled for 12:00 to 1:00 with Dean Riley, but I know you have a lot of stuff to talk to her about."

"Actually, she and I met today for lunch and decided to cancel the lunch for tomorrow."

"Super," said Shelley disappearing back into her office.

Before I even had a chance to sit back down at my desk, Shelley yelled through the hallway from her office to mine: "How about if I just pencil Ms. King in for that lunch?"

I stood up and walked back to her doorway so that I wouldn't have to yell. "That's fine, Shelley. Thank you."

I settled back down in my desk to hear Shelley yell one more time: "All set!"

I pulled up my calendar for Wednesday and saw that I had ended up with three meetings in the morning: Caroline Cruz at 8:30, Aaron Cartwright at 10:30 and Kiana King at noon. I spent the rest of my day jotting down discussion topics for all three of them. I sent an e-mail to communications about Riley as interim dean. When I called Natalie a few minutes after 5:00 to see if she wanted me to bring anything home, she was in a state of panic. Alyssa had actually slugged two neighborhood boys. Even though I tried to joke it off, these were never-before-seen behaviors for Alyssa. It wouldn't be surprising to see a normally passive kid react with a little aggression to a move. I tried to convince Natalie that Alyssa was attempting to adjust to a new environment where other kids would want to see how much they could push her buttons, and that she would just need time before everyone got on with the mundane life of playground politics. Natalie could not be easily convinced, and it took a bottle of Cabernet Sauvignon and Chinese take-home to get her to relax. It must have worked as I never even had to uncork the second bottle.

Chapter Six

Caroline Cruz arrived early for our meeting at my office on Wednesday. I'd read about half of a *Chronicle of Higher Education* article on the increase of cheating among students at elite universities when she rapped loudly on my open office door. Turning around, I was surprised to see her in a Boan sweatshirt and black slacks. Her black hair had been pulled up and held by barrettes, although a few strands of the hair fell over her right eye in a potentially seductive way. Given how early it was in the morning, I couldn't help wondering if she had styled her hair to do exactly that.

"Mark," said Caroline, almost as if purring. I instinctively pulled my chair farther under my desk and sat upright in my chair. 'Does this woman have this effect on all men,' I wondered, 'or, am I the only idiot?'

"Why the casual look, Caroline?" I asked.

"It's Super Wednesday in the advising office."

I waited for her to explain more, but no explanation followed. Instead, she settled down in a chair across from my desk and pulled a small notepad and a pen from her purse.

"Meaning what?"

"Everyone is trying to hit their final goals for the fall. With online classes beginning Friday, we've always considered this day to be our last day to make our goals. I've ordered everyone in my unit to wear Spiritware and work through the night if we have to in order to make goals. Staff loves it."

'I'm sure they do,' I thought sarcastically. "Sounds fun. By the way, I didn't expect you to schedule a meeting with me so quickly."

"Why not? It's never too early to get your support."

I leaned back in my chair. So, the positioning and jockeying for the provost's time and support had officially begun. 'That's o.k.,' I thought, as this came with the territory.

"For instance, speaking of Super Wednesday, I really need your support for Spirit Week, Mark. I'm tired of students not being able to participate in all my staff's events."

"Now, Caroline, I said at cabinet that I ..."

"I know what you said at cabinet, but that's the official record, Mark. Unofficially, can I count on you to push the faculty to encourage more student participation?" Caroline flashed that cold smile I had seen several times on Monday.

"I need to find out from the deans the academic schedule that week," I stammered, my will separated from my voice.

"Well, have you talked to them?"

"Barely. It's only Wednesday morning."

"Don't let them dance around this, Mark. I've worked with these people before. They're slicker than a politician's PR man."

"Or woman," I added. Caroline completely ignored me.

"I'm sure they have valid reasons **if** they don't encourage their faculty." I did my best to emphasize the "if."

"Poppycock."

I burst out laughing. "Poppycock? Weren't you in an Agatha Christie novel?"

"I'm not kidding, Mark. Push them."

I rose out of my seat, my voice gaining courage. "I will, Caroline. I did talk to Jennifer Riley yesterday, and she said she'd spread the word. Let's not assume the worst."

"Sit down, Mark. There's no reason to stand up. We're just having a conversation."

I laughed in astonishment at her description of what seemed to me a confrontation. I looked at her for several seconds, then sat down. 'Keep cool,' I told myself.

"On to another topic, Mark. Living and Learning Community. How familiar are you with that program here at Boan?"

"I know of it," I said, taking deep breaths to stay calm, "in fact, I have that on a list...." As I turned around to grab my list, Caroline cut me off.

"Dave Duncan quit on that program last winter. He really upset the students and the advising staff who have worked so hard to make that work. Riley never did anything about it, and we still haven't got a replacement for Duncan." With her clipped voice, she made it sound like 'Dunkin.'

"I've got notes from Jennifer Riley saying it was discussed at the June retention meeting." I waved my list at Caroline as if it was enough evidence to end the debate.

"Well, yes, but she recommended eliminating it."

"I know that and we discussed it very quickly yester...."

"Retention's your and my goal together, Mark. Riley didn't care, as she wasn't the permanent provost. You need to make this a priority."

"Damn it, I will, Caroline, it's just that...."

"Mark, don't swear. This is just a discussion." Somehow Caroline never rose to a challenge, maintaining the same intense looks and vocal patterns, whether she disagreed with you or gave you the weather report.

"You're right, Caroline. My apologies." I took another deep breath and wished I had refilled my coffee cup. "It's just that I feel put upon. It's only the third morning I've been here."

"I know, Mark, and all I'm asking for today is your support on these things. We can hash out the details later." Caroline's thin lips formed a partial smile.

"I appreciate that, Caroline. I really do. However, there are several sides to every story, of course, and the little bit I heard from Jennifer about the Learning Community suggests there's no evidence that students in it were more successful." I was amazed that I had been able to even articulate such a lengthy monologue without Caroline interrupting me.

"Poppycock!" This time I didn't laugh. "I can e-mail you the evidence. There's plenty that says it works, and would have continued to work if Duncan had fulfilled his responsibilities."

"Well, forward me the information and I'll review and get right back to you." I paused. "I promise," I vowed although immediately regretted being the one to kowtow.

"All I want is your voice of support, Mark," sighed Caroline.

Before I could respond, the phone rang. I held my finger up for a second toward Caroline and checked the phone display. It was home. "I better get this," I said. "I won't be a minute."

Caroline didn't offer to leave the room, and I was too tired to ask.

"Hey," I said, picking up the phone.

Natalie was crying again. "She just did it again, Mark."

"Who? Alyssa? She did what?"

"She hit the Cunningham boy again."

I closed my eyes and leaned back in my chair. "You're kidding me? Why this time?" I'm not sure I ever understood why she hit him or the Klein boy the day before.

"She says she's sticking up for herself. I don't know." Natalie started sobbing harder.

"Have you talked to the Cunninghams?" I asked.

"Not yet. I can't face them after their rudeness yesterday."

"Look, just ignore it for now. Ground Alyssa for the day. Keep her inside.

Take her to a movie. I don't know. Just do something and when I get back tonight, we can talk to the Cunninghams together."

Natalie sniffled for a few seconds, saying nothing, a pattern I'm accustomed to. When she's bothered by something, she calls me, I give her advice, and she says nothing for a long time.

"Look, honey, I'm in a meeting. Do what I suggest and we'll talk more about it tonight. I promise. And if I get time later, I will call." I glanced over at Caroline looking at her notepad.

"O.k.," answered a resigned Natalie.

As I hung up, I looked at Caroline. "Kid problems?" she asked.

"Yeah, fighting."

"Your daughter?"

"Yep."

"Just a couple of more items for me." Caroline undoubtedly would stay on track. "Let's talk online."

"O.k., give me your e-mail address and I'll IM you later tonight."

"Very funny, Mark," Caroline said without a smile.

"The advisors don't know how to advise students in terms of online expectations. Can we get some talking points?"

"Is that true? Our own people don't know how to advise for online?"

"Of course, it's true, Mark. Why would I say it if it wasn't?"

"Sorry, Caroline," I said smiling, hands in a surrender pose. "A verbal habit. Just something I say when I am in disbelief."

When Caroline didn't say anything, I scratched my head. "Who would be responsible for coming up with those?" During my interviews online emerged as a nebulous area without clear leadership. I hated to admit I had no clue who on my team would be responsible for this.

"That's part of the problem, Mark. I have Rochelle Wallace as my Director of Distance Advising. She would normally be my point person for all things online. But, she doesn't know what the academic expectations are."

"Has she talked to people on my team?"

"I believe she's talked to a lot of people on your team. The problem is that you have no dedicated person for online."

I wrote some notes down on my yellow pad, underlining "talk to Jennifer about online" twice. Thank goodness I liked Jennifer. I would lean on her a lot these first few weeks. Caroline continued to stare at me, barely moving.

"You'll have to give me some time on this one, Caroline." As she opened her mouth, I held my hand up to stop her. "And, don't worry, I completely support you on this one. I'm definitely on your side here."

If Caroline was pleased by my response, her expression gave nothing away.

"Has Rochelle at least tried to direct students to some general web resources about online learning environments?" I asked.

Caroline sighed. "Of course. Most of the ones are very generic, and don't seem to fit our model, whatever **that** is. If you could at least help us define our learning model, we could probably cobble together our own talking points."

"Remind me," I said, leaning back in my chair, "of the development of our online programs. Who was involved in their development?"

"We had a limited use of learning management systems until about four years ago. Then, Berrian decided we needed to tap into online education more aggressively. We created a Vice President for Online Offerings, brought in some hotshot from out west, allowed him to create a model, and then denied him the resources to support it. He apparently had a shouting match with Berrian one evening during **the** basketball game, and quit on the spot." The way Caroline referenced the basketball game unmistakably revealed disgust. I assumed she saw it as merely another way the boys hung out with the boys, while the girls got left out of the bonding.

"And when he left?"

"No one replaced him. Berrian said that we had developed what we needed, and that functional areas could manage their parts of online: Howard has to deal with online admissions, you have online academics, and I get online student services."

"And how's that worked out?" I chuckled. Before Caroline could speak, I stopped her with a wave of my hand. "That's one of them rhetoricals," I cracked. "Anyway, none of this helps us immediately. Given how close it is to the first day of online classes, I guess there's not much we can do before Friday."

Caroline exhaled loudly. "Probably not."

"That's o.k. I promise I will make this a priority. I'm just as bothered by this as you are."

"Excellent. And that brings me to my last agenda item. Average class size."

"I know. I was looking at those notes...." I attempted to stop Caroline with my hand-held-up routine. It failed.

"We need to be of the same belief on this, Mark. Palmer and Riley were too cowardly to help me take on Hank with this one. After all, both student services and academics want students taking classes and earning credit."

"What do you mean by 'cowardly'?"

"Palmer simply wouldn't speak about it, either way. Riley claimed that smaller class sizes were detrimental to a good learning environment."

"I hate to say this, Caroline." And, yes, I did hate to say it. "But, I might agree with Riley."

Caroline flicked her hand at me in disgust, or perhaps, worse, in annoyance. "Poppycock!"

"Any class that requires group work is hampered by small class sizes. Any class, such as speech, that requires a lot of time on the part of students is hampered by small class sizes. Any class that requires intense interaction among students is hampered by small class sizes."

Caroline shook her head. "Such conservative answers. Why can't faculty adapt their classes?"

I took a deep breath. It was 9:30. I couldn't use my next appointment as an excuse to end this discussion. There also would never be enough time to counter any arguments, because Caroline would reject or deflect them all.

"Look, Caroline," I said, deciding on a deflection tactic. "I'm not saying I can't support you on some of the average class size issues. In fact, based upon what I heard in cabinet, I would say the real problems are all the damn, sorry, dang, delivery options. That's what's hurting your class sizes."

"I know that, Mark, but those are Berrian's babies and we're not going to get him to change his mind about those."

"So, what you are saying is to ignore the hole in the hull of the Titanic and fire the band instead? That's insane."

"That's reality. That's all that matters." Caroline's thin lips tightened in a weak smile.

I ran my fingers through my hair in frustration. "I'm not sure I want to give up on the bigger issue so quickly, but how about if you set up a meeting with Hank and me. If you think he could be open to certain stipulations (kinds of classes that can go with smaller class sizes), maybe we can get some compromises that help some."

"Anything would help, Mark." Caroline grabbed her purse from the floor, stuck her pad and pen in it, and stood up. "Very good." She gave me a firm handshake and slid out of the room before I had any time to say anything more. She certainly was something. I just wasn't exactly sure what that something was.

As compared to Caroline, Aaron Cartwright resembled a lamb. He laid out for me the complete academic budget (thirty-five million, as I already knew) and showed the various sub-budgets. While I was not surprised that the nursing and allied health colleges had the largest budgets, the size of the adjunct budgets within each college did shock me. Aaron couldn't give me a whole lot of insight as to why that was, so I made a note to talk to the deans about their adjunct costs. I wasn't overly surprised to see a bare bones library budget. At Farrington, the library budget had been slashed so dramatically that the librarians referred to their unit as the "Abridged Farrington Library."

While good-natured about it, they rightfully felt frustrated by the de-emphasizing of the library through budget cuts.

Aaron hadn't brought me a report on salaries, which sat in the HR budget, but when I asked him about it, he texted someone on his BlackBerry, and it arrived in my mailbox within minutes. As I pulled the printout from my printer, I was shocked to see that Michael Hartley, even in death apparently, was the highest paid person on my team. This surprised me, as he had been a more recent hire than many of the other deans. Aaron admitted he couldn't speak to the salaries, and I made a note to talk to Victor.

By the time Aaron had left, I knew little additional information about my budget and how we managed it. Aaron was a nice enough kid, with "kid" being the appropriate word, as he looked about twenty-three with his spiky moussed hair and barely-full goatee. He kept reassuring me that if I had any questions to give him a call. That offer comforted me in the way that Mayberry must have felt secure under the eye of Barney Fife.

As I crossed the square for my lunch meeting with Kiana King, a cool breeze that cut through the summer heat invigorated me. Indiana summers can be pretty miserable, but the last three days had been reasonably comfortable.

King arrived about five minutes late, and by the time she set her pile of materials down at my table, I had already grabbed a panini and some iced tea. I waited until she returned with her food. She went through the cafeteria slowly, looking and sniffing at many of the options judiciously. A short woman, maybe 5 feet 2 inches, she did not attempt to add to her height via her sensible brown sandals. One of the workers in the cafeteria must have known her, as she smiled at him and they chatted for several minutes. Eventually after about ten minutes, she returned to the table, her tray populated by a bowl of soup, a dinner roll, and a fish sandwich.

"So, what are you hearing about Hartley's death?" asked Kiana.

I hesitated, stopping myself from saying, "I wanted to ask you that." I assumed the police had questioned King rather pointedly, given what Caroline Cruz had said about her potential motives for wanting Hartley dead.

Instead, I responded in a safe way. "Actually, nothing. How about you?" I took a small bite of my panini sandwich, glad it hadn't gotten too cold while Kiana took her time getting to the table.

"You didn't hear?" she asked.

"Hear what?"

"They grilled me for almost two hours Monday night."

"You don't say." In order to avoid eye contact, I looked at her prominent necklace, a yin/yang symbol the size of a ping pong ball.

"Yeah. I had the feeling that someone at cabinet had told them about my disagreements with Mike."

"It could have been," I stammered. "Detective Marsh did interview us at length, although I'm not sure I caught all the discussions with individual cabinet members." It was almost the truth, although certainly not the whole truth. I certainly wasn't privy to the conversations Marsh had with Victor and Bob prior to coming into the meeting. "That's a cool necklace, by the way."

King glanced at it and shrugged her shoulders. "Nothing spectacular. Look, Mark, you probably need to know that I had a strained relationship with Mike, as did many others around here. He was such an opportunist; some of us simply didn't yield to his bombastic self-serving presentations. Not that I would have killed him, though."

I choked briefly on lettuce in my sandwich. "Hey, don't worry, Kiana, this isn't an interrogation. I have no idea if you would kill Hartley, and it's not my place to determine that." I sipped on some iced tea.

"You'll hear more of this from the others. Rumor had it that he had a beeline to Berrian's office. Certainly Riley's told you that?"

"Uh, actually not." I looked desperately for some other fashion accessory to compliment.

"Well, she should. Anyway, since education has been the cornerstone of this university for years, he wore that like a badge. And, you know, he and the president both have that educational leadership Ed.D., which certainly opened a door for him."

I nodded and kept eating my sandwich. I figured I had no choice but to let Kiana rant for a little while.

"And another thing: Mike was an outright liar. You couldn't believe a word he said." She used her soup spoon to play with her soup, but she hadn't taken a bite of anything yet. "For instance, he promised to develop with me a health education certificate program. This was on my goals two years ago. Then, he put off and put off meeting with me, and at the end of the year, when I had to discuss my goals with Palmer, Mike denied ever having a conversation with me. Ugh, what a jerk."

I nodded again and glanced at my watch. How quickly could I get out of this meeting? Would it be better to come back another time and try to catch Kiana when she wasn't so wound up? Jennifer Riley had been right on target with her advice to not ask Kiana about her public blow-up with Hartley.

"I'm sure you've already heard about his faculty being pissed that he didn't support their tenure."

"Oh, yeah," I said, drinking some more tea. "Jennifer and I discussed that some yesterday."

"Plutowski was fit to be tied. I saw him and Hammer at the Heartland the night after they were denied tenure, and they were three sheets to the wind. Hammer, perceptibly down, cried in his beer, but Plutowski ranted and raved and scared me half to death." I had heard of the Heartland, a bar populated mostly by Boan employees. The Heartland was, according to our realtor, not the place to go if you didn't want your business heard and spread around campus. 'Chalk one up to the realtor,' I thought.

"Did you tell the police this?" As soon as I asked, I regretted it. I had encouraged her to rant and rave more.

King rolled her eyes. "Duh! Of course, I did. They're not interested."

"Hmm?" I was at a loss for words. Finishing my panini, I wondered how adeptly I could get the heck out of there.

King must have thought my primordial grunt invited her to continue. "They didn't give it much credence since it was three years ago. When I told them my blow up with Hartless was in the past, too, they sure didn't act convinced."

I tendered an uneasy smile. "Hartless! I get it. Were others likely to call him that?" I asked.

"Hartless. Hardly. Harshly. Harmfully. Fartley. You name it, he was probably called it."

"Fartley! You've got to be kidding me?"

"That was Plutowski's favorite name for him." King finally took a bite out of her fish sandwich. I figured I had my opening to pursue other lines of inquiry. "Look, let's cover a few things in the time I have." I had plenty of time, but I quickly needed to utilize the trick of leadership, which is to suggest your calendar is always full so that you can duck out of unwanted situations. "What can you tell me about the status of your college, Kiana? I know we talked about it some at the interviews, but what are your main concerns right now?"

Kiana sipped some of her soup. "Well, as Ms. Franklin sang, R-E-S-P-E-C -T, respect. That's what we need, Mark, respect."

"How have you not been getting it, Kiana?"

"Look around you, Mark."

I exaggeratedly looked around the cafeteria as if I expected to see homeless allied health faculty, dim-witted allied health students, and a war-zone of allied health despair.

"Not literally."

I laughed. "I know, Kiana. Just trying to lighten the mood."

"This is no laughing matter, Mark."

"Jesus, Kiana, I know that. Please continue." Boy, with King and Cruz, there wasn't much frivolity.

Kiana took another bite of her fish sandwich. I drained my iced tea. "Marketing! Find me any pieces dedicated to phlebotomy or medical assisting or medical records programs. I dare you! Find one."

I'm sure I looked helpless.

"None! Not a single damn one, Mark. We're afterthoughts on promotional materials for nursing degrees or even educational programs." Kiana was waving her arms so wildly that her yin/yang had flipped over her left shoulder.

"I thought Hartless," Kiana smiled at my obvious attempt to curry favor, "never followed through on a specific health education certificate."

"Partially true. The next year, he grabbed a few of my junior faculty, hammered out something way too quickly, and got the university's approval. Bastard."

I made a mental note to avoid mentioning Mike Hartley around Kiana King, perhaps ever again. "O.k., so back to the lack of respect. No specific marketing materials. What else?"

"Lack of faculty. We have two full-time faculty and we can't get any more. The adjuncts we pull in off the street are pathetic."

I pulled a pen out of my notebook and began taking notes. "Go on."

"Signage! If you go into Weaver Hall, there is no signage directing students to our area." The necklace had now bounced over to her right shoulder.

"I still need to get to Weaver Hall, so help me out here. You're saying that there are no signs directing students to your specific allied health offices?"

"That's correct. We're on the fourth floor at the end of the hall. No stupid signage."

"Who's 'we'?"

"Gladstone, Quick and me."

"Would have made a great power trio."

"What?" Her expression was the definition of dumbfounded.

"Gladstone, Quick and King. A 60's power trio. Like the Jimi Hendrix Experience?" It was her turn to appear helpless. "Never mind, Kiana. I assume Gladstone and Quick are your two full-timers."

"Yes. Monique Gladstone and Kathy Quick."

I wrote their names down in my notebook and added "check out fourth floor of Weaver."

"O.k., anything else?"

Kiana veered off into petty jealousies about nursing and conspiracy theories about the admissions staff. I pretended to listen and to take notes, but her remaining comments lacked any substance. Her initial comments might bear some validity, so I made a note to look into her first three examples of lack of respect. I had a few more things to discuss with her, but all of a sudden, she interrupted her own chain of thought. "Oh my goodness, what time is it, Mark?"

"Uh, it's 1:20."

"Shoot. I've got to go. I'm going to be late for Peter Robinson."

My ears pricked up. "Peter Robinson, the mystery writer?"

"Oh, yes, he's doing a book signing at the Barnes and Noble downtown."

"Honest to god? I love Robinson. Do you read a lot of him?"

"All of him," she said, grabbing the keys next to her tray and heading to the door. "The signing starts at 1:30." As she ran to the door, I heard a clanking on the ground. Her yin/yang had come undone and fallen to the floor.

"Hey, Kiana, don't forget your duality!" She looked at me dumbfounded again. I pointed to the floor. She grabbed it and hustled away.

As I watched her race out of the cafeteria, I thought about going to the signing myself, but with my car behind the Administration Building, I couldn't even see myself getting off campus by 1:30. Who knows how long the book signing would go or how many people might be in line? I decided not to risk the time. Instead, I went out the backdoor of the cafeteria and took a short cut to Weaver Hall. With the afternoon free, I might as well get out and about a little bit.

Crossing volleyball and basketball courts to get to Weaver Hall, I entertained myself with the surprising thought that Kiana King, initially a tiresome woman, was a Peter Robinson fan. Maybe I had hope with her. The world of mystery writers is quite immense, so I wondered if we would share other writers of interest: Rankin, Connelly, Sanford, Harvey and Larsson. I would have to explore her mystery interests more. I could always use another mystery buff to compare notes with.

Weaver Hall had recently been renovated, and it stood out, in an ugly way, from many of the other buildings on campus. Whereas many of Boan's buildings were either traditional ivy-covered or modern brick-and-glass structures, the attempts to renovate Weaver had resulted in a pretty hideous collage of both. I stood facing the older part of the building now, at its front doors, near the sign that listed the various health-related departments within the building. To the west side of the building a wing had been added, which is evidently where the various laboratories were built when Boan added nursing and other clinical-based programs less than a decade ago. This addition on the west side comprised of two stories, while the rest of the building stood four stories high. On top of the addition, on the flat roof, someone had set some folding chairs.

Entering the older part of the building, I immediately took the stairs up to the fourth level. Out of breath by the third floor landing, I stopped briefly for a rest at a window at the end of the fourth floor hall. As I looked down the dimly lit floor, I could see six doors on each side of the hallway. The hallway was stuffy and not surprisingly in an old building like this, there wasn't much cool air.

I walked down the hallway, noting that most of the doors led to dark classrooms. Each room had been outfitted with about twenty uncomfortable-looking chairs and blackboards straight out of my school years. I wondered if allied health typically got relegated to these classrooms. Probably not, as certainly Kiana would have itemized that disrespect too in her litany. Her office stood at the end of the hallway. Over her door window, she had placed a poster promoting the benefits of a health professions career. A pictograph showing the increase of jobs in health professions used obvious nurse icons to represent the numbers of available positions. At the bottom of the poster, someone had scrawled "Nurses: God's gift to doctors. God hates doctors." I wasn't exactly sure what to make of it.

I looked on the walls outside her office. She did have a small nameplate reading 'Dean Kiana King,' but as she'd said, nothing else, besides her own poster, told potential visitors they had located the health office areas, let alone allied health. A little further down, I found an open door, with the nameplates saying, 'Katherine Quick' and 'Monique Gladstone.' Inside, two cubicles split the office in half. The two offices were separated only by half walls, and the window, being held open by a book, was split by the wall separating the office.

A petite black woman sat at one of the desks, using her mouse to navigate through something on what appeared to be MSN.com. "Hello," I called out.

"What!?" she screamed, jumping out of her chair.

"I'm so sorry. I didn't mean to scare you." I walked a little further into the office and presented my hand. "Hi, I'm Mark Carter, the new provost."

The woman slumped back in her chair. "Yes, you certainly are. My goodness, you gave me a scare." Her face had a magnificent bone structure. With my mind still on Peter Robinson, I had a fleeting thought of her as Detective Winsome Jackman.

"I'm really sorry. I should have knocked on the door."

"Don't worry about it. It's just so bloody quiet around here this week. And, I'm a little jumpy from the Hartley murder." She quickly closed the window on her computer. The one above her desk was not allowing much air into the stuffy room.

"I understand. Are you Monique or Katherine?"

"Oops," she said, putting her hand out to shake. "I am Monique. Welcome to Boan, sir."

"Please, no 'sir' to me."

"Have you been looking for Dean King? Because I think she has left for the day."

"No. In fact, I just had lunch with her. She had told me there was no signage for your programs, so I decided to check it out."

Monique quietly chuckled. "Kiana has such a good heart, but if you look around, you'll see that nobody in this building has any signage. Nursing doesn't. The labs are hard to find the first time you look for them. So, it's not just us."

I took a deep breath. "Well, that is interesting. The signage in the other academic buildings is better?"

"I think for the most part. I spend most of my time here in Charlie Weaver Hall."

"Charlie Weaver Hall? That's great. Any particular reason you call it that?"

"Most of us here call it that. We figure that's because we're not the center square or even the corner squares; as a result, people only care about us when we can help them achieve something else."

"I'd say that's really cynical, but I have already met the people at Lynde Hall, and they do think the world revolves around them." Monique laughed very loudly, reminding me how great it feels to make a beautiful woman laugh.

"If we had a Paul Lynde Hall, we'd put education smack dab there."

"Anyway, has the signage for the whole building even been addressed?"

"I think off and on for years."

"What's been the problem? Money? It can't cost that much." I looked around her office, noting that it could use new, brighter paint and new carpeting.

"To be truthful," said Monique, lowering her voice. "Dean King and Dean Linares can't agree on anything, so nothing happens. It's true for more than just signage. Sometimes I wish we had just one dean for all the health professions, but that is never going to happen."

"Well, let me see what I can do. I appreciate the information."

I left her office and took the backstairs to the third floor. Peering down that hallway, all the rooms were dark. On the second floor, I found the same thing. On the first floor, as I got out of the stairwell, I faced two hallways; the one that went straight would take me back to the front doors while the one to the right would almost certainly take me into the new addition. I saw only a couple of doors in the hallway in the old building, and all looked dark and closed. I considered walking down to the labs, but decided to get back to my office, review my notes from my meeting with King, and see what awaited me.

When I got back to my office, I shot Kiana King an e-mail: "Hi Kiana. Hope the book signing went well. I investigated the missing signage and discovered it is not an isolated case. Will talk to the Chief about a full-fledged probe of the matter." I signed it as Peter Robinson's leading man, "Alan Banks." I hoped she had a sense of whimsy.

As I looked back through the forty or so e-mails that had piled up during the course of the afternoon, I surprisingly discovered a response from the president to my e-mail regarding the appointment of Riley as interim dean of education. I clicked on it, nervous that he had had second thoughts since our conversation yesterday afternoon. However, he had completely forgotten that conversation: "Sounds like a plan. Work with communications!"

I noted that his e-mail had been sent twenty-six minutes later than the communications' e-mail about Riley as the interim dean. 'That could have been ugly,' I thought, 'if he had changed his mind.'

Later that night, after gnashing our teeth about Alyssa's sudden bouts of physical altercations, Natalie and I asked Alyssa why she was fighting.

"The boys in this neighborhood are jerks," she said pouting.

"Why, honey?" I asked.

"They cheat. In kickball, in soccer, in everything."

I looked at Natalie, who had a tear forming in the corner of her almond-shaped eye. "Well, honey," I said, turning back to look at Alyssa, whose white pants had grass stains on the knees, "that doesn't give you the right to hit them."

"But I just get so mad. And they only cheat against us girls. Staci and Kristy just roll over and let them do it." Alyssa crinkled her crooked nose as she frowned.

I had to suppress a little laughter. Alyssa would not be like a lot of other girls.

After an hour of her pouting while Natalie and I pleaded and tried to reason with her, I convinced her to go apologize to Spenser Cunningham. Natalie, who had experienced tense moments with the Cunninghams the night before, decided not to join us. That was fine. I could only deal with one angry female at a time. In fact, I think god must have equipped man to deal with only one angry female at a time. After all, we're pretty lousy at it.

"Hello, Walter," I said, when Walter Cunningham opened the door and immediately frowned. "Truce," I declared immediately, holding up my hands in surrender. "Alyssa here has something she would like to say to Spenser. Is he around?"

"Yes, he is. Spenser!" he yelled. "Get in here."

Long-haired, shuffling, x-box-t-shirt-wearing Spenser lumbered to the door. I wanted to smack him based on his attitude alone, but instead pushed Alyssa to stand in front of me.

"Spenser, I'm sorry I hit you. I won't do it again." Alyssa tugged at the hem of her shirt, barely looking at Spenser. I figured it was best to take what we could get.

Spenser grunted something and walked away. I looked at Walter Cunningham and shrugged my shoulders. "Damn kids," he muttered, closing the door without saying anything. The look on his face suggested he might be angrier with Spenser than with Alyssa and me. It's too easy to imagine what the father of five boys might think about a son getting beat up by a girl.

As Alyssa and I walked back to the house, I held her hand and talked to her about how I walked the long way to school to avoid getting beat up when in middle school. I'm not sure if I meant it as a cautionary tale or a parody.

Chapter Seven

Thursday was destined to be a great day. My meetings were with Charlotte Webb, Director of the Libraries, and Gertrude Fulbright, Dean of Arts and Sciences, areas I considered my turf. I had also scheduled for the mid-morning a webinar for new provosts, as part of a professional development opportunity.

The webinar ended up being about 75% useless, but some valuable insights about vision and direction came from it. I tuned out at one point to check Snopes.com, just for fun. I signed off the webinar just in time to see Charlotte Webb standing at my door.

"Hi, Charlotte. Come on in. I need to duck into the restroom and then refill my coffee. Can I get you something to drink on my way back?"

"No, I'm fine," said Charlotte, a thin, waif-like creature with salt-and-pepper hair and big round glasses. Not quite the stereotype for a librarian, but close.

When I returned with my coffee, I found Charlotte thumbing through the few books set up in my office. While I had three boxes of office books sitting at home, without a whole lot of available bookshelf in my office, I still needed to pick out what would fill out the shelves.

"Not much there, yet. See anything interesting?" I asked her.

"I was looking at your copy of *What the Best College Instructors Do*. You probably don't know this, but five or six years ago when that book first came out, we ordered ten copies and encouraged the faculty to come check it out. I bet only three or four faculty members ever took us up on that." Charlotte carefully slid the book back into its spot on the bookcase and headed back to her chair.

"That is sad. Is it likely that a number of them have it for themselves?" I pondered.

"Who knows?" sniped Charlotte.

"Anyway, did anyone else tell you, yet, the good news that the library renovation will be put off until next summer?" I waited to see Charlotte smile.

It never came. "Oh, good lord, they put it off. What are we supposed to do now?"

I stroked my forehead and took a deep breath. "I thought you'd be happy. The way I understood it is that the library staff didn't want the renovation to happen this fall. It would create too much chaos and deny students more services and space."

"We had a plan in place. We've been meeting about it for five months, planning, anticipating and preparing communications for students."

"Frankly, Charlotte, I'm flabbergasted. I could have sworn that Hank Turing said that some of the library staff, at least, favored the postponement. Could there be some members of your staff who mis-conveyed your intentions?"

"No, Mark."

Later, after Charlotte had left, I tried to replay the scene from cabinet where we discussed the library renovation. After struggling to recollect anything from that discussion, I remembered that the conversation occurred during my dazed state. Caroline had taken the lead on the discussion, something about surveys showing we would disrupt students less.

I called Caroline quickly, before heading back to the cafeteria for my third lunch meeting this week, this time with Gertrude Fulbright. Caroline answered on the first ring.

"Caroline, let me ask you a quick question. In the discussion Monday at cabinet about the library renovation, did either you or Hank reference the opinions of the librarians?"

"No. I referenced a student survey, but I certainly never asked a librarian."

"And you don't think Hank did either?"

"No, I don't think so. We would have expected the provost to survey the librarians."

"It was my first day, Caroline. How could I have already asked the librarians?" I fought to keep my voice from rising too much.

"I figured Riley might have prepped you."

"First day, Caroline. First morning of first day. What's so hard to understand?"

"Settle down, Mark. It's not that big of a deal. What's the problem? Are the librarians storming the metaphorical Bastille, seeking justice or the provost's head?"

"Very funny, Caroline. No, I just had a quick conversation about it with Charlotte and she was disappointed, hardly angry. I am just following up."

"Hold on a second, Mark." I could hear a male voice in Caroline's office. He said something about payment plans. Caroline brusquely told him that it should have been taken care of a week ago. The male voice then clearly whined about something. 'Good Lord,' I thought, 'Caroline, just put me on hold.'

Finally, Caroline said loudly and plainly, "It's your fault. Get out there and fix it, and don't come back until you have." After a couple of seconds, she spoke back into the phone. "Sorry, Mark, where were we?"

"I'm getting a sense I need a compass to know where I'm at sometimes around here, Caroline. Don't worry, you've told me enough. I'll follow up with Charlotte." I started to hang up the phone.

"Oh, Mark?"

"Yes, Caroline."

"You wanted course schedules?"

I snapped my fingers. "Thanks so much for remembering. I forgot to bring it up at our meeting yesterday morning." Actually, bringing up anything at that meeting would have felt like requesting a death squad.

"Go to the website. Click on the right side where it says 'important information,' then click on the left side of that page where it says 'essential student information,' then on that page, click at the bottom where it says 'records and databook.' Then, there, you want to click on number four, 'academic calendars and course schedules.'"

Anxiously, I attempted to jot down everything she told me. "Hold on, Caroline. That's 'important information/essential student information/ records' and what? And then what?"

"'Records and databook,' then 'academic calendars and course schedules.'" Caroline sounded as if she had already tired of dealing with her fresh, new provost.

I jotted down the rest of the chain. "Not exactly the easiest site to navigate, is it?" I said, reading through the chain.

"Cry to Yost. I'm tired of tilting at that windmill." Caroline hung up, and I left the phone cradling over my right shoulder as I clicked through the pages to get to the course schedule. Why the schedule had been combined with the academic calendar was beyond my comprehension. A loose relationship existed between the two, but students would be searching for information related to the two in much different ways. When I went to print off sections of the schedule related only to the time relevant for my needs, I stupidly printed the entire schedule. Given that the full schedule would be forty-four pages, I panicked. I hit the stop button on the printer, but then in turning it back on, caused it to jam. I had the first three pages of the schedule, virtually useless for my needs, a jammed printer, and a rapidly developing headache.

I hit the speed number to IT support and while on hold looked at the back parking lot where most of Boan's administrators parked. The lot was populated by more than one Mercedes Benz, all grey or black, at least two Audis (one black, one cream), one Cadillac, and any number of cars resembling a Lexus. My Honda stood out like the tall girl with braces at a middle school dance.

I finally got a chance to leave IT support a voice-mail, thank goodness, because in another minute or two, I'd be late for my lunch with Fulbright. I told them of my jammed printer, then hung up, grabbed my notebook and pen, and headed outside to go to the cafeteria. The sky was overcast and to the west lurked a potential storm front. I had no umbrella with me, so hopefully after lunch I would be able to get back to my office unscathed.

A few minutes late, I slid into my chair across from Gertrude Fulbright. Despite her name, she was young, and she exhibited a powerful sense of peacefulness. She wore casual clothes, but still looked neat and presentable. I had met the auburn-haired Gertrude, or Trudy, at my interviews, and we shared a lot of interests, most notably in the areas of popular music. I looked forward to working with her.

"So, what are you hearing about Hartley's death?" asked Trudy, after we had settled down with our lunch. I had chosen from the salad bar. Trudy had ordered a Reuben. Her lunch did look better than mine. As with the previous days, the cafeteria remained fairly empty, although I could see Hank Turing lunching with Aaron Cartwright and three women I didn't recognize, probably members of his finance/accounting team.

"That's the question of the week, isn't it?" I commented. "All I hear are rumors. No one has talked to me about it since Monday."

"Nor me. One of the detectives talked to me for about twenty minutes on Monday but that was it."

"You must not have made a very good suspect," I laughed.

"I beg your pardon, Dr. Carter. Don't think I'm so innocent."

While I picked through my lettuce, Trudy went on. "Actually, I probably had the least amount of issues with Hartley as anybody. I found him laughable and even contemptible, but I lost no sleep at night over Mike."

"You might have been the only one."

"Uh-oh," said Trudy, looking toward the cafeteria entrance.

I turned around and looked beyond the tables that still had chairs set on them from a recent cleaning. This would all change in the matter of a few days. "Is that Berrian?" I asked Trudy.

"Looks like it is him and Victor Woo. I wonder if Victor has come to taste the president's food."

"Dr. Fulbright! That's not nice."

"I suppose it isn't."

I hesitated for a moment. Then, in a low whisper, I asked, "was that a slam against Woo or a slam against Berrian?"

"Good question. Let me get back to you." Trudy leaned back in her chair, looked over my shoulder, and flashed a magnificent smile. "Dr. Berrian. Victor. How nice to see both of you."

I could feel Berrian's stern hand on my shoulder. I tried to stand up but his grip held me down. "Stay seated. Don't want to interrupt your lunch. We just thought we'd say 'hi.'"

"Hi," said Trudy with just a hint of impishness.

"So, what's good today?" asked Berrian. Victor looked nervously around the room.

"The Reuben is always good, Dr. Berrian."

"Boring salad bar for me. I'd recommend the Reuben too." I used my fork to show a few pieces of wilted lettuce I kept pushing around my plate.

"Difficult decision. Difficult decision. Luckily, we're used to making tough decisions, aren't we, Victor?" Berrian removed his hand from my shoulder and slapped Victor on the back. Victor looked like he might crumble like a wobbly tinker toy set.

As they moved away, Trudy leaned back over the table and murmured, "So, how was the cabinet meeting? You survived?"

"That happens to be the second most asked question this week." I hesitated, thinking of my response. "You know Aimee Mann?"

"Do I know Aimee Mann? I've only seen her three times." Trudy slapped her hands together in delight.

"Two times for me, including a dark little club in Cleveland, where there couldn't have been more than two hundred of us. I probably still haven't washed those clothes."

Trudy hooted in an incredibly feminine way. Apparently, she had suffered through two failed marriages and showed no interest in romantic relationships. A lot of single men around Boan had to be disappointed by that.

"Then you'll know why cabinet reminded me of the line 'we're only flogging the horse, when the horseman has up and died.' In fact, I have thought of that line several times this week."

Trudy laughed loudly again, drawing attention from Victor who waited for the president near the cash register. "Don't get too cynical and pessimistic so quickly, Mark. We'd like to keep you for a few years."

I smiled. "Don't worry. Among other things, I saw enough at Farrington to know that many of us suffer through the same banalities. My favorite moment at Farrington was the two-hour debate about whether our ultimate service award should be called 'the lifetime achievement award' or 'the career achievement award.'"

"Sounds like our great debate last year about whether pencil sharpeners should be replaced in bulk or by building."

"Ah, academia. Nothing like it in the world. Still," I said, as I worried that the rumor mill around Boan would circulate stories that the new provost was already fed up, "I have lots of hopes. I think maybe I can influence leadership," and I looked over to see Berrian taking a French fry from Victor's tray, "for the better."

"All you want to do is something good, eh?" smiled Trudy.

"So I better be ready to be ridiculed and misunderstood. Thank you, Aimee."

We finished our lunches and slipped into work talk. I asked about the expansion of arts and sciences, learning that Berrian had requested this, but that few in the university seemed to want to take it on, including herself. Through the conversation Trudy revealed her skills as an effective administrator. She was loved by her faculty and respected by administration. Sadly, when one has a direct report like that, one needs to meet with her less. That's the cruelty of management. The people who you can most enjoy are the ones who need the least management.

Right as I started to tell Trudy that I should get back to my office, she was surprised by someone coming up from behind me again. Before I could turn around, she had welcomed Detective Marsh.

"Hello Dr. Fulbright. Dr. Carter. Apparently I can find the president in here. Have you seen him?"

"He and Victor are right over there, detective," I said, pointing to the far wall where they had set up their lunches. I noted Berrian taking another one of Victor's fries. "Looks like we're mistaken, Dr. Fulbright. It appears that the president is the food taster for the EVP of HR."

Even Detective Marsh laughed and thanked us before heading over to the president.

"By the way, detective," Trudy called out before she got too far away, "anything you can tell us about the investigation? Catch the murderer yet?"

"No, ma'am," she responded politely. "But we will."

"Aren't you tempted to go eavesdrop?" asked Trudy after Marsh had made it to the president's table.

"Not really," I said, looking at my watch. "Besides we've had way too much fun and it's almost 2:00. I've got to go get stuff done. See you later."

"I'm going to sidle over there. Take care."

When I got to the door, I turned around and saw Trudy standing next to

Detective Marsh, hands on hips, apparently welcomed into the conversation. Somehow I wasn't surprised.

As I walked back to my office, in a slight drizzle, I realized Veronica still had confirmed nothing about a potential one-on-one with Berrian tomorrow. I walked past my office to hers. I found her muttering under her breath while she fiddled with her computer.

"Hi, Veronica. Everything o.k.?"

"Yeah, just some computer problems. In fact IT is going to look at it after they are done in your office."

"Oh, that's right. My printer problems. Do I have a one on one tomorrow?"

"Yes, I finally got it scheduled about an hour ago. It's on your calendar for 3:00." She tapped repeatedly on the 'enter' button with her finger.

"What should I expect? Will he send me an agenda in advance?"

Veronica scoffed. "No. You should bring one in advance, and if you can, send it to me the day before so that I can print it out for him. Don't worry about that for tomorrow."

I looked at my watch. "I might still get one to you. I had been half working on one all week. Anyway, thanks."

"Oh, Mark?"

"Yes."

"Realize that your one-on-one is right before the basketball game. Be ready."

"I never really got invited to the basketball game."

"Oh, you're expected to go. Bob calls it the end-of-the-week-bonding experience."

"I do like basketball, so it's not that big of a deal. How long do they play?"

"Depends how many show up. I think they play until 5:30, 6:00 at the latest." Veronica had stopped fighting with her computer.

"Who else will likely play? I better start assessing my competition."

"Bob, Howard, Hank, Victor, Garrett, Adam, Aaron, I forget who else. Mike Hartley sometimes played."

"Did he? I wonder if he provided any motives for his murder on the basketball court."

Veronica smiled. "I hear it can be pretty brutal. Hank came in one Monday with a black eye, and it sounds like they spend all weekend nursing the damage to their out-of-shape middle-aged bodies."

"Great. I'll fit right in. Thanks for the information."

Back in the office, I saw two IT guys unplugging my printer and getting ready to take it away. "Can't fix it here?" I asked.

"Can't fix it at all," grunted the stockier one.

"You're kidding?"

"No, unfortunately not, Dr. Carter," said the thinner, better groomed one. "We'll put in a request for a replacement and hopefully you'll have one by early next week."

"You're kidding?"

The stockier one just shook his head and placed the printer on a cart, while the better groomed one held his arms up in the universal "sorry" gesture.

Frustrated, I sat down at my computer and finalized my agenda for my afternoon one-on-one with the president. When finished, I looked for Shelley across the hall, who, while not at her desk, could be heard over the partitions of the other cubes.

"Shelley," I called rounding the corner.

"Oh, hi, Mark," she said, turning from talking to an older, long red-haired woman.

"They just took away my printer, which was jammed. I need to print something out. What's the next best printer to print it to?"

Twenty painful minutes later, Shelley had finally matched up her printer with one on my list of available printers. When two copies of my one-on-one agenda materialized in Shelley's printer ("like magic," she gushed), I took one to Veronica to give to Berrian. I went back into my office and then e-mailed the agenda to both Berrian and Veronica. Redundancy, redundancy, redundancy. I had learned long ago to be careful.

The rest of the afternoon progressed slowly, so I slipped out of the office a little after four. It helped that I could see the president at ten minutes before four hop into his Mercedes Benz and leave. On the way home, I bought two six packs of beer, two bottles of wine, and orange soda for Alyssa. At home, no one talked about hitting a Cunningham or other minor crises. We played a game of Monopoly Junior, and then Natalie and I sat on the porch and read. I was devouring the latest Nick Hornsby, Natalie read a Margaret Atwood. I had stopped worrying long ago that she read more "prestigious novels" than I did. I found my reading to be exactly the kind of mind-munchies that relaxed me at the end of a day. By the time I dragged my half-asleep body up to the bedroom where Natalie already slept, I fantasized about how quickly my jump shot would come back.

Chapter Eight

In my forty-five years of life I had never before taken a bubble bath at 8:00 PM on a Friday night. Yet, here it was, that time on a Friday, and I lay submerged, all but my head, in a hot bubble bath, glass of Glenfiddich on the toilet seat next to the tub, and Sigur Ros' *Takk* on the CD player in the bathroom, the minimalist sounds serving as a superb complementary coolness to the water temperature. My head leaned back against the wall, and I felt the water, scotch and music work their magic on my tired and sore muscles. My calf muscles, which had cramped up at the end of the Boan basketball game, slowly began to loosen up. My feet, which had barely been able to make it up the stairs after dinner, started to resemble their former selves. I couldn't be the only Boan leader recuperating in this way. Many of us limped off the courts to the locker rooms, or in some cases, directly to our cars.

I wondered how Michael Stewart was faring. He had tripped ("been tripped," he argued to me) over Garrett Jones. He'd grabbed his ankle and writhed on the floor, while Berrian grabbed the ball that had sprung loose from Stewart and drove the court for an easy lay-up. Poor Michael had already hit the floor twice before that. On this third occasion, he picked himself off the floor and left the court without saying anything to anybody but me.

I felt somewhat guilty because I had encouraged Stewart to join the game. Earlier in the day, on dean lunch meeting number four, I admitted to being anxious about the game that afternoon.

"I used to play in those," he said. "Haven't done it in months."

"Why? What happened?"

"Nothing, really. A few things came up. Friday afternoons can sometimes be the worst time to do these things. I guess I just didn't miss it that much. Perhaps too competitive for my tastes."

"Excuse the stereotype, Mike," I said, giving his graying head and soft body a once over, "but I guess I am a little surprised that a 60-year old fine arts dean would even be interested in playing."

"I'll accept your apology for such unfair criticism, Dr. Carter. You'll quickly see that I am not the old fuddy-duddy artist people think I am."

"I stand corrected. Well, why don't you come back this afternoon? I'd like to see somebody there who doesn't intimidate me!"

"Gee, when you say it like that. Do they still start at 4:00?"

"I believe so. All I know is that I should expect to go play as soon as my one-on-one is over."

Stewart pushed his plate of spaghetti to the center of the table. "I better not eat any more of that stuff." He then paused and looked out the window. We sat at the same table where I had been with Jennifer Riley, and as I looked out the window, too, the same workmen could be seen working on the same exposed underground pipe.

"I think I might. I can easily get home and get some clothes."

"You said the games were competitive. Did you mean that they were ruthlessly competitive?" I asked.

"They could be," replied Stewart. "But, one should expect, when playing with presidents and vice presidents, a certain element of ruthlessness."

I grinned at his cynicism. "Well, that may mean I don't play often. I don't get into that ruthless competitiveness."

"Speaking of ruthless," said Stewart, looking at a few notes he had brought to the lunch meeting, and getting us back on task, "what have you heard about the proposal to eliminate fine arts?"

"A little, Mike, to be honest. The perception of some people is that your enrollment is so low that the program is losing money, and, more importantly, that there is no strategy for changing that."

Stewart heaved a sigh. "That's what Riley believes. Has she already talked to you about that?"

"She and others." I lied about the others, just to avoid making this a Stewart vs. Riley confrontation. The truth is that I planned to discuss with Howard, whom Jennifer said agreed with her proposal, but I hadn't had the time.

Stewart played with the label on his Coke bottle. "I can't argue some of the facts. Enrollment is down and has been going down substantially for a decade. I don't believe it's to the point where we lose money, but it's so damn hard to get accounting and finance to show me clear data on costs versus revenue." He continued to play with the Coke label, while I leaned back in my chair and stared at the workmen.

"The college probably needs a new dean, Mark," continued Stewart. "I've been leading it for sixteen years now, and I'm tired and out of ideas.

The problem has been that the university refuses to do anything for the college. I've been looking for a sculpture full-timer for several years. The three full-timers in the department teach their classes and go home. They have absolutely no interest in leadership. They just want to teach and work on their own stuff."

"I've heard about the open sculpture position, Mike. We can talk about that in greater detail another time, but it's clear that some people on cabinet don't support that position."

"**Cabinet**. Oh, yes, the infamous cabinet. There is much speculation around here about the secretive, nefarious creations that come from cabinet."

I snorted. "It's not like it's Dr. Caligari's cabinet. Although, I'm getting a feeling a lot of the faculty and staff think it is." One of the workmen dug around the exposed pipe; three other ones stood around and talked. "I will admit to one thing, Mike. Given my one day in cabinet, I can't speak to anything 'creative' coming out of that meeting. It's no wonder you artists want nothing to do with it."

Mike shrugged his shoulders and continued peeling the Coke label. It was almost off, with just some remnant of the glue left on the plastic bottle.

"I'm not a knee-jerk kind of guy, Mike. As far as I know, the decision to keep or eliminate the College of Fine Arts rests entirely with me. Trust me when I say that you will be fully involved with all the data and the decision. We may have to decide to eliminate the college, but you will have been involved and may even have discovered alternatives for you, or your faculty, or even your students, through the process."

Stewart did not particularly cheer up. I felt desperate to give him something of a lifeline. "Look, before I leave today, I'll contact Tanya Tyler in institutional research and set up a meeting with you, me and her to look at data. O.k.?"

"We have an institutional research department now?" asked Stewart.

I tried to maintain a straight face. "Yes. I believe Boan has had one for five or six years now."

"Wow. I remember when the faculty senate recommended one to President Johnson. That must have been ten to twelve years ago. He practically laughed us out of the meeting."

"I have to go, Mike, but, I'll set up that meeting. I promise." I began packing up my things to head back to the administration building.

"Well, I do appreciate that," said Stewart with a little more enthusiasm.

"And I do hope you're still going to come to the basketball game."

Stewart responded hesitantly. "Oh, maybe not. Maybe I am too old and out of shape."

"Oh, forget that stupid thing I said. Come on."

We had reached the cafeteria doors and stepped outside. The temperature was back to a typical Indiana summer day: 90 degrees and high humidity.

"Probably shouldn't play in this heat," observed Stewart.

"I'm going to give it a shot. I think it's required of me—certainly the first week. I hope you come, Mike."

"We'll see. Thanks for the invite. The problem is this weather is murder."

I stopped and turned back to Mike. "I just realized something."

"What?"

"You're the first person I've met this week who didn't ask about Hartley?"

Stewart waved his hand as if to brush off the suggestion. "Jesus, why would I even want to talk about that?"

"I don't know, Mike. Sometimes the guilty party likes to act like he or she has no interest in the case. Seriously, though, did you get a lot of questions from the cops?"

"Not many. I didn't particularly care for Hartley, and so I mostly avoided him. I stayed away from all the politics."

"A smart move, Mike."

"I'm not so sure. That may be part of why my college has declining enrollment. That may be part of why Mike Hartley got trotted out in front of governors and fat cats and whatever, while I only trotted with myself." Stewart waved at me as he turned the corner of the cafeteria and left my line of sight.

I was roused from my sleepy recollections of my meeting with Stewart by Natalie, who had sauntered into the bathroom with the one offer that I couldn't resist: the bottle of Glenfiddich.

"Need a hit there, Kobe?" she asked.

"Oh, please." I held up my empty glass and she slowly poured me half a glass.

She set the bottle down on the sink, and sat on the edge of the toilet seat. I swished the elixir in my glass and took a hefty sip. "So, how are those muscles feeling?"

I pushed some bubbles away and carefully balanced my scotch on my belly. "Much better. Especially the calves and the feet."

"How about that **groin injury?**" she asked, mimicking the pathetic rap Sam Malone had once done about a groin injury on *Cheers*.

"It still hurts."

"Luckily, that's a part of your body you don't use very often."

I held my scotch with my left hand and pushed some bubbles at her with my right hand. "Don't be so sure, woman."

"MOOOOOMMMM!" came the cry from downstairs.

Natalie smiled and wiped the bubbles from her shirt with my towel. "Try not to fall asleep in there. It might be hard for me to explain to the police when I report it tomorrow morning." As she started to leave the room, she stopped. "By the way, I haven't heard you talk about Hartley's death. Any news?"

I chuckled. "If I had a dollar for every time someone asks that question? The problem is that my answer is always the same: don't know. Well, that's not entirely true. There was some discussion about it during the game tonight."

"MOOOOOOMMMMM! I need you."

"Uh, maybe you should see what our princess needs. Don't worry I won't go anywhere."

As Natalie left the bathroom, I took another sip of my scotch and set the glass back on the toilet seat. Actually the discussion about Hartley's murder had occurred before the basketball game even started.

Bob, Hank, Victor, Garrett Jones and Eddie Stevens, the volleyball coach for our girls' team, were changing in the staff locker room a little before 4:00. Stevens, whom I had just met, had asked the question: "So, what's the story with the Hartley case?"

Victor pulled on a faded Cincinnati Reds t-shirt. "The police seem to think they have narrowed the list of suspects, but they're not telling us much."

"Idiots better wrap this up soon," snapped Berrian while he carefully folded his suit pants and laid them on the top shelf of his locker. "I'm getting tired of seeing that Detective Marsh on campus every time I leave my office."

"There are worse things to have to look at than Allison Marsh," said Garrett Jones. This was the first time I had met Garrett, and I prayed I wouldn't have to guard him during the game. His body didn't look that far removed from his college football days at Ball State, even if that had been more than ten years ago. Not surprisingly, he wore a sleeveless t-shirt that showed off every ripple and muscle. As I quietly undressed and put on my vintage Clash concert t-shirt, I sized up my comparative physical shape to the rest of the group. I was near the bottom. Perhaps only Hank could compete with me for the out-of-shape middle-age jock-wanna-be in this group.

"Allison!" declared Hank in a sing-song voice. "My, my. How have we got on a first name basis, Mr. Jones?"

"I have had to spend a lot of time with her. It came out."

"What else are you holding back on?" asked Berrian, snapping Jones with a towel next to his gym bag.

"Really! Have you shown the fine detective your night stick, Mr. Jones?" Stevens slapped Jones on his back. The lines flew fast and furious.

"Did you let her handle your gun, Garrett, old boy?"

"Did you ask her to frisk you or did you frisk her?"

"Did she try out her handcuffs on you?"

"Did your snake find a nice warm home in that Marsh, Jonesy?"

Jones smirked as the double entendres flew around. "Are you all finished?"

We all looked at each other. "Are we?" asked Hank. "Yep, I guess we are."

"Good. Because I'm pretty sure they've decided the murderer is incredibly strong." Jones had begun stretching in the corner of the locker room.

"How the hell could they know that?" asked Berrian.

"All that science stuff like you see on *CSI*."

"I have to ask," said Hank, beginning to put on a pair of dark blue Boan shorts. "What exactly was the murder weapon?"

Berrian had finished tying his tennis shoes. "The award that Hartley got from his alma mater."

Hank stopped with his gym shorts still at his ankles. "You're shitting me? That one from Texas?"

"Oh, yeah."

Hank grimaced. Victor stifled a laugh.

"Am I missing something?" I asked.

"The award, Mark," disclosed Berrian, as he headed to the door, "was a bronze longhorn. You know, like the emblem on their helmets?"

"No!" Stevens instinctively slumped back toward his locker.

"Yep, 'hooked 'em horns.'" Berrian flashed us the Texas horns finger salute as he left the locker room for the gym.

Hank shivered, even though he had finally pulled his shorts up, ready to play. "I can only imagine one of those horns stuck somewhere in Mike Hartley." He grabbed his gym bag, shoved it in a locker and followed Stevens out of the room.

Jones had finished stretching and was leaving too. Victor and I dawdled. "Is that what you heard too, Garrett?"

"Yeah, basically stabbed by a bronze horn. I'm guessing the killer really had to thrust that sucker deep into Hartley's heart." Jones paused as he opened the door. "That is, if he had a heart."

Out on the main floor of the field house, a number of men had already grabbed a few balls and were practicing jump shots, lay-ups and free throws. Besides the group I had already seen in the locker room, Howard Shue was already out there, white Boan t-shirt, white shorts, and black socks inside black tennis shoes. Alan Yost, the CIO, drained some pretty jump shots from the corner. Aaron Cartwright tied his shoes on the bleacher seats. I walked by him and held out my hand. "Good to see you, Aaron."

"Oh, hi, Mark. Welcome to the game."

"You have to be twenty years younger than most of us geezers out here. That should give you a distinct advantage."

"Don't worry. What I have in youthful energy I counter with what I don't have in talent."

"How many we got?" yelled Berrian.

"It looks like we got nine," responded Victor.

"Who else might come?" Berrian stood at the far end of the court shooting free throws, three dribbles and a pause before every shot.

"Howell should be here."

"Who's Howell?" I asked Aaron.

"Athletic Director."

"Is he any good?"

"He's o.k. None of us are that good, Mark. Don't sweat it." Aaron had picked up a loose ball and launched a three pointer. It hit Victor Woo, standing two feet short of the basket, in the head.

"I think Mike Stewart might be coming too, Bob," I yelled.

"Stewart? I thought he gave up on this months ago." Berrian sank his fourth straight free throw.

"I kind of encouraged him. I hope no one minds."

"Of course. No one minds, Mark." Free throw number five hit nothing but net.

"Let's give them a couple more minutes," suggested Victor. "It's only 4:00 on the dot right now." Victor pointed to an ugly clock above the modern scoreboard at the far end of the court.

"Whose got tunes?" asked Berrian, heading back to our side of the court.

"I do," said Alan Yost, racing to the bleachers. He rummaged in his gym bag and pulled out a CD case. "Aerosmith's Greatest Hits. *O, Yeah!*"

"O, yeah," shouted Berrian. Alan scrambled up the bleachers to the section where the public address system was housed. Within a minute or two, "Mama Kin" blasted out at high decibels on the sound system.

I walked over to Victor. "Do we play it this loud during the game?"

"O, yeah," said Berrian, walking by us.

"Anybody ever bring any Cocteau Twins?" I paused for effect. "I didn't think so."

"Let's start. Hank and I are captains." Not surprisingly, Berrian did not ask this as a question. No one challenged it. "Free throws to see who picks first, Hank?" Berrian tossed the ball to Hank, who bobbled it.

Hank lumbered up to the free throw line, his bony knees barely bending as he put up his free throw. It bounced high off the back rim and off to Aaron standing to the left. Aaron bounced the ball to Berrian, who promptly took it to the free throw line and started his three dribble routine.

"I need to warm up more," announced Hank to no one in particular.

Berrian sank his free throw. "I pick first. I pick Jonesy." Garrett loped over to stand by Berrian.

"Gee, there's a surprise," cackled Howard from under the basket.

Hank pointed at Eddie Stevens. "I take Eddie."

"Don't forget me guys, I'm here," shouted a young-looking man with a crew-cut and long, athletic legs.

"I take Howell," shouted the president, pointing at the newcomer.

"Don't forget me, either. I'm here." A couple of seconds behind the young man with the long legs came the older guy with a paunch and thinning grey hair. "Hey, Mike," I yelled, waving at Stewart, "glad you could make it."

For a couple seconds of silence, Hank thought about his pick. "All the former athletes are gone. What is Coach Turing to do?" muttered Howard.

"You any good, Carter?"

I shrugged my shoulders. "It's been awhile since I've played. Even then I was amazingly mediocre."

Hank looked around at the rest of the group. "Anybody see Carter shooting during warm-ups?" He turned to Stevens. "How about you?"

I shrugged my shoulders. "Actually, Hank. I didn't even get a chance to try a shot."

Berrian, who had been holding the ball, fired a one-bounce pass to me. I looked down to see my feet just past the three-point line. 'What the heck,' I figured. I gave the ball my customary high arc and it went right through the net.

"I pick Carter," went Hank.

As I walked over to join him and Eddie, I whispered under my breath, "that was all luck, Hank."

"Well, keep riding Lady Luck as long as she'll have you."

"Yost." Alan jogged over to stand behind Berrian.

Hank thought again for a minute. "I'll take Aaron."

"Going for the fresh, young legs, are you, Turing? I guess I'll take Howard."

"Victor."

"What are we going to do with the extra player?" I asked, pointing to Mike Stewart.

"We'll do what we always do. Since you picked last, Hank, you get the extra player and can substitute at will." Stewart hustled over to join us.

"What are we playing to?" asked Stewart.

"To avoid injury," I cracked, although it was **my** primary goal.

Berrian ignored me. "Twenty-one. Have to win by two. Three pointers count as three."

"Do we call fouls?" I asked.

Berrian stared at me. "Only if it's a real foul?"

"What the hell does that mean?" I asked Aaron.

He shrugged. "You'll see how that goes."

The teams separated onto the two halves of the court. "I'll sit first," offered Stewart.

"Since you got the extra player, we get ball," Berrian barked.

"Full court?" I asked Hank.

"What else?"

As Bill Howell dribbled up the right sideline, we all naturally sought out a player to defend. Howard had floated into my area, making me more than happy to guard him. I didn't think he could embarrass me.

Howell passed the ball inside to Jones, who tossed the ball back out to Berrian, who drove into the lane. There in the middle stood Aaron Cartwright. The two men collided, and Berrian tossed the ball toward the basket hitting the underside of the rim.

"Foul!" cried Berrian.

"Charge!" screamed Hank.

Aaron slowly picked himself up off the floor. Garrett Jones had recovered the ball and stood in the left corner. Berrian yelled at him to give him the ball.

"Charge, Mr. President."

"No way! Foul!"

"It's o.k., Hank," said Aaron. "I moved into the lane."

Berrian missed one of the two free throws and the game quickly gained its rhythm. I floated around the outside of the three-point line, mostly handling the ball from Stevens, who served as our guard, and trying to dump passes into Hank and Aaron in the paint. Most plays were punctuated by the sounds of hands hitting arms, knees hitting knees, and balls hitting rims. On several occasions, as I back-pedaled down court to play defense, I could see Victor holding his hands on his knees and barely making it to half court. He wasn't alone, though, as Howard did the same for the other side, allowing me to float around on defense.

Several minutes into the game, I had no idea of the score. Our team might have hit two baskets, and Berrian's team might have made three baskets, at least one a three-pointer. After Alan Yost went flying into the basketball post under his offensive basket and the ball rolled to the field house wall, I waved for Stewart to come in for me. As I hobbled to the bleachers, I yelled over "Same Old Song and Dance," "What's the score?"

"We're up 8-2," yelled Berrian.

"It's 8-4," shouted Hank back.

"Bullshit." Berrian, guarding Hank, took a swipe at the ball, and missed. Hank drove past him and passed the ball to Stewart at the top of the key. Mike lowered his shoulder and drove into the lane. For some reason, Garrett Jones actually moved to his left, probably confusing Mike. He stumbled on his lay-up, tossed up a shot that barely hit the backboard, and fell awkwardly under the basket, while Stevens rebounded the ball.

"Traveling!" shouted Howard. "Don't you know that you need a BUS One Card and Pass for that trip, Mike?"

"It's 8-2, Turing," declared Berrian, who had cornered Hank near the bleachers.

"What are you talking about?" asked Stewart, holding his knee.

"8-4. Christ, Bob, I hit a shot from the corner, and Aaron made a shot off a rebound."

Jones leaned over and pulled Stewart up. "I didn't expect you to move out of my way," admitted Stewart.

"Whatever," said Berrian, "come on, let's go."

Jones shrugged and took the inbounds pass from Howell.

Hank stole the ball at half court and had a clear path to the basket. Hank drove the hoop, sailed about two inches into the air, screamed, "Slamma Jamma," and missed the basket completely. Play temporarily stopped while we all doubled over in laughter. "What's so funny?" asked Hank with complete deadpan.

After Berrian sank a jump shot from the corner, Victor waved me in, as he walked over to the bleachers, completely stumped over. "It's too fucking hot to play today!" he mumbled.

Almost immediately I got the ball from Aaron, and I found myself posting up against Howard. I backed him up with butt, felt his body give nothing away, faked to my right, turned to my left and put up a perfect … air ball. Luckily, Hank was under the basket and rebounded for the basket. "Nice shot, Mark," teased Howard as we both headed back down the court.

All of a sudden a few of us started making shots, helped almost certainly by most of us losing the interest in playing defense. With Howard sweating entirely through his white shirt and panting so loudly that you could hear it over the deafening Aerosmith, I got several open looks at the basket from the top of the key. I sank three in a row, the third of which brought us to within two points at 18-16.

"Next time down, I take Carter," yelled Berrian at Howard, bending over near the half court line.

After Jones hit an easy lay-up to make it 20-16, Hank hit Mike with a perfect bounce pass through the lane. Mike bobbled it and then tried to go up with a shot off the backboard. Alan Yost went up and came down, hand entirely on ball, body entirely on Stewart. Mike collapsed to the floor and the ball bounced off of him and went out of bounds.

"Where's the foul?" yelled Victor, still standing on the sidelines.

"All ball. All ball," yelled Alan back.

"You o.k., Mike?" I asked, pulling him off the ground.

"I'll be fine." He brushed my hand away and took off to guard Howard. I switched to guarding Alan. Berrian missed a wild circus shot at their end of the court, Hank rebounded and fed Mike a pass going down the right sideline. Jones moved over to guard him, and that's when Mike had his third and final fall. As the ball bounced loose, Berrian, the last man getting up the court, grabbed the loose ball for an easy lay-up and the victory.

Half of us stood over Mike, trying to see what help he needed. The other half (Bob, Garrett, Hank, Eddie and Victor) argued over whether there had been a foul. Meanwhile, "Big Ten Inch Record" blared at unneeded decibels all around us. Alan stayed on the side singing, "then I whip out my big ten inch record of the band that plays the blues."

"I don't think I can handle any more of this, Mark," said Mike, as I brushed him off and helped him stagger to the bleachers while he avoided putting weight on his left ankle.

"Can't say I blame you. What hurts the most?"

"Right now, I'd have to say..." Stewart paused and tilted his head so that one ear positioned toward the ceiling. The opening strains of "Sweet Emotion" filled the field house. "I'd have to say that it's a tie between my ears and my pride."

"Who was responsible for beverages?" asked Berrian.

"I was," admitted Victor. "My team lost last week. There's a cooler down by the door to the visitor's locker room."

Everyone else headed to the far end of the court. "Anyway, I'm going home."

"Thanks for coming, Mike. We'll talk soon," I said, rubbing his shoulder as he picked up his bag and limped out of the gym.

"See you, Mike," shouted Victor as Mike walked away. Mike offered a half-hearted wave to the group.

We broke into Gatorades and bottled water and wiped our faces with our already soaking shirts.

"Looks like you lost your man advantage," declared Howard.

"Hardly," mumbled Hank.

"It's just not the same without old Mike Hardly, is it?" exclaimed Bill Howell.

"We all would have been like old Stewart, wouldn't we?" chortled Aaron.

"Was he a dirty player?" I asked.

"Mike approached basketball like he approached everything in life. Like it was his ball and his gym." Victor had picked up a loose ball and kicked it off the wall.

"By the way, speaking of missing guys, where's Berninski?" asked Howell.

Victor stopped kicking the ball. He and Garrett Jones visibly tightened up.

Berrian finished drinking some water, then dumped a little on his head. "He's gone. Let's get playing again. Remember, it is best of three."

Jones grabbed Howell and pulled him back. "He was let go. Didn't you hear?"

"I didn't know either," said Eddie.

"How are you supposed to know?" asked Aaron. "These things happen in secret and we all kind of figure it out later."

"Shit," said Howell. "I liked Bil. What the hell happened?"

"Come on. Get back to the game," prodded Victor, trying to discourage the speculation; unfortunately, his authority carried no weight with the participants.

"I guess he didn't respond quickly enough to the Hartley death." Aaron had bent over to tie his shoe. He, Eddie, Alan and I were the only ones left at the far end of the court.

"How sad? Bil usually covered Hartley in these games. Remember how miserable he made Bil's life?"

"Well, it looks like he did that in his death also," responded Alan, sprinting back to center court to join the others.

The rest of us strolled to middle court. "It still sucks," said Howell.

Game two picked up where game one had ended. The defense was minimal, and the offense took advantage. Hank asked me to guard Berrian, but Jones guarded me. I took it as a sign of respect that the ex-football player drew me for his defensive assignment. The first few times down the court, I tried to work my way into my sweet spots just outside of the lane, but could gain no territory. Luckily, for us, Eddie Stevens had caught fire, perhaps because Jones no longer guarded him. However, Berrian, Jones and Howell proved unstoppable, no matter whom we had guarding each one. Even I got into the sniping, as I took offense to the president's permanent camp in the lane.

"Three Seconds!"

"No way, Carter. I've been moving in and out."

"Sure!" I said sarcastically.

"Nobody calls three seconds in these games."

"So, you admit you've been camping in the lane?"

"Shut up and play."

About the time Steven Tyler's raspy voice spat out "Checkmate honey/ Beat you at your own damn game" at the beginning of "Draw the Line," we were clearly going to lose. The score was 19-9. Not only had we not scored in at least five trips down the court, but we had only got one shot off, an ill-advised three pointer by Hank, who had already shown that his range extended no further than his height. Finally, as Jones put in a rebound off a failed Howard shot, game two ended and several of us collapsed on the floor.

"So, how quickly can I replace Berninski, Victor?" asked Jones as we all sat or lay in various spots on the court.

Victor hesitantly looked at Berrian. "We might not replace him, Garrett."

"What?" Garrett, who had been leaning on his elbows, sat upright. "You're kidding, right?"

"This is news to me, Victor," chimed in Hank. "What the hell are we supposed to do with one less security officer?"

"Alright, simmer down, you two," snapped Berrian. "I told Victor that we might not replace Bil."

"Why not?" asked Hank, who had stood up, holding hands on hips.

"I'm not sure we have the best plan for security. The morning of Hartley's murder, Jonesy should have been on campus and should have been the person who took charge of the situation. If so, I might not have had to wait forty-five minutes to learn that there had been a murder on my campus."

"I was at Central High that morning for a planned recruitment event." Jones had stood up too.

Berrian remained lying on the sturgeon logo in the middle of the court. "I know that, Jonesy. Settle down. Why would I want my head of security at a high school talking to high school students, leaving some inept, fumbling bozo in charge of the campus?"

"With all due respect to Bil Berninski, sir, he was a good man. He can't help it if the murder he discovered was the **first** one ever at Boan. He ended up in a trial by fire." Jones' agitation led to him pacing up and down the sideline.

Berrian pulled himself up to a full sitting position. "I said to settle down, Garrett. You, Hank and Victor can figure this out. I just don't want my security guys worrying about anything but security."

"I was promoting the security and safety management programs." Jones had stopped to open a bottle of Gatorade.

"I know, Garrett. And I know that's your interest and background. But, truly, that recruitment has to be the responsibility of Howard's team."

All of a sudden Howard stood up. "Hey, we appreciate Garrett's support, Bob. Since that program is so new, we have never had a dedicated admissions rep for it. Garrett's a valuable source for us."

"Well, then, maybe that needs to change too, Howard." Berrian had stood up. "Give me the ball, Eddie," he shouted at Stevens, lying down with his head leaning against the ball.

Eddie rolled it slowly toward Berrian. Hank put his foot down on the ball before it got to the president.

"It sounds like both security and admissions will end up with holes because of this decision, Bob. Certainly that's not what we want to do."

"Dear god, it's not that big of a deal, all. Security just goes back to handling security, and there is ample staffing for that. Admissions just handles recruitment. Howard will need to figure that out."

"Can I hire someone specifically?" asked Howard.

"Look at the options, Howard. Maybe there is someone who is already able to pick up this."

We all sat for several seconds in silence. "Are we ready for a third and last game?" Berrian asked. "It won't change the best of three, but, let's get at it. I'd like to get out of here before 5:15."

As we set up for the third game, Victor shouted above the song that represented the depth of Aerosmith's career, "Angel," "you know, Howard, I think Maggie Long has some background in the public safety area?"

"Who's Maggie Long?" asked Howard as he back-pedaled the court, watching Jones dribble up the court.

"She's one of the business advisors," panted Victor.

"Cute red-haired girl? Looks like that chick from *That 70's Show*?"

"Laura Prepon," I told him, as I guarded Howard again.

Victor moved closer to Howard. "Yeah, her." Alan Yost, who Victor should have been guarding, broke down the baseline for an easy pass and basket.

Eddie Stevens stormed back up the court but proceeded to bounce the ball off his knee and out of bounds.

"Anyway," said Victor, moving in close to Howard and me, "maybe we could use her to pick up the recruitment for the program."

"Jesus, Victor. Let's just switch. I swear you're guarding me," I yelled, turning around and racing, as much as it could be, after almost fifty minutes of basketball, called that, to guard Yost, who had drifted unseen under the basket. I got my hand in just in time to deflect a pass from Berrian.

"That's off me," I shouted, quickly bending over to catch my breath.

Victor continued hounding Howard. "She has expressed before to Wanda her interest in getting out of student services. Maybe this is an opportunity for her."

"Wanda?" asked Howard.

"You know. Wanda Joplin, my employee relations director?"

"Hot blond girl? Legs that go to Lake Michigan?"

"Yes," sighed Victor.

Howard took a pass from Jones and pulled up for a short jumper. It hit the back of the rim and bounced over the back of the backboard.

"Our ball," shouted Hank, who scrambled to get the ball and throw it in to Stevens.

Down at our offensive end of the court, I took a long pass from Eddie Stevens, turned to drive the rim, saw Jones moving into the lane, and at the last second threw a perfect pass to Victor, who watched it go right through his hands. Meanwhile, I fell into Jones and tumbled to the ground.

"You o.k., Mark?" asked Jones, giving me a hand.

"Yeah, just give me a second." I sat up, pulled my knees to my chest and took a couple of deep breaths.

"If she's interested and she has the background, I'm fine with it," said Howard, picking the thread back up with Victor.

"Call Wanda on Monday. I'll send her an e-mail over the weekend telling her to expect your call." Victor had grabbed a bottle of water off the bleachers.

"Would you be o.k., Bob, with that?" asked Howard.

"C'mon, Carter, get your ass off the ground! O.k. with what, Howard?"

"There's a girl in student services who has background and interest in the public safety programs. I'd like to ask her to pick some of the recruitment work Jones is going to have to give up."

Hank dribbled the ball at center court, while I got up and limped down the court. "I still don't think we should give up the security position," he argued loudly.

"It's fine with me," said Bob. "Come on, let's play. Bring the ball down the court, Bill. I think it sounds like a plan best for all."

"Uh, wait a second," I interrupted, back-pedaling and watching Howard walking up court. "Shouldn't Caroline get a chance to speak about this? We are now talking about somebody on her staff."

Steven Tyler's voice crashed around us: "I'm rippin' up a rag doll, like throwing around an old toy."

"Jesus, do we have to make this so complicated? Pass the damn ball, Howell."

Howell threw the ball at an exhausted Alan Yost, who had it bounce off his foot into the waiting arms of Aaron Cartwright. Aaron threw a softball pass to Victor Woo hanging back and cherry-picking. Victor blew a wide-open lay-up.

Berrian rebounded and headed back up court. I moved over to guard him as they had a four-on-one fast break. Berrian faked to my right, threw to my left, and fed Garrett Jones an easy lay-up.

"Hot time, get it while it's easy," crooned the president.

We never made it a game. Eventually, Aaron Cartwright and I stayed on the defensive end, with our teammates staying on the offensive side. It was a strategy of self-preservation. Quickly and mercifully, the third game ended, 22-4.

"Oh, gentlemen, that was truly pathetic," said a gasping Berrian.

No one responded. Some of us writhed on the floor; others of us crawled to the bleachers. Meanwhile, Steven Tyler wailed around, relentlessly: "Workin' like a dog for the boss man/Workin' for the company."

"Can someone finally turn that fucking music off?" screamed Hank.

"Sure thing," responded Yost, who slowly climbed the bleachers to the p.a. system. It took most of "Love in an Elevator" for him to drag his tired body up there.

And that's how I had ended up this bathtub, sipping on good scotch and listening to much more calming music than Aerosmith. The water was now cold and the scotch was warm, so I decided to get out of the tub.

Downstairs, Alyssa and Natalie cuddled on the couch watching Disney Channel. "Hey, girls," I said.

"Daddy! We weren't sure you'd ever get out of the tub." Alyssa's eyes sparkled whenever she teased her parents. It made it difficult to be mad at her.

"I'm not sure I wanted to, but figured you might like a father who hadn't prematurely wrinkled."

"Feel better?" smiled Natalie.

"You bet. What's on the tube?"

"One of those saccharinely sweet Disney shows. Something like *The Suite Life of the Cheetah Girls*?"

"Hmm? Shouldn't you be heading to bed soon, Alyssa?"

"I have six minutes until my bedtime."

"Oh, excuse me. I don't pay such close attention to time." I tousled my daughter's hair as I plopped down on the couch and put my feet up on the coffee table. Outside the window, as darkness started to fall, a couple of chipmunks chased each other.

"Any altercations with the boys?" I asked to either Alyssa or Natalie.

Alyssa rolled her eyes but stayed focused on the television. "No, Dad. I got your point about hitting them."

"That doesn't mean there couldn't have been an altercation."

Alyssa looked over at me and then to her mother. "What does that mean?"

"That means that they still could have said or done something that made you mad. You just decided not to hit them." When Alyssa continued to look at me nonplussed, I continued. "You could have just walked away after one of them said or did something to hurt you. You could have yelled at them. You could have made fun of them. There are a number of ways to handle people who make you angry."

"Like, for instance," continued Natalie, talking to Alyssa but looking at me directly, "you could have tried to explain to the boys what bothered you."

I faked a look of surprise for Natalie, but continued with the line of reasoning. "Your mother makes a good point, Alyssa."

"Whatever."

I laughed. "Seriously," I said to Natalie, "did anything happen today?"

"Not that I know of. She and the girls played kickball with some of the boys. I heard no tears, saw no bruises, learned of no tantrums."

"So, it was a good game, Alyssa?"

"I'm trying to watch my show."

I laughed again. "I asked a simple question. I didn't expect the Spanish inquisition."

Alyssa rolled her eyes again. "Dad's such a dork."

"But he's a lovable dork, honey. Now it's time to brush your teeth and go to bed."

"Let me take care of it, sweetheart. Stay here. I'll be back down in a few minutes."

After I got Alyssa tucked into bed and kissed her forehead, I came back downstairs to find Natalie had turned off the television. She leaned back on the couch staring out the window, sipping on a glass of red wine. I sidled up next to her and stroked her knee. "How are you doing?"

"Good. I hope this all works out, Mark."

"I'm sure it will—if I can survive the Friday afternoon basketball games?"

"Now I see why they're on Friday. You need all weekend to recover."

I chuckled. "You might be onto something." I took the glass from her hand and took a drink from her wine. "Ah, very nice."

"You survived your first week."

"Yes, I did." I paused. "I certainly did."

"Any real surprises?"

"Everything and nothing. I knew there'd be some craziness and frustrations, so that's why there are no surprises. However, the specifics can sometimes come out of nowhere and bite you."

Natalie laid her head on my shoulder and we both glanced at the night enveloping our backyard. After a couple of minutes, Natalie jerked up. "Wait, you never told me how the one-on-one with Berrian went?"

"I didn't? I guess I didn't. How the hell did I block that out?"

"Will I want to refill my glass before you start?"

I contemplated thoughtfully. "Probably a good move. Give yourself a big glass to share."

As Natalie filled her wineglass, I thought back to the low-key start to that meeting in Berrian's office. I showed up with copies of my agenda, including another one for him in case Veronica didn't have one for him. He sat at his desk with an accordion folder on top, label clearly reading "provost." He did pull out a copy of the agenda from that folder. We started with simple banalities about my first week, his day, weekend plans, and so forth.

Natalie returned and offered me the glass first. I took a nice, long glug of wine, certainly in a fashion not appreciated by any connoisseur.

"At the beginning, when I covered my agenda items, and at the time still had no idea if he had an agenda for me, it was pretty good. I believe I started with some of my observations about the deans. He listened well and supported my general conclusions about each dean. When I got to Kiana King, the Dean of Allied Health, he asked me if I had thought she could have killed Hartley."

"What? That seems a strange question." Natalie sipped the wine, saving the entire Carter family from being dismissed by any wine aficionados.

"Not really. She was one of the prime suspects. She'd had a pretty ugly public row with him."

"Hmm? Still seems a strange question to ask the new guy. How would you have known?"

"I don't know. Maybe he thought I would outright ask her. 'Did you kill Hartley, Kiana? Go ahead, you can tell me. I won't tell anyone.' The funny thing is that at my meeting with King this week, she did ask me if anyone at the cabinet level had identified her as a potential suspect."

I pushed the pillow that I leaned on farther down so that my lower back rested on it more. My body still felt some aches from the basketball game.

"Anyway, from there, I asked about some topics that had yet to come up during the week, such as research dollar issues, stuff like this. Pretty boring stuff, and he didn't provide a whole lot of guidance. Just a 'look into it more and keep me posted' kind of response.

When I asked him about the accelerated programs, then he became more aggressive and I became uncomfortable. I merely asked him what the university was doing to gauge the effectiveness of those deliveries. He took exception to the implication that they might not be successful. I kept trying to suggest that I wasn't condemning them, but that I wanted to know how we could be sure students could succeed, given these deliveries were new. He would cut me off and cite any number of reasons why we had to be creative in graduating students more quickly. I tried to comfort him with the fact that I also believed universities had to make it easier for students to graduate on time, but that **that** wasn't the point. None of this registered with him. As he kept getting more and more agitated, he kept pushing his chair farther and farther away from me, so that eventually his entire lanky frame stretched out behind his desk. It was incredibly disconcerting. After ten or fifteen minutes, I punted and told him I would drop it."

Natalie presented me the wine glass, which I gladly accepted. "Will you?"

I smiled. "Good question. Common sense tells me I should, but common sense also tells me not to. Did I tell you that Boan has four of these accelerated deliveries, all started within the last year? All proposed, as far as I know, within the last year? That scares the hell out of me, Natalie."

"I understand. Why don't you quietly look into them over the next few weeks and then decide if and how you want to present the argument to Berrian again?"

"You're right. It was stupid to take on that discussion the first week. I guess I was underprepared for how much he felt ownership of these deliveries."

"Uh-huh. What else? Any fireworks after that? Did he stay visibly upset with you?" She sipped at the wine again; at this rate, I would consume three-fourths of the glass.

"No. I'll give him credit for that. His mood changed almost immediately. I forget what my next agenda item was—maybe something about budget. No matter what, it led to the easy 'look into it and get back to me' response. When I covered my last item, retention, he got pretty animated again, but not so much with me, or against me, as the case may have been with the accelerated deliveries. I had a sense his anger focused on Caroline Cruz, although I'll give him credit that he never named her. He went on and on about the unpredictable numbers for retention over the years."

"Unpredictable?"

"Oh, you know, one year about 60% of our students might be retained, the next year 51%, the following year, 57%, the next year 49%, the next year, 56%."

"I could see why that would be frustrating."

"Caroline Cruz and I will have to work closely on figuring that all out."

"Cruz? That's the kind of frightening one you mentioned, right?"

"Uh, did I say that?" I paused and thought about it. "I guess I did. Yes, she can be kind of frightening. I don't think she takes 'no' for an answer."

Natalie cackled. "And you're such a softie. Seems like a match made in heaven. Despite that, do you think she's good?"

I paused and took the wine glass off the table. After a sip, I tilted my head back and closed my eyes. "You know, if I think about it, I would say she may be the best person on the leadership team. She is incredibly smart. She knows how to hold her own. She knows what she needs and she tells you. I'll take those characteristics any day of the week over the conniving, self-centered, ruthless characters one could meet at this level."

We sat in silence for a few more minutes.

"Is that how your one-on-one with Berrian ended?" asked Natalie.

"Oh, that's right. No. Interestingly, after I told him we'd reached the end of my agenda, he shoved his chair back up to his desk, and placed his hands on his temples. 'Let me think of what I've got,' he said. He then proceeded to pull a discussion topic from his head, jotted it down on the bottom of the agenda I had provided, and then proceeded to say a few things about it. Nothing serious, and he only had about three or four items. He told me that he wanted me to make a decision on the College of Fine Arts by the end of the year. I had avoided that topic in my agenda, but I had no problem with that. I don't remember the other ones, but as I said, nothing earth-shattering. Luckily, after he pulled the second one out of thin air, I got smart enough to write them down on my agenda."

"What a fascinating approach," Natalie declared with all sincerity.

"Isn't it? I don't know if this is what he does with others, or if he'll do it all the time. Part of me thought that maybe he had been unprepared for my first one-on-one because the appointment had only been set up about twenty-four hours earlier. Part of me thought that the approaching basketball game may have changed how he does things. I just don't know. I would have asked Howard or Victor or Hank at the basketball game, but there was never an opportunity."

"Do you have these meetings every week?"

"God, yes. I can see that I'll be in a lot of meetings in this job."

"Then, I guess you'll get the answers to your questions soon enough." Natalie had finished off the wine. "Come on, let's go to bed. Maybe it's time for a one-on-one where you can see everything up front."

I groaned as I lifted my tired and sore body off the couch. "If this is going to be full contact, I'm going to be in a lot of pain."

"I'm already interested, Mark. You don't need to try to convince me." She grabbed my hand and dragged my sorry body up the stairs.

Part Three:
Experiential Learning

Chapter Nine

Natalie, Alyssa and I spent Labor Day weekend on Diamond Lake, the largest of the many lakes surrounding Boan. It was less than an hour away, so we drove up early Saturday, Sunday and Monday mornings, and then came back in the evenings on each of those days. The frequent driving worked out rather well. By the evening, the various cabins and campgrounds around Diamond Lake turned into raucous scenes of who-knows-what. Since we didn't want to know what, going home each evening to a quiet neighborhood where almost everyone had gone away for the whole weekend provided our perfect nighttime setting.

Heading home Monday evening, Alyssa asked us why so many of her friends had gone away for the weekend.

"Families use Labor Day weekend as one last chance to have a family vacation," responded Natalie, who drove. Against better judgment, I had partaken of a couple of beers at Charlie Durant's campground. Charlie, Boan's Vice President of Marketing, had seen Alyssa and me splashing about in the water and had invited us to a cookout at their campsite. We had gone and had an enjoyable time, I more so than Natalie, who, when she saw that Busch beer was the only alcohol, agreed to be our designated driver for the trip home. Feeling in the moment of the festivities, I took Charlie's offer of Busch, but after a couple of them, felt in no mood to live, let alone drive.

"We never took a vacation this summer," Alyssa said from the backseat, while playing with her gameboy.

"That's because daddy took the new job, honey. Moving to Indiana ended up being our vacation."

"Sure didn't feel like one. The Fosters went to South Carolina earlier this summer and went to Lake Michigan this weekend."

I groaned and turned sideways in the passenger seat to be able to see her better. "We're not the Fosters, though, are we?"

Alyssa gave me the exasperated look reserved just for me.

"What happens if on the first day of school my teacher asks all of us to talk about our summer vacation? I'll have nothing to say."

"That's not true, Alyssa. You can tell them about your exciting move from Ohio. You can talk about your new house. Your new friends. How you've explored this area, including Diamond Lake." Natalie sped up to pass a rickety old pick-up truck on the kind of deserted two-lane road that defines much of this portion of Indiana.

"But, it won't look as good as someone else's story about going to Australia."

"Who went to Australia, sweetheart?" I asked, pulling the window visor to my side window to cut out the light.

"Well, I'm sure somebody did." Disgusted with her gameboy, Alyssa tossed it onto the seat next to her.

We drove in silence for several minutes. The sun crept closer and closer to the horizon and soon the evil brightness should stop coming in the side window.

"Maybe I should tell them the story about the dead fox, daddy? Remember when we saw the dead fox?"

"Of course, honey."

"That would be exciting. That would get people's attention."

I closed my eyes and my head drooped farther into the seat. "Yes, a dead body does tend to get people's attention."

The truth of the matter is that Michael Hartley's dead body had stopped grabbing most people's attention. His death faded into deep recesses of memory as we launched into a new fall semester and the typical activity of a college campus in September. Detective Marsh never made an arrest, never even held anybody for questioning. Occasionally she or her partner, Jerome Klinger, came on campus to ask us a few more questions. One time, Klinger brought a sketch artist's rendition of a man a student had supposedly seen loitering outside of Muswell Hall before 7:00 AM the morning Hartley was killed. No one recognized him, and when the local newspaper published the artist's sketch, Natalie said it best: "Good god, that could be anyone from Willie Nelson to LL Cool J and you wouldn't be able to tell." It is unclear if that is a testament to the eyewitness's lack of memory or of the sketch artist's poor skills.

The memory of Hartley lay in what he represented, and what we wanted to avoid, as I put together a search committee to find his replacement. Dewayne Wilson agreed to chair it, and Christina Llewellyn begrudgingly consented to be on the committee also. She questioned me as to why she didn't serve as chair, but I convinced her that the difference between the chair and any other committee member was minimal. The only thing the chair got that others didn't was more time with me and the president. "Put it that way," she said, "and I thank you very much for the non-consideration."

In developing the search committee for a new dean, the university positioned itself for one of the on-going conflicts in the world of higher education: the great clash of Ph.D. vs. Ed.D. In some ways it's our Civil War, common ground bloodied by the petty differences of two cultures who fundamentally hate each other. For the Ph.D.'ers, the population with the longer history and the conservative view of the world, the Ed.D.'ers were carpet-baggers, charlatans, and great pretenders. To the Ed.D.'ers, who had created their own kingdom and sought to apply its decrees to the very culture the Ph.D.'ers promised to protect, the Ph.D.'ers were snobs, narrow-minded, and the resistance.

The Ed.D. programs mass produce their graduates in fields such as educational leadership, educational policy and research, teacher education and the opposition's most detested credential, higher education administration. Meanwhile, Ph.D. programs kick out graduates in fields such as conflict resolution and peace studies, post-colonial theory, macromolecular science and engineering, and the guaranteed-to-send-the-enemy-into-convulsions gender studies. There is little hope of getting these differing groups on the same battle field and not having it turn into a blood path.

Actually, I lie. Lure some poor M.B.A. into the middle of the field and watch all differences fade away in the interest of protecting their common interests.

When Victor, Berrian and I sat down to write the job description and advertisement for Hartley's replacement, the president pushed us to list a doctorate as "preferred." It was a single word in a job description of seven hundred and fifty words, a single word in advertisements that often ran two columns, but it was the word that drew the ire of so many faculty members.

"I hope you know I could never report to someone who doesn't have the same level of degree as me," admitted one poorly dressed, bad-breathed faculty member to me as he grabbed me crossing the square.

"Hartley had a lot of problems, but at least he had a freaking doctorate," said another, a rare moment out in the light, whispering to me as we waited in line in the cafeteria.

"God help us if we get an M.B.A.," bemoaned another, while he discreetly tied his shoes next to me before a meeting. "Let them ruin the educational system like they ruined the banking industry."

"I never thought I'd say it," disclosed one faculty member who obviously didn't appreciate the beauty of an unexpressed thought, "but even an Ed.D. is better than an M.B.A."

My standard response: "don't worry about it." The search had barely begun and I was confident that qualified candidates who could make some of the faculty happy would emerge. I had no hopes of finding anybody, whatever position, who would please all faculty.

In working with Victor and Dewayne Wilson on the timeline for the dean search, we planned to hold first round interviews before Christmas, with second round interviews occurring in the first week or two of the winter semester. Overall, we faced a five to six month search process. "Why the rush?" joked Natalie when I first told her about it.

"That is a rush," I responded. "These things often take nine months."

"You're kidding. Nine months to deliver a dean. That's a heck of a long gestation period."

"You forget that it took thirteen months to deliver me to Boan. But, in that case, they used a search firm."

"Doesn't that put you in with the rhino population? I know it's one of those big endangered species."

"Are you saying that I'm a dying breed, even with the thick skin? I thought that skin would keep me alive in this job?"

When we publicized the anticipated timeline for the search, a number of faculty complained about the potential dates for interviews. Those who would participate in the first rounds didn't want to have to schedule interviews during the week of fall finals or the brief break before Christmas. For all the rest, who would participate, if they wished, in the second round interviews, they lamented that the interviews would happen in the first few weeks of the winter semester.

On top of all that, faculty assumed that winter storms would wreak havoc on these interviews. Dewayne revealed a lot of angst as we worked it through with him. My standard response to him, and to the number of faculty who confronted me about their concerns, continued to be, "don't worry about it."

In general, the day-to-day persisted at Boan as if the provost wasn't new and in exploratory mode. Cabinet meetings came and went every week. Howard produced his weekly goal reports, and the on-going squabble between Hank and Howard about the differences between "actual," "goal," and "stretch" made for mildly amusing interludes in the marathon sessions. Subjects that had appeared vital in that first meeting were temporarily forgotten, and new issues introduced, perhaps not to be seen again. I brought my own general updates, but no weighty topics.

The students returned and commotion became the norm in hallways, the commons and the square. I did my first week meet-and-greets in the hallways, shaking hundreds of students' hands, thanking as many faculty as possible for their dedication. By the second day of classes, a student had apparently taken squatter's rights on a couch in the lobby outside of the cafeteria. Day after day, we would walk by the couch, and this student (no one knew if it was a he or a she; the long blonde hair suggested a female, but the lack of hips intimated a male) would be snoozing, head turned toward the wall, backpack under the feet. No faculty member recognized this student from any class.

September also became the month to navigate through the continuing saga of accelerated deliveries. One student in the adult accelerated program, a Jamie Viola, told her advisor that she wanted out of the accelerated program and to be put immediately into a regular fifteen-week semester. She made this request at the beginning of the second week of the fifteen-week semester. The advisor, a skinny, long-necked new guy named Frank Pollen, switched her automatically to all the same courses in the fifteen-week semester. However, she showed up to all of her classes with the wrong textbooks and without any context as to where she had landed in the class. The faculty members, all who had never taught any of the accelerated courses, recommended she talk to the bookstore about the textbooks and to find a classroom buddy to get caught up.

By the end of Jamie's first week in a standard fifteen-week curriculum, even though it was the end of the second week of the fifteen-week curriculum, and the end of the third week for her (now discarded) accelerated curriculum, she was so confused and frustrated that she broke down at her family's formica-topped kitchen table, causing her three middle-school kids to freak out, and leading her husband, Hector Viola, to call the president directly to complain about the way the "college had made his wife cuckoo." Berrian passed the phone call directly on to me, and I dealt with the angry Hector, who was so wound up that I had to hold the phone away from my ear. When I told him that the Family Educational Rights Privacy Act prevented me from talking directly to him without his wife's written consent, he went over the edge. According to him, the advisor was a son-of-a bitch, the teachers were bastards, and I was an asshole. Instead of praising him for his adept use at increasingly pointed curse words as insults, I gave him the name and number of someone who could talk his wife through the infamous FERPA.

At that point, he finally handed the phone over to his wife. Through the twists and turns that make up any conversation with a complaining student, we agreed that at this point in the semester, she would drop all of her classes, and that I would work with the Boan financial aid office to scholarship these three classes when she registered again for them in the winter.

"Just as long as I don't have to take them accelerated, Dr. Carter," she reiterated when I summarized our mutually agreed upon solution.

"I know, Jamie. They'll be regular fifteen-week classes."

"Those accelerateds are too hard."

"You mean that they are too **difficult**, Ms. Viola," I said.

"That too. The teachers ask us to do too much in those courses."

"Well, in all fairness to them, they expect the students to do the same amount of work that is done in fifteen weeks in the five weeks or the seven weeks."

"I wish I had known that." One of Jamie's kids could be heard screaming in the background. Something about leaving her stuff alone.

"Weren't you told?" I asked, dreading the potential answer.

"No. Frank told me nothing about that."

"What were you told?"

"I'm not sure I remember." The screaming had resumed again. "I need to go."

After I hung up, I played with the twisted cord on the phone and stared out my window at the administrative parking lot. A student looked to park a car there. He parked front first in a back corner spot, probably figuring that it would make it more difficult for someone to notice the lack of a permit on his front window. He guiltily looked left and right as he leapt over the short wall of the parking lot and worked his way around the side of the Administration Building. I considered for a minute whether I should report him. Instead, I decided to call Frank Pollen.

"Hi Frank," I said when he answered on the first ring. "This is Provost Carter."

He responded with absolute silence. He probably never expected to receive a call from the provost.

"Don't worry. I just wanted to ask you a few questions about Jamie Viola."

"Yeh," he grunted. "What do you want to know?"

"Well, first off, she will be calling you in the next day or two to drop her classes for this semester. I'll be working with financial aid to scholarship them next semester when she signs up again."

"Is that next adult accelerated semester or next full semester?"

I sighed. "Next full semester, Frank. But, tell me, what kind of information did you give her, or do you give students, when they first register for an accelerated course?"

"Uh, just the usual information about course degrees and policies and stuff." I could hear the nervous tapping of his fingers on his desktop.

"Yes, that's good, but how about for delivery options? What information would someone like Jamie get to decide what option they want?"

Frank's tapping increased. "You probably need to talk to admissions, sir. That comes out of their area. If you're willing to hold, I can transfer you...."

"No, Frank," I yelled. Then I took a deep breath. "Sorry to yell. What is the 'that' you referred to?"

"What 'that'?"

"You just said that 'that comes out of their area.' I'm trying to discern what you meant by 'that.'" I had grabbed a pencil from my desk.

"I really think that's something you should ask Admissions, sir."

"Fine, I'll contact them myself, Frank. Thanks." After he hung up, I added, "for nothing."

I flipped through a pile of papers on my desk looking for my quick phone reference. I didn't particularly want to call Howard on this one, preferring to get someone more in the trenches. Before I could find a name that fit that need, my phone rang. Picking it up, I noted Caroline Cruz's name on my display.

"Hi, Caroline."

"Mark, Frank Pollen said you just called him and grilled him about how a student had been advised. What was that all about?"

I blew air out of my mouth in an exaggerated sigh. "Good lord, Caroline. It's not that big of a deal. I had to talk with one of his students who called the president and was transferred to me. She practically had a nervous breakdown when she switched from her adult accelerated class to a regular fifteen-week class. I took care of her, but wanted to follow up on the kind of information she would be given about choosing her courses."

"That's admissions, Mark. Why didn't you call Admissions?"

"Caroline, that's what I was just getting ready to do. Frank made it very clear that he couldn't speak for them. However, why the hell wouldn't your staff know what admissions hands out regarding this?"

"Mark," responded Caroline in a calm voice, "there is no reason to curse."

"I know. I'm sorry, Caroline, but I'm exasperated by the inanity of this." I looked down to see I had snapped my pencil in half.

"Look, it's no big deal. I've got Howard with me right now. Let's put him on speaker phone and get you what you need to know."

"No, it's o.k. I was hoping to talk to...."

"Howdy, Mark. What's up, besides your blood pressure?"

I rubbed my left temple and leaned back in my chair. 'Oh well,' I thought, 'let's see what I can get.'

I took a moment to ask my question as succinctly as possible: "What information do new students get about delivery options?"

Silence hung over the phone line for several seconds. "Hello. Hello. Are you guys still there?" I asked.

"Yes, Mark. I was just trying to think." Howard's voice sounded like he had a cold.

"Ah, then that's what threw me."

"What?"

"The silence, Howard. I wasn't accustomed to silence from you." After several seconds of additional silence, I clarified more. "Since I had never experienced you 'trying to think' before, Howard, I had never experienced you silent. Oh, come on, surely you get that."

"Hold on, Mark," said Caroline. "Howard's run over to his office to get an application."

I sighed and watched a security officer walking toward the student's car in the back of the parking lot. "Good lord, Caroline, we're all in the same building. We could have accomplished all this by walking to each others' offices. How difficult is it for us to walk up or down one flight of stairs?"

"Hold on, Mark. I'm getting a text on my cell." I could hear the beeping of her phone as she apparently read and responded to the text. After about thirty seconds, enough time for our security officer to write a ticket and leave it on the student's windshield, Caroline came back on the line. "O.k., sorry about that, Mark. It was Bob, so I texted him back."

"Any sign of Howard?" I asked.

"He's not back, yet."

"O.k., then hold on a sec. I have to step away from the phone." I had to find out if people in this building also texted each other rather than walked to each other's offices.

I laid the phone down on my desk, as opposed to putting Caroline on hold, and stuck my head out of my office, peeking down the hallway toward Berrian's office. I could see the door open and the light on. Curiosity got the best of me and I had to determine if he was in there. As I got closer to the door, I heard him talking to Veronica. I turned around and went back into my office. At least Bob and Veronica weren't texting each other.

"You there, Mark?" I heard Howard say as I got closer to the phone.

"I'm back."

"Where did you go?"

"Sorry. Just needed a second to confirm something. I'm good." Little did Howard and Caroline know of the humor I saw in that statement. "So, Caroline told me you got an application. Planning to go back to school, Howard?"

"We don't have a degree in Pimpology, do we, Mark?"

"Crimminy, Howard, do you ever turn off that sexist, banal chatter you think is humor?" asked Caroline. I could imagine the scowl on her face.

"Isn't that educational leadership, Howard?" I interjected.

Caroline howled uncontrollably and I could even hear Howard cackling over the phone.

"I have to be careful going one and one with you, Mark. Anyway, the application has a place...." I could hear Hank evidently ruffling through an application. "There's a place on page five that the admissions rep fills out after the student has completed all the information. The admissions rep checks the box.... Hmm, do you think that might even be multiple boxes, Caroline?" I could hear the papers ruffling as he apparently passed them to Caroline.

"It doesn't say anywhere. I would assume they can check more than one box," replied Caroline.

"The admissions rep checks the boxes for deliveries the student is qualified for. And there are six boxes, ranging from online to fifteen week in-seat."

"Yes, but are there explanations?"

"Hmm? Not that I can see anywhere."

I could feel myself getting older by the second. How can the simplest of questions ("Did you have sex with that woman?") not be answered in any way, simple or complicated ("it depends upon what box you mean.")?

"O.k., this is only partially helping me. I'm just going to come downstairs and talk to some of your staff, Howard, and see if they can help me understand what is being told to a potential student. Is that o.k.?"

"Of course, it is. You're welcome to come ask them whatever you want." I couldn't prove it, but I was sure Caroline glared at Howard as he said this.

I spent the better part of all my free time, the little I had, for a week talking to admission reps and advisors, usually after Caroline had given me begrudging approval, about how they talked to students about these accelerated deliveries. Responses ranged all over the map, from lengthy, detailed discussions to apparently mimed explanations, none of which properly armed students with a knowledge of what they might get into. The prevailing message was, "we can help you get done as quickly as you want."

In the middle of this investigation, I had told Natalie in complete frustration: "we might as well call this Liposuction Education! Your degree looks good without any effort on your part."

Natalie had responded, "market it, Mark. The Liposuction Education Degree: LED. 'Taking too long to graduate. Get the LED out, people!'"

Still feeling the burn of Berrian's response to my accelerated deliveries questions at my first one-on-one, I decided to say nothing to him, but to continue to work with the admissions' and student services' teams to identify problems and potential solutions. I first asked Howard if I could join one of his staff meetings. Howard was supportive and told me to come to his next Wednesday morning meeting. He put me on at 9:30, near the end of his agenda. I showed up about 9:25 and quietly slipped into the meeting's classroom.

The desks in the room had been arranged in a huge rectangle, necessary to fit more than twenty people. Since they were still discussing an earlier agenda item ("military scholarships") I did a quick count around the room. Counting me, twenty-three people were enduring the meeting. All but three of them had laptops open in front of them, and while a member of Howard's team whom I did not recognize (buzz cut hairstyle, baby smooth face, white shirt, yellow tie) talked about military scholarships, at least ten of the participants typed on their laptops.

Since I had found an open seat next to Howard's assistant, Kathy Gutenhuis, whom I had met several times as she loitered around Shelley's desk, I leaned to my left and asked, "are all these people paying attention? Or sending e-mails?"

Kathy smiled and turned her computer so that I could see it. She had an open IM box on her screen. "Most of them are like me, trying to take care of things. It's multi-tasking." She said it with no hint of embarrassment.

"Ah, I see." Looking at her IM screen, I saw a message come in from Howard. Amazed, I looked across the table at Howard, one of the few without a computer. However, he remained hooked to his BlackBerry. Had I really just seen Howard IM a person merely across a table from him? In a meeting? I snuck a glance to my left, disgusted with my desire to confirm what I feared. Sure enough Kathy was responding to him, typing "you're to pick it up tomorrow" before she hit send.

Meanwhile, baby-faced, crew-cut kid kept talking about increasing military scholarships. A few members of the committee watched and nodded their heads in approval. Interestingly, all were bright-faced young women.

"Cecil," interrupted Howard, looking up from his BlackBerry, "let me stop you there. Thanks for the report. We can continue with this at next week's meeting. However," he looked across the table at me and gestured with his right arm in an exaggerated way, "we have Provost Carter with us today, who wanted to spend a few minutes … right, Mark, just a few minutes?" I nodded in agreement. "Who wanted to spend a few minutes talking to us about accelerated deliveries. Mark, go ahead."

"Thanks, Howard." I stood up to see everyone better. Howard immediately went back to his BlackBerry, and I resisted the urge to look down at Kathy's laptop to see if he had IM'd her. "I've talked to a few of you," I said, nodding at Wayne Wellington and Kim Christopher, "about the way we inform, or in some cases, not inform, new students about all our delivery options."

Several of the bright-faced young women who had been enraptured by Cecil's presentation bobbed their heads in vigorous agreement with my comments. Had I talked to them? They didn't look familiar.

"So, my first question, were any of you given anything last year in terms of talking points about these deliveries?"

One of the bright-faced young women raised her hand.

"Yes?"

"The College of Nursing gave me a sheet telling me what students couldn't take."

'Carla Hoopsnaggle!' Now I remembered her.

"Yeah, I got that, too," spoke a dour-looking woman sitting next to Howard. She looked ten to fifteen years older than most of her compatriots in this meeting. "Two pages of information that might as well have been one line: 'nursing students can only take fifteen-week in-seat.'"

"That's not entirely true," countered Carla. "Some courses can be taken online, and a few can be taken in the accelerated honors deliveries."

"Come on, Carla, stop drinking the Kool-Aid all the time. Those exceptions are few and far between and almost always require the approval of Dean Linares." This admissions rep nearly spat Rachel Linares name out. I made a note to remind Shelley to get a meeting set up with Linares; scheduling conflicts apparently kept preventing that from happening.

I held up my hand. "If you don't mind, I know Carla, but you are?" I asked the woman, who had evolved from dour to severe in front of my eyes.

"I'm Lucy Walsh," she said without smiling.

"Pleasure to meet you, Lucy. This is great information already. I have unfortunately not had a chance to meet with Dean Linares, so this is news to me. Since I'm mostly in an information-collecting mode right now, could either you or Carla forward me a copy of that nursing sheet?"

"It's part of the nursing handbook, Dr. Carter," responded Carla. "You can find it on the website under nursing admissions."

'Ugh, not the website,' I thought.

"I can scan you those pages and send those to you, sir," offered Lucy.

"Thanks, Lucy. So, nursing has its own guidelines. How about the other colleges?"

A girl in a tie-dyed blouse with flowers in her hair raised her hand. "Fine arts has a very limited range of what can be taken."

"I bet you're Emma Firth," I hypothesized.

She blushed demurely. "I am."

"Do you have a sheet or something similar to nursing?"

"Thank god, no," said Emma.

"How many times has that been the response to 'are you similar to nursing?'" cracked military Cecil, jumping in, and the room burst into laughter.

Emma flashed a very girlish smile. "Dr. Stewart and I met and talked about these after they were developed. I jotted down a few notes, but have them committed to memory. There are quite a few upper-level courses that are blocked given the hands-on nature of the fine arts."

I jotted down a note to myself. "Do you think you could write those down in an e-mail and send them to me?"

"Couldn't Dean Stewart give them to you?" asked Cecil.

"I'll ask him, also." The concerns of some of the folks in this room needed to be addressed. Howard was lost in his BlackBerry. I needed to deflect his staff's belief that they were being criticized.

"I probably should have set this up better," I said. "I'm not criticizing anything that's been going on. I want to provide you with the best, consistent information about academic matters like deliveries. At the moment, I don't even know if you need anything more. This really is a fact-finding mission. As a matter of fact, I didn't even know until right now that you had different guidelines by colleges."

"Welcome to our world," pronounced Cecil. He had nicked himself with a razor recently. Given how young he looked, was shaving even needed?

I laughed. "I'm picking up on a theme. Are you a rep for a school, Cecil?"

"Yes, sir. I'm one of the business reps."

"Excellent. And are your guidelines different for the College of Business?"

"Luckily, ours are pretty easy. We have some accounting classes that can't run in all deliveries, but I would say that all our other classes can run in any form."

"Don't forget the internships," said Emma.

"Oh, yeah. Internships are an exception."

"I would hope," I replied. "Are internships exceptions across the colleges?" I asked the group.

Several people nodded and a few replied, "yes." No one responded in the negative.

"Education? Who are the education reps?"

Wayne raised his hand.

"Yes, Wayne, I know who you are and we talked. You said you had no directives and understood that all courses could be taken in all deliveries. Is that correct?"

"Yes. Dr. Hartley promised that all education students would have every opportunity with these deliveries. He pretty much demanded it."

"Was that received well?"

The second hand on the wall clock could be heard ticking as I waited for an answer that didn't appear to be forthcoming.

"Hey, speaking of Hartley. Are the police having any success finding his killer?" asked Cecil.

I flashed a tired smile. Could this university go several days without someone asking that?

Howard perked up from his BlackBerry. "It doesn't appear so, Cecil."

"Wow," responded Cecil, " a bona fide cold case developing."

"How about allied health? Are those reps here?" I asked.

There was quiet again. "Neither of their reps could make this meeting, Mark," said Kathy.

"Oh. What are their names so that I can contact them?" I asked her.

"Michelle Myers and Donita Banks."

"O.k., thanks. I'll contact them. What about ... ."

I was interrupted by dour Lucy Walsh. "They have something similar to us in nursing, but just not as extensive in the exceptions." As if to offer explanation, she added, "my cubicle is next to Donita's and we talk a lot."

"Ah, so there is someone who admits to being similar to nursing."

"Well, notice that they didn't want to show their faces in public and admit it," joked Cecil.

"Good point. And, finally, how about arts and sciences?"

Two young ladies, part of the bright-faced young women contingent, raised their hands. "We have nothing written down, sir," admitted one of them. "Dean Fulbright meets with us before every semester, and we discuss stuff like this. Basically, for students in these programs, there are no limitations. However, for students not in our programs, like nursing, but taking our classes, there can be confusion."

"I can only imagine, Ms...." I left the sentence hanging so that the woman could tell me her name.

"I'm Trish. Trish Adams."

"Thanks, Trish." I looked at the clock, having already gone five minutes over my allotted fifteen minutes on the agenda. "I don't want to take up more of your meeting time. If all of you could e-mail me a brief summary of guidelines for your respective colleges, I would really appreciate it. The sooner, the better. Maybe Howard will allow me to come back to this meeting in a few weeks and we can talk about standardizing some of this information—to make your jobs easier."

Most of the bright-faced young women nodded in clear agreement. Most of the rest of the participants were lost to the virtual world via their laptops. I left the meeting to the sounds of Howard asking for open floor items.

Within a couple of days, the various members of admissions had forwarded me the requested information. All of the deans had given feedback, with the exception of Rachel Linares. Eventually, I ended up in Shelley's office trying to discern the problems setting up a meeting with Linares.

"You should probably ask Cicely Irons, Mark. I always work through her to set up these meetings."

"That makes sense," I said. "What's her extension?"

"663. I have to tell you, though, that this is not unusual. I always had trouble setting up appointments between Dean Linares and Dr. Palmer, or even with Dr. Riley."

"You don't say," I fingered a miniature Dalmatian on her desk.

"She frequently goes off campus to clinical sites. You know, hospitals and such."

"I do know, Shelley." I smiled. "Anyway, I'll call Cicely and see what I can find out."

Two minutes later I had Cicely on the phone. An incredibly sweet, overweight girl, Cicely, even though she served as the administrative assistant for all the deans, had an office in Muswell Hall, just one office down the hall from Michael Hartley's former office. Apparently activity stirred outside of her office, because she answered her phone in an excited frenzy.

"Hi, Dr. Carter. Guess what? The police are back searching Dr. Hartley's office again. They had some more questions for me."

I groaned. 'Would there come a time when the phantom of Mike Hartley didn't permeate everything we did,' I wondered.

"Really? The reason I called is...."

"Yes, apparently they think something **was** stolen during the murder."

I couldn't help getting sucked in. "I thought they discounted robbery as a motive."

"Yeah, yeah. Me too. But, a few days ago, Mike's ex-wife came through here and the police showed her the office. Since then, I think she has identified something missing."

"Hmm," I mumbled, playing with the stress ball. "I wonder what it could be."

"I don't know. I asked Detective Klinger if it was a rare book or some rare artifact. You know, something like what Indiana Jones would keep in his office."

I almost popped the stress ball across my office. "He was a dean of education, Cicely. There are no rare books or artifacts in that field."

"I don't know, but this is so exciting. I'm going to go back and peek through the door."

"Wait, Cicely. Remember, I called you." I took a deep breath and traded my stress ball for a pencil.

I could hear her stop in her tracks. "Oh, that's right. What can I do for you?"

"As you know, Shelley and you have been trying to set up a meeting between Dean Linares and me. It's now going on more than three weeks. What's the problem?"

"Yeah. I know and I'm sorry about that. Dean Linares is the only dean who prefers to maintain her own calendar. All I can do is e-mail her suggested or required appointments; otherwise, she tells me if times are open or not. Every time I e-mail some suggestions from Shelley for meeting times, she responds that she's busy."

I chewed on the eraser end of the pencil. "Does she give you reasons?"

"Oh, sure. Usually, it's a site visit, or it's a meeting for the accreditation visit. She's constantly prepping for that."

"As she should," I said. "Anyway, would you let her know that I really need to talk to her? Just tell her it's a basic one-on-one and nothing to worry about. However, she needs to give you three or four open times in the next week that you can offer to Shelley. I'll let Shelley know to move my appointments around, if necessary, to accommodate one of those."

"Drat!" Cicely practically shouted it in my ear.

"What?" I exclaimed, nearly jumping out of my office chair. "Is there already a problem?"

"What? Oh, no, I was just upset to see Detective Klinger and that other cop leave. I guess they're done searching the office again."

"Well, don't let me keep you," I said, knowing my sarcasm would fly thousands of feet above Cicely's head.

"Thanks, Dr. Carter. Maybe I can catch them before they leave the building."

I tried to fight off the image of a toddling Cicely chasing after two cops.

I finally got up my nerve to call Caroline Cruz to ask to be a part of her staff meeting. I had collected enough information from the admissions reps and my deans, Linares, notwithstanding, to explore how the advisors worked with students once they had been admitted. The hand-off of a student from admissions to advising remained unclear.

I walked down to Caroline's office and found her intently studying some papers.

"Hi, Caroline. You got a second?"

She looked up, recognized me, took off her glasses, and leaned back in her chair. "Sure, Mark," she responded with a hint of a smile. "Anything is better than GAP reports."

That same pile of paperwork was stacked un-reviewed in my office. "Oh, yeah, I should look at those, too."

"Please," said Caroline in a snarky voice.

"I will. What I'd like to ask you is if I can come to your staff meeting to discuss communications with students about delivery options."

"Oh, that again. I thought you cleared that up with Howard several days ago."

"Oh, I'm not that lucky. I'd have better luck clearing up the Hartley case."

"That bad, eh? Well, I have a meeting every Tuesday afternoon. Do you want me to get you on the next agenda?"

"That would be great. I can have Shelley juggle my appointments if need be. When do you meet on Tuesdays?"

"Two to four." Caroline had put her glasses back on.

"Just give me twenty minutes in there somewhere."

"Will do. I'll let Shelley know the exact time." Caroline had risen from her chair, putting a blue pinstripe jacket over her grey blouse. "Excuse me, Mark, but I need to run for my one-on-one with Berrian." She grabbed a thick pile of papers from next to her printer.

"Good luck. I have mine tomorrow."

"They're the highlights of our week, aren't they?" She stood in her doorway with her arm extended to show me out.

"Absolutely." She followed me up the stairs and headed to Berrian's office as I turned into mine. "Good luck," I said again. 'That went well,' I thought. Working with Caroline appeared to be easier than I thought.

Shelley bounced across the hall as I entered my office. "Cicely's got back to me with dates and times to meet Dean Linares. The earliest one is next Friday."

"**Next** Friday? Jesus Christ. I'd have better chances at seeing the Pope."

"Keep taking the Lord's name in vain, and you'll need to, Mark." Shelley poked at me with a rolled-up piece of paper in her hand.

"Touché. Anyway, I don't care. Just confirm the stupid appointment."

"You got it." Shelley drifted away as only twenty-something administrative assistants are able to do. I felt a little bad reacting so strongly. I had an appointment set with Linares. Cruz had openly agreed to allow me to talk to her advisors, and I was collecting solid information about accelerated deliveries. Maybe this job would work out after all.

Chapter Ten

The next day, I spent most of my morning collecting all my materials for my one-on-one. Subsequent one-on-ones after my initial one had been surprisingly low-key, always the same routine: I spent several hours identifying key topics, sending out the agenda and key materials ahead of time, copying the agenda and key materials for the actual meeting, and reviewing exactly what I wanted to discuss with Berrian. For his end, the routine stayed the same, too. After I had completed my agenda, he'd lean his head back, think of anywhere from three to six topics, write them down and tell me his expectations in regard to all of them. Since none of those 'top-of-his-head-moments' had been direct challenges to what I did or didn't do, they became endearing, in the same way that one finds a dog urinating on the same mailbox post everyday on a walk endearing. This was just part of who my new boss was.

However, at this one-on-one, after I had finished my last agenda item, he launched directly into his first agenda item with none of the Carnac the Magnificent flourish of scanning his brain.

"What the hell are you doing with this investigation of the accelerated deliveries, Mark?"

Taken aback, I stammered for a couple of seconds. 'Could Caroline have already said something to him? Howard?' It would be more likely that Caroline had. Ultimately, **investigation** suggested more to my questioning than it deserved.

"Oh, that. 'Investigation' is hardly the word. I would call it 'follow up.'"

"Follow-up!" exploded Berrian. "Follow-up to what?"

"It's o.k., Bob, settle down," I said, feeling my blood pressure rising. "Remember that angry husband who called you a couple of weeks ago?"

"Angry husband? What the hell are you talking about?"

141

I laughed at my own unfortunate set-up. "Don't worry. I'm not talking about infidelity or jealous spouses."

"Well, I would hope not." The vein in Berrian's forehead throbbed.

"I meant the guy, Viola, who called to complain about how his wife had been moved, accelerated to regular courses, and how she was so stressed out that she was, uh, I think he put it as, 'well on the way to the loony bin.'"

Berrian visibly relaxed. He leaned back in his chair, and his eyes became a little softer.

"Oh, yeah, that guy. Did you take care of him?"

"You mean, in the way the mafia might take care of him?"

Berrian even cracked a smile. "If you had to resort to that, then this conversation ends right here. What I don't know can't hurt the university."

"Anyway, yes, I took care of her. I worked with financial aid to help her out. However, as I looked at the way she had been advised, obviously she had no clue about what she was getting into, whether accelerated or even regular deliveries. I've merely been following up with Howard's and Catherine's groups to see how academics could give them better information."

Starting to take a few notes, Berrian asked, "and what are you finding out?"

And just like that, I dropped my guard. I forgot my audience.

I monologued.

"All sorts of interesting stuff, Bob. For one thing, each college has different restrictions about what courses can be done in accelerated formats. Sometimes these restrictions...."

Somehow I missed the initial steam coming out of the president's ears. No one could miss the slew of fury that came out of his mouth, though.

"What the hell? Those deliveries were supposed to be for all courses. How the hell did this happen?" I could see the vein on his forehead again.

"All courses? Did Riley or Palmer support that?"

"What kind of question is that, Mark? Of course, Palmer did." Berrian had risen out of his chair to pace around his office.

"It appears the colleges never knew that."

"You say the 'colleges,' Mark," declared Berrian, "but don't you really mean the deans?"

A chipmunk once got its head stuck in the hole in the plastic cap that sealed the well on my property in Ohio. That chipmunk was now me. No matter what I said, I would be flailing like that little guy, with the truth of the matter being that my behind stuck up where it could be kicked.

"I'm still trying to figure that out, Bob. I have found nothing in Palmer's files, and Riley says she wasn't involved in the planning. She merely was told to represent business in discussions with admissions and advising."

"Have you thought of calling Palmer? He could clear it up in a minute."

Berrian kept pacing the room, causing me to have to turn and gyrate to see his reactions. Still, no matter how I turned, my backside remained vulnerable.

"No, I hadn't called Palmer. I figured the intentions at the time didn't matter, per se; what mattered was the way everyone dealt with these deliveries now."

Berrian stopped pacing and stood at the corner of his desk, hands firmly pressing onto the desk, his feet splayed apart as if he was positioned to take my best punch. Unfortunately, his opponent was cornered and in no position to come out swinging. "Alright," he said, taking a deep breath, "let's back up this train a minute. The **deans**," he enunciated quite strongly, "each submitted different restrictions. What exactly does that mean?"

"For instance, education pretty much blessed all their courses."

"Thank god for Michael Hartley," he responded. I avoided making any joke about whether god had been looking out for Hartley.

"I would say that business and arts and sciences have approved over 90% of their courses to be run in any format." I didn't know for sure about the percentage, but I figured I'd err on the safe side—my safe side.

Berrian smacked his lips. "I suppose we can live with that."

"Fine arts may have more like...." I paused to make my best estimate.

"Ah, who cares about fine arts?"

"Really?"

"Yeah, move on."

"What do you mean 'who cares about fine arts?'?" My hands started to shake, and I wondered if I had a visible vein on my forehead.

The president rolled his eyes. "Get off of it. They have virtually no enrollment anymore. And you're going to eliminate them by next year anyway."

I held my hands up in front of my chest, palms extended to Berrian. "You told me to make a recommendation by Christmas. We discussed nothing about elimination."

"A recommendation to eliminate the college." Berrian sat back down and leaned back in his chair.

I laughed nervously. "Why should I bother, then? Let's just eliminate it now."

"Don't be such a pain-in-the-ass. Get the data and then we can make the recommendation. We do nothing without the data."

"What if the data shows … ?"

"Oh, shut up about it, Mark. What about health and nursing? How many of their courses are approved for all deliveries?"

Taking a deep breath, I twisted my neck trying to work some of the tension out. "They are the two with the most limitations. I'm guessing allied health only allows 40% of their courses, while nursing probably allows 25% of their courses."

As expected, Berrian did not react well, slamming both hands down on his desk. "25 fucking percent! 40 percent! Unacceptable, Mark!" He must have hurt his hands because after noticing how bright red they were, he rubbed them together.

"Maybe so, Bob, but let's take more time to see the results once we weed out the clinical/practicum courses."

"Don't weed out anything, Mark. This isn't some garden where only the roses get room to grow. Everything grows in here. And everything grows because students expect it and deserve it."

"I know what you mean, Bob, but remember that a clinical and a practicum are experiential in nature, taking place at the worksite. That, in itself, dictates what can and can't be done."

Berrian had risen from his chair, pacing the room again. I had no idea if he'd heard me. "I don't like this, Mark. This smells like King and Linares through and through. They fight these kinds of innovations, all in the name of the tradition of health education. You talk to them, Mark. You understand! You talk to them, and you tell them that those kinds of shenanigans might have worked with Palmer and Riley, but you're the new sheriff in town and things are going to be done differently. Do you understand that, Mark?"

"Yes, sir, I will work with them." He didn't pick up on my lack of a direct confirmation.

"Damn it." Bob paused for a moment, clearly in thought. "I had asked you to look into something with Linares several weeks ago. What the hell was it? Do you remember? It was something like this where I told you to talk to her and set it straight. What was it?" He disheveled papers left and right on his desk. I had no idea what he sought. "Come on, help me. What was it?"

"I probably have it in some notes in my office, Bob. I haven't had a chance to meet with Rachel yet, so it will come out when I put together all my notes related to nursing."

Berrian stopped his frantic searching. "You haven't had a chance to talk to her? Why not? You've been here a couple of months and you have yet to talk to one of your deans?"

"It's not been a couple of months, Bob. It's not even been a month. We've had a couple of passing discussions in the hallways, but our calendars have not matched yet."

Resuming his frantic disturbance of the papers on his desk, Berrian finally pulled out an old agenda. "Aha. Here it is. Cabinet meeting. I wrote 'nursing faculty. Why the hell can't we hire them?' See, Mark, right there." He waved the agenda right under my nose.

"That's right, sir. That recommendation is in my notes in my office. I do plan to discuss that with her."

"Do that. Look into it, Mark, and keep me posted." He had settled back down into his chair and looked back on an even keel. For several minutes, he said nothing, alternating between note-taking and looking at me.

I had to ask the question I really wanted to avoid. "Did you have anything else, Bob?" He looked puzzled. "We're still on your part of the agenda."

"Oh, that's right. Let me think." He leaned back in his chair and touched his temples with his fingers. "Have you given me your goals, yet?"

"Not officially. We discussed the concept of goals quickly last week, but I haven't put them in any orderly form, yet."

"Do that for the next one-on-one."

"You got it." As I scribbled a note as a reminder, I thought to ask, "Do you have some? It might make sense for me to tie mine into yours."

"Absolutely. Ask Veronica. I'm sure she can get you a copy."

"What else?"

Berrian thought for a few minutes, but instead of writing anything down or saying anything, he clapped his hands. "I think that's all. Playing Friday?"

"Oh, yes. I'll be there." Despite the aches and pains from week one, basketball continued to be part of my weekly ritual.

"Watch your elbows. My nose still smarts from where you hit me last week." With his left hand, he tenderly touched his nose.

I tendered a half smile and grabbed my materials. "See you, Bob."

My exploration of the accelerated deliveries took a hiatus as scrutiny of the fine arts and nursing situations took greater precedence. My infamous goals also now stood as a priority. Even having presidential goals that Veronica sent me, I struggled. Goal-setting was never a clear process at Farrington, and when asked about them during my interview, I mumbled vague responses, although they must have been good enough to mislead the interviewers about my goal-setting abilities.

By the beginning of the following week, I called Victor for assistance.

"Victor, how are you doing?"

"Hi, Mark. Could be better?"

"What's the headache in the HR world?"

"Ha. What isn't? The police want to interview people again about Hartley's murder. Berrian's furious about the two candidates for the EVP of Communications position. Five lawsuits are pending. And I got two staff members on maternity leave."

"Can't you prevent that, Victor?" I joked.

"No one ever listens to me when I tell them to not have children. Anyway, what do you need?"

"Goals."

"What about them?" Victor sounded as if he was unwrapping something.

"I mean, goal-setting. Bob wants me to get a draft of my goals together for my one-on-one this week, and I have never really understood goal-setting in the academic setting."

Victor chewed on something. "Simple. Make them SMART."

"I'd settle for DENSE goals, Victor, just to get something down on paper."

"SMART means 'specific'..."

"I know what they mean, Victor."

He hurtled on: "measurable, attainable, realistic and timely."

"I know, Victor." On my note pad, I wrote DENSE and tried to think of a word to be represented by each letter of the acronym. "For instance, 'measurable' can be pretty difficult to do for academics."

"I would challenge you on that, Mark. Isn't student success in classes 'measurable'?"

"Sure. And I've seen academics with goals that say 85% of students will earn passing grades. And, lo and behold, the next year, grade inflation has set in." 'D'—Daft, Doctored, Droll, Dim, Dreary.

"Then, that's not a realistic goal."

"Au contraire, my HR friend. You could argue it is the most realistic goal ever. No one has to do anything, and at the end of a course, a faculty member slaps a 'B' or an 'A' on the paper." 'E'—Elastic, Exasperating, Endless.

"You're missing the point, Mark. The goals need to be specific, measurable, attainable, realistic, and timely. If they're not all of those things, then they're not appropriate goals." I watched a fly beating itself against my window.

"I understand, Victor. But, in our example, I could put '85% of Boan students will earn passing grades' —there are your specific and measurable parts—'by the end of the academic year' –there's your timely. It can be realistic if faculty know that tenure and pay raises are tied to that goal. And if it's tied to performance evaluation, it will be attained." 'N'—Nefarious, Noxious, Numbing, Naïve.

"You're on the right track, Mark. Each faculty member and employee should be able to tie their own goals with your goals and the university goals." His chewing had been replaced by drinking.

"Are you listening to me, Victor?"

"Yes."

"Let me put it this way. You got anything I can use: a guide, a how-to manual, old goals, anything? My desperation must equal Lindsey Lohan's while on house arrest."

Victor laughed. "Not one of your best, Mark. But, yes, I can send over some materials."

"I did panic on the Lohan line. That's an indication of my depths, Victor." 'S'—Simplistic, Stupid, Smarmy, Sketchy, Short-sighted. "Anyway, could you leave some things at your desk? I'm in a bit of time rush. I'd like to pick them up today." The fly had moved higher up the window, but still hammered away.

"I can do that. Give me an hour. I will leave them at the front desk to our offices."

"Thanks, Victor." As I hung up, I had my DENSE Goal-setting: Doctored, Elastic, Naïve, Short-Sighted, Endless. 'I ought to get these on business cards and hand them out.'

I barely had hung up the phone when it rang. The display showed Caroline's name.

"Mark, are the faculty in full support of Spirit Week next week?"

"Hi, Caroline. A good day to you, too."

"Yes or no, Mark?"

"How about a partial 'yes?' It's the best I can do. Most of the deans promised to strongly encourage their faculty to strongly encourage students to go to Spirit Week events."

"Sounds weak to me."

"Honestly, Caroline. Riley is in full support." I could hear Caroline's snort of skepticism. "So are Fulbright and Stewart. King dragged her feet a little, and I haven't had a chance to talk to Linares."

"Health!" uttered Caroline with loathing.

"Mazel tov!" The fly had landed on the windowsill. If I didn't think it was crazy, I would have said I could see it hyperventilating.

"I'm counting on your faculty, Mark."

"Don't worry, Caroline. You'll have enough students for your 'how many people can we get in a Boan booth' contest."

"Very funny, Mark. Just know I'm counting on you."

I sighed. "Yes, Caroline." As I got ready to hang up, I remembered something. "Oh, Caroline?"

"Yes."

"Is it alright if I don't come to your staff meeting this week to discuss accelerated deliveries? Too many other things have come up."

"Doesn't matter to me. Berrian wasn't real happy when I told him you were looking into that."

"Why the hell did you tell him?" I prodded the fly with my pencil. It flitted back up the window.

"Settle down. If there's one lesson you need to learn, Mark, it's that the president likes no surprises."

"Couldn't you have told me that and recommended that I discuss my activity with Bob?"

"There wasn't an opportunity." The fly resumed batting against my window.

"What does that mean?"

"If you remember, I went straight from our discussion to my one-on-one. When he asked how we were doing in terms of credits scheduled, I felt I had to bring it up."

"Couldn't you have just answered his question without raising the specter of my inquiries?"

"What part of 'no surprises' do you not get, Mark? Look, I've got to run. I'll fill up your twenty minutes with something else at the meeting. And remember, there better be fighting sturgeon spirit from the academics."

The fly had come to rest again on the windowsill. I kicked my chair out and put my feet on my desk. It was a toss-up as to who was the more evolved species.

To satisfy Caroline, I decided to wrap up the Spirit Week commitment. A memo went out quickly to all faculty thanking them in advance for encouraging any student participation during spirit week. As with a gumball machine, I couldn't be sure what I'd get in return. Immediately, sixteen out-of-office messages bounced back to me, all but one announcing that said faculty member wouldn't be back until a date that had already passed. Within hours of my e-mail, a handful of e-mails came in declaring that said faculty member was fully behind Spirit Week, including the oft-repeated line, "Go Sturgeons!" Within a few more hours after that, the malcontent retorts filtered through, ranging from mild annoyance to outright resentment at having class time taken away for the trivialities of student life. Three days later, sooner than I expected, the requisite "When is Spirit Week?" e-mail came in. Shelley and I had placed bets on the college represented by the first "When is Spirit Week?" message. She had picked fine arts; I had chosen nursing. The prize was lunch off campus, which after several weeks of eating in the cafeteria, appealed to me even if I did have to pay.

In the long run, an education faculty member, fairly new to the university, sent the first "When is Spirit Week?" e-mail.

A routine of urgency followed by stagnation permeated almost every issue. The trend had spilled out of cabinet into the day-to-day life of the university. After making this observation to Henry Van Wyck one afternoon in the square, she appropriately labeled it "Sturgency."

"Sturgency" affected me at the highest level. Despite racing to get my goals done, my one-on-one that week with Berrian got cancelled at the last minute—something about some board member's daughter's stepchild's birthday. Veronica apologized over and over for only letting me know of the cancelled meeting five hours before the scheduled time. I felt relief, despite the mountain of papers assembled for the meeting. The agenda could be re-used for the subsequent meeting, and the goals could continue to be refined. It would be over a month before the president and I would ever discuss those goals.

Finally, during Spirit Week, I got my meeting with Rachel Linares. She could only meet in her office, so as I walked there, the festivities of the week surrounded me. All the events led up to our soccer game Saturday against Defiance College, a small liberal arts college across the border in Ohio. Students and staff had decorated doorways, field house walls, parking lots, sidewalks around buildings with various "Crush the Yellow Jackets," "Take the Sting out of the Jackets," "Swat the Yellow Jackets," and other versions of obvious battle cries.

Outside of Weaver Hall, Caroline Cruz and two of her staff members were hanging what appeared to be an ugly gray blob across a line that had been tied between two massive old oak trees.

"What in god's name is that, Caroline?"

"A yellow jacket nest piñata."

"What?"

"It's not a real nest, Mark. It's made out of paper maché. Candice, over there," she pointed to a frumpy girl near one of the oaks, "made it in her fine arts class."

"Naturally," I laughed. "And is it actually filled with candy?"

"Not only that," said the young lady helping Caroline. "It's candy in the shape of yellow jackets." She handed me a sample. Sure enough, it was candy molded in the shape of a wasp. I unwrapped it and popped it in my mouth.

"Lemon. Of, course. Cute." I watched as Frank Pollen carefully secured the nest from the line. "So, students will be blindfolded and hitting the nest with a stick?"

"Oh, much better than that," answered the young lady. "They'll be hitting it with fish."

"You're kidding me? Sturgeons, right?"

"That's right."

I shook my head and walked up the steps of Weaver Hall. I turned around, and squinted to be able to see the three of them. "Hey," I yelled. I saw all three of them turn to me. "That's not live fish, right?"

"Don't be silly, Dr. Carter," shouted Frank from atop his ladder.

"Good. Hate to have PETA all over us." As I got to the door, I turned around one more time. Frank had descended the ladder. "Hey, that's not dead fish either, right?"

They must not have heard me, as all three headed back toward the commons, ladder in tow.

Making my way to Linares' office, I noticed that the nursing students had decorated the third floor hallway of Weaver Hall. Cut-outs of fish, soccer balls and yellow jackets populated the walls on both sides, sprinkled with mundane "Go Sturgeons" and "Boan #1" signs, alongside clever "Nurses always love a good Sturgeon" and "Yellow Jackets: when crushed, take two aspirin and call us in the next millennium." Caroline had to be pleased with the spirit of the nursing students. Linares had picked up on my e-mail to encourage participation.

Linares stood at her window on the phone when I rapped on her open door. She motioned for me to come in, and waved for me to sit down at the small, round table in the corner. She listened intently to the person on the other line. Looking out the window, I saw the table and chairs on the roof of the Weaver addition. If anyone on this floor opened their windows fully, they could easily walk out on to the addition's roof and sit at the outdoor table. As Linares asked the person on the phone, "what else would you need?" I made a quick note in my notebook to confirm with facilities that this set-up met code.

"Thank you, Dr. Eggars. We should be able to do that. I'll get the paperwork faxed over to you shortly." Linares hung up the phone and held out her hand. "Dr. Carter, good to see you. I thought we'd never get to this meeting." I was struck by her bright red lipstick.

"Luckily we have time now."

"Yes. Sorry about that phone call. That was Dr. Eggars from the NLNAC. It's non-stop trying to keep her happy."

"No problem. By the way, love the hallway. Thanks for encouraging the Spirit Week support. You've curried me some positive mojo with the daunting Dr. Cruz."

Linares shook her head. "I had nothing to do with that. Pearl Young did that. She got her Fundamentals of Nursing students to do all that. I wasn't real happy when I came in the other day and saw it."

"Why did it bother you?"

"She spent class time doing it."

"Not the worst thing in the world if she's confident the students aren't falling behind."

"You don't understand, Mark," Linares said, reaching into her purse. "You mind if I smoke?"

"You can't smoke in the building." Despite my desire to be open-minded with Dr. Linares, I quickly was growing irritated.

"I know. I go outside. You want to join me?" Sure enough, she had opened her window completely and had stepped outside onto her makeshift patio on the addition's roof. I uneasily followed her out.

"I seriously doubt this meets the university policy on smoking." On the plastic table sat an ashtray full of cigarette butts, bright red lipstick stained on every butt.

"It does, Mark. I checked the policy in the HR manual. It says that all smoking must occur at least twenty feet from a building. Get a tape measure and see how far it is to my window: Twenty-one feet."

"But, you're not even an inch or two from the building, Rachel," I said, pointing to the roof we stood on.

"Nonsense." She lit a cigarette and sat down in one of the two chairs. "Anyway, let's get started out here."

"Let's start with your faculty issues. I know you have three open positions and that all your positions are revolving doors. Help me to know how to help you get and keep faculty."

"What are we to do?" Linares drew a deep breath and stared off into the distance. "Nurses can make a lot more money on the floor."

"Victor said that money had become an issue with new hires versus some of your long-term faculty. Is that true?"

"Probably. Frankly, I told HR not to give any credence to what Tina and Janet said when they left."

"Those are two of the three who quit recently?"

"Yes, at the end of July."

"Wasn't there a third?" I asked, knowing the answer.

"Well, that had nothing to do with money. Stacy Vrbosky decided to have a baby." Linares had finished her first cigarette and had started her second.

I waved away a wasp. "A spy from Defiance, perhaps?" I chuckled.

"What?"

"Nothing. So, Vrbosky didn't want to take maternity leave and come back?"

"No. Her husband is **loaded**. She doesn't need to work."

"Was there any attempt to try to at least convince the other two ... who were they again?"

"Tina Rolls and Janet Elizabeth Ward. Yes, we tried to keep them, but they were head-strong on leaving."

"What did we offer them? Was it simply about the money?" I waved to try and shoo the wasp away.

"For the most part. The new nurses we brought in were making $7000 more than Tina and Janet. HR wanted to offer them half of that this year, and the other half next year, but I suggested we not cave."

I now stared off into the distance. "That wasn't much money over the course of two years. Why wouldn't you support that?"

Now the wasp flew around Linares. She waved at it. "You don't understand, Mark. Nurses are an emotional group. I've found that you can't give in to the emotion." From inside her office, Linares' phone rang. "Hold on, let me get this." Rachel ground her second cigarette into the overflowing ashtray and scrambled back to her window to answer her phone. I made several notes on follow-up with HR, about both the attempt to keep Ward and Rolls, as well as about the smoking policy. 'How long has she been getting away with this?' I wondered.

Linares stayed on the phone for more than fifteen minutes, enough time for me to get steamed, enough time for me to walk to the edge of the roof and see a group of students sitting on a bench below me, enough time for me to check my voice-mail (one message from Mike Stewart), enough time for me to contemplate if I could get away with murder in the same way that Hartley's killer did. Finally, Linares stepped back through her window with a sheepish grin. "Sorry, that was the NLNAC again. They want to add another person to the visiting team. I had to get all the information about her, some bigwig from San Francisco."

"Why didn't you tell her you were meeting with your boss and you'd call back?"

Linares staggered back from my response. After a couple of seconds, during which she lit another cigarette, she finally responded, "You don't understand, Mark. For the next five to six weeks, I'm basically the NLNAC's slave."

"Make a note, though. From now on, if you are in a meeting with me and the NLNAC calls, you tell them you'll call them back."

Linares blew several circles of smoke. "Really, Mark, this is a side of you I didn't expect. Riley was an arrogant prig as interim provost, but that didn't seem you at all."

"Everyone has their limits, Rachel. It's taken Shelley a month or so to even get this first meeting scheduled. Almost half of our allotted time has been spent with you on the phone or lighting up another cigarette. I'm simply encouraging us to remember our priorities."

Linares looked down at her cigarette. "Are you saying I can't smoke, Mark?"

"Jesus! Of course not, Rachel. Although I'm going to suggest you find a more suitable smoking place than this roof."

"Whatever," she replied, grounding her unfinished cigarette back in the ashtray. "Do you want to go back into the office? I have less than twenty minutes before I go teach."

I took a deep breath and exhaled. "Teach, eh? How convenient?"

"What do you mean, Mark?"

"Nothing." I struggled to maintain my composure.

"It's pharmacology. I have no one credentialed to teach it. To be honest, I'm not credentialed to teach it. But, what's a girl to do?"

"This is a good point, Rachel," I said, settling back into the chair in her office. "Start making some notes of topics for one-on-ones. I'm going to suggest we meet every other week at the beginning to make sure we're both on the same page. After that, we'll meet as needed." The wasp had followed us back into the room and Linares agitatedly tried to shoo it away with her yellow writing pad.

I didn't wait for Linares to be ready to write. "Agenda items: 1) Full-time nursing staffing issues; 2) Credential problems; 3) Accelerated deliveries."

Linares groaned. "Oh, god, what about those?"

"Let's just talk. For now, let's just say that Bob and I are in disagreement about them."

"I hope that means you hate them. I sure do and have forbidden them in all classes coded nursing."

I jotted that in my notebook. "As you might imagine, the president isn't keen that we have forbidden students from participating in the 'If you have the need, we have the speed' scheduling campaign."

"Damn wasp!" she muttered, swinging her writing pad at it again. "I hate those damn things."

"Ignore them and they usually ignore you."

"Anyway, nursing doesn't do well with speed, Mark." Rachel had begun gathering up some textbooks and papers for her class. From outside, the sound of laughter could be heard.

I passed on any obvious joke and pressed on. "Every discipline could argue that, Rachel. And for the time being, I'm still more on your side than on Bob's side. I'm nervous about all of these deliveries too. However, we are representatives of this university and we must open-mindedly approach these kinds of discussions."

"So, what is it you want me to do about these deliveries?"

I grabbed a hard candy from a jar on her table and began unwrapping it. "For now, just be ready in our next one-on-one to discuss them—open mindedly."

"I'm not sure what good it will do, but o.k. Do you mind walking with me to class?"

I looked at my watch. "You have more than 10 minutes."

"I need to go over to Jordan Hall."

"You do? I thought all your classes were here in Weaver?" I couldn't help but be suspicious with almost everything she told me.

"Have you smelled the classrooms on the second floor?"

"Have I what?"

"Smelled the classrooms downstairs. Every year in the heat of summer, some ungodly odor permeates our classrooms over here. Last year I got smart enough to schedule my classes in the other buildings on campus."

I took out my notebook to make a note. "I assume facilities know about this."

"You bet they do," she said, holding the door open for me to exit. "Doesn't mean they do anything about it?"

"Do they refuse?"

"I don't know, Mark. I try to just do my job and stay away from everything else around here." I made a mental note to add 'attitude' to our next meeting. "One thing I'd like to add to our next one-on-one, Mark, is a review of the accreditation visit. Were you associated with one at... where did you come from again?"

"Farrington." I held the door to the stairwell for her. "And, yes, we had a nursing accreditation visit there."

"Good, then you know how we need to show the NLNAC exactly what they want to see?"

"Exactly what they want to see? That phrasing concerns me a little."

"You don't understand, Mark."

"Rachel," I said, grabbing her shoulder before she headed to the front door of Weaver Hall. "If you tell me one more time that I 'don't understand,' I will scream. Stop being so bloody patronizing."

Rachel looked me up and down with a superior attitude. For the second time this day, I understood how Michael Hartley's killer might have felt. I took a deep breath, released her and held the door open for her. Outside, the laughter and cries of students could be heard. Off to the left, the yellow jacket piñata event had begun. I could see a tall boy waving something, presumably a fish, wildly at the paper maché hive. The hive already looked pretty beat up. A piece of candy dangled already.

Rachel dug in her purse and almost missed the first step outside Weaver Hall. She dug out a pair of garish sunglasses and put them on. As we walked away from Weaver, Rachel on my left, she turned toward me. "With all due respect, Mark, nursing is a pain-in-the-ass. I've heard the president say it in front of hundreds of alumni, donors, and members of the community. I made up my mind several years ago to just keep my head down and do what I know needs to be done for the students and the program. Provost Palmer never got it. Riley sure as hell doesn't have a clue. At least, Palmer left us relatively alone."

If her gaze was locked on me, I couldn't tell because of the sunglasses. "Oh wait," she exclaimed, looking forward and seeing us heading toward the commons. "Jordan Hall is back that way." She began back-pedaling, all the time continuing her monologue. "Anyway, I'd like to talk about that at this one-on-one. I appreciate very much what you want to do and what you **think** you need to do, but this is the first time you've ever overseen a nursing program. In many ways, accreditation forces the hand of the University."

As Linares continued to back-pedal and talk to me, I could see the inevitable chain of events that would occur. To this day, I cannot say if I had enough time to warn her or not. In memory, I've come to believe that I could have uttered a caution but had enjoyed seeing the scene play out. Linares backed right into the boy with the fish swatting at the jacket hive. With her additional momentum pushing into him, he struck the hive fully and the hive burst open. Suddenly the sky around the students filled with candy yellow jackets scattering everywhere. A swarm of them descended directly onto Linares, who had turned her head upwards with a look similar to what some colonial explorer must have had when stumbling into a cannibal settlement. Linares dropped her bags and started waving her hands.

"Help! Help! Oh Christ! Stop them!" Her arms waved wildly and the crowd of onlookers watched stunned. Finally, Rachel dropped to the ground. She lay there for several seconds, surrounded by yellow jackets, student papers, and something I couldn't quite make out. Walking over to get a closer look, I noticed it was a dead fish that had fallen next to her face. Frank Pollen raced over to her, brushing candy jackets off of her.

"She's fainted. A nurse! We need a nurse! Someone get a nurse!"

Chapter Eleven

Rachel Linares' concussion and Michael Hartley's murder dominated the October board of trustees' meeting. Berrian's displeasure showed from the moment he told us the board chair wanted discussion of these incidents as the first agenda item. Two cabinet meetings had been devoted to the October agenda, with the primary focus being enrollment. Hank, Howard and Berrian had pored over every actual, budget and stretch goal imaginable in an attempt to present the fall enrollment in the best possible light. That topic would now be diminished by, as Berrian put it, "the sordid soap operas playing off stage."

The Linares "incident," as we lightly called it, deserved no discussion. After a paramedic revived Rachel (none of the nursing faculty could be found in her time of greatest need), she complained of dizziness and informed HR that she would work from home for a couple of days. After a couple of days passed, she faxed me and HR a doctor's report that said she had suffered a concussion and needed to rest. She claimed she couldn't afford to rest completely, since the infamous accreditation visit loomed, but that she wanted to continue working from home. Upon Victor's recommendation based upon employment law, I told her that was unacceptable: she either couldn't work at all or she could return to work. At that point, the media, which had hovered around Boan since Hartley's death, smelled a story, even if a weak one, and ran a scathing editorial regarding the safety of Boan employees.

The Hartley investigation probably did deserve priority. More than six weeks had passed since the murder, and the longer the police took, the more the media attempted to cast the story in the harshest light so as to keep readership. One student had been detained for a full day, leading to speculation that the murderer had been caught. However, the student was released when three other students finally came forth and accounted for the

156

accused's whereabouts in the hours leading up to Hartley's murder. He (the student, not Hartley) had been passed out in the bathtub of a friend.

The police never spoke of any other suspects. They now confirmed that something had been stolen from Hartley's office, but refused to say what. That stolen item became the clue they held back to separate the real culprit from a few crazies who showed up at police headquarters to turn themselves in. Everyone at Boan speculated about the stolen item: the leading possibility was a manuscript that Hartley planned to publish. However, Hartley's scholarship history revealed a piecemeal approach to publication. Poorly written, unacknowledged articles and presentations made up his scholarship. Why would anyone want to steal something he wrote?

The next favorite hypothesis surrounded the idea that the stolen item revealed the killer's identity. In this case, the rumor mill conjectured a gift from a lover. Given that he had three ex-wives and a countless string of lovers, this potentiality didn't get anyone much closer to identifying the killer.

Howard joked that Hartley's soul was stolen, which explained why no one had even thought to look for it missing, or why it was fruitless to wait for it to be found.

During the last cabinet meeting before the October board meeting, Berrian requested that Detectives Marsh and Klinger bring us up to date on the investigation. He evidently had to pull some weight with the police chief to make this meeting happen.

This visit, Detective Jerome Klinger, who stood about six and a half feet tall, with an iron-clad body that could put Garrett Jones to shame, an acne-scarred face, a cleft jaw straight from Kirk Douglas, and, I didn't notice it immediately, a right arm longer than his left, took charge. "What exactly do you want, President Berrian?" he said, still standing at the foot of the U, while Detective Marsh stood off to his right.

"Detective Klinger, thanks to you and Detective Marsh for coming." Berrian's placation attempts fell upon dear ears, and he moved on. "Please, take a seat." Klinger cast his eyes around him as if wary of a communicable disease.

"We'll stand."

"Fine. We have a board meeting in a week and the board has requested an update on the Hartley investigation. As you might imagine, they are very concerned about the impact of this unsolved murder on the Boan image."

"Image, sir?" asked Klinger.

"Yes, image. Parents send their eighteen-year olds to Boan because it is a safe environment and they know their kids will be protected."

"I see. And, have you had a number of complaints from parents, sir?"

Berrian hesitated. He had taken to standing also to diminish the impact of Klinger's towering presence. Even with his 6 feet 4 inch height, he looked insignificant compared to Klinger's bulk. "We'd prefer to avoid them, detective. However, this is the time of year we recruit in the high schools very heavily for next year, so our image is of utmost importance."

"Image? You like that word 'image,' don't you, President Berrian?"

"It's not a question of liking it, detective…." Berrian's voice attempted to take on his usual bravado and conceit, but he had no follow through. He was like Shaquille O'Neal trying to force a free throw through sheer brute force. "It's a question of perception."

"Perception?" Klinger finally broke his gaze from Berrian and turned to Marsh. "These academic types love their fancy words, don't they, Marsh?"

Berrian sighed. "What's the big deal? We're on the same side here, detective. All we're asking you is for some information we could use to comfort our constituencies, you know, our stockholders, shareholders, if you will?"

"I'm all for helping, sir, when there appears to be a real need. However, if you ask me, it appears that the only need is to protect Boan's 'appearance.'"

"That's hardly fair, Detective Klinger."

"Perhaps I can help," spoke up Victor. Berrian nodded at him to continue. "Boan is well-known as a solid Midwestern university in a small town; that picture appeals to many of our students and their parents as a refuge from the danger and chaos that can be Indianapolis or Chicago or Cincinnati. So, what the president is expressing is our concern that one murder can damage that brand."

"Brand! Isn't that like what they do to cows? Sear a brand on their backside?" Klinger allowed himself the first smile since he had arrived. "Detective Marsh, perhaps we should ask the Boan students around here to drop 'trou' so that we can make sure each shows they are 'Property of Boan'?"

"Damn it, detective," said Berrian, finally gaining his courage, "why the aggression? As I said, we are on the same side here."

For the first time, Detective Marsh stepped forward. "You have to understand, President Berrian, that being called to a meeting to explain any development on this case is not the best use of time. Heck, Jerome here hates having to do that for the chief, let alone for you."

"O.k. Then don't call it 'developments,' just call it, 'update.' We certainly deserve that, don't we?"

Klinger held his longer arm out to indicate to Marsh that he would take over again. "With all due respect, sir, I'm not sure what you expect. One of your deans was killed in his office in the middle of an open and well-populated building in a way that was so gruesome, there is no way he didn't die without making a lot of noise. Your security measures, both before the murder, then during and immediately following, were, let us say, 'lax.' Upon investigation, we have uncovered a list of potential suspects that runs longer than the awards at the Oscars. Apparently, twenty to thirty people hated your dean so much that they admit they were happy he was dead, even if they didn't do it. Upon our additional investigation, most of those motives are somewhat understandable. It **appears** that this University let an unethical, narcissistic, jerk do whatever the hell he wanted to for many years. If you ask me, Boan University has gotten off pretty easily in terms of the media." Klinger stopped and swept his eyes around the table, resting them back on the speechless Berrian. "How's that for your update, sir?"

The president attempted to regain control of the moment. "So, we can say that the list of suspects continues to be reviewed and that possible motives are emerging? Veronica, did you capture that?"

Veronica jerked back to attention. All of us had been reduced to statues. "Uh, hold on, Bob," she said, trying to get her computer to fire back up. A painful ten seconds or so of waiting resulted in the absolute silence of the room until the laptop beeped that Veronica's access rights had been restored. "O.k., so 'the list of suspects continues to be....' What was it you said, Bob?"

Berrian's voice increased dramatically: "the list of suspects continues to be reviewed and possible motives are emerging."

"Got it."

"Well, detectives, keep us posted. Hopefully, this murder can be solved quickly and we can all lose our surliness."

"Don't worry, Mr. President," replied Klinger. "The second we turn up anything new..., uh, should I say 'turn up anything **brand** new'..., we'll let you know."

After they left, Berrian exploded into a fury. "Of all the god-damn gall. What an ass. I have half a mind to report him to the chief. Where did he get off copping that attitude with us? And, yes, Howard, I know there's a damn good pun in 'copping.'" He slammed his fist on the desk, causing Hank's coffee to somersault onto the floor. Berrian continued, "unbelievable. You'd think we all were criminals. Hell, we're the victims here, even more than Hartley. He's dead, but we're still living in this fucking nightmare."

"Uh, Bob," said Howard, "perhaps we can take a quick break. We all could probably cool down."

'Sure,' I thought, '**we** need to calm down.'

In the end, we decided to tell the board that the investigation was going slowly because of few solid clues, more than one suspect, and multiple motives. If the board pushed, it could be said that Hartley had apparently not been the public figure we all thought, and that as the police discovered potential motives, everyone, ranging from Boan administration to the police to even the media, desired to err on the side of Hartley's memory. Once the murder got solved, then only the relevant motive or motives would be revealed.

It was a lousy strategy, obviously, but we were in a boat without a rudder. We were going to be taken wherever the strong waves pushed us, and all we could hope was that we could run ashore without capsizing or being dashed against the rocks. As it turned out, I played the part of a mere spectator in how that would play out at the meeting.

During the board meeting, Chairman James K. Oliphant, a retired lifetime military man, challenged us immediately.

"How many suspects are more than one?" Oliphant twirled an outrageous handlebar mustache.

"Well, the police won't be specific."

"Take an educated guess?"

"Three or four?" Berrian hesitated in a rare moment of weakness. Board member Selma Wellington, a former superintendent of schools, sprang into the discussion.

"Three or four? After almost two months of investigation? That doesn't make sense to me, Bob."

"That's about all they're telling us, though."

"Surely you have an idea of who they are. Staff members, faculty, students?" Wellington, a diminutive black woman, could barely be seen above the massive conference table in the Boan board room, a recent addition to the Administration Building. According to faculty opinion, the room cost an outrageous amount of money and it only got used for board meetings. It was also the reason Victor Woo now had his office in a different building. His office and something called the "Executive Reading Room" were sacrificed for the Oliphant Board Room.

"No, not really, Selma."

The third member of the inquest jumped in the fray. Wilson Greystone III, heir to the multi-national Greystone Mortuary Supplies Company, stood out during the meeting. The only board member under the age of sixty (he was only forty-one), he had come to the meeting in a Polo shirt and khaki pants, stuffing a clove cigarette out in the ashtray next to the board room entrance. "With so much uncertainty, wouldn't this mean there is still the chance of others being hurt?"

"What do you mean, Wilson?" asked Oliphant.

"Well, the police can't identify the killer, can't pinpoint a single motive, and can't identify additional clues. Nevertheless, they're hanging around campus virtually every day doing their investigation. If I was the murderer, I'd get a little nervous. Who knows what I might do?"

"Well, first off, Wilson, the police are hardly hanging around there every day, and secondly, there is no indication of additional danger."

"I beg to differ, Mr. President," spoke up Trent Dejeerling, second youngest board member and partner in the Gaylord, Dejeerling, and Poindexter law firm. "I can see the police cruisers on campus almost every day from my office." Gaylord, Dejeerling, and Poindexter towered over most of Boan from its eight-story law offices across the street from the Administration Building. I had been afforded the honor of visiting his eighth-floor corner office upon my introduction to him a few weeks earlier.

"More importantly, we have no concerns of additional violence." For the first time since I had met him, I saw a bead of perspiration trickling down Berrian's forehead.

"How can you be so sure?" asked Oliphant.

"Because nothing has happened," responded Berrian, perhaps a little too forcefully.

"Not real comforting, Bob."

"Mr. Chairperson, may I interject?" asked Wellington. Selma was the first, and last, person to attempt to hold to Robert's Rules of Order for the meeting.

"Ms. Wellington has the floor."

"What strikes me every time I read about this story in the paper is the sordidness of Dean Hartley. Three, or is it four, ex-wives? Reputed affairs? Angry colleagues? Desperate students? If you ask me, it's the victim that's killing us here!"

I smiled at her characterization of the issue. She had emerged as a board member in which to place some hope.

Wellington continued. "My question, therefore, is how we had allowed such an apparently repugnant man to be in leadership for as long as we did. I'm not sure who to ask this of, whether it's Bob, or Victor, or perhaps even, Mark, but certainly you knew of this man's trail of tears, did you not?"

"Unfortunately, most of it came out after the murder," said Berrian. Sitting across from me, Caroline Cruz visibly winced. The rest of my colleagues had their heads down at their places.

Dejeerling followed up for Wellington. "I am aware of at least three lawsuits in the last several years."

"And what about that student teacher with us a couple of years back?" asked former superintendent Wellington. "Remember, Bob, that I called you with the concern. You said that Palmer looked into it. What did he find out?"

Berrian still responded with slight hesitations, which almost everyone in the meeting had to be picking up. "Come to think of it, I don't think Palmer ever did follow-up for me."

If I wasn't mistaken, that was the sound of a bus backing up and running over John Palmer that I had just heard. More and more victims related to this murder emerged every day.

Victor finally spoke up. "HR did deal with some random complaints and grievances against Hartley over the years. Maybe we should have acted differently or more aggressively, but I would really encourage all of us not to drag his reputation through the mud. He is the victim here."

"Come on, Victor," responded Oliphant. "Save that for the employee handbook. It is the function of this board to serve and protect the interests of this university. If a man has been allowed to get away with murder—in a metaphorical sense both professionally and privately—then that murder needs to be addressed as equally as his actual murder."

Several seconds of stillness ensued. No one knew how to move forward. Finally, Berrian broke the silence. "Is there a particular action step on this item, Mr. Chairman?"

"I'm not sure. Does anybody else want to speak to this matter?"

"Mr. Chairman," said Quincy Ashland, the Vice President of Human Resources at northern Indiana's largest hospital, "I would like to confirm that Rachel Linares' accident had no relationship to Hartley's murder. Is that true?"

"I can speak to that, Mr. Chairman," I declared, raising my hand.

"Please do, Mark."

"I was there when it happened. There is no relationship. Dean Linares had an unfortunate accident where she unknowingly stumbled into a Spirit Week student activity. Thinking she actually was being swarmed by a nest of angry yellow jackets, she fainted, hit her head and may, or may not, to be truthful, have gotten a concussion. In other words, it is exactly like the newspapers have reported it."

"Is that so?" responded Ashland, with a heavy dose of skepticism. "It sounded too ridiculous to me, even for Linares, which is why I asked."

Victor raised his hand. "Go ahead, Victor," said Oliphant.

"A point of clarification and a question for Quincy. Clarification: Mark has pointed out that she may or may not have a concussion. We are asking her to give us confirmation of that. I'll make sure the board is updated. And then the question: why did you say 'even for Linares'?"

For the moment, Quincy looked like us from a few minutes earlier, as if he didn't know how to respond. Finally, he replied. "She's an odd duck when she comes to the hospital. To be truthful, she puts off a lot of our staff. In all honesty, if I didn't know and you told me a dean had been murdered, I might have thought she'd been killed."

"Really, Quincy," responded Victor. "That's surprising."

"Are you saying she is a poor representative of the university?" I asked, timidly.

Ashland squirmed in his seat, noticeably uncomfortable with opening this line of discussion. "That seems overly harsh. The best I can say is that some of our staff believe she is a bit pushy and difficult to work with."

"That's good to know, Quincy," said Berrian, finding an opportunity to regain control of the meeting. "Mark, please make note of that, and work with Victor on addressing these concerns?"

"Will do," I answered, nodding at Victor.

"Wasn't it this woman who the papers initially claimed was the main suspect?" Matilda Upton, eighty-five-year old matriarch of the Boan legacy, she being the great grand-daughter of Horace Boan, spoke up, her voice barely audible above the ventilation system in the room.

Howard, sitting next to Matilda, patted her on her liver-spotted arm. "You're confusing her with someone else, Matilda, dear."

"Are you sure? I thought it was the dean of the school. I know it was some woman who at a meeting one time had yelled out, 'You'll rot in hell, Hartley.'" Matilda's eighty-five-year old face broke into a lovely smile. She apparently still had some kick in her.

"That would have been the Dean of the College of Allied Health, Matilda," said Berrian.

"I'm confused, Bob," admitted Greystone stepping in. "I thought this Linares was the Dean of Allied Health."

"No, she's the Dean of Nursing."

"Oh, so you have two deans for health?" asked Greystone.

"Yes. Don't you remember? The NLNAC practically blackmailed us with no accreditation if we didn't make nursing a separate college. That happened the last time they visited us, so, what, about four years ago?" Bob looked at Victor and Hank, the two longest-tenured members of his Cabinet for confirmation.

"That would have been five years ago, Bob," corrected Hank. "At that time Linares became dean."

"So, when did Linares say this thing about 'Hartley rotting in hell'?" asked Wellington.

"She didn't say that. King said that." Berrian struggled as he lost control of the meeting again.

"Let's move on from this topic. I believe there are no action items or resolutions about either Hartley's murder or Linares' injury. It is expected that Boan leadership will continue to keep the board posted on the incidents." Oliphant scanned the participants around the table and seeing no reactions from his colleagues, continued. "Next on the agenda is enrollment. Mr. President."

"Thank you, Jim. Howard is passing around the latest enrollment numbers. We have had a fantastic fall." Berrian quickly got back into his stride. If he was a peacock, he would have needed more room for his feathers. "Now a couple of things to keep in mind before Howard takes you through these numbers. One: some programs are declining in enrollment. We're not going to mislead you there. Fine arts continues to see dramatic drops in students. The media communications degree is losing students. And, the public safety degree program continues to stay flat. The great thing is that Carter is now on board, has been able to look into these programs a bit, and will be making recommendations on all of them by the end of the fiscal year."

'I was?' My look, hopefully, did not betray my stunned reaction. We had never talked about anything but the College of Fine Arts, in which case I had already been surprised by Berrian's pre-determined "recommendations." Who knows where Berrian had come up with the "media communications" concern, so I flipped through Howard's report frantically to locate the reference. Finding nothing about any programs, I started to panic. The "public safety" issue I hadn't heard anything about since the first Friday basketball game. I tried to glean if Cruz or Shue were panicking in the same way I was, but as usual Caroline gave away nothing, and Howard stared at Berrian.

"Howard, go on and talk everyone through the enrollment report."

While Howard droned on about the report, I drifted into a place where I had been dwelling way too much the first six weeks or so at Boan. In talking to Natalie about it, I called it the Oz Effect. Every time I felt confident with how the university operated, the curtain got pulled back to reveal the true workings of the place. The latest surprise about declining enrollment in programs should not have surprised me at all after several months in this job.

All of a sudden, Howard had stopped talking and Oliphant had asked for questions from the board. At least three hands had gone up. Oliphant recognized Matilda Upton first.

"If enrollment is up overall, why is enrollment in the dormitories down?" she asked.

"We're getting a lot more adult students, Matilda," answered Berrian.

"We are? That's a surprise. I thought we decided to put our efforts toward traditional students to get those huge dormitories filled. Am I not right, Mr. Chairman?"

"You are right, Matilda, that last year we expressed concerns about the empty dormitory rooms."

Berrian looked at Chairman Oliphant as if expecting additional clarification. When it didn't come, he leapt in. "Yes, that was one of the critical areas of concern noted last year. But, if you also remember, the board said that overall enrollment must be the most important goal."

"'Critical area of concern?' Are you saying that we didn't make it an actual goal, Bob?" asked Dejeerling,

"Well, yes, it was a goal, but the number one goal was overall enrollment." Berrian's head vein had appeared.

"I thought it was the first sub-goal under the overall enrollment goal."

Berrian tried to push Dejeerling's comment aside. "I don't remember, but it's all semantics."

"Mr. Chairman?" Upton had raised her frail hand again.

"Yes, Matilda."

"Can we ask the secretary to review the minutes from last year for confirmation of this?"

Richard Finley, board secretary, turned to Matilda. "Give me a sec, Matilda. I'm trying to find them. The wireless in this room is pathetic."

"While the secretary looks, Mr. Chairman, may I ask a question?" asked Quincy Ashland.

"Go ahead, Quincy."

"The goal for students enrolled is up, and I commend the administration for that, but the goal for credits is down. Isn't that a concern?"

Everyone turned to Berrian for an explanation. His staff knew better to reply unless directed by him. Berrian took a drink of water, I'm sure, to buy himself a few more seconds.

"Yes, Quincy, you are right. That is a huge concern. Our credit hours have gone down rather dramatically. We're not exactly sure why, but institutional research is getting us data on that."

"I am correct, aren't I, Hank," asked Ashland, turning to face Turing to his far left, "that credit hours are much more important than basic enrollment for the bottom line? It is the more realistic indicator of money coming in, right?"

"You are correct, Quincy." Hank didn't have any distress about speaking without the president's expressed consent and approval ahead of time.

I, on the other hand, still struggled with how to assert myself. In all the cabinet meetings planning this board meeting, we had never considered having to address this differential in credits vs. bodies. In fact, given that the credit information had been buried on the middle of page three of Howard's report, I was impressed by Ashland's attention to a detail that we had fully expected to be glossed over.

Greystone joined the discussion. "It would seem to me that Boan needs to understand that better and do something about it quickly." His statement posed no threat; he sounded simply like an astute businessman.

"We'll do that. I promise you," said Berrian.

Finally I raised my hand. "Provost Carter?" Oliphant recognized me.

"I will throw out a hypothesis about the decline in credits. Granted we have no data yet, so this is just my gut speaking. If our enrollment in bodies is going up because of additional adult students, then the goal for credits can't go up at the same rate. Adults take fewer classes a semester than traditional students." After a moment's pause, I had to throw in, "you know, those pesky things like kids and work that detract from coursework."

"That would make sense. Thank you, Mark," responded Ashland.

Berrian didn't glare at me, so I had to believe all was o.k. with him. "Let's see what the data tells us."

"May I ask a question, Mr. Chairman?" Greystone had taken off a shoe to rub his foot.

"Please."

"Where does online fit in all this?"

"I'm not sure I understand your question." Berrian checked his watch, almost certainly exasperated that an hour into the meeting, we still hadn't moved past the first two subjects on the agenda—the two subjects he most wanted to keep in his control.

"Where would I find online enrollment?" Greystone leafed through Howard's report.

"I'm still not sure we understand what you're wondering about, Wilson," said Berrian.

"Why don't we see how many students are enrolled for online?"

Howard jumped in. "Because we code them by program. We don't code them by online vs. in-seat."

"Don't you think you should have two codes, though, Howard?"

Berrian stepped in for Howard. "Two codes?" He responded in the same way he might if Greystone had commented that he should have two heads. "Wouldn't that just get confusing, Wilson?"

"Maybe 'code' is the wrong word. I don't know." Greystone showed his growing frustration.

"Let me help you out, Wilson," suggested Ashland, stepping in. "What is it you would like to see concerning online enrollment?"

"How pervasive is it?" The looks, or lack thereof, from around the table caused Greystone to push on. "My daughter spends all her time online. I know some of her friends who have already graduated high school talk about taking classes online. And these are from some prestigious and traditional schools: Penn State, Maryland and so forth. I'm just trying to get a sense of whether online is an important piece of student enrollment, not only at Boan, which is the immediate question now, but across the country."

"That's a good question, Wilson," said Upton. "I see advertisements for University of Phoenix all the time. They're primarily online if I'm not mistaken."

"You're not, Matilda," responded Berrian.

"I'm not what?"

"Mistaken."

"Oh, thank goodness."

Caroline raised her hand. For the first time, she entered into the conversation. After being acknowledged by Oliphant, she cleared her throat and spoke in her characteristic clipped speech pattern. "We do have a large number of students taking individual classes through online. The last data I remember showed 38% of credits taken online. I have dedicated staff for handling only online advising, and it's frankly not enough staffing. I have recommended to Mark that he do the same for academics."

Greystone whistled. "38%! That's much higher than I thought. But, if I'm hearing you correctly, you are saying 'individual classes.' So, does that mean there are few students taking entire programs through online? I know the Higher Learning Commission blessed Boan to do that."

Howard took up the discussion. "We do offer complete programs via online. It's unclear how many students do that because they mostly live in the tri-state area, and we're pretty sure they come to campus to take some classes or to get many of their services." Howard looked toward the president and the chairman sitting side by side. "Perhaps, Mr. Chairman and Mr. President, we can bring you more specific data on this at a future meeting? In the interest of today's time."

Berrian smiled at Howard, almost certainly to thank him for the steering of the discussion. Oliphant, however, acted as if he hadn't even heard Howard.

"It would seem to me," announced the chairman, "that this coding thing is what's holding you up. I can't believe you haven't run into this problem before."

"With all due respect, Jim, I'm still not sure what the problem is." Berrian radiated a level of smugness.

"The impact of students taking online."

"Impact on what? Tuition is tuition."

"But if I understand Caroline correctly, the university is not staffed appropriately to manage online, especially if it does a third of the business."

"And then there's the question of quality." Selma Wellington's comment came literally out of left field. She had gotten up, mostly unnoticed, and gone to the far left of the room to refill her coffee.

Berrian sighed. "What does that mean, Selma?"

"The public school system debated ferociously the quality control of online even when I was still working with the schools. No one had any specific evidence as to whether online students performed better, worse, or the same as in-seat students. The perception certainly was that they didn't."

"Mr. Chairman, may I then recommend that my leadership team bring data about the online delivery, both in terms of enrollment and quality, to a future meeting. With all due respect, there are other items on the agenda that should be addressed."

The board agreed to postpone discussions of online until more concrete data could be identified. The rest of the meeting became, to put it bluntly, downright boring. The concern about Taylor's name on the field house was a non-issue. The board supported pulling his name **if** anything concrete came out about the relationship between this potentially Nazi dead sympathizer and Boan University. Hank led the board through a humdrum conversation of the financial numbers, producing merely a couple of pointed comments that tied back to the opening debate about credits vs. bodies.

The damage was done, though. Even before board member Dejeerling had crossed the street and ascended to his eighth floor office at Gaylord, Dejeerling, and Poindexter, Berrian had called us all into his office to seethe about the direction the meeting had taken. We had less than two weeks to get relevant information together before our retreat. Even before board member Matilda Upton buckled herself up in her chauffeur-driven Rolls Royce and drove out of the specially reserved parking spaces for the Board meeting (student parking was not affected; apparently the career services staff had to find alternate parking for the day), Veronica had sent an e-mail to a number of vice-presidents, deans, and other second level management to clear their following Tuesday for a special University Council meeting. This group typically met every semester, and Berrian essentially moved the November meeting to October. Finally, even before board member Wilson Greystone III could light his second clove cigarette, my phone rang off the hook, as those called to the meeting attempted to clarify why they were being called to it.

As the Administration Building cleared out at the end of the day, Hank, Caroline and I ran into each other in the parking lot. Knowing Berrian had already left for the day, I felt comfortable broaching the unstated: "that was certainly an interesting meeting."

"Bob worked with Jim Oliphant well into the evening last night. I have to imagine there is some tension there." Caroline had changed her heels for tennis shoes.

"Is that typical?" I asked.

"Not for that long a time. Usually he meets with the chair for about an hour prior to the board meeting. Last night he must have been with Oliphant for three hours."

"What kept you here that late, Caroline?" asked Hank.

"Are you kidding? I'm so backed up that I need three or four more nights like that."

Hank veered away from us to get into his green Explorer. "We'll see what carry-over there is to University Council."

Chapter Twelve

T he key person at the center of the University Council meeting turned
out to be Tanya Tyler, Executive Director of Institutional Research. She
and I joked that this would be her coming out party. Despite being hired
five years ago to oversee a completely overhauled research department, she
soldiered on in obscurity, a mistake in several ways. For one, Tanya was a
gorgeous dark-haired woman hired straight out of graduate school. Even
now, as she approached thirty-two years old, she still turned men's heads.
She kept in excellent physical shape, admitting an addiction to her two daily
exercise regimes, and needed little make-up to highlight a delicately soft face.
I reacted with amazement when any man at Boan admitted to not knowing
Tanya Tyler. Second, though, she possessed, more importantly, extraordinary
talent. With an advanced degree in statistics, she remained an under-utilized
resource at the university. She also had enough confidence to call out anyone
who misused or abused data and statistical methodology. And in a university
environment, chances abound to call out those foolish enough to tread where
they don't belong.

Tyler's office was buried in the basement of Dred Hall, alongside human
resources. Tanya had a staff of one, a research assistant who also carried
flawless credentials. When I first started as provost, I asked her about the
underutilization of her expertise and how she managed to stay motivated.
She shrugged her shoulders, saying, "we are happy to fly under the radar. If
people want us, they know where to find us."

Now found, Tanya needed to present to University Council an overview
of data related to program enrollment, online enrollment, trends in online
education, and measures of excellence. In our inability to hone to a single
concern, we in essence asked her for the kitchen sink. When we met with
Berrian prior to the meeting, he reiterated repeatedly that he wasn't expecting

Tyler to have all the answers. Instead, she was charged with identifying the prevailing data trends in any of these key areas.

Get upwards of fifteen to twenty academics in a room, which is what University Council amounted to, and you might as well cut off the gas and turn out the lights. No good can come from it. Some presidents can go into a group setting like that believing with the best intentions that they will receive good feedback, information and advice that in the interest of transparency will help frame leadership's decision-making. Other presidents know that the get-together is symbolic, that there are no expectations for information or epiphanies, but that the participants believe they're part of the decision making.

University Council served as an exemplum of all those councils, committees, task forces, circles across the country. Many members of this group approached that meeting as they would approach a panhandler on the street—with enough cynicism to choke a horse. Other members imbued the University Council with an unnatural sense of enthusiasm and optimism. They were immediately identified by everyone else as the weakest part of the pack, and thus great enjoyment could be found from the anticipated devouring of Mr. or Mrs. Enthusiast by, usually, Dr. Cynic. And the final cadre of council members simply bided their time. Show up with five minutes to spare, enough time to grab a Danish and coffee, speak only when asked a question directly, smile blankly through all presentations, and nod occasionally and appropriately when the president or some other administrator said something profound.

Content ultimately mattered less than sound bites:

"The numbers don't lie."

"There are three kinds of lies: lies, damned lies and statistics."

"The numbers can be twisted to justify everything."

"The math is a little fuzzy here."

"Surveys are useless instruments anyway. No one answers them honestly."

"Yes, but what proof do you have for that?"

"Garbage in; garbage out."

The highlight of the meeting came between Tyler and Kiana King, who, buoyed by a number of cynics with more axes to grind about online than about the meeting itself, attacked the data senselessly, even though most of us in the room recognized she wanted to attack the online education itself.

"When you say, Tanya, that 58% of all credits are taken online, does that mean students choose online 58% of the time?"

"There's no way of knowing that, Kiana," replied Tyler. "That's a whole different set of questions."

"I would think the more important question is student choice. After all, it is 58% of all credits, but in allied health, it is only 28% and nursing, only 17%. So, not all students are choosing to go online."

"That could appear to be true, Kiana, but if you look at page five, you'll see that allied health only offers 25% of its courses online in any one semester, and nursing only offers 15%. Students can't choose something that doesn't exist."

"That's because we know many of those classes can't run effectively online."

"So, how's that student choice?" jumped in Jennifer Riley, who didn't miss many opportunities to highlight faulty logic.

"But, that's my point," responded an exasperated King, looking around the large table for support. She wasn't getting it from me.

King continued to open her mouth and make things worse for herself. "We have to help students make the right choices. It's like it is with my kids. If I put vegetables, grains and chocolate on a plate for them, and let them choose, they'll always choose chocolate."

Howard pretended to awaken from slumber: "There's chocolate? Where?"

Gertrude Fulbright, sitting next to Howard, tapped him a couple of times on the wrist, "now, now, Howard, don't get excited. There is no chocolate. Dean King is using a figure of speech."

"Maybe she can abuse that 'figure' as well as she can abuse the mathematical figures presented here today," muttered Aaron Cartwright sitting directly to my left. I half-turned to smile at him, but maintained superficial visual support of King's commentary.

"What I'm saying is that if we don't give them the right choices, then they will make the wrong choices. What Rachel—and I don't want to speak for her since she's not here—and I have tried to do is limit the online options so that students don't get into an environment where they can't succeed."

Even university politics make strange bedfellows, I thought, listening to Kiana. Here she was aligning with Rachel Linares, when in every other situation, Linares represented her anti-Christ.

"We have to look out for all our standardized testing," King screeched on. "Nursing has its NCLEX results, and again not to speak for Rachel, their students are in the 85% and better pass rate range every year, while our scores for health information exams are in the 90% range every year."

"And those are great results, Kiana," continued Tyler, getting back into the debate. "But, those are exit exams and we really don't have any clue if online courses that **would** have been available would have changed the scores. You're begging the question!"

Victor sought to play peacemaker. "Have we asked students on the student satisfaction survey about their preferences for courses in the online environment?"

"Yes, Victor, we have," responded a calm Tanya. Add grace under fire to beauty plus intelligence for her total package. "The problem is that we have never asked students about individual course preferences. We just ask if they like online courses—and I direct everyone to page seven, where 56% say they do—and whether they would like to have more online course options. Also, on page seven, you'll see that 63% would like more options. We have never been allowed to ask by program or specific course, though." Tyler, who had her long hair braided, twisted a braid with her left hand.

"What do you mean, 'never been allowed'?" asked Berrian.

Tyler hesitated, making sure she got her wording correct: "The decision from academics has been to not drill to that level of detail. The concern was that the survey would get too long and we'd get a poor response rate."

"Is that true, Mark, or Jennifer?"

I looked to Jennifer to confirm the history. "Yes, sir, that is pretty much correct, although in all honesty, academics split on this. Some of us," she pointedly looked toward Fulbright, "believed this could be accomplished with just a few more questions. But, with a house divided, Provost Palmer supported not changing the survey."

"Again, not to speak for Rachel...." King was cut off by Hank.

"You know, for someone who doesn't want to speak for someone, you sure do it a lot."

King paused. For the first time during this discussion an executive leader had stepped in, and she now needed to weigh her strategy. "For me, then, it's just too complicated. We have practicums and laboratory classes, and it just didn't make sense to do experience-based courses online."

"O.k., that's enough," barked Berrian. "In the interest of moving forward, I've heard that Mark will re-assess the questions on the student satisfaction survey related to academic course offerings. He is directed to consider the needs of the students as much as the needs of the colleges."

I nodded my head in confirmation. However, Michael Stewart offered a comment out of nowhere. He'd been so quiet, I'd forgotten he was in the meeting. "The question about student choice is still a reasonable one. I'm not sure I would ever have found myself aligning with my colleagues in health professions, but sometimes students, even in fine arts, don't know what the best thing is for them."

Along side of me I could hear Berrian drawing in his breath to respond.

I used my right arm to encourage him to pause and let me speak. "Michael, your point is certainly relevant. If we give students the choice to sit in a class and do four papers and take four tests and do a team project, but then tell them they can also choose to 'take a class,'"—I did the dreaded quotation marks symbols with my fingers—"where they meet in the commons once a week to play twenty questions about the material, they will choose the easier approach. What we have to do is identify if online can achieve the same outcomes as the in-seat class, whether through the four papers, four tests, and a team project, or through other assessment measures. I certainly have seen nothing to indicate that online can't do that. When we know that, then we can present to students these two different options with the same level of work."

"With all due respect, Mark," jumped King back in, "there isn't that same level of work. Let's face it, courses are much easier online."

"To quote others today, and I can't believe I'm saying this, 'do you have any proof for that?' If you don't have the proof, then get it."

King visibly shrunk from my rebuke. I decided to cut her some slack. "This is an on-going controversy in higher education right now. It is up to all of us to, first, see if we can verify that an online class has the same objectives as an in-seat class, and if so, to confirm if the outcomes for the student are the same. And until we do that, I don't want to hear anyone on my team falling back on the unproven statement that online is somehow 'easier.'"

"Well said, Mark." Berrian slapped me so hard on that back that I lurched forward.

"Be careful, Bob," interjected Howard. "He's finally had his first good idea; don't beat the crap out of him."

"Can I ask a question, then?" said Charlie Durant.

"Go ahead, Charlie," responded Berrian.

"Are we going to do the same for the accelerated deliveries?"

The meeting after that became a blur. Berrian's mood turned dark, and even though I attempted to deflect the discussion of accelerated by saying it was new and we'd have to see, the tension in the room had increased. It's amazing how an elephant can walk into a room, maneuver itself under or over (who knows how he did it) a large rectangular set up of tables, plop his huge butt on the floor in the middle and proceed to be mostly ignored.

In the brief period between University Council and the cabinet retreat, all of executive leadership fought to unbury ourselves from a mountain of e-mails and reports. As the list of topics to be discussed at the retreat increased, the more and more I leaned on people throughout academics to give me information that might be relevant for the retreat. The night before the retreat, I had compiled three notebooks worth of materials. Frankly, everyone had come through for me, with the exception of Linares, who continued to work from home while she and HR debated the extent of her injuries. In order to manage all the various initiatives that ran through the provost, I had set up an elaborate spreadsheet (which I called the Provost Task List) that ran three pages, allowing me to capture and categorize priorities for each, as well as needs related to each one.

In the end, only Charlie Durant, because he oversaw marketing, joined us at the retreat. Several days before we left Veronica sent out the tentative agenda, "tentative" being an overstatement given its formlessness. Apparently the theme for the meetings was the "Boan assurance to Boan stakeholders." Seeing Howard in the hallway minutes after the agenda had been e-mailed to us, we both deliberated about the potential acronym "BABS."

"Barbra Streisand could be a helluva spokeswoman."

"Boan memories may be beautiful and yet," sang Howard.

"You have a lovely voice, Howard," I said, half in jest and half in seriousness. He actually could carry the melody.

"And to our apathetic alumni, she could do 'You Don't Bring Me Sturgeons Anymore.'"

"Please," I begged, "don't bother to sing that one for me."

"So, you think this agenda could be any more non-existent?" asked Howard, lowering his voice and looking around the hallway to make sure we were alone.

I looked at the printout in my hand. After the heading of "Boan assurance to Boan stakeholders," Veronica had listed a rough schedule that was comprised of "brainstorming" for Thursday afternoon, "key findings" for Friday morning, and "next steps" for Friday after lunch. At the bottom, a series of enumerated general questions apparently provided more direction:

1) "What can Boan realistically assure?"
2) "What in the past has Boan assured?"
3) "How do we market assurance?"
4) "What needs to change to deliver our assurance?"

"Ugh, we haven't even gone to Chicago, yet, and I already hate the word 'assurance.'" I crumbled up the printout in disgust and threw it in the nearby wastebasket.

"And we can be pretty sure that at some point in the next year, we'll meet again about this for the purposes of 'reassurance.' Anyway, I'm getting out of here, Mark." Howard also crumbled up his agenda and tossed it into the wastebasket.

Given that we hadn't been spending much time together, I convinced

Natalie and Alyssa to accompany me to Chicago for the retreat. We would
be in the Hyatt in the heart of Chicago, so there would be plenty of things
for them to do while I sat in meetings. The hotel extended our room through
Friday and Saturday nights, meaning the three of us would spend two nights
and almost two days together. With Alyssa in only fourth grade, we justified
pulling her out of school for two days.

We left early on Thursday morning, as the meetings started at 1:00 that
day. Our plan was to get there in time to grab a quick lunch either at the hotel
or nearby before I headed to the meeting rooms.

While I drove into the city, Alyssa, anticipating her visit to Chicago,
and her mother cooed about their plans for shopping and museums. Paying
little attention to their conversation, I tried to organize my thoughts about
the possible meeting discussions. Given the imprecise agenda, I needed to
be prepared to talk about anything even peripherally related to academics.
During our rest stop, I had pulled the Provost Task List out of my briefcase
to review all of the pertinent issues already identified. Not knowing just what
I might be accountable for, my nerves were frayed.

Natalie interrupted my thoughts to needle me about the "retreat" idea.
"Why do they call it a 'retreat' anyway? What is the dangerous situation you
are escaping from?"

"Good point. Crazy students? Insane faculty?"

"Maybe it's the threat of Hartley's murderer still being free?"

"No, that can't be it. I think most of the place would make him king if
he came forward."

"Do you think it was a man?"

I paused. "No, not necessarily. The speculation that the killer had to be
really strong lends credence to that hypothesis, though."

Alyssa, who had been in her own little world, perked up during our
discussion. "You mean they still haven't caught the person who killed that
dean, daddy?"

"No, honey."

"Why not?"

"I really can't say, honey. Sometimes these things aren't easy to figure out.
Mistakes are made, bad luck happens, the investigation gets stalled."

"Being a detective must be a hard job." Alyssa twirled the red hair on
her doll.

"Probably so."

"Doesn't seem fair."

I thought about her point for a few minutes. Natalie searched for a
radio station that didn't promise Rush Limbaugh in the next half hour. "It's
not about fair or not fair, Alyssa. A detective probably has a dozen different

suspects to consider, and must constantly stay on top of information related to all of them. Some of that information may be relevant; some may not be. Some of that information may be outright false; some may be true. The detective has to sort through all that. And somewhere in the middle of investigating all of those possibilities, one suspect emerges as the one to pursue. The detective better hope he's pursuing the right one, because if not, he's lost valuable time chasing other leads." I laughed as I neared the first toll booth for metropolitan Chicago. "I think I just convinced myself that it's not fair, honey!"

Natalie waved my Provost Task List under my nose while our car idled in the long line at to the toll window. "Sounds like you just described this, bucko."

"Great. So, have we just come to the conclusion that being a provost is unfair?"

"Not necessarily. Maybe we've come to the conclusion that the best provosts are like the best detectives."

"Am I Holmes or Clouseau?"

"That depends. Say 'monkey.'"

My spirits thus improved as we managed the nightmare that is driving the Dan Ryan Expressway. Apparently, we lucked out that we hit the Dan Ryan in the mid-to-late morning, after the morning rush hour, but nevertheless more traffic encircled us than we would see anywhere in northern Indiana. We crept and crawled and got to the Hyatt about 11:45. Our room was immediately available, and as we headed to the elevator, we saw Caroline Cruz and her husband entering the lobby. I waved from the elevator, but Caroline either didn't see me, or wouldn't wave. Her husband, Miguel, served as her beast of burden, dragging a heavy suitcase on rollers, while also carrying two briefcases over his right shoulder.

After a quick lunch, I kissed Natalie and Alyssa goodbye at the Italian restaurant close to the Hyatt. I had to hurry to get to the meeting room by 1:00. Natalie and Alyssa would be back in the room by 5:30, the time our afternoon session would, supposedly, end. Everyone, families included, would meet at 6:30 to go to dinner at Brasserie Jo's. Natalie had the afternoon to accomplish the near-impossible task of convincing Alyssa that it would be fun to go to a French restaurant with more than a dozen adults and no other kids. Some days, I'll take the challenges of being a provost over being a parent.

The meeting room provided way too much space for the eight of us. Victor and I moved tables around to create a better central working location. Five easels with flip charts had been left in the room, which also seemed too much, so we brought two of them over to the central work area and left the other three in the corner. Along the wall, the hotel had set up enough cold drinks and cookies for the Chicago Bears. "Is this the set-up we asked for?"

boomed Berrian as he looked around the room. Berrian wore pressed jeans and a pressed red golf shirt, which he kept buttoned all the way to the top button.

"I think so," responded Veronica. "I can check when we get a break."

All of us except Charlie Durant had come in casual clothes. The poor guy probably never received much information about what to expect. As a result, he stood out quite dramatically in his tie and white dress shirt that kept unbuttoning around his beer gut.

Bob settled himself at the head of the table. "Who wants to be the recorder?" he asked, waving a blue marker at us.

"I can do it," said Victor, hopping out of his seat and pulling one of the easels over to where he sat.

"Write down 'Boan's Assurance,' Victor."

Victor did so. He wrote long-hand with elongated tails at the end of the 's' for Boan's and the 'e' for Assurance.

"So, let's have it, gang? What do we mean by the 'Boan Assurance'?"

Only the sound of Veronica continuing to get her laptop set up could be heard. Charlie, the outsider of the group, sat next to Howard and avoided eye contact with Berrian. Given his small eyes and small framed glasses, this was easy for him to do. The rest of us looked at each other, waiting for the first volunteer.

After about a minute, Caroline, in her Boan sweatshirt, raised her hand. "May I ask a question?"

"Certainly."

"Why did you choose the word 'Assurance,' Bob? That's come out of nowhere."

Howard, Hank and I nodded our heads in agreement. For the first time, Charlie raised his head from his notes in front of him.

"It's just a word," responded Berrian.

"Maybe it's just me, boss," confessed Howard, intervening, "but it makes me think of State Farm or Geico, not higher education."

Can't we fall back on "brand'?" asked Caroline.

"I haven't liked that word since that policeman Klinger mocked us for it. I thought about 'guarantee,' but a lot of community colleges use that word. I definitely want to distinguish ourselves from them. So, I just chose 'assurance.' Anybody got anything better?" he asked.

"'Pledge?'" said Victor.

"Windex," responded Howard.

"Don't start already, Howard!" chastised Berrian.

"How about 'promise'?" Durant had made his initial contribution.

"Land-o-Lakes."

"God damn it, Howard."

"Maybe the point behind Howard's jokes," I offered, "is that this pre-occupation with language and labels leads us into the world of commercialization. Is that really where we want to be as an institution of higher education?"

"First off," Howard acknowledged, "there is never a point behind my jokes. Secondly, though, I agree with Mark. Is it really the place for a university to brand itself like a furniture cleaner, or an insurance company, or a, I don't know, pet food, or a television network or, hell, like a tampon?"

I almost spewed my Coke. Howard could surprise with his deft moves between profound thought and superficial wisecrack. "Howard!" shouted Caroline. "Must you always go to the gutter?"

"With all due respect, Caroline, this time there was a point to my joke. Brands are for products and services. Products and services are mass produced and mass consumed. A college education is much more than that."

"I won't disagree with your point, Howard. I just despise the way you deliver it." Howard stuck his tongue out at Caroline, who did at least crack the fraction of a smile.

Excited by this initial round of discussion, I ventured in. "I'm also inclined to agree with Howard. Branding of education lends itself to a certain superficiality that is diametrically opposed to what an education is."

"I think we can have both," asserted Victor, setting the blue marker on the easel and sitting down.

"You can't really have both, because the brand ultimately becomes bigger than the educational experience." I had removed my windbreaker, as the room had heated up.

"Isn't this discussion a superficial way to describe a brand?" asked Charlie. "After all, we're not really looking for a marketing slogan, are we? We're looking for a declaration of what Boan is, right?"

"Well said, Charlie," responded Berrian. "Let's not lose focus of the deeper issue here."

"I think this is the deeper issue, Bob." Howard was hell-bent on this point, and I found great joy in being able to support him.

"And really, Bob, if you think about it, the problem here is that we are working backwards. We're sitting in a room wanting to know what our assurance is, wanting to know who we are, or what we represent. The truth is who we are and what we represent should already be defined. And from that, Charlie takes that definition and forms his marketing strategy."

"University brands develop because of an institution's history. The big guys, Harvard, Stanford, are untouchable and have been for years. The next level of established institutions—Purdue, Butler, Southern Illinois—is just a few steps away from Harvard, Stanford, and Princeton. That's because they've been cultivating and building from their core educational experience. For those of us unfortunately dumped in with the community colleges and DeVry and Indiana Tech, even Phoenix, we often don't want to take the time to cultivate and build our core experience." Caroline had taken three Hyatt writing pads and had built a small teepee while talking.

"But, we don't have the time to do that," proclaimed Berrian.

"I agree," followed up Victor. Charlie nodded his head in agreement.

"Maybe we can look at it this way," said Hank, chiming in for the first time. "Is our educational experience one to be proud of?"

"Of course it is, Hank," bellowed the President.

"If that's really the case, and everyone believes it—and I don't just mean everyone at this table, nor everyone within academics, but if every admissions rep, every custodian, every administrative assistant, every adjunct faculty member, really, truly believes that—then we can say we have that core. I would think, then, we could start to define ourselves around that."

We all sat in silence for a couple of minutes thinking about what Hank had said.

"I didn't mean to do a Dexter Lake Club."

"What the hell, Hank?" asked Bob.

"I'll buy a drink tonight for anyone who knows the reference."

"You mind if we dance with your dates," I responded in my deepest voice.

"*Animal House,*" muttered Howard, slamming his hand on the desk. "How did I miss that?"

"I still have no clue what you are talking about," said Caroline.

"I just always wanted to use that line," admitted Hank.

"Back on point, people. Before Hank went all Howard on us, he brought up an interesting idea. I guess the question is, 'do we all have that pride in our educational experience?' What do you all think?" asked Berrian.

"I'm guessing that beyond leadership this is not the case. Not that people are ashamed of the university, just that they don't know." Caroline turned toward me. "Mark, you're the first key element. You've been here less than two months. Have you found the educational experience something to be proud about?"

I drew in my breath. "That's going to be hard to say at the moment. What I have found is that there are too many languages that require too many interpreters. As we all know, nursing's got its way to describe why its programs are **superb**. Meanwhile, that's significantly different than the allied health programs, where even the definition of a superb medical assisting program can be different from a superb health information management program. And that's just in the health professions. Then, throw in the areas of business, and it gets muddier. The difference between accounting and marketing, for instance, can be tremendous. After that, let's throw in education, or arts and sciences or fine arts, and there's little likelihood of ever getting a common way to phrase what is unique and exemplary of our educational experience."

Hank started to say something, and then noticeably backed off. Bob definitely noticed it.

"What, Hank? You were going to say something."

"I just don't know if this is the place."

"Nonsense. This is the place to say anything and everything."

"Well, I hate to speak about others' reports."

"I want this to be an open discussion." Bob looked around the table. "Let's make a pact now that everything is up for debate the next twenty-four hours. Nothing is sacred, me included."

"You're not sacred, Bob. You're divine." Howard was at it again.

"Christ, Howard."

"Exactly."

"Shut up."

Sitting next to Howard, I leaned over so that only he could hear me. "Are you saying Bob's a cross-dresser?"

"Ooh, a John Waters reference after an *Animal House* reference! This retreat is going to be special."

"Come on, you two," barked Berrian, "Anyway, Hank, what did you want to say?"

"If you ask me, the deans have always taken too narrow of an approach to their programs. Mark's right in that if you asked each dean what makes a quality educational experience, they each would say something different."

"I actually agree, Hank. If you remember, at my interviews, I talked a lot about collaboration and inter-disciplinary approaches to academics. I just haven't had time to get to that. By the way, to be entirely clear, the phrase I've heard everyone saying today is 'educational experience.' That's broader than course and program outcomes. Is that what everybody means?"

"Absolutely," replied Caroline, with everyone else nodding their heads. "It's the life-changing environment that is a college education."

"Great. That should help us. We can initiate an approach to this then that is more than just simply academics. I can use that as the leverage to make sure the colleges get on the same page, or at least in the margins of the same page."

Victor suddenly realized he had not been recording anything. "Uhm, what should I be writing down here?" he asked.

Berrian got up and ripped off the top sheet of Victor's easel with great force. "For one thing, we start anew. Get that marker ready, Victor. Let's capture everything that needs to be considered for the students' educational experience."

And with that charge, all of us proceeded to bombard Victor with suggestions and ideas. In the spirit of true collaboration, we strayed from our own realms of comfort into others' areas to snatch an important piece to consider. Examples weren't simply itemized to be prioritized, but scrutinized and analyzed. Caroline listened openly to a number of critical observations about her advising staff. Hank accepted that some behind-the-scenes functions in his area needed reviewing. I certainly felt no need to defend areas within the curriculum. In fact, Charlie managed to suggest "deliveries" as a crucial piece of the educational experience and Berrian didn't blink an eye. Perhaps we were helped by the frantic pace of all of us being as one in our pursuit of the Boan educational experience. Perhaps Bob just fell asleep at the switch for a moment, considering "deliveries" to be a topic related to stocking the bookstore or supplying the dormitories.

We brainstormed, full of untapped energy, without a break, and when Veronica pointed out to all of us that it was 5:10, we recognized that we had worked pretty much straight through four hours. Nineteen pages of easel notes had been completed and taped to the room's walls. Hyatt staff had apparently come several times to clean up empty beverage containers and plates. For the life of me, I couldn't remember seeing one of them. For the first time since stepping on the Boan campus, I felt like I had finally been part of visioning.

Bob encouraged us to leave the meeting room exactly as it was, and Veronica went to ask Hyatt staff to lock it. "We'll be back here tomorrow morning at 8:30. This isn't going anywhere."

Later when we all met for dinner at Brassiere Jo's, the positive feelings continued to dance around the table. Victor had relaxed so much that he started beating Howard to the obvious double entendres. Berrian, relaxed by at least two whiskey sours, charmed his guests, especially the family members who saw a Bob Berrian that had never been seen, metaphorically, around the family kitchen table.

Even Alyssa enjoyed herself. As is often the case with a single child at a large dinner surrounded by adults, everyone's attention went to her. On the few occasions when we forgot about her, or ignored her, she talked to the stuffed shark she had gotten at the aquarium. Later, in our room, she told me she had named her shark, "Brucie."

"Why?" I asked.

"Someone told me today that Bruce was the name given to the shark during the making of *Jaws*."

"I have no idea, honey, but that sounds right. I thought *Jaws* scared you." Besides, she had never seen *Jaws*.

"Of course not, Daddy," she said, rolling her eyes. "But, one still wants to be wary of any shark."

"I still don't get why that led you to name him Brucie."

"It's just a name, Dad. Get over it."

And seeing how pumped up I still felt about the day's discussion and its future potential, whether during Friday's conversation or how we'd pick all this up once we got back to campus, I did get over it. As was the usual case when we traveled, Alyssa requested that she and I share one of the queen-sized beds in the hotel. Knowing I would only have such opportunities for another couple of years, I gladly acquiesced. Sleep took quite awhile as my mind raced, buoyed by the warmth of Alyssa's body next to mine, Brucie tucked in between us.

On Friday morning, I casually strolled into the morning session, well-rested, primed for the next stage of discussion. Even though I arrived ten minutes early, Berrian and Veronica evidently had been busy for quite awhile already that morning. They'd rearranged the nineteen pages of easel notes taped onto the walls all around the room. The one that took the dominant focal point had "deliveries" boldly highlighted across the top.

Victor and Howard were already in the room. I stood next to Howard while getting my coffee.

"Be careful of the big guy today, Mark," whispered Howard.

"What do you mean?" I whispered back, looking at Berrian deep in quiet conversation with Veronica about the notes she had taken on Thursday.

"Victor and I aren't sure, but something's clearly gotten under his skin. Victor says Berrian came to the meeting room by 6:30. Look, let's step in the hall." As Howard left the room, he moved near Victor and grabbed him by the arm to pull him to the door.

Out in the hallway, Howard nudged Victor to stand between him and me. The hallway was empty, although somewhere a vacuum could be heard.

"Tell him what Bob said to you this morning, Victor."

"I was the first one here besides him and Veronica. Before I even had a second to say 'good morning,' or to grab my coffee, Bob said, 'I'm taking control back again today, Victor.'"

I must have looked as perplexed as I felt. "He said, what?"

"He said, 'I'm taking control back again today.'"

"What the hell does that mean?" asked Howard. "What the hell does that mean?"

"Do you think he meant that Victor had control yesterday? That's insane. You only recorded, Victor."

"I don't know. But he said it in that way that we all know tells us to give him a wide berth."

Down the hallway came Hank. Even from a distance, we could tell that he was not his normal self. Howard grabbed his arm before he went into the room.

"Hank, Bob's sending weird signals this morning. He seems pissed about something."

"Of course he's pissed about something. He called me at 3:00 AM to let me know he was pissed." Hank looked as if he had gotten little sleep.

"He called you at 3:00 AM? Christ." I counted my blessings that I wasn't his early morning call.

"What did he vent about?" asked Victor.

"Accelerated deliveries. I got a 3:00 AM briefing about how leadership better understand that the need for speed represented the future of higher education."

"I wondered yesterday," I offered, "how that topic slipped through without him saying something. I guess he must have figured it out in the middle of the night."

"Yeah, I think we all held our breaths when Charlie first brought that up."

"So what does this mean for today?" asked Victor.

"Bunker mentality. Keep your head down. And when he lobs the grenade labeled 'accelerated deliveries,' protect your family jewels." Howard covered his crotch with his hands.

"I know the first thing to do to save my goodies. I ain't going to be late," said Hank, pushing open the meeting room door. The rest of us promptly followed.

"Well, well, if it isn't the four horsemen of the apocalypse," announced Berrian.

"Shucks, I thought we were your four apostles, Bob," said Howard, counting on humor to please the president.

Berrian ignored him. "Let's get settled. As soon as Caroline gets here, let's get going."

"Don't forget, Charlie," said Veronica.

"Charlie? Oh yeah, Durant. What a waste to bring him along."

His remark came across as spectacularly unfair, as Durant had been a valuable member of the discussion yesterday. However, Berrian must have remembered that poor Charlie mentioned the accelerated deliveries, or more fairly, all deliveries, as a point of analysis. I was determined to throw myself on a mine or two to support Charlie here, not because of Charlie, per se, but as a statement regarding the integrity of this whole process.

Within five minutes, Charlie and Caroline had arrived and Berrian wasted no time launching into a diatribe. "This notion that accelerated deliveries need to be examined as part of the 'educational experience' is bullshit. Once we identify that education experience, it has to be delivered in whatever manner suits the students. The deliveries will carry the Boan experience, not be subjected to the analysis of it."

"Bob, I'd like to disagree," I said, even before Charlie Durant had probably processed what Berrian said. "The deliveries...."

"Everyone here knows you disagree, Mark. These have been on your radar since you started."

"Hold on a minute, Bob, let me finish the thought."

"I'm saying, Mark, that deliveries need to be pulled off this list. They are not relevant to the core discussion of educational experience." Berrian walked up to the sheet of the paper with "deliveries" written across the top and crossed through it with a red marker.

"Damn it, Bob, didn't you say yesterday that 'nothing is sacred, not even you'?"

"There's nothing sacred, here, Mark. It's just an irrelevant point."

"Well, evidently, some of us think it is relevant."

"He's right, Bob," said Caroline.

"I concur," said Howard.

"It at least needs to be discussed," responded Hank.

"Heck, I'm the idiot that brought it up," admitted Charlie.

Only Victor said nothing, although he did offer barely visible nods of agreement.

The debate went on for a half hour about whether to include deliveries in the analysis. Later in telling Natalie about the sequence of events, I would call it the "decelerated discussion of accelerated deliveries." Finally, Berrian demanded we take a break and the argument died. When he came back, he requested Victor to start recording our committee recommendations for every topic from Thursday except deliveries. The rest of us, spent, discouraged and wary, never brought up the topic of "deliveries" again. We figured we would find out soon enough its fate.

Perhaps, dampened by our lack of energy and stricken teamwork, Berrian called the retreat over at lunchtime. We all scuttled out of the meeting room with our specific assignments regarding committee formation and the definition of Boan educational experience. A few of us grunted 'have a good weekend' to each other, but even those of us staying in Chicago for the extended weekend consciously avoided the others. Because Natalie and Alyssa were on Michigan Avenue shopping, I decided to not even try to reach them to ask them to return to the hotel or to meet elsewhere. Instead I walked to the lakeshore, picked up small stones, and tossed them into the lake, watching the concentric ripples until my arm started to hurt.

Part Four:
Comprehensive Exams

Chapter Thirteen

Autumn paradoxically gave my work new life and energy. As the leaves changed color and fell off the trees, most of my projects and interactions with others blossomed into spring-like blooms and gave me a sense that I was finally firmly rooted at Boan. It wasn't easy to see this forest through the trees, though, but I never stopped wanting to look.

Rachel Linares returned to work on the Monday following the cabinet retreat. Her doctor gave her a clean bill of health, and Victor and I decided we wouldn't challenge her fifteen days of leave. The nursing accreditation was still scheduled for November 2 and 3, and Victor suggested that none of us wanted to risk that by antagonizing the dean. Linares understood this dilemma, and, according to many people who saw her in the halls, wore a smug look that confirmed it. I definitely walked a fine line between supporting her and confronting her.

In the final two weeks before the visit, she blustered about campus, getting the university ready for the accreditation visit. She requested that everyone from the president down to administrative assistants attend mock site visits, where we would be prompted to say what needed to be said and coached to act the way we needed to act. All of us, she claimed, must convince the NLNAC visitors that no expense, no support mechanism, no necessity, or luxury for that matter, had been spared for our nursing students.

Despite my better judgment, I did dedicate time at a provost's circle meeting to Rachel's accreditation checklist.

Her requests started immediately. "Shelley, make sure all the provost's circle minutes are up to date for the last five years."

"The last five years, Dr. Linares? I only have the last year since I've been in the position."

"Well, that's ridiculous. Certainly someone saved copies of the previous meetings?"

"I'm not sure. That would have been when Candi Philpott was Provost Palmer's secretary."

Rachel flashed an exaggerated grimace. "Well, can anyone contact her to see if she saved minutes? Or, Mark, can you contact Palmer?"

Jennifer Riley stepped in for Shelley. "Don't worry about it, Shelley. Rachel, you know as well as the rest of us that minutes from Palmer's meetings were sketchy and often never completed. I'm sure the minutes you saved are as comprehensive as anything we could find hidden in Palmer's basement or Philpott's attic."

"Well, all I have in my office is a fairly thin file that barely captures one-third of the previous four years."

"That's all any of us are going to have."

Rachel drummed her fingers on the table and thought for a minute. "O.k., here's what we'll do. Charlotte?"

"Yes," said Webb, with a jaundiced look.

"In the resource room, what I need you to do is put all the old provost's circle minutes into the deepest part of the highest filing cabinet you have. If we're lucky we'll get some short, tired site visitor who just won't want to take the effort to dig that deeply into the file cabinet."

"That's who we'd get if we're lucky?" I laughed. "If we're unlucky, do we get Nurse Lockhart from 'ER'? Because if we do, I'm walking under a ladder tomorrow."

Charlotte either ignored me or hadn't heard me. "I don't have those minutes, Rachel. I've only been attending provost's circle for about a year and a half."

"Don't worry. I'll send mine over to you. Don't lose them, though!"

Charlotte rolled her eyes, which Rachel completely missed as she focused on her checklist.

"Next, labs. We need all the labs completely stocked and spic and span. Gertrude, you have directed the science lab coordinators to review their equipment and materials lists, correct?"

"Absolutely, Rachel, ever since you first reminded us to do this in September."

"Excellent. Excellent. According to the schedule, we will bring the visitors through during a lab session with students. That's scheduled to be Warren Everest's class. Can I count on him?"

"Count on him. Subtract on him. Divide on him. Just don't multiply on him."

"Very funny, Jennifer."

"All kidding aside, Rachel, 'count on him' to do what?"

"Not to embarrass me in front of our visitors."

Jennifer looked disgusted. I gave her a smile to suggest she just grin and bear it. "You can count on him to be his wonderful self teaching the class," Jennifer finally responded. "The rest is up to you."

I fought back the urge to laugh. I couldn't make eye contact with either one of them. Instead, I watched a squirrel looking for food outside the window.

Linares paused and gave Riley a pained look.

"He'll be fine, Rachel."

"Excellent. Excellent. O.k., let's see, what else?"

"Uh, Rachel, we may have one problem?" Trudy had the hint of a smile.

"Yes?"

"If you remember, some of the refrigeration units in the biology lab were vandalized a few weeks ago. As a result, we have had some issues with the cats."

"The cats?" I asked.

"Uh, yes, the dead cats."

"Damn it, Gertrude. What's the problem?" snapped Linares.

"Well, with no place to store them, Jackie Walton has taken to keeping them in the trunk of her car."

"What the hell?" I said.

"I wish this was a joke, Mark, but sadly not. We have no place to store them, so Jackie keeps a huge cooler in the trunk of the car, leaves the cats in there and transfers the cooler to and from the labs and her car every day."

"Just when I think things can't get stranger. Dead cats? Really?" I said flabbergasted. "And who is Jackie Walton?"

"She is the lab coordinator," said Fulbright.

"Wait a second," interjected Kiana King. "When you say 'cooler,' is this that olive green one she brings to the spring picnic every year?"

"Yep."

"The olive green cooler that is usually loaded with fruit and veggie trays?"

"Oh, yeah, that one."

A collective "ewww" went up from the table. "Remind me to pack my own for next year's picnic," I said.

"Stop it, everybody. We've got a lot of ground to still cover here. Gertrude, is there any hope of fixing the storage units by November 2?" Rachel looked exhausted.

"As you know, it's not my call. It's facilities."

"Mark, could you push facilities to get that fixed? There's no way I'm going to allow a site visitor to see a cooler of dead cats lying around." Linares wrote herself a note, and then proceeded down her checklist.

"Other last minute things to discuss with facilities, Mark, include improved signage, new chairs for the faculty offices and the nursing student lounge, damaged lockers, the carpet in the nursing labs hallway, and more filing cabinet space in the faculty office lounge. Here, I'll just give you this list." She handed it to Shelley, who exchanged a quick glance with me, as she passed it along.

I looked at the list. "There are some things here, Rachel, that we're not going to be able to do anything about in the next two and a half weeks. Like new carpet or new chairs."

"We have to have the chairs, Mark. The NLNAC looks at the physical environment very closely."

"What the hell do you want us to do? If they weren't budgeted back in June, I'm not going to force that now."

"Oh, come on. Move the money around as need arises."

"I still don't like it. Are there chairs elsewhere you can move into those areas for those couple of days?"

Linares gave me the same unpleasant stare she had given Fulbright earlier. "Why does this have to be so hard?" Finally she tossed her hands up in despair. "O.k., plan B. The library has those new chairs. Let's swap them out with the ones in the offices and lounge."

"Don't you dare," snapped Charlotte. "It took us almost three years to get those chairs."

"Hold on, Charlotte, I'm only asking for them for about three days total."

"No. They'll get beat up and destroyed." Charlotte looked pleadingly at me. "Mark, I know this sounds stupid and selfish, but it was a nightmare. We put in requests for new chairs every year and had them ignored. Meanwhile the old chairs were falling apart. They looked ratty; many of them were unsafe. The only reason we finally got these new ones is that we found out Berrian was going to bring some big-time donor through the library, so we put the worst ones where they could see them."

Jennifer Riley laughed. "This is true, Mark. In fact, Bob went to sit in one and the wheels came flying off and he collapsed on the floor."

"Oh, I would have loved to see that," I admitted. "Any chance it's on YouTube?"

Charlotte giggled. "We really didn't want it to be that blatant, but it worked. Within two weeks we had all new chairs."

"Don't laugh too openly about it, Charlotte. I did a lot of damage control for you."

"I know, Jennifer, and I appreciate it."

"How is all this helping me to get better chairs for the accreditation visit?" demanded a pouting Linares.

"Chill down, Rachel. I'll talk to facilities and see if there are other temporary solutions."

Rachel took a deep breath. "O.k. Thanks. Now, has everybody seen the schedule for the mock visits?"

"How could we not? They're plastered everywhere," said the usually silent Michael Stewart.

"You can't swing a dead cat and not hit one of the signs, Rachel," proclaimed Gertrude.

"And she should know. She knows where the dead cats are kept," said Jennifer.

"Dang you beat me to it." One had to be quick around this place, that's for sure.

"Stop joking around." Linares turned bright red.

"Cool off, Rachel. Forgive us for a little bit of mockery surrounding a mock visit." Unmoved by my argument, she stared at me for several seconds. "So, will there be anything else, Rachel?"

"No."

Linares didn't speak the rest of the provost's circle meeting. Undoubtedly, in her eyes no other topics related directly to nursing. I raised this with her immediately after the meeting, when everyone else had left.

"Rachel, one of the things I want you to continue to work on is more collaboration and support of areas outside of nursing. You did it again today. As soon as your section of the meeting ended, you checked out."

Linares tried to maneuver around me so that she could get out the door. However, I had effectively blocked her escape route.

"Is that an order, Mark?"

"Good lord, Rachel. No, it's a 'directive.' Call it whatever you want."

"I have to say, Mark, I really resent … ."

"Stop it right there, Rachel. I've been patient but you are crossing a line."

After a few seconds, she sighed, "Yes, Mark. I will do that." Based on the fact that she left the room by slamming the door behind her, I was pretty sure she wouldn't.

I let out a primordial yell. A facilities guy opened the door and asked, "You o.k.?"

I assured him I'd be fine, especially once the accreditation visit faded into memory. He showed no sign of understanding my pain.

As the visit got closer, I made an appointment with the president to review the accreditation visit to discuss our roles. Berrian had been low-key since the cabinet retreat and lacked the emotion and vigor that characterized his personality. Regardless of the unpredictability of his moods, his core nature of bravado and high energy had initially attracted me to working for him.

I set up the discussion of the accreditation visit outside of a normal one-on-one meeting. This had been upon my request, as I planned to make it a fairly quick meeting in my office. He made few comments regarding the logistics of the schedule, such as our welcoming the visitors when they first arrived, or about the way they would have complete access to our resource room and to any staff member, faculty member or student. Berrian had survived dozens of accreditation visits and recognized the standard operating procedure of them. When I pointed out that the board chair, he and I needed to meet with the visitors, then he took umbrage. Just not in the usual fiery Berrian way.

"Do we really need to have the board chair there?" he asked with a touch of resignation in his voice.

"I don't know for sure, Bob. The trick is always to figure out what the NLNAC demands and what our dean demands. I can double check. You're saying that you'd prefer it just be you and me?"

"Yes. Oliphant is much too busy to have to come to campus for thirty minutes to meet some ditzy nurse."

"Uh, sure." I hesitated, waiting to see if he might say more. When he didn't, I continued. "In fact, I will just tell Linares that the board chair is unavailable and that if the NLNAC has a problem with it, you and I can discuss it with them."

Bob nodded sluggishly. He turned and stared out my window.

"Do you mind if I ask you something personal, Bob?"

"Uh, sure, go ahead."

"Are you o.k.?"

"Oh, yeah. Just a little burned out today to be truthful."

"If you ask me, you've looked this way for over a week."

"I have?" He paused to think about that. "Yep, I suppose I have."

"Do you need a vacation? You haven't taken any time off since I started here."

"That might help. Luckily, the holiday season is almost here."

"Well, if you're like me, that's no holiday. My parents will come to town for Christmas, so there'll be a lot of work in getting ready for them."

Berrian stood up and walked over to the window. "Nah. That's not the case for us. We're going to go to the Bahamas for the Christmas break."

"That sounds great."

"I suppose so." He continued to stare out the window.

"Bob, would you like to do this later? In fact, I'm not sure there's a whole lot more to brief you about. You've gone through more of these things than I have."

The president looked at me for a couple of seconds. Instead of answering me, he changed the direction of the conversation. "I forget, Mark; did we talk about your long-term ambitions at your interview?"

"I think we did. I don't remember what I answered, though. Why?"

"Is being a university president one of your ambitions?"

"I don't think you asked that specifically. I'm not sure, actually. I climbed the career ladder so quickly always enjoying the challenges that came with each successive step. Four years ago I'm not sure I would have said I wanted to be a provost."

"A presidency is a whole different world."

Unsure how to respond I waited for him to provide direction.

Berrian pulled a book off my book shelf. I couldn't tell which one. He opened it, leafing through the pages aimlessly. Finally, he looked back at me. "I've got another meeting with Oliphant tomorrow. He has been all over me regarding the board's concern about Boan's stability."

"Are we unstable? How does he mean?"

"Mostly, it's that fucking Hartley thing. God, I wish the cops would arrest somebody. But, the truth of the matter is they picked at us even before Hartley died."

Still not knowing how to respond, I merely nodded.

"They're all over the damn place about enrollment. You heard it at the board meeting. Do they want traditional students or do they want adult students? Do they understand the different needs for those kinds of students? They want more sports visibility, but they don't support us having a football team. They want big donors, but they're not willing to donate the big money themselves." He slammed the book down on the table. It was John Baldoni's *Lead by Example*, a present from Natalie a few years ago.

"This does explain a lot, Bob. Some of the questions at the board meeting did puzzle me."

"One of them will read something in the paper and will expect us to follow suit. For instance, a few years ago, Matilda Upton read that Oprah Winfrey had set up an endowment scholarship for students at Morehead College. She pushed and pushed for us to set up something similarly. To this day, I still don't think Matilda really understands the personal relationship Oprah has with Morehead."

'Thank god, Howard isn't here,' I thought. 'He wouldn't have allowed that line to slide by.'

I smiled. "I can only imagine how that went."

"Oh, I'm not sure you can, Mark. She demanded that we ask Mike Douglas to do something similar for us. We pointed out he was dead. She then said Merv Griffin. We pointed out he was dead. She finally got us with Larry King. We, unfortunately, couldn't point out that he was dead. So, I put her off and eventually told her that he wouldn't return our call."

I laughed loudly, and the humor began to work on Berrian a little too. "I'll pass on the obvious 'Larry King corpse jokes,'" I said, "but will point out that he probably wouldn't if you did ask, so you can take solace in that."

"Then, there's that freak Greystone, who has been asking for a mortuary science degree even since I've been here. And if that wasn't bad enough, he discovered that his kid's new nanny had a professional nanny degree from some college in Kentucky, and he requested us to start a nanny program."

I laughed even more loudly than before. "My god, Bob, I had no idea how bad it could be."

Berrian began to laugh uncontrollably also. "Wait, wait. Here's the pièce de résistance: just last year, Matilda read about the University of Virginia partnering with some website, something called 'Doostang,' I believe, and told us we were missing the opportunity to partner with the 'hip internet thing.' Howard, in his typical way, wouldn't let it drop, and kept asking who she wanted us to partner with. Finally, she said we should partner with 'Faithbook.'"

We both laughed so loudly that Shelley popped her head in. "Everything o.k. in here?"

"We're fine," nodded Berrian. After Shelley had shut the door and we had stopped laughing, he spoke again. "What's most frustrating is that they're so unpredictable."

No matter how comfortable I had felt the last few minutes, I wasn't going to tell him what I thought ("Mr. Pot meet Mr. Kettle"). Instead I bit down on my tongue so hard that I almost drew blood and figured the time had come to move on. "Anyway, Bob, I'll let Linares know that Oliphant will not be available for the accreditation visit. We'll be fine."

And we were fine. The NLNAC site visitors came, snooped around a lot, and kept Linares running. Berrian turned on the charm when we met with them and they left satisfied that nursing was our primary academic priority. We almost certainly received help from an opportunistic and coincidental meeting between the lead nurse for the accreditation team and a famous alumnus.

The men's basketball team would play its first game of the year the night of the nurses' visit, and we had an unannounced appearance by Sherman Head. He arrived on campus in the late afternoon, and was being escorted around campus by Athletic Director Howell, when the lead of the site visit,

Bertie Muldoon, saw Head from afar while Linares and I escorted her from Weaver Hall to the resource room in the library.

"Oh my goodness," said Muldoon, a tall, stately woman with silver-grey hair, rings on six fingers, and a genuine New England accent. "Is that Sherman Head?"

"If I'm not mistaken, I do believe it is, Dr. Muldoon," I replied, squinting across the square.

"Oh, please call me Bertie. What is he doing here?"

"He's one of our alumni. I assume he's shown up for the opening game tonight."

Linares tried to grab Muldoon's arm to turn her towards the library, but she certainly would have nothing to do with that.

"Please introduce me to him!" she begged.

"Dr. Muldoon," said Linares. "The resource room is this way. I'm sure Dr. Haygood is waiting for you there." Haygood was the second member of the visiting team.

"Frederika can wait. I must meet Sherman Head."

"I've actually never met him either, Bertie," I stated, "otherwise, I'd gladly introduce you."

"Come on," responded Linares begrudgingly, "I've met him before. I'll introduce you."

"Oh, goody," replied Muldoon, sounding more like a fifteen-year old girl than a leader of a powerful nursing association.

Getting closer to Head, who had stopped to talk to some students, I realized he was thinner than he looked on television. Standing just under seven feet tall, his dark, ebony skin gleaming from the late afternoon sun, he appeared almost brittle. A Boan coed, probably just under five feet, talked to him, her beaming face looking up (way up) at him.

"Sherman?" called out Linares as we approached. "Dean Linares. Remember, for the nursing program?"

"Uh, sure," he responded, although he probably didn't have a clue.

"I wanted to introduce you to a big fan of yours, Dr. Bertie Muldoon. She is with the NLNAC." Muldoon held out her hand, practically shoving the coed out of the way.

"NLNAC? What's that?" Head inquired, shaking Muldoon's hand.

"The National League for Nursing Accreditation Commission." She held tightly onto Head's hand, refusing to let go.

"What? Is there an American League, too?" Head asked with a big smile.

"Oh, boy, as if we haven't heard that one before," muttered Linares.

"Very funny, Sherman. Can I call you Sherman?" If Muldoon had been any more obsequious, she would have needed to drop to her knees.

"Why wouldn't you?"

"Thank you. By the way, I was always so disappointed that Boston traded away that draft pick the year the Nuggets picked you. You would have looked great in Celtic Green."

"Ugh. Not the dreaded Celtics. Sorry, Ma'am, but I hated those SOB's on that team when I played."

Muldoon laughed so awkwardly that my skin crawled.

"You know," she went on, "I played basketball when I was in college. Mount Holyoke College."

"You don't say." Head looked over at me and Linares as if expecting us to step in. Figuring I still hadn't been introduced to the man, I wasn't going to interrupt.

"Starting center for three years. Averaged almost 10 points and 8 rebounds a game over my college career."

"You must have been something."

"Still am, hot stuff. Don't think I can't give you a run for the money."

"I'm sure you could, Ma'am."

Bill Howell, who had been on his cell phone during the exchange, came over and tried to extract Head from the situation.

"Hey, Rachel," said Muldoon, breaking eye contact with Head for the first time, "you got a nice field house over there. Think Sherman and I could go over there and shoot a few hoops."

Linares rolled her eyes, looked at her watch, and started to say something. I jumped in.

"There will be a game there in a few hours, Dr. Muldoon. That's probably why Mr. Head came in today." Turning toward Head, I held out my hand. "Hi there. Mark Carter. New provost. We haven't had a chance to meet."

As we shook hands, I continued. "If you both want to come back Friday, I could probably get you in with the administration basketball league." Head raised a skeptical eyebrow. Muldoon ignored me. "Undoubtedly, Berrian has you on his team even before we show up, Sherman."

"Anyway," interjected Howell, "I need to drag Sherman to meet some parents. We're already late." He pulled Head to his right, toward the field house.

"And we have to get you to the resource room, Dr. Muldoon," encouraged Linares, pulling her to the left, toward the library.

"I would like to see that game tonight, Rachel. Can we fit that into our schedule?" Without waiting for an answer, she turned back toward me and the retreating Head and Howell. "I'll see you at the game tonight."

Linares turned around and gave me a dirty look, as if I had done anything to create this situation. I watched Muldoon and her walk into the library, then I raced to catch Howell and Head.

"Hey, Bill," I said, getting him to turn around. "Don't worry, I'm not with the creepy groupie brigade." Bill smiled and slowed down his pace. Head also turned around.

"If you can," I said, "let Dr. Muldoon see Sherman again tonight. Nursing accreditation is a big thing, and I'm not above whoring our most famous alumni for five or ten minutes more to make sure we get it."

Howell looked horrified, but to his credit, Head smiled and nodded. "By the way, if you're provost, can you help expedite the decision about me getting a name on a building? I got this mighty big check that you people don't want to cash."

"I am aware of that, Sherman, and I promise to look into it and help out. Feel free to call me anytime. Bill can give you my extension number."

In the end, Muldoon went home with a Boan t-shirt signed by Sherman Head. Head went home with a member of the executive team ready to support whatever naming opportunity he wanted. And six weeks later, Boan received a letter from the NLNAC saying that we would have our accreditation extended with no citations.

Chapter Fourteen

Not everything revolved around nursing, although Linares believed so. Going for a couple of quick fixes within the faculty ranks, the university rolled out two changes related directly to the faculty. Supported by human resources, the tuition support policy for advanced degrees for faculty was blessed and vetted through a faculty task force. Along side of that Victor and I proposed a faculty recognition program supported by cabinet. At a full faculty meeting in early November, I laid out the parameters of it. Many faculty fought with the usual vim and vigor reserved for any program "passed down" from administration:

"What will prevent this program from just being another popularity contest?" asked a perpetually grumpy faculty member, who legitimately had little chance of ever winning such popularity contests.

"You're going to get the same faculty from the same 'chosen' programs and disciplines receiving it every year," argued a math faculty member whose failure rate in his classes would have embarrassed even a WB network executive.

"If you don't publicize the nominating committee and the criteria they use, then this is just hogwash. Where will be the transparency?" challenged another faculty member who refused every year to submit her syllabi to central administration on time.

"Is there money attached to it?" asked a fourth faculty member who with overloads made more money than I did.

However, these were the usual cranks, and most challenges were shot down by faculty members who saw the program's best intentions. People like Henry Van Wyck who weren't afraid to stand up in a meeting and call out the wolves in sheep clothing.

A more challenging subject during this period concerned the fate of fine arts. Although Berrian told me he expected it to be eliminated, even if it had to be supported by forced data, I knew that if the data showed differently, I would fight for the college. In an initial meeting with Tanya Tyler and Michael Stewart, we talked at length about the minute amount of data we already had. It did not look promising, but Stewart was appreciative of being part of the discussion. I'm also sure he was smitten by Tyler. He wasn't a fool if he was.

"If you look at this enrollment report," said Tyler at this first meeting, "you'll see that enrollment in the college has fallen most dramatically among returning students. See, your new students, Michael, are about the same for the last six years...." Sure enough, the report showed anywhere from thirty-three to forty-seven new students per year. "However, on page two, you can see that a lot of your students don't make it to graduation. Most don't return between the sophomore and junior year."

"That's odd," I commented, looking at the table on page two. Fine arts had a 10% drop in returning students from freshman to sophomore year, 21% drop from sophomore to junior, and then only a 3% drop from junior to senior year. "As both of you probably know, attrition is usually between the first and second years. You have any thoughts about this trend, Michael?"

Stewart stared longingly at Tyler. She appeared unaware of his interest. "I'll ask some of the faculty, Mark, to see what they think," he said. "Ironically by the junior year, they would be almost entirely in their major courses, so I would hope that's when they really want to stay."

"That's unfortunately not the case, so we'll need to figure that out."

"Competitive analysis is our next hurdle," said Tanya.

"Ugh," uttered Stewart. "Does this have to involve the competition metaphor?"

"Don't blame me," replied Tanya. "Does it make you feel better to know that my whole life has been about sizing up competition? After all I did track and field and tennis in college." Tanya attempted to make light of the serious conversation, but she didn't realize the effect she had on the visibly licentious Stewart, who no doubt imagined her in a tennis skirt.

I tried to snap him out of it. "What's our competition doing? That's got to help, right, Mike?" He looked at me like a cow lost in thought in the middle of a large field.

Tanya continued, "What we also need, Michael, is information about enrollment in similar programs around the country? Would you have any of that?"

"Uh, not really. I mean, generally, the feeling is that students aren't as attracted to the arts as they once were." Michael glanced quickly at Tanya than looked away.

'Good lord,' I thought, 'this is like a high school dance. The nerd is completely intimidated by the girl.'

"Data, though, Michael. Data is what we need." Tanya was either oblivious to Michael's reactions or doing a heck of a job at working through them.

Michael sighed. "I know. I know."

"What professional journals do you subscribe to? Are they likely to have this information?"

Michael hung his head in embarrassment. "I'm afraid I haven't subscribed to anything in years."

"Really?" I said with more incredulity than I intended, given that Tanya was also in the room.

Tanya ignored me and continued pushing Michael for additional data resources: "Do you belong to any listservs where you might get this information?"

"Lip service? What?"

"A listserv. It's, uh, oh, never mind." Tanya laid her pen down and looked at Michael and then me. "Tell you what, Michael, I'll do some research on how other universities are doing. Do you have any colleagues at other schools you could talk to and ask them how their enrollment is and what they are doing? I'm not sure we're going to build a case on their anecdotal responses, but it's something."

"I'll do that. How soon would you like that information?"

"It's your neck, Michael," I joked, speaking for Tanya. "I would suggest you get whatever you can as soon as possible. You want to save the college, right?"

"Of course I do, Mark."

Tanya reinforced that she would share as soon as possible whatever additional information she could get, and then she said goodbye. Michael's eyes followed her as she swayed out of the room.

"Michael? Michael? Attention, Michael."

"Uh, sorry, Mark. I'm probably not really subtle, am I?"

"As subtle as a Fox News reporter."

Michael gave me a half laugh, then started to gather up his things. "Truth be told, Mark," he said, "I'm not sure I want to save the college."

"Nonsense, Michael. That's just fatigue talking."

"No, in all honesty, I don't think the fine arts programs fit with the way Boan has changed over the last decade. We're a remnant of an older Boan where arts and sciences and fine arts were the premiere colleges. Now, it's education, nursing, and business that get all the press. Just a sign of the times."

"Well, let's just see what the competitive analysis shows us."

"Either way, Mark, I really do appreciate the effort you've put in regarding this. I just wish I believed it could do any good."

Good lord, if he was more of a wet blanket, he'd have to be dry-cleaned. Nevertheless, I sat there knowing that the president already believed in an outcome that offered no reason for optimism. Sometimes it is better to be Billy Pilgrim than Don Quixote. Nevertheless, touched by Michael's appreciation, I vowed to continue to explore every avenue possible for the College of Fine Arts.

Later that night, as Natalie and I sat on the couch, staring at our backyard, enjoying our peace and quiet with Alyssa in bed, I described the bizarre dynamic with Stewart and Tyler. She commented that she grew tired of only hearing about this cast of characters in my work life and wanted to meet some of them.

"That's actually a great idea," I responded. "Let's have a holiday party."

Natalie revealed her panic. "Uh, which holiday?" Thanksgiving was barely two weeks away.

"Christmas."

"Thank goodness. I almost regretted opening my big mouth."

"I'm not sure who I want to invite, though. I'm not comfortable mixing executive leadership with my direct reports."

"Why not?"

"You've heard me talk about all of them over the last few months. I'd say they mix as well as oil and water, but that's an insult to oil and water."

"Well, you decide. I don't care either way. I'll just need to know how exemplary my behavior will have to be."

"You have exemplary behavior?"

I barely dodged the low-flying pillow.

In the end, I did decide to mix the two groups. We chose a date at the beginning of the university's Christmas break, when Berrian should be on his trip to the Bahamas. Apart from him, I had no great trepidations of the conversations that might ensue.

Meanwhile, curriculum vitae and cover letters for the dean of education arrived in droves. Many people around the world believed they could answer the call, almost as many wasted our time. The search committee and I met right before Thanksgiving to identify candidates to interview. We wanted to interview five or six candidates for the first round, but an initial pass around the table revealed thirteen potential candidates in terms of basic credentials and our expectations for the position. As a result, we had to set aside significant time to discuss all thirteen and whittle the list down.

I let Dewayne Wilson run the discussion. He was the chair and while everybody in the room knew that decision eventually ended up with me, it still made sense to let him control the discussion, with me jumping in as needed.

"Let's look at Bonnie Niedermeyer first," said Wilson. "She's the Ed.D. from Eastern Michigan University who has been an assistant dean at Wisconsin-Green Bay the last five years."

"Oh, yes, I remember her materials," spoke Greg Friend, education faculty member on the committee. "I liked her. She has progressively advanced through her career and this seems like the natural next step."

"I don't like her," responded Sarah Kennedy, arts and science faculty member asked to assist on the committee. "The cover letter is tooooooo long, and she has a couple of typos on her C.V."

"Where?" asked Friend.

"On page five, her third publication on the page: it says, "Autistic 'Kinds.' That should be 'Kids.'"

"Wow, you actually read all that crap on the publications pages," said Friend. "No wonder I missed it."

"It's not good," criticized Christina Llewellyn in support of Kennedy, "when someone has a typo in their own publication."

"She also did it on the last page. Twice. Once on the year of her Master's degree. She typed 1984, when she probably meant 1994." Wilson held up his copy of her C.V. to show the group the mistake.

"I see what you mean," said Friend. "Her Bachelor degree is listed as 1991, so it would stand to reason that the Master's is meant to be 1994. Hmm?"

"Finally, note that she says 'References Available Upon Respect.' She got killed by spell-check on that one."

"I see that, Dewayne," responded Friend, "but I still think she is someone to consider."

Debate about the second candidate did not improve. Friend immediately expressed concern that the man had a New York background: degrees from the State University of New York, faculty positions at Buffalo University and more recently St. John's University. "Why does this guy even want to leave New York?" he pondered.

"Isn't it a bit premature to even speculate about that?" asked Wilson. "If during the interview we found we liked him, we could ask that kind of question, then." He looked at me for confirmation: "Right, Mark?"

"Definitely."

Friend continued. "I don't think we want one of them fancy-talking Easterners here. Boan is a mid-western institution with mid-western values. The pace out here is a little different than it is in New York."

"I should be offended by that remark," countered Kennedy.

"Why?"

"I lived in New York for ten years. Don't you remember?"

"You did?" asked Friend incredulously. "With a name like Kennedy, shouldn't you have been in Boston?" Kennedy ignored him.

Llewellyn didn't. "What's your point, Greg? Afraid lox and bagels will end up on your menu at Denny's?"

"Jeez-o-Pete! Relax," declared Friend. "I'm just reminding the group about the bad luck we've had bringing in people not from the Midwest. Most have barely survived before moving on."

With another candidate, the dispute concerned gaps in the work history; for a fourth candidate, concerns were expressed about the candidate jumping from position to position almost every year. For a fifth candidate, there weren't enough scholarly publications; a sixth candidate had too many scholarly publications. Others had cover letters that were too lengthy; some were criticized for having cover letters too brief. One candidate was mocked for listing electronics as a hobby ("does he play with ham radios in his basement?"). Sadly, one candidate, a former Boan faculty member who had moved to Western Kentucky University to be an associate dean, was eliminated because of an extremely ill-placed typo: she wrote that she "wanted to be a member of Born again." Llewellyn offered to forward her materials to Huntington College, the small Christian-based institution southwest of Ft. Wayne.

Eventually, Dewayne decided that we would all vote for each of the thirteen possible candidates. We would either vote 'yes,' 'no,' or 'maybe' in terms of interviewing them. Kennedy suggested that we do our votes by secret ballot, because if everyone saw how I voted, then their votes might change. Her suggestion reeked of overkill, and I almost volunteered to stay out of the voting until I realized that put too much influence in the hands of these well-minded, but often small-minded, faculty members.

After we tallied up the votes, we had two candidates with enough "yes" votes that we decided to interview them. Another five were "maybes" and all the rest were predominantly "no's." I confirmed that none of the candidates in the negative pile needed to be interviewed on my behalf, and so the discussion turned on what, if anything, we should do with the pile of five "maybes."

"Would two be enough candidates to interview?" Wilson asked me.

"For a first round, that makes me nervous. As all of you know, you often have duds in the first rounds. Then perhaps one backs out because he's accepted a job elsewhere, then we have to start all over. My preference is that we add two or three more to the 'yes' pile and give us a larger pool."

"But, none of those five clearly stood out to us?" challenged Friend.

"Well, that's not quite true. There are six of us voting. Most of the ones in the 'maybe' pile," I suggested, while looking through Wilson's hand-recorded tabulations, "have two, even three, 'yes' votes. And all but one doesn't have a single 'no' vote. So, there is just less certainty with them."

"How about if we assign them point totals? 3 points for a yes, 1 point for a maybe, -1 point for a no," suggested Friend.

"Oh, god, please no," begged Kennedy. "Does **everything** in education have to involve a freaking rubric?"

While most members of the committee laughed, Friend took exception. "You folks in arts and sciences might want to use a few more rubrics. They make the standards nice and clear. Lord knows, I'm tired of seeing students get to my classes who can't write or perform basic math."

"Well, first off, Greg, I teach psychology and sociology, so don't cry to me. But, secondly, have you been attending the WAC sessions?"

"I don't have time for those."

"Greg and Sarah," interrupted Wilson, trying to stay on track, "now is not the time." His effort was in vain.

"Then you have no right to complain." Kennedy didn't even acknowledge Wilson's comments. My role of hanging-in-the-background might have to change here.

"All these stupid 'across the curriculum' initiatives that come out of arts and sciences: Writing Across the Curriculum, Math Across the Curriculum, Diversity Across the Curriculum, Scientific Method Across the Curriculum. WAC, MAC, DAC, SMAC. Aaaaccccckkk!!"

"O.k., people, that's enough," I said. "Let's stay focused. I'd like to wrap this up by Christmas."

"I thought we weren't doing second round interviews until January?" asked Llewellyn.

"I meant this meeting!"

Eventually, we decided we would do brief half-hour phone interviews with each of the candidates in the "maybe" pile. Because of schedule challenges, Wilson and I would conduct all of the phone interviews, and other members of the search committee could join as available. We conducted all of these the few business days in the week of Thanksgiving, fortunate enough to schedule the interviews at this time with each of the five candidates.

We first called Dr. Jeremy Boorst, the candidate from St. John's University. While Friend had concerns about bringing a Yankee to Indiana, more of the committee had concerns about the jump Boorst would have to take from being a chairperson (he had only been the chair for over a year) to being a dean. So, Wilson and I worked out a couple of questions aimed to get at this concern. On the day of the interview, Friend and Llewellyn joined us.

From the opening, the interview went poorly. In retrospect, we should have cut the interview off after about ten minutes, but even if we had the foresight to do that, we probably never would have gotten a word in edgewise. Dr. Boorst flew out of the gate with our opening question about why he wanted this position, and proceeded to lull all of us to sleep with rambling observations about the state of secondary education, the cost of higher education, the need for qualified teachers, the crisis of the Obama administration, and the importance of bilingual education. Along the way, he threw in metaphors related to baseball (St. John's was like the Los Angeles Dodgers; Boan was like the Milwaukee Brewers; if he would have shut up long enough, I might have asked for clarification); misquotes from Confucius ("he who will not economize will have to strategize." Before the phone interview had even ended, Wilson had googled the quote to confirm that Boorst had substituted "strategize" for "agonize."); and colloquialisms ("the city"). All of this delivered in a quintessential New York accent.

At one point, I looked around the room to see Llewellyn grimacing, Friend wearing a smug "I-told-you-so" look and Wilson doodling. A few minutes later, Wilson held up two pieces of paper. One showing the profile of a handgun he held so that that the barrel was facing his head. On the other side of his head, he held a picture of his brains splattering. He mimed pulling the trigger and thrust his head away from the imaginary bullet's impact. Luckily, I hit the 'mute' button on the phone before any of us broke out laughing.

When Boorst finally paused for a breath, Friend made the mistake of asking him why he wanted to move to the Midwest. While curious about that, also, I did not care enough to sit and listen to the blowhard for another fifteen minutes. At that point, I did hit the 'mute' button and asked Friend, "What the hell did you do that for? Now, he'll never shut up."

"I just have to know." If Boorst told us, we weren't listening at this point.

"And I thought you were my friend, Friend," I replied.

In the end, Dr. Boorst and one other exaggeratedly affected candidate had eliminated themselves via the phone interviews. While phone interviewing both of them totaled more than an hour of our time, it was worth it to save us the unimagined horror of spending two hours with each of them in a cramped room. We could now set up campus interviews with five potential candidates to replace Michael Hartley. Shelley now had the wonderful task of trying to coordinate those interviews for early December.

The Monday after Thanksgiving, I also lost my unofficial title of "the new guy" on the executive team. Tim Stevens began as the new Executive Vice President for Communications. He was almost as tall as Berrian with sandy blond hair, a well-groomed goatee, and a big nose. Recruited by Tina Noone through Kraft and Selbst, Stevens had left Baker College in Muskegon,

Michigan, to join Boan, and was easily likable with a quiet personality. Berrian had raised concerns about his unassuming manner after Stevens' campus interview, so there had been doubt in my mind about whether we'd hire him. I learned of most of this from Noone, who, since she had recruited me, had dropped by my office after she'd had a particularly arduous conversation with Berrian about Stevens in the days before we offered him the position.

Noone looks too young for her position, which almost certainly led to Berrian often challenging her. While she looks twenty-something, she is in her late thirties, a devoted wife and mother of three children. She had spent ten years right out of college working in the human resources department at Wake Forest University, and then had been recruited by Kraft and Selbst to assist with academic searches across the country. She was sharp, knowing a lot about higher education through her experience, contacts and reading. Her ability to understand institution and individual, at least as I saw in my recruitment, was unparalleled. However, as she sat across from me, grumbling, in that quaint southern accent, about Berrian's unpredictability, I realized I had an opening to explore some unanswered questions for myself.

"Tell me, Tina," I said, after letting her ramble for awhile about working with Berrian. "I was surprised from almost day one here how unpredictable, sometimes psychotic, Bob can be. Had you been aware of that from the beginning of the provost search? You certainly never mentioned it to me."

She hesitated in responding. "That's an interesting question, Mark." She paused and continued to reflect upon the question.

"To be fair, Tina, a lot of what you told me about Boan is very true. The academic side of the house has pockets that need real leadership. The personalities of my colleagues on the executive team run the gamut, and we both agreed after my interviews that Bob was demanding but fair. I'm not now going to say he isn't fair, and am in no way blaming you, or even myself, for not seeing a different side. I'm also not saying I made a mistake. However...."

I paused to watch Tina remove her glasses to clean them. "However, we both sit here today with a different perspective on the man. I'm interested in what you've learned."

"Let me see if I can explain. I saw some of Bob's sudden irrationality during the provost search. At one point early in the search, he called me from his car as he drove back from meeting some community college president. Apparently, Berrian told this president that his community college provost had applied for the Boan position. The other president was upset. It took me fifteen minutes to get Berrian to understand that he had the wrong 'James Long.'"

I grinned. "Do you know if he ever went back and told the president about his mistake?"

"I told him I would call the president and explain the mistake." She grinned. "As soon as he heard I was from Kraft and Selbst, the community college president proceeded to give his Jim Long the worst reference I'd ever heard. I kept trying to interrupt him, to tell him that not only was I not calling for a reference, but that I had no interest in his Jim Long. It must have taken me ten to fifteen minutes to get him to understand that."

"Do you think he lied about his Jim Long to keep you from recruiting him?"

"I don't know about that. I really didn't care about his Jim Long. I only wanted to smooth over Berrian's mistake. But, the story doesn't end there, Mark."

"Holy crap. This is a long story."

"I've used that pun myself when telling it. No, the story gets better when I get a call from the other Jim Long."

"No," I cried in disbelief.

"Oh, yes. He was the president of a small college in the middle of West Virginia. He had been applying to some provost and president positions because he wanted to get out of there. He hadn't told anybody at the university or his board."

"Let me guess. Someone found out anyway?"

"Yep. It turns out the first Jim Long knew a board member at the second Jim Long's college. They'd had an on-going series of jokes about coincidence of the Long name, and so when he found out he had been mistaken for Jim Long number two...."

"He called his buddy on the board, who called out Jim Long number two." I smirked. "Let me guess. Jim Long number two was relieved of his presidency."

"Eventually. At the time he called me he didn't know that. But he called me up and cursed me a blue streak. I couldn't get a word in edgewise for twenty minutes."

"What eventually happened?"

"He threatened to sue us, but he had no case. Kraft and Selbst never actually breached his privacy concerns. As we prepared to go to court, Wilhelm Kraft, our CEO, put him in touch with a small college in Los Angeles, he got the job, and everything was dropped."

"Wow, from West Virginia to L.A. Well, he got his wish. He got far away from West Virginia." I looked out my window. "So, what's the point to this long story?"

Tina smoothed her skirt. "University presidents are pretty much the same, Mark. They are in highly visible positions where a faculty affair, or a student shooting, or a hazing incident, or an athletic scandal can shake their whole foundation, pun intended. They spend most of their time either shaking down donors for money or handling pesky media and/or board members. Their every move is scrutinized; they by nature are the scorn of the very people who 'run their business,' the faculty. In this way, they are like hospital CEO's who face the wrath of the medical staff daily. I'm not surprised that some of them can come across as a little schizophrenic. I'm only surprised you weren't aware of that until you started at Boan."

I chewed on the end of my pencil. At Farrington, stories about President Hansen were fairly run-of-the-mill, stuff like the size of his yacht, or his fawning over politicians, or an apparent disinterest in the day-to-day academic activities. Had I missed stories that showed him more like presidents Noone had described? Had I not picked up on Provost Jensen's commentary about Hansen? Finally, I shrugged my shoulders. "Maybe I was a bit naïve."

"As long as that's past tense, I think you'll be o.k., Mark."

I laughed. "I have to admit. Some recent conversations with Bob have given me a little more insight into what he's dealing with. All of this gives me something to think about."

"Excellent. Then my job here is done." Noone got up, brushed her skirt once more, and slung her purse over her right shoulder. "Take care, Mark."

Before she got out the door, I yelled toward her. "Wait a second. If you believe all that, why the hell did you just stop at my office to rant about Berrian and the EVP of Communication search?"

"Mark! Even though everything I said is true, that doesn't change the fact that presidents like Berrian drive me crazy. Why the hell do you think I left Wake Forest?"

I laughed again as she shut the door. Not long after, she must have eased Berrian's concerns about Stevens. He accepted our offer and agreed to start within a couple of weeks.

That's how I ended up meeting Tim Stevens again the week after Thanksgiving. Since Natalie and I were already in a decorating mood, I had brought some decorations from home to help Shelley decorate my office for Christmas. Victor and Tim stopped by as I unpacked decorations from a box.

"Hey, Mark. I wanted to bring Tim by to see you. It's his first day."

"Welcome, Tim. I'm glad you accepted the position."

Tim held out his hand to shake mine. He didn't say anything, although he may have grunted a "hello." It was difficult to tell.

"Excited to get started?" I asked.

"I guess. I won't have much time to think about it with cabinet starting in an hour."

"Consider yourself lucky. When I started, the Monday meetings began at 7:30."

"Yeah, I heard. Thank goodness that's no longer the case."

"That's no longer the case now," said Victor, "but don't be surprised if we go back to that schedule after the holidays."

"Why?"

"I've seen it happen before."

Tim eyed the piece of tinsel and miniature stocking I prepared to hang on the edge of my desk. I felt I had to explain my actions. "I know it's way too early, but I'm a sucker for Christmas. It helps when you have a 10-year old. You have kids, Tim?"

No." He paused a moment. Then he turned to Victor. "Certainly HR doesn't condone this?"

"Condone what?" asked an immediately panicky Victor.

"This public display of a Christian holiday. Where is the respect for Hanukah? Or, Ashura? How about Rophatsu?"

Victor looked at me in puzzlement and fear. I couldn't read anything from Tim's expression. "If it counts for anything, all my decorations are miniature Santas, reindeer, and stockings. I couldn't get more secular if I tried, Tim."

"Damn it, brothers, not even Kwanzaa?" He remained straight-faced but the joke clearly was on us.

"He's joking, Victor."

Victor stuttered. "Uh, I'm, I'm not so sure."

"Of course. Tell him you're kidding, Tim."

"But I'm not. Equal time for equal faiths, right, Victor?"

Victor looked like he would crumble in his place.

Finally, Tim broke into a big smile. "He's right, Victor. I'm kidding. Boy, are all of you going to be this easy?"

"If you can be that dead-pan, we will all be at your mercy," I replied, finishing with the tinsel on my desk.

As they left, Victor looked back at me finishing my decorations. "You know, Mark, you really shouldn't have religion-specific decorations."

"Victor, give it a break."

Meanwhile, at home the Christmas decorations went up without fear of offending any faith or nationality. We quickly realized that we had neighbors dueling for the most elaborate decorations. Our house only had a few basic strands of lights outside, which served us well, because the light coming from the neighbors' houses spilled through our blinds and lit up the inside of our house. The three houses immediately around ours, including the Fosters, covered every tree and every window frame with colored lights.

The Fosters even managed to put a ten-foot Santa in the nativity scene in their front yard. Natalie and I joked about how lost he looked. Later in the month, when I went to write directions to our house for the holiday party, the Fosters provided me the perfect landmark for our guests: "Turn left into the driveway just past the house where Santa has come begging Jesus for forgiveness."

Chapter Fifteen

My original intention was to take some time off the first weeks of December to help Natalie prepare for the party and, after that, the arrival of my parents for the holidays. Unfortunately, as The Counting Crows sang, it became "a long December," mostly because of on-going personnel issues. Nothing is more draining to an institution than the efforts needed to address staffing issues.

Thanks to continual pressure on Rachel Linares, we filled her three open nursing positions for the soon-to-begin winter semester. Normally, a provost would give his dean plenty of room to review candidates, interview them, and recommend whom to hire. If business or arts and sciences, for instance, needed to replace a faculty member, I would ask only for the opportunity to have a one-on-one interview before we made an offer. One needs to have faith in direct reports to pick good people, and should stay mostly out of the way. However, in the case of nursing, I needed to stand firmly in the way. In the end, Linares and I agreed that the two of us would interview each candidate together as part of the process.

The first candidate for whom Linares forwarded application materials to me, a Fiona Staples, represented the Ob/Gyn specialty. "Gee, thanks," I told her, "I hoped to work my way up. Maybe start with a Proctology specialist?"

"There are no proctology specialists among nurses, Mark," responded a completely humorless Linares.

"I know, Rachel. It was a joke." When she didn't smile, I had to add, "maybe it's because they're usually the pains in the ass."

"Very funny." She pushed a one-page resume under my nose. "Fiona has fifteen years experience as an Ob/Gyn nurse on the floor. She's spent the last nine years at NorthEast Indiana Hospital and comes with a great reference from her supervisor."

"What's her teaching history?"

"Clinicals."

"For those nine years?"

"Off and on for about the last three years."

"Where's that on this resume?" I flipped the resume over hoping page two had been copied onto the back. It was blank.

"She doesn't list the clinical teaching."

"Why not?"

"She just didn't. Figured it was assumed, I guess?"

I frowned. "Any classroom teaching experience?"

"No."

"Doesn't that concern you?"

"We can teach her what she needs to know."

"Did she do a teaching demonstration?"

"No."

"Why not?" As with all my discussions with Linares, this conversation resembled pulling teeth.

"Was she supposed to?"

"I would hope so. Shouldn't any faculty member we're hiring have to demonstrate the ability to teach in the classroom?"

"Mark, you don't understand...." As my eyes almost certainly widened, she backed off. "Oh, sorry. I forgot you hate that. Nevertheless, the point, Mark, is that we can't make these nurses jump through so many hoops. They don't have to take faculty positions, and as we know can often make more on the floor, especially with overtime."

"Good lord, Rachel. Name me a damn discipline where someone can't make more money in the field than in teaching. Ours is supposed to be a noble profession."

Rachel shrugged. "I can only speak about nurses, Mark. We might lose Fiona."

"Are you saying she's indifferent to being a faculty member?"

"Oh, no, she really wants to teach for us!"

"Then, she should be willing to do a teaching demo for us."

"Well, she'll be here in a few minutes, so let's interview her and then figure that out after the interview."

I frowned again. "Is she fully credentialed, at least?"

"Oh, yes. She finished the MSN just last year from Phoenix."

"Oh, great," I muttered. "Won't the NLNAC require us to have more Ph.D. qualified candidates?"

"Absolutely."

"Then, why are we even interviewing her?" I held up her single-paged resume to the light, as if I might see a watermark bearing more information.

"She's the only Ob/Gyn candidate we have. If we hire her, we will tell her that we expect her to get a Ph.D."

Stunned, I sat back in my chair. "The only one? How long did we advertise the position?"

"For a month."

"Christ, this is hopeless. And if we do hire her, when will she have time to complete the terminal degree?"

"She'll manage. I assume she'll apply probably to Phoenix or some other online program."

"Wow, we must be a great supplier for our competition."

Rachel turned on a smug smile. "Not if we start our own Ph.D. in nursing."

"Oh, that's a solution," I mocked in frustration.

In the end we hired Staples, although I did require her to present a classroom demonstration. I didn't go to it, but Gertrude Fulbright showed up unannounced, much to Linares' resentment, and Trudy reported that while not stellar, Staples did well enough. Upon my directive, Linares required her to go to the faculty development office for additional workshops.

"But she'll walk if we require that," whined Linares.

"It will be a miracle. 'Look, she can walk. She can walk.'" As usual, Linares frowned at my humor.

Amazingly, Staples stayed.

We did end up with three candidates for the pediatrics specialty. I wasn't sure if that meant that kids were the happening place in nursing, or if pediatrics was so bad that those nurses would flock to the underpaid world of academics. One of the three could barely form complete sentences (Linares never could appropriately explain why she even got to the interview stage), but the other two were surprisingly strong, and for a few moments, we speculated about hiring both. However, given the strict restrictions nursing had regarding credentials for their faculty, it would have been a waste. The first one to whom we made an offer turned us down anyway, as she had accepted a position at a nursing school in the Cayman Islands. Northern Indiana can't compete with the sandy beaches of the Caribbean.

The third position required a nurse with an infectious disease specialty. It sounded like an incredibly narrow specialty, but Linares cited the NLNAC and showed similar faculty profiles from other universities; apparently the specialty was merited. As with Ob/Gyn, we had only one candidate to interview. In this case, such a small pool of qualified candidates comforted me. Who would dedicate their life to working with patients with infectious diseases?

Linares dominated this interview, as there's only so much a provost with a liberal arts degree could add to discussions of anthrax ("Gang of Four's greatest song?"), Candidiasis ("Is this the best of all possible rashes?"), Q-Fever ("I almost had that once but cut it off in the early stages; it was Q-Tip fever."), Chickenpox ("I've always been scared of getting that!"), Shingles ("Is that better than *tin roof rusted?"*), and everybody's favorite infectious disease, Herpes Simplex ("I heard that wasn't doing so good ever since they opened that Gonorrhea multiplex out by the mall."). To her credit, Dr. Imogene Vane emerged as the strongest of these three new nursing hires, probably in part because of the need to constantly educate idiots such as me on the seriousness of these diseases.

As we neared Christmas break, three new nursing full-time faculty had finally been hired. Linares and I met with the current nursing faculty to discuss the new recruits and to create some sense of a nursing team. We attempted a proactive strike to fend off current faculty wanting to leave Boan out of resentment, frustration, or whatever else related to their new colleagues.

Linares did not get asked to be on the interview teams for the dean of education. She was noticeably not happy with that exclusion, but I justified it by pointing out the frantic pace she had been maintaining through the accreditation and the nursing faculty hiring. In addition, by also not including Michael Stewart in the dean interview process, I hoped to soften the blow for her. Stewart barely blinked an eye when told, and for all I know probably resumed stalking Tanya Tyler. Linares still did voice her displeasure, trying to drag Stewart in with her, when she had an opportunity alone with Berrian, but he saw through her and cast her concerns aside brusquely.

We lost the best candidate for dean before we could even get any of them to campus for interviews. Dr. Darren Hockney possessed the rare quality in a potential dean of education that is often heard of, but rarely seen: the Ph.D. in education. Earning it from George Mason University, he had been toiling as the chair of education at Creighton University for more than five years, emerging as a top scholar in his field, with numerous articles and presentations. Several faculty members in the College of Education had met Hockney at a conference and raved about his presentation on "Rich Media in the Poorest School Districts." He had wowed the whole search committee with his C.V. and his application.

Unfortunately, when Shelley called him to set up the interviews, he disclosed that just that week he'd decided to step down from his position at Creighton. Fed up with higher education apparently, he now pursued a new career in the non-profit sector. While I was disappointed, members of the college were outright devastated. I spent the better part of an hour consoling

Stefan Hammer, who asked that I join him for a beer at the Heartland. He had three large glasses in less than a half hour and eventually, through all his whining and moaning, made Michael Stewart look strong.

Shelley and Cicely Irons must have been the only ones pleased that Hockney had chosen a new career path. They needed to manage a series of interviews with the remaining four candidates to occur over the same few days. Traditionally for higher education, academic interviews might involve candidates on campus for several days, with elaborate dinners and generously timed sessions between candidates and small groups of university faculty and staff. However, those kinds of interviews had gone the way of typewriters. The key objective was to inconvenience the Boan staff as little as possible. As a result, we ran dueling interviews with two candidates on one day, and then repeated the insanity for the other two candidates just two days later. Candidates were rushed in and out of sessions, maneuvered around campus, and at all costs kept from running into each other. The prevention of those accidental meetings rested on the shoulders of Shelley and Cicely.

Both shared their plans with Victor and me prior to any phone call going to a candidate.

"Candidate one will come into town Sunday night and we'll put him or her at the Radisson," said Cicely. "Candidate two will come into town Sunday night and we'll put him or her at the Hampton."

"Then," interjected Shelley, taking over, "candidate three will come into town Tuesday night and stay at the Radisson, with candidate four coming into town Tuesday night and staying at the Hampton."

"Sounds like a good start." I'm good at stating the obvious.

"Oh, that's the easy part. Now, if you look at the sheets in front of you, we have Shelley meeting candidate one at the commons at 7:45 on Monday morning. I will meet candidate two at the Administration Building at 8:00." Cicely looked tired already.

"Cicely will immediately take candidate two to meet Dean Riley and Mark in the board room, while I will take candidate one to Room 112 in Muswell Hall," continued Shelley.

"Are you sure Room 112 is available?" I asked. "When I was in that building last week, that room had been flooded."

Shelley looked at Cicely frowning. "O.k., I'll double check and assign a different room if necessary." She wrote down a hurriedly captured note to herself. She continued where she left off, "at 8:00, in whatever room, candidate one will meet with the search committee, minus Mark. That session will be done at 9:45; after a brief break, I will take him or her to Room 304 in Muswell Hall to meet Dean King and Dean Fulbright at 10:00."

"Meanwhile," pronounced Cicely, resuming the candidate number two thread, "I will get my candidate at 9:30 and escort him or her to Gray Residence Hall to meet with students. Dean Riley will take care of getting students for that session. At 10:45, candidate two gets a brief break and then meets with the search committee at 11:00 in Room 112 at Muswell Hall."

"Assuming it's available," Victor said, maybe with or without humor.

"Yes, assuming it is available."

"Meanwhile, back in my hell," cracked Shelley, "I will be moving candidate one at 11:00 to the Administration Building to meet with Mark and Dean Riley. Immediately after that, at 12:30, he or she will stay in that room to meet with Caroline, Howard, Hank, Tim and Victor over lunch, which will be Caesar salads, rolls, and blueberry cheesecake."

"To continue with candidate number two, his or her lunch period will begin at 12:45 in Room 304 of Muswell Hall with King and Fulbright." Cicely clearly showed impatience. If I attempted to coordinate what she had to, I would have been just as impatient also. "At 1:45, my candidate number two gets a brief break, but by 2:00, I have shuffled the candidate to the administration board room for the meeting with Cruz, Shue, Turing, Stevens, and Victor."

"Now, that's a law firm!" I interjected.

"Thing number one," said Shelley, clearly influenced by my banter, "gets a break at 1:30. At 1:45, there is the session with the faculty in the Butler Hall auditorium. At 3:00, as that ends, I will then give him or her a campus tour before meeting with students at 3:30 in Gray Residence Hall."

"At 3:15, candidate two goes to the Butler auditorium for the faculty interviews, after which at 4:30, I will give the campus tour." Cicely tapped on the table with one of those five-colored pens I hadn't seen in ages.

"Sounds like they get the campus tour all day," I said.

"It will feel that way," commented Cicely. "Wear your walking shoes, Shell."

"My candidate leaves campus at 4:30," said Shelley, "and Cicely's leaves at 5:00. Then, we all take a deep breath and repeat the same schedule for Wednesday. I'll take candidate three and Cicely will take candidate four."

"And both of us take Thursday and Friday off." Cicely was not joking.

"And that's all, ffffollks," I cracked.

"Do you have to put up with him like this all the time, Shell?" asked Cicely.

"He has gotten worse," responded Shelley smiling.

"The key all day, ladies," reinforced Victor, "is to avoid having the candidates meeting each other. As I look at the schedule, the key time will be at the end of the day, when one is finishing with the faculty and the next is ready to be ushered into the faculty. I would recommend, Mark, you ask one of the faculty members to be watching the clock and to ensure everything gets wrapped up on time."

"Already taken care of my HR comrade. Henry Van Wyck has volunteered."

"I have a question," requested Shelley. "Why isn't the president involved in any of these?"

"He will wait until the final round of interviews in January."

"We'll have to do this again in January?" Cicely whined.

"Don't worry. At that point we'll bring back maybe two candidates just to meet with Berrian and me. It should be fairly straightforward."

Once the week of these interviews arrived, all of Shelley's and Cicely's hard work went to naught. It began poorly on Monday, when candidate one, Glynnis Proust, proceeded to pepper the search committee with dozens of questions about details most of them couldn't answer. Wilson failed to interrupt her to tell her she needed to stick to her schedule, and Shelley never felt comfortable disturbing the session. As a result, Proust arrived fifteen minutes late to King and Fulbright. Kiana, miffed that the session started late, proceeded to dominate Proust's time with her and Fulbright, so much so that Fulbright and King got into a shouting match that Shelley said could be heard as she and Proust walked away. Each successive session started later and later.

Cicely had better luck with candidate two, Dr. Harley Wells, who managed, with Cicely's direction, to stay on schedule. However, at 3:00, the faculty remained early in their session with Proust; Cicely and Shelley, communicating via cell phone at every opportunity, had developed a back-up plan to move Wells' campus tour to 3:00 and then to have him end the day with the faculty. However, that meant she brought Wells from the north part of campus and not the south part. Shelley, believing that once she had extracted Proust from the faculty wanted to avoid heading south, and headed out the north entrance of Butler Hall at the exact moment Cicely endeavored to sneak Wells in that entrance.

Shelley and Cicely disputed the sequence of events at this point. Shelley claimed she played dumb and pretended not to even know Cicely, trying to push past both her and Wells without making eye contact. Cicely maintained that Wells acknowledged Shelley's and Proust's presences with a "fancy meeting you here!" declaration to the two of them. Proust apparently held her hand out stiffly toward Wells, who avoided the handshake and hugged Proust. At this point, Shelley admitted to lifting her head up so that she could see the full effect of the train wreck. Cicely acknowledged that she was left standing there holding the door open with Proust on the inside of Butler Hall, Wells on the outside, and Shelley awkwardly straddling the threshold.

"What exactly did they say to each other?" I asked both of them later that evening.

"Wells said, 'you look wonderful, Glynnie,'" claimed Cicely, "as he let her go from the hug."

"No, he said, 'you took one for Lennie,'" countered Shelley.

"Are you nuts, girlfriend?" snorted Cicely.

"I have to admit, Shelley, that doesn't make sense." I had already called Natalie to tell her I would be late for dinner.

"No, it makes sense, because she then said, 'Hardly!' She was angry about seeing him."

"She wasn't angry, Shelley, just puzzled, because she then said, 'Harley?'"

"No way, Shell."

"Yes way, Cicely."

"O.k., ladies, slow down. Let's take our time. What happened next, Shelley?" I had grabbed a piece of paper to better keep track of the two story lines.

"He said, 'I was aware of the whole thing.'"

"Damn it, Shelley, what he said was 'I wish you were over our thing'. To, which she replied, 'what thing, Harley?'"

"What? Are you saying they had an affair?" I asked, slapping my hand on my forehead.

"I'm not saying anything, Mark. I'm just telling you what I heard."

"And I'm telling you, Cicely, that you heard wrong, because she said, 'One thing, Harley.'"

"'One thing?' I'm completely lost, Shelley."

"You know, he said he was 'aware of the whole thing,' and she kind of challenged him that it was 'one thing,' which led Wells to say, 'tell that to Lennie.'"

Cicely shook her head. "Shel! What's wrong with your hearing? Wells then said, 'hell to that, Glynnie!'"

I looked at my hastily scrawled dual plot lines. "Jesus, is it possible neither of you heard them right? Could they have been talking about the weather? Surely by this point, one of you had recovered from your initial shock?"

Shelley grimaced. "Well, I did start to pull Proust away from the door, but Wells grabbed her other arm and I couldn't move her."

"That is true, Mark," confirmed Cicely.

"And then ... ?"

"Right before I wrestled Proust from Wells, she turned to him and said, 'I'll never forgive you for what you did, Harley.'"

"Actually, that's right," confirmed Cicely. "It is what she said to Wells. He yelled at her retreating figure, 'No hard feelings, right, Glynnis?'"

"Unfortunately," declared Shelley, "that made Proust stop again. She turned back to Wells, yelling, 'you have a lot of nerve.'"

"Is that what you heard, Cicely?" I questioned, fearing an alternative memory.

"Oh, I didn't hear anything, Mark. By that point we were in the building and the door had shut behind us."

"And from there on out, we got them wrapped up and off campus, right?"

"I'm not sure about that, Mark," continued Cicely. "Wells asked me if Proust was also on campus for the dean interviews. I told him I had no idea, but I did hesitate at first, so I think he figured it out."

"Proust was preoccupied during the remaining campus tour. When I left her at her car, she clearly lingered." Shelley chewed her fingertips.

"Anything else from either of you?" I asked.

Cicely looked at Shelley, who shook her head. "I guess not, Mark."

I looked at the hastily sketched storylines on my piece of paper—both interesting plot lines. However, they didn't appear to have that much relevance to the hiring process. At most one of them figured out the other one had been on campus for interviews, and the fact that others are interviewed in the first stages of the process should not surprise any candidate.

I dismissed the administrative assistants, telling them not to worry and to get ready for Wednesday. My notes from my interviews with Proust and Wells hardly left me optimistic. Proust had at least a dozen questions for me about the work environment, benefits, and opportunities for advancement. She reflected no strategic thinking through her questions, although some of her answers revealed pat answers that did tie loosely to a comprehensive strategy for the College of Education. She also clicked her tongue quite a bit when she talked, a nervous habit that drove me crazy by the end of our time together.

Wells, in contrast, came across as superficial and too happy-go-lucky. When asked to address some of the challenges he had to overcome in the course of his career, he referenced time management issues that didn't help convey whether he could dig his heels in and work through some of the obvious challenges in the post-Hartley era College of Education.

My guts tightened, because on paper Proust and Wells stood out as the best candidates of the four remaining. Wednesday's candidates might impress me beyond expectations, but they had both been part of the phone interview sessions, and I already had a basic sense of their capabilities and their limitations. I couldn't fathom re-opening this search. Tough decisions loomed ahead.

On the day between the interviews, some of my precious unscheduled hours were purloined by Gertrude Fulbright, whom on most days I would have gladly seen. "Trudy, can this please wait?" I asked when she knocked on my door unannounced.

"I'm afraid not, Mark."

I sighed. "Then, come on in. What is it?"

"I have a faculty problem. HR suggested I come to you."

I waved for her to sit down. "Go ahead."

"Actually, do you mind if I come around to your computer? I need to show you something."

"Show me something? And HR recommended you come to me? I knew Victor's crew was losing it."

As with many others at Boan these days, Fulbright ignored my sophomoric attempt at humor. She bent over the computer, pulled up my Internet Explorer and proceeded to type something into the address bar. An image popped up, but Fulbright blocked my view. She moved out of my way to reveal a picture of a group of men at a bar or a restaurant. The men barely showed in the dark environment, but I could see two pitchers of beer, countless glasses, and in the far right corner of the picture wrapped and unwrapped birthday presents.

"So, what's this? Some of our students celebrating someone's birthday?"

"Almost," said Fulbright, now settling into the chair in front of my desk. "Take a closer look at the guy behind the presents. He's the actual birthday 'boy.'" The way she said "boy" made me a little leery.

I rolled my chair to my computer screen and peered into the corner of the picture. The boy, a blond haired, barely-stubble beard, freckled kid, looked familiar.

"Should I recognize him?" I asked, hoping he would be some star athlete drinking in a bar before his twenty-first birthday.

"You should, although you have only met him a couple of times, probably, for short periods of time."

"Why do I have a feeling I'm going to need some pain medicine very soon?" I looked frantically around my office for my stress ball.

"That's Dwight Sax."

I bowed my head and closed my eyes. Opening them again, I spun the chair back around to face the computer. "Sax? He's the whiz kid young English faculty member."

"The one and only."

"Not such a kid that this picture is from his twenty-first birthday?" I found the stress ball in my desk drawer. I commenced squeezing as if my life depended on it.

"No, he turned a whopping twenty-nine when that picture was taken."

"And it was taken recently, right?" Not waiting for the expected answer, I continued. "And those are our students with him, correct?"

"Oh, yeah! All students in his advanced writing course."

I turned back to face Fulbright, taking a deep breath before attempting to minimize the situation. "If we can confirm all the guys in that picture are over twenty-one, then big deal—an unfortunate lack of discretion on Sax's part. We can reprimand him for that, tell him to make sure it never happens again."

"Mark, look more closely at the present he's unwrapping."

"I don't think I want to. Do I have to?" My stress ball was not helping. I let it roll onto the desk.

"You really should." Trudy picked up the ball.

I rolled the chair back around and peered again into the dark right corner. Whatever object he held, long and cylindrical, was difficult to make out. Then I saw the packaging lying on the table in front of him. The light from behind Sax projected perfectly on the packaging. Clearly readable was the single word, 'Roor.'

"I see it says 'Roor.' What is that? Who is that?"

"You don't know? Good. If you do a search on that brand, Mark, you'll see that they make bongs."

"Bongs?"

"Yes, bongs."

"As in water pipes?"

"Yes, as in water pipes?"

"A hookah?"

Trudy tossed the stress ball at me. "Yes, Mark, a damn hookah!"

"Where did you find this picture?" I asked, scrolling to the address bar to see the web address.

"It's all over the internet. It started on one of the student's FaceBook page, but it's spreading."

"Have you confronted Sax yet?"

"Yes. He claims innocent fun. He says no marijuana was involved."

"Oh, boy, as if a lot of people are going to care if marijuana was involved or not." Fulbright said nothing, merely waiting for me to continue.

"What's the kid's record been like with us?"

"Positive student evaluations through the roof."

I sighed and bounced the stress ball off the wall. "Heck, he teaches English. That's no real surprise. He probably cites Kesey, Angelou, Bono and the Beat poets at all turns."

"Still, he has had a good record and, as I say, is beloved by his students."

"Well, who wouldn't be if the midterm is 'quarter bounce' and the final is rolling a blunt?" I ran my fingers through my hair and yawned. It had been a long first day of the week. "Anyway, what did HR recommend?"

"They suggest a written reprimand for his file, but they leave it up to us."

"Why don't you have another talk with Sax, and if you get any sense that he really doesn't understand the boundary he must establish with his students, then let's do the written reprimand?"

In the end, Fulbright did write a formal reprimand and the waiting lists for Sax's classes doubled by the winter semester.

In the meantime, Shelley and Cicely managed to shepherd their two dean candidates around campus on Wednesday without any accidents, surprises, or confrontations. No solace could be found from that, because neither candidate rose to the occasion. One of them, Dr. Patrick Yeats, was universally scorned by every person with whom he met. The strongest responses came from the faculty, who after their session with Yeats forwarded evaluation sheets that bordered on vicious.

"A complete idiot," summed up one faculty member, "even beyond our standards."

A second faculty member wrote, "What he lacks in vision he complements with personality."

A third faculty member suggested that Yeats would be "better suited to be Dean Jones than the Dean of Education."

I found him uninspiring also. Had I missed something on the phone interview? Dewayne Wilson confirmed that he too discovered a whole different person once Yeats stepped on campus. "Oh, well," I expounded, after Wilson and I debriefed at the end of Yeats' interview, "the hour's come at last for this rough beast."

Wilson's blank stare told me the reference had sailed so far above his head that it might bring rain.

"Don't you people in education read any poetry?" I exclaimed to Wilson.

"We much prefer the limerick form, Mark."

"That's something, at least."

The second candidate on Wednesday, Dr. Janice Courtland, came armed with an exam for everyone that she met. Since Jennifer Riley and I were the first victims of Courtland's aggressive turning-the-tables on the interview, we were caught completely unprepared. At least by the time Courtland left the administrative conference room, we spread the news to the other interview teams.

She wasted no time. I opened the questioning: "What is it that you will bring to Boan's College of Education that makes you unique?"

"I'm so glad you asked that Dr. Carter," smiled Courtland. "I think the best way for me to show that is to work with some feedback from you." She had opened her portfolio and pulled out two stapled handouts. She slid one across the table to me, and handed one to Riley, seated to her left.

"What is this?" I asked hesitantly.

"A quick exam. It will help facilitate our discussion."

"You're kidding, right?" I said, looking at Riley who had leafed through the four pages of the handout with a pained expression on her face.

Courtland saw me looking at Riley, and pushed her thick glasses up her nose and fixed a few strands of her red hair falling around her head. "Don't worry. It will take you about two minutes." When the expressions on our faces did not change, she grabbed Riley's copy and held it up. "See, they're all multiple choice!"

"With all due respect, Dr. Courtland," I said, after a few seconds of deep breaths, "I don't think this is appropriate."

"Dr. Carter, you haven't even read a question. Go on, look at it." She turned to point at Riley. "See, Dr. Riley is on page two already."

I gave Riley an annoyed look. "Et tu, Brute?"

Riley shrugged in a "if you can't beat them, join them" mode.

I shook my head and looked at the first question: "If your university was to offer a new graduate program in education, which would it be? A) Distance Learning Education; B) Geriatric Education; C) Lifelong Learning Education, or D) Accelerated Education." I couldn't suppress a laugh. Riley looked at me with a faint smirk, but continued to keep her head down.

I composed myself and tried a new tactic. "Dr. Courtland, how about if you just answer a few questions for us, and then maybe we can talk through this uh, very interesting, instrument?"

"Come on, Dr. Carter. Trust me."

I looked at Riley who had reached the last page. Maybe it didn't take that long. I flipped the pages absent-mindedly.

"Uh, Dr. Courtland, can I ask a question?" Damn Riley actually raised her hand like a student in an exam.

"Yes, Dr. Riley."

"On the last question, when it asks what historical period corresponds to the state of higher education today … ?"

"Yes."

"For choice C, when you say, 'Roman Empire,' do you mean pre-Constantine the Great or post-Constantine the Great?"

I looked at Riley to assess just how far her hand had gone up Courtland's leg in order to pull it. Riley, bless her heart, had a perfect poker face.

"I don't really know, Dr. Riley. Do you think it matters?"

"Oh, it matters tremendously. For instance, I could argue that the Edict of Milan is Brown vs. the Board of Education."

"Interesting. Well, it really doesn't matter. Choose what makes you happiest."

I watched in amazement as Riley marked "C" on her exam with a big swooping circle, laid her pen down satisfied, and pushed the exam back to Courtland.

"How about yours, Mark?"

I tamped down my seething. "I'm really stuck on question two. Can you just work with Riley's?"

"Would that be o.k. with you, Dr. Riley?"

"Oh, whatever makes you happy would be fine with me." I would make Riley pay later—probably with several beers at the Heartland.

Both Riley and I humored Courtland for the rest of the interview, during which she actually answered a few questions interspersed with her strange connections to exam answers. I gladly excused Courtland when Cicely came to move her to the next interview team. While Courtland stepped into the ladies' room, I pulled Cicely aside.

"If you can, warn upcoming interviewers that they may get a test."

"What?"

I showed her my copy of Courtland's exam. "She handed this out to us at the beginning."

"Gee, Dr. Carter. You didn't answer any of them. Didn't you study at all?"

"I studied the pinholes in the drop ceiling above us. I believe there are four million, two hundred thousand holes in that sucker."

At the end of that day, several of us sat in the Heartland and joked about the exam. By the time Courtland got to the faculty, a mini-revolt broke out when she handed out the exams. Van Wyck allowed the chaos. I wasn't proud that so many of us didn't take Courtland seriously, but interviews are grueling enough, even without a pop quiz from the crazy interviewee.

Unfortunately, that meant we recommended no candidate to come back to campus for a final interview. I discussed this at my one-on-one with Berrian, and we agreed to discuss moving forward at the Monday cabinet meeting. However, even before I walked into that meeting, I had a bombshell to share with the rest of the executive team.

Chapter Sixteen

"D r. Linares just handed me her resignation," I announced, arriving last to cabinet. "That's why I'm late. She came to my office and handed me her resignation letter right as I left for this meeting."

"What the hell?" asked Hank. "Where did that come from?"

"Apparently she feels unappreciated by new leadership. Since all of you have been here awhile, I assume she means me."

"Don't count me out," said Tim.

I grinned at him. "Unless communications has embarrassed her in front of her peers and made unfair demands on her, you're safe."

"Gee, that was on my to-do list for this week."

"I can't say I'm heartbroken, but what does that mean? Is she leaving immediately?" asked Berrian.

"No, she gives us two weeks' notice, which means she'll stay through finals."

"Do you have anyone waiting in the wings?" asked Berrian.

"I seriously doubt it. The nursing program has had so much turnover of faculty that few veterans remain on board."

"Can one of the other deans handle the interim?"

I nearly choked on my coffee. "I hardly think so. Riley's already covering education along with business. Stewart would be lost. King would start a riot throughout all the health programs. Maybe, I could ask Fulbright, but I like her too much."

"You're not going to decide that today. Nevertheless, Victor help Mark get an advertisement out soon." Berrian seemed content that Linares' departure would cause no great hardship. As much as she frustrated me, I wasn't as sure.

"Mark's now missing two deans," Berrian continued. "In fact, it's the first item on the agenda." Veronica had already passed out the agenda to the others, and she slid one down the table to me. "Apparently interviews last week didn't go so well. Why don't you fill the rest in?"

"I'm not sure there's much to tell," I said. "Everyone except Bob and Veronica met the four candidates and judging from your feedback no single outstanding candidate emerged. Responses from faculty were hardly endorsing, and the trend continues that way no matter who the interviewer."

"So, our problem now is, do we re-open, how long might that take, and what do we communicate?" Berrian scratched his face with his well-manicured fingernails.

"There's no one else in the pool you'd like to bring in for interviews, Mark?" asked Victor.

"Nope. Some of our best candidates never even got to this stage. They have chosen other career options."

"Then, I say we simply re-post the position and say 'open until filled.' As soon as any application comes in that looks pretty good, let's try to get them on campus."

"Do we contact all the ones in this first pool and tell them they haven't made the cut?"

"Definitely contact the ones we interviewed. Did the ones not interviewed receive any status updates?"

"I don't know, Victor. That's your staff's role."

"I'll ask them." Victor wrote himself a note.

"We should also communicate something to the faculty, if not the university at large." I got up to get some coffee.

"Why say anything?" asked Berrian.

"Come again?" I asked.

"Why communicate anything? Wait until you have someone in place, then let people know."

"That only fuels speculation and rumor, Bob. I say we nip that in the bud."

"Bullshit. To say anything makes the speculation and rumor happen. No matter what, people will read what they want into any communication." The ever-present vein began to throb on Berrian's forehead.

I glanced at my colleagues around the table to see if anyone would openly side with me. As usual, the only eye contact was either with a BlackBerry or a spot on the table in front of that person.

"I can make a suggestion," said Tim, finally. "Let's bundle the news about ... what's your nursing person's name again?"

"Linares."

"Let's bundle the news about her resignation and the on-going search for a dean of education in a message about steering the university in new directions versus new academic leadership. You're still new enough in your position, Mark, that we could make this work."

"Do we have to?" asked Berrian.

Stevens played with a paper clip in front of him. "We have two potential negatives: an open position that may stay open for several more months, and the departure of a person in a second similar position. A lot of staff and students might see these as signs of instability. We cut that thought off at the pass, by suggesting that our strategic vision is stable and that we're just waiting for the final few pieces in the manner of two deans."

"Well, if we have to say anything, this sounds right, Tim," said Berrian. "Can you write something up for Mark?"

I ran my fingers through my hair. "Tim doesn't need to write anything for me, Bob."

"Don't be proud, Mark. Tim can write this up for you."

"Jesus, Bob. I'm not even sure we need to spin the communication this way. I just want to make sure people know what's going on."

Tim jumped in to save me. "How about if Mark and I work on something together? We'll share it with you, Bob, after we hammer it out."

Berrian grunted his approval and looked for his agenda. Before he could move on to another item, Howard spoke up.

"We have an additional problem."

"What, Howard?"

"Sherman Head is still expecting naming rights for his multi-million dollar donation. If you all remember, he last requested naming the College of Education. Hartley supported that, but then he had to get himself killed. We never did decide what to do."

"Hey, if the guy's got money to burn, let's accommodate him. We could do worse than the Head College of Education, right?" asked Hank. He paused for a moment. We all looked toward Howard.

"Too easy!" he grumbled.

"You think we could request that we use his first name: 'Sherman College of Education?'" asked Hank.

Caroline changed the nature of the conversation. "Are you sure it's the College of Education that he wants to name, Howard? When you brought this proposal last time, didn't he choose education primarily because it had no name yet? Is there some other naming opportunity we could offer, Howard?"

"There's not much. We could put his name on the new tennis courts, or the track, or even a room. But those typically go for a lot less money than he's offering now."

"Look it's just a name," I said. "Let's just let him name the College of Education. No one will really care or think about it a year from now."

"But your faculty, Mark, were the most upset by that possibility," interjected Victor.

"They'll live with it. I can talk to them again. Point out the 'there is no such thing as bad publicity' angle."

"I tell you what," suggested Berrian finally, "we need to move forward. Howard, you work with Sherman and lay out every possible scenario. Pin him down on the one he wants and bring it back to cabinet for final approval as soon as possible. And maybe work with him a little on the exact name he wants on the building. See if we can avoid the unfortunate associations with Head."

"No, Howard!" I declared from across the table. "Don't go there. It's still too easy."

The rest of cabinet that day focused on a number of HR-related issues and, as usual, once we got into policy and word-smithing, I disengaged. With the fall semester wrapping up, my thoughts drifted to preparations for both the upcoming winter semester and for the holiday party to occur at my house on the Saturday after finals.

Not surprisingly, I was anxious and on edge during the hours leading up to the party. They are a great idea when you plan them weeks before they occur, and, once they get started, are a lot of fun. However, the few immediate days preceding a party are akin to torture.

We expected about twenty-four people and so, less than two hours before guests would arrive, we anxiously moved furniture around to create a traffic flow from our screened-in porch, looking over the back yard, through our open kitchen to finally our family room. Wine and beer cooled in the garage, and a caterer would deliver all the food around 5:30 PM. Guests would start arriving around 6:00 PM. Card tables had been bought and set up in corners and recesses. Alyssa flitted around us, setting out plastic plates, cups and silverware.

"Will I like these people, daddy?" asked Alyssa.

"I would certainly think so, pumpkin. You've even met a couple of them."

"I have?"

"Remember when you came into work with me that one morning I needed to pick up some stuff to work from home. You met Ms. Ford, remember, the one with the Dalmatians on the desk." A stain on one of the card tables wouldn't come out no matter how much I scrubbed. "Natalie," I yelled, "do we have an extra table cloth for this one table?"

"Oh, yeah," my daughter said, smiling, "the one with a bunch of little Dalmatians."

"Certainly more than a hundred and freaking one," I muttered under my breath.

Natalie emerged from the laundry room. "For that table?" she asked.

"Yes, this table." Taking a deep breath, I then responded more softly, "yes, this one."

"We might, but then we probably don't have matching ones for the other four card tables."

"Shit!"

"It will be alright, Mark."

"Who else, Daddy?"

"What, honey?" I said, scrubbing ridiculously hard on the impenetrable stain.

"Who else have I met?"

I sighed resignedly. "You also met Mr. Shue that morning." I continued to scrub the spot violently.

"Let me try a different cleaner on that, honey," spoke Natalie, grabbing the rag from my hand.

"He's the really funny one, isn't he?" Alyssa had run out of silverware and leaned against the wall, playing with the buttons on her dress.

"Who? Shue? He certainly thinks so, sweetie." After a moment's pause, I clarified. "Yes, he's the funny one, honey."

"You're just waxing poetic, tonight, Mark." Natalie used a different cleaner on the table; the stain was coming right up.

"I got that started for you, you know."

"You used a wood cleaner on a vinyl table top. Read the label on the bottle first, Mark."

'Read the label on the bottle,' I thought to myself, adding an irritating voice.

"Anybody else I'll know?"

"What, Alyssa? Oh, I don't think so, but don't worry. You'll like all of them and they'll think you're adorable."

Stain fixed, Natalie began arranging flowers on the card table. "Who was the woman we all met that one day at the pool? You remember, don't you? The one Alyssa said looked like Edna from *The Incredibles?*"

"I liked her," giggled Alyssa.

"Oh, yes, Henrietta. Henry, to her friends. She is coming. But, Alyssa?"

"Yes, daddy?"

"Don't tell her she looks like Edna Mode." My attention was now focused on arranging glasses on the countertop.

"Why not?"

"It might hurt her feelings. It might not, but let's not take a risk."

"I thought people liked it when they are told they look like someone famous. I **loved** it when your old boss said I looked like Christina Ricci in *Mermaids*."

"I liked that too. Let's hope no one ever says you looked like her in *The Ice Storm*. Anyway, it's different when someone is compared to a cartoon."

"But, why?"

"Let's just drop it, Alyssa. Here, help me set these coasters on all the tables."

She walked around the family room, dumping the coasters all over the place. "Alyssa, honey, we don't need ten coasters on the family room table. We're probably only going to be able to seat six around it."

"Whatever!" My daughter was well on her way to teenage sarcasm.

"Well, here's a surprise!" Natalie's voice came from behind me in the kitchen.

"I don't like surprises less than an hour before our party starts," I said. Cautiously, I walked over to Natalie, bent down, peering under the built-in desk area of our countertop. I couldn't see what she was doing. All of a sudden she backed out, holding a snake.

"A fucking snake!" I screamed. "Where the hell did that come from?"

Alyssa shrieked, although instantly I recognized her shriek as a sound of delight. I looked at my daughter as if meeting her for the first time. "Jesse!"

"That snake has a damn name? Get it out of here. Now!" I screamed.

"Jeez, Mark, settle down," said my wife. "It's just a little garter snake."

"Here, I'll take her," declared Alyssa, grabbing the disgusting thing from my wife. I went back and forth between staring at each one of them.

"Do I know you people?"

Alyssa raced down to the basement, Jesse flopping off her arm.

"Where the hell is she taking it?" I asked.

"O.k., settle down, Mark. The Cunningham boy gave it to her a few days ago. She's got a temporary terrarium down there for him."

"A few days ago? How long have I been unaware that there's a snake in my house?"

"A few days. Duh!"

I tried to calm myself down. "You know how I feel about snakes, Natalie. Jesus Christ, I have the snakes-crawling-all-over-me nightmare at least once or twice a year." I started to pace around the kitchen. The clock said 5:15. The caterers would be here any minute and a snake had been given a cozy home in my basement. "Wait a second," I said, stopping and looking at Natalie. "The Cunningham boy gave it to her? I thought all those troubles were over."

"They are, silly. It was a Christmas present."

"A Christmas present! Has everyone lost their minds?"

"It was very sweet, Daddy," cooed Alyssa returning up the stairs sans Jesse. "He said he caught it in his back yard a few weeks ago and decided to keep it for me until Christmas."

I could feel myself hyperventilating. "Spenser ... Cunningham ... gave ... you ... a snake ... for ... bloody Christmas! What did you give him, a freaking tarantula?"

"No, I just gave him a kiss."

"I can't deal with all of this. You gave him a kiss?"

"She knows how to get you all riled up, Mark."

"Of course she does, she brings a damn snake into the house. Where's the little bastard now?"

Natalie had resumed preparing for the party. "In a temporary terrarium in the basement. Go down and look for yourself."

"I'll pass, thank you very much."

"Honey," Natalie asked, turning to Alyssa, "did you put the lid securely back on that bowl?"

"I did."

I had slumped into one of the folding chairs waiting to be placed at a card table. My heart pounded so hard I could hear it. "Good lord," I said to no one in particular. "Were you ever going to tell me?"

"Of course, dear. We were going to wait until after the party. We knew you'd overreact if we told you before the party."

"Well, I did. Are you happy?" Admittedly, the humor in the moment had started to emerge.

"It could be worse, Mark," said Natalie, as the doorbell rang. "That will be the food. I'll get it."

"How could it have been worse, Natalie?"

"Jesse could have shown up during the party."

Luckily, Jesse didn't and when the guests started to show up, many of them found it fascinating that my daughter had a pet snake, and so people made a trail to the basement all night long to see Jesse. Apparently some of them handled and petted Jesse. Since I wanted to still respect them come Monday, I told everyone I didn't want to know who touched Jesse. Only Jennifer Riley shared my common sense about the evils of snakes.

Besides Jesse, much of the talk centered on the departure of Linares. She had been invited to the party before she submitted her resignation; however, several people at the party, including Kiana King and Garrett Jones, had seen her the day before as she cleared out her office. She vocalized to anyone who would listen that she would be glad never to see Boan again. We all speculated where she would work next. Linares had been silent about her future plans, and few of us knew her well enough to draw that information out.

About 7:15, just as I bit into a heavenly piece of rhubarb pie, the phone rang. Natalie waved at me that she would get it, so I remained at the family room table, listening to Caroline Cruz, Gertrude Fulbright, and Veronica Miller talk about the upcoming season of *American Idol*.

"I guarantee that they'll have a female win it," said Veronica. "You know that they try to 'fix' the results to some degree."

"Come on, Veronica. Conspiracy theories and *American Idol*?" Caroline emphatically made her point with her glass of red wine. My carpet looked dangerously close to being introduced to a cheap merlot.

"Mark, it's for you," announced Natalie, walking toward me with the phone.

"Who is it?"

"I don't know and I didn't ask."

"Hello?" I walked toward the stairwell that would lead upstairs, in case the noise got to be an issue.

"Dr. Carter?"

"Yes."

"This is Amy from the Call Center."

"Call Center?" What a time for a solicitor to call. "Look, this is not a good time. I'm not interested in whatever you're selling." I started to walk back to the kitchen to hang up the phone.

"Wait, Dr. Carter. I'm with the Boan Call Center." I stopped in my tracks.

"Oh, sorry, about that. What's up?"

"Well, Dr. Berrian is unavailable, and I had someone from Channel 11 call wanting a statement from Dr. Berrian."

"A statement?" I said puzzled. All around me, the buzz of conversation diminished. I could see several heads turn to look in my direction.

"Yes, sir. About the arrest for Dr. Hartley's murder."

"An arrest? Holy cow." By now, the only sound from the party was the cackling of Kiana King from the screened-in porch.

"Anyway, Dr. Berrian is out of the country. Can you call this person back?"

"Uh, sure. Give me the name and the number. Natalie, bring me a pen and paper," I yelled into the kitchen. She handed both to Jennifer Riley, who handed them to me.

"O.k., Amy. Go ahead."

"It's Consuela Rodriguez. 555-542-8058."

"Thanks, Amy. Call back if you have similar requests."

"Yes, sir. Sorry to have bothered you."

As I hung up the phone, I looked out at a sea of astonished faces. Everyone had squeezed into the kitchen or the living room, watching with great expectations.

"As you've probably figured out, there's been an arrest. Channel 11 wants a statement."

"And Bob is in the air now, somewhere between Indiana and the Bahamas. So they called you."

"That's right, Caroline. Look everybody, go back to enjoying yourself. I'm going to go upstairs and call the police to find out more."

As I handed the phone back to Natalie, I headed up to the phone in our bedroom. I could hear murmurs about the "arrest" among my guests. The last thing I heard before shutting the bedroom door was Howard's voice: "You want to bet it was one of the ex-wives?"

It took me ten minutes to get someone at the police station that would connect me with either Detectives Klinger or Marsh. No one else would tell me anything. Downstairs, I could hear the joyous laughter of my colleagues. Eventually, someone at the police department told me Detective Marsh would call me right back. While waiting, I wandered downstairs, grabbed a bottled water and filled my plate with a few more goodies. A beer called out my name, but I resisted. A few people asked me what I had learned, but the word got around quickly that I had been stonewalled so far.

When the phone rang, I bolted back upstairs, shut the door, and answered it. "Dr. Carter? This is Detective Allison Marsh."

"Hello, detective. Thank you for calling me back."

"I'm sure you're wondering about the events of the last few hours."

"Oh, yes, someone from Channel 11 wants a statement, but the president is out of the country, and frankly I have no idea what statement to make."

"We've left messages with the president and his secretary." Marsh offered the statement as a mere announcement of fact, not as an explanation, nor as an apology.

"Veronica Miller? She's here right now. I'm having a holiday party. Did you try her office, her cell or her home number?"

"I don't know, Dr. Carter. We left messages at the numbers we had."

Perhaps Marsh had transitioned into the Klinger bad cop role, as she offered up nothing. "Anyway, none of this matters now. Who did you arrest?"

"Karl Billingsley."

"Who is Karl Billingsley?" I collapsed on my bed and stared at the cobwebs in the corners of my ceiling.

"You don't know who he is?"

"No. Is he a student? Is he not connected to Boan at all?"

"He was his student worker. They worked on the IMET proposal together?"

"What's IMET?"

Marsh clicked her tongue in disapproval. "International Military Education and Training."

I looked at the bottled water in my hands. Someone didn't sneak vodka into it, did they? "I'm really sorry, detective, but I'm completely at a loss here. Can you start from the beginning?"

Marsh proceeded to explain that Karl Billingsley was a rough-neck senior student with a crew-cut in Boan's education program. Earlier in the day he had confessed to Hartley's murder. Hartley's student worker for just under a year, Billingsley had worked closely with the dean on a proposal for teaching international militia and civilians via Boan's online deliveries. Initially, Billingsley had been excited because he thought Hartley intended to educate these foreign students about the American educational system in the hopes of encouraging more American-style schools across the world. However, during the summer, while Hartley vacationed on the Riviera, Billingsley saw some documents that showed that the proposal could be used to train terrorists to infiltrate the United States more easily. He confronted Hartley upon the latter's arrival back from vacation, and Hartley blew off Billingsley's concerns, telling him "someone's going to teach those bastards. We get the tuition dollars and we let our own intelligence and military handle them." Billingsley stewed about that response for several weeks, obsessed about "kill the terrorists"-type blogs over the internet, and on the morning of Hartley's murder, went to confront him one more time. They got into a heated argument; Billingsley completely lost it, stabbing Hartley several times with his Longhorn Award. In a panic, Billingsley took a folder full of all the materials for the proposal with him and got out of Hartley's office probably only a few minutes before the body was discovered. It was a folder Hartley's ex-wife had seen Hartley with just a week earlier when she went to his office to fight over alimony. She had no idea what it contained, but he clutched it tightly the whole time they argued. Luckily, she thought to tell the police to look for it.

When she finished, I stretched out on my bed flabbergasted. Words, let alone coherent thoughts, escaped me for several seconds. Finally, I thought to ask Marsh why it had taken so long for them to figure this out.

"Well, that's one of the questions we'd like to ask you. We had dozens of leads for several months and no one ever mentioned this angle. No reference to a student worker. No mention of the proposal. No suggestion to look into IMET. Why did everyone there hold back on this information?"

"If you haven't noticed, Detective Marsh, this is news to me. I knew nothing about it."

"I could hear that in your responses, Dr. Carter, and given you were brand new this fall, it is understandable that **you** might be one who didn't know."

"Wow! I just don't know what else to say, Detective Marsh. Anyway, the president will be out of the country for close to two weeks. Would you like me to have him call you?"

"Yes, thank you. And make sure he understands as soon as possible, not when he gets back."

"I'll make sure of that, detective."

As I hung up, I thought about what statement we should make to Channel 11. Berrian would probably not be available for three or four more hours. I decided to gather the rest of the executive team, who hopefully weren't too much into the holiday cheer, to discuss how we should respond.

Downstairs, Howard was taping a big piece of construction paper on the wall. Columns and rows were visible on the paper, and numbers had been written in some boxes. I couldn't make out exactly what he was doing.

"What's this, Howard?"

"Oh, wait, Mark, don't tell us what you found out. We need another five or ten minutes."

"What the heck?" I walked closer and saw that the names of various people had been recorded across the top in the columns. At the top, "Ex-Wife #1," "Ex-wife #2," and "Ex-Wife #3," followed by "Palmer," "Linares," "Plutowski," "Hammer," "Palmer's wife," and finally "Student," with "Other" hastily scrawled at the far right of the board. Under most were numbers. That's when I realized what was happening. My guests had made odds as to the murderer's identity. Since within each of the various boxes were the signatures of my guests with dollar amounts, my house had instantly been transformed into a gambling den.

"What the hell?" I growled, ripping it down. "What kind of idiots do I work with? We could get arrested ourselves."

"Oh, lighten up, Mark," said Howard, trying to pull the board away from me. "Really, just give us another ten minutes to finish up the board and the rest."

"You people are nuts." I looked at the board in my hands. The biggest odds had been given to Linares, 10-1, with Kiana King in for $100. Four of my guests apparently liked former Provost Palmer's odds of 7-1; I'd need to watch those four a little more closely. No one had yet to write in their name for "student," which had 1-1 odds. "Sorry, guys, to break up the game, but a student allegedly did it. Everyone keep their original bet." I looked at Howard in disgust. "Really, Howard, don't you think this went too far?"

"Which student, Mark?" yelled Shelley from the kitchen.

"Someone named Karl Billingsley. Caroline, Hank, Howard, Veronica, Tim, Victor, can we talk upstairs for a minute?"

"Karl who?" asked someone.

"I think he said Billingsley. Ever hear of him?" That sounded like Michael Stewart.

"Don't know him," said the first person.

"Anybody ever hear of him?" asked a third person.

Almost everyone shouted or shook their head "no," but as I headed up the stairs with the executive leadership team, Victor's body language revealed that he probably knew him. I pulled Victor's arm to slow him down and let the others get ahead of us.

"So, you knew of him, Victor," I declared angrily.

"Of course, I did, Mark."

"Why is it such a big secret?"

"I'll try to explain once we get upstairs."

My other colleagues loitered at the top of the stairs, not sure which room to go into. "Go into the room on the left. That's my office."

We all squeezed into the smallest room in our house. The people who built the house had made this room a nursery. For us, it served as my study. The room could barely fit my desk, a bookcase, and a chair. However, it seemed more appropriate than the bedroom as an impromptu executive meeting for the seven of us. The phone in my study also had speaker capabilities in case we needed it. We all squeezed in. Veronica sat in my desk chair, while the rest of us stood, filling any available space.

I provided a quick rundown of what I'd learned: "The police have arrested a student worker named Karl Billingsley, who apparently was working with Hartley on a proposal to the International Military Education and Training program. Billingsley got upset with Hartley when he discovered the proposal could support the training of extremists out to destroy America. Hartley did not share this concern, and in the heat of an argument Billingsley allegedly killed Hartley, then took the file with all the documentation for the program."

Judging by the reaction of everyone but Victor, the Billingsley connection was obviously new information. I turned to Victor and challenged him. "Victor, why did none of us know of this situation?"

Victor was pressed against the door, sweating and squirming, although he had little room to do that. "Hartley convinced Berrian and Palmer that this proposal needed to be done completely hush-hush. All the arrangements, including the use of Billingsley as a student worker, were done in secret. To be honest, I basically got dragged in when Berrian told me to help Hartley find a student worker or two and to keep it under the radar."

"Why the hell did Hartley want it done hush-hush?"

"Apparently, he thought the faculty would resist the project, so he convinced Berrian to work around the faculty."

Caroline pointed her finger at Victor. "The faculty wouldn't have been the only ones," she said bitterly.

"And how long ago was this set up?" asked Tim.

"Probably about fifteen or sixteen months ago."

"Damn," muttered Caroline. "So, this had been going on for about a year before Hartley's death."

"What do you know about Billingsley?" I asked.

"We pretty much let Hartley find a student. Berrian asked me to free up potential restrictions to help Hartley get the right student. Since Billingsley took only one class at the time, we had to set up independent study credit to reach the necessary credits for him to be in our student worker program." Victor had slumped completely against the door.

"And none of this was noticed by the appropriate department chair, the advisors, or the records office?"

"Hartley was the dean. He had the ultimate power to request and approve anything like this."

We all looked at each other in silence for a few minutes. Victor eventually lowered his eyes and examined his fingernails. Finally, Hank broke the silence. "So, what's next?"

"I still owe this ... ," I had to look at my notes to remember the name, "Consuela Rodriquez a call. Her media request for a statement caused the call center to call me."

"I know Rodriquez," said Caroline. "She's actually o.k. We can call and tell her that the university has no official comment yet, as well as that we need to wait for all the information before we respond. She's one of the few reporters who probably won't push us too much on that. We should be ready to explain why Bob can't respond at this point."

"Go ahead and tell her that he's on vacation," said Tim. "There's no crime in that. Tell her that if more information comes out that requires his response, we will be glad to connect her to him. Whenever Berrian lands, we call him."

"Everybody o.k. with this plan?" I asked looking around the room.

Getting no response, I clapped my hands. "O.k., Caroline, would you be willing to stay with me and make this call? We can use the speaker phone. Since you know Rodriquez, that may help. Everybody else, out!"

Victor turned to push open the door. However, it opened inward. We all stumbled over each other trying to get turned around and situated so that Victor could open the door. "We're a scene straight from Richard Russo," I exclaimed as Victor tried to inch the door open while moving his body out of the door's way as it came into the room. Eventually, he got it open and my colleagues began to spill out of the room not unlike a Keystone Cops routine.

In the end, Caroline and I reached Rodriquez who graciously accepted our "no comment" response. Almost three hours later, after all the guests had left, Natalie began to clean up the house, while I disappeared to my study again to call Berrian.

"Bob, how was the flight? Are you there safe and sound?"

"Yes, Mark. Flight was smooth and we're just getting settled in the hotel. Beautiful beach right outside my window."

"Great. Great. Look the reason I called is that they have arrested someone for Hartley's murder."

"Oh, sweet mother of Jesus, thank you. That's the best Christmas present anyone could get me."

"Hold your horses, Bob. This might be the lump of coal in your stocking. The murderer was Karl Billingsley."

"Who?"

"Karl Billingsley. Michael's student worker." I looked fondly at my instructor of the year award from Farrington and longed for those simple days of being merely a faculty member.

"Hmm?" The name certainly meant nothing to Berrian. "So, some student offed him? Why the concern?"

"That name doesn't mean anything to you, Bob?"

"Why the hell should it? What's your point, Mark?" Berrian's sudden agitation was palpable, even over the phone. "I got a vacation to get to, so stop dicking around."

"He was the student worker helping on Hartley's IMET proposal."

"I met whom? Christ, between cell phones and being out here in the middle of fucking nowhere, I can't understand what you're saying."

"IMET, Bob. The International Military Education and Training program—the proposal Hartley was putting together to offer some classes for them."

"International military ... I'm sorry, Mark, I really am drawing a blank on this."

"You, Palmer and Hartley set it up about a year and a half ago. Apparently you all did it rather under the table because Hartley feared faculty might not support it."

"Oh, wait. You mean that thing where Hartley wanted to provide online education to foreign troops. Hell, yes, I remember that." Bob's agitation had abruptly shut down.

"Well, Billingsley supposedly believed the proposal would help terrorists, which is what he and Hartley fought about."

"So, the kid is some nutcase right-winger? Perfect! This will be easy for the university to dismiss. *Conspiracy theory fruitcake kills well-meaning Dean.*"

I sighed and looked at my watch: 11:40 PM. I just wanted to curl up and go to sleep. "Bob, first off, the media has called the school and we have issued a standard 'no comment.' There may be a need for you to talk to them over the break. If you do, are you o.k. with us giving you a heads up and having you call them?"

"No problem."

"Secondly, you need to contact Detective Marsh as soon as possible."

"I'll do that in the next couple of days."

"I promised her that you would do it right away."

"Mark, I'm on vacation, damn it!"

"Fine, then thirdly, Bob, this will not play out well. Why didn't we make Hartley's intentions public?"

"What?"

"Why all the under-the-table crap?"

"I don't know. Who cares?"

"The faculty will care. The staff will care. Lord knows, the media will care. A top-secret project was occurring...."

"It wasn't top secret."

"What the hell do you mean, Bob? Only you, Palmer, and Victor evidently knew about it."

"We gave Hartley the room he needed to pursue this opportunity."

"Don't give me that bullshit."

Berrian remained calm as my agitation grew. "Mark, step back a second. It's pretty late and I just got to my hotel. Let's save this conversation for when I get back. I really think you are making too big of a deal about this. The good news is that they have arrested somebody. The better news is that the murderer may be a freaking loony tune. All of this other stuff is nothing to worry about, o.k.?"

"Bob, it is something to worry about. At the minimum, it shows that Boan administration is not transparent."

"When I get back, Mark! Let me know if the media needs more from me in the meantime. I promise I'll call the cute little Detective Marsh." And with that, he hung up the phone. In frustration, I smacked a small Duquesne University globe sitting on my desk with my left hand, causing it to bounce against the wall, smashing and sending pieces of Pittsburgh all over on my floor.

Almost immediately, Natalie showed up at the study door. She saw me slumped over at my desk, head in my hands.

"Let me guess," she said. "That did not go well?"

"About as well as twenty-five-cent beer night at a White Sox game."

"Want to talk about it?"

"Not really. Suffice to say that I'm to talk to Berrian when he gets back."

"When's that?"

"After the New Year's."

Natalie rubbed my shoulders. "Sorry, honey. I don't know what else to say."

I patted her hands on my shoulders. "There's nothing you have to say."

"New Year's isn't that far off."

"Hell, for me, this evening officially starts a new year."

Break

Chapter Seventeen

As much as I tried differently, I couldn't avoid brooding over the holidays. I spent as much time as possible away from my office, phone and e-mail. Luckily legal bureaucratic procedures are similar to university procedures, and so the various next steps in dealing with Billingsley crept along through the holidays. Still, as Alyssa and Natalie watched *The Grinch Who Stole Christmas*, I sat in the other room muttering about "those fools in foolsville." When my daughter and wife immersed themselves completely in the Christmas spirit by watching *It's A Wonderful Life*, I walked through the neighborhood cursing Frank Capra's sentimental claptrap. When a group of carolers actually came to our house and broke into "It's The Most Wonderful Time of The Year," I mumbled from the other room, "stick a fork in it."

On December 23rd, my parents flew in from Arizona. I drove down to Indianapolis to pick them up, and we weren't in the car for more than twenty minutes when my mother picked up on my discontent.

"You don't seem yourself, honey. Is there something wrong?"

"I'm o.k., Mom, don't worry."

"Don't worry! Don't worry? He says, 'don't worry,' Ralph," she said turning to my father staring out the window at the flat Indiana landscape. "How's a mother not to worry?"

My father did not respond. He had grown much quieter in his old age, and at times could completely disconnect from the conversations around him. Medical tests had shown no signs of Alzheimer's or other neurological disorders. He simply participated less and less with those around him. This didn't affect my mother, who went on as she always did, fussing and bustling around her loved ones.

"It's just been a tiring first few months at work, Mom, that's all." I offered her a half-hearted smile.

"Why don't I believe you? Why don't I believe him, Ralph?" My mother, Constance Carter, is a small woman, four feet ten inches tall, barely one hundred pounds. She keeps her white hair short, wears hats even at home in Arizona, and always wraps her body completely with sweaters and scarves to keep warm. As I looked at her in the rear view mirror, all I could see was her still lively face, strengthened by the lines and wrinkles that she's never worried about hiding.

My father, sitting in the passenger seat, still did not turn away from the window to acknowledge my mother's protestations. He sat rigidly, his five-foot-nine inch frame carried like a soldier's. Given he stared out the window, I had a prime view of the growing bald spot on the back of his head. I estimated it to be about the circumference of an orange.

"There's nothing to believe or not to believe, Mom. It's the truth. I'm just tired from a busy first few months." Why was I reticent to share my frustrations with my parents? Was it because I didn't want them to worry? More accurately, did I hope to avoid any histrionics from Mom and indifference from Dad?

"Is it something with Alyssa? Are those awful boys upsetting her again?"

"No, Mom. In fact, she accepted a snake from one of them as a present."

"She did!" said my mother in a sing-song voice. "Isn't that sweet?" Not the reaction I intended. I looked to see if my father reacted. After all, I inherited my Ophidiophobia from him. Yes, I know the word for fear of snakes. That's how much they scare me. Dad, however, still looked placidly out the passenger window.

"Natalie?"

"What about her?"

"Is there something wrong with her?"

"No, Mom."

"Everything all right between you two?" She hesitated. "Still a spark between you, isn't there?"

"Jesus Christ, Mom! Yes, there still is." Distracted I had almost rear-ended a pickup truck in front of me.

"All right. No need to take the lord's name in vain. Especially not during the season."

Despite my desire to remain calm, I found myself unable to stop from slipping into sarcasm. "The season? What's that, Mom? Is that like the football season? Are there a couple of pre-season games for the worship of Christ's birth? What's the post-season, Easter?"

"Mark Allan Carter, that's terrible." My mother's eyes had welled up. "Isn't that terrible, Ralph?"

My father turned slowly from looking out the window. His world-weary face looked at me. I had no idea if my mother could see the glint in his eyes. He caused her to collapse back into her seat with his response. "I thought that was pretty good."

"Don't encourage him."

"Oh, come on, he could have done worse and made a joke about 'sudden death.'"

"You both are going to burn in hell."

We drove in silence for several minutes, my mother sulking in the backseat, my father resuming his meditation with the Indiana landscape. Finally, I had to break the silence.

"How about you, Dad? Are you o.k.?"

My father turned towards me slowly. "I'm fine."

"I hope so. You haven't seemed so the last few times I've seen you."

"I'm fine, Mark."

"There," said my mother from the backseat. "See where you get it from! Two peas from the same pod."

By the time we made it to the house, where Alyssa had charmed her grandparents, and Natalie showed them the house and served them wine, the tension from the car was forgotten. I did recognize in me my father's inclination for silence. The day after Christmas, a postcard arrived from Berrian in the Bahamas. On it he had merely written, "Not a care in the world. Happy Holidays." I ripped it up and dumped it in the trash can. My mother watched me do it, started to say something, but then thought better of it.

A few days later, my father and I sat watching the Champs Sports Bowl on television. Boston College was annihilating Iowa, and we sipped good bourbon, waiting for something exciting to happen in the game. Finally, during the thousandth Geico commercial, my father turned to me and said, "I'm tired, Mark."

"Feel free to go to bed, Dad. This game's a snorer anyway."

He looked at me and sighed. "No, I meant overall, Mark. I'm incredibly tired these days."

I paused, not sure how to respond. I watched as Iowa tried a fake punt, only to come up short on yards. Boston College players, already up thirty-one points, ran around the field as if the play had decided the game. "So, there is something wrong, Dad?"

"When I retired a couple of years ago," he started, not necessarily answering my question, "I thought for sure retirement would recharge my batteries. It just isn't happening."

I swirled the bourbon around in my glass. From upstairs I could hear bath water running, probably Natalie's. "You know, Dad, I'm sorry I haven't been around much to see you in the last four or five years. This is not something I should be hearing for the first time now."

My father waved his hand at me as if to discard the thought. "Nonsense. You have had plenty going on with family and work."

"It's no excuse, though." On the television, the Geico lizard started up again. I hit the mute button. "Anyway, go on."

With the television on mute, the silence was punctuated only by the sound of water in the pipes and the wind rustling through the trees outside. Finally, my father laid down his glass on his coaster and leaned back on the couch.

"When your mother and I moved from Pittsburgh to Phoenix for retirement, I really thought I could put all those years as a principal behind me. I can remember driving our car through Ohio as we headed to Arizona, thinking 'no more meetings, no more policy discussions, no more standardized testing and on and on and on.' I can remember having a list of fifty-two things I wouldn't miss from the job before we even reached the Mississippi River. However, almost as soon as we got settled in Arizona, I found I couldn't cut myself off. My friends e-mail me almost every day with news of the ineptitude, of the corruption, of the cronyism, of the mistakes, of the indecisiveness, of the politics, of the, I don't know what to call it …" He paused to wipe his glasses with the sleeve of his shirt. "Of the general vacuum that the public school system has become. I just can't separate myself from it."

I stared at the TV, watching Boston College cheerleaders flinging themselves into the air in a dangerous and pointless spectacle. Dad took another drink of his bourbon and continued. "I also can't stop reading about education in the newspapers and on the internet. Your mother gets that damn online subscription to the *New York Times*, so every day she calls me to come downstairs to read some article on education. And the truth of the matter is that I want to. I'm still obsessed by the field, still compelled by an insatiable desire to fix everything. What I really need to do is turn it off, to not care anymore. Can you understand that?"

"Very much, Dad. Very much. Probably more than you know." I took a swig of my bourbon. "I thought, though, that you had developed some interests and hobbies in Arizona. More golf. Volunteer activities. Are you saying these things bore you?"

"Not at all. Just that my mind keeps returning to the scene of the crime, so to speak. And even though I feel more like the victim than either the criminal or the detective, I can't help wanting to go back to see what I missed."

Iowa had just recovered a fumble. A fan with a face painted half in black and half in gold thrust his head up to the television camera to flash the ubiquitous "number one" sign with his finger. The score remained Boston

College 38, Iowa 7. "You know, Dad, I really think I can understand. Do you feel like you made this huge personal investment and have come up short?"

"Yes, to some degree." From upstairs, we could hear my mother cough. "More so, I think it feels like a hairshirt. I believe I've paid my penance and deserve to be freed from the discomfort, but it isn't coming off."

"Hmm? Do you think you need to cut off e-mail with the old gang back at work?"

"I don't want to, but I have thought about it."

"How about asking them not to mention their work?"

"Not really possible. That's the common bond we shared, for some, for well over twenty-five years."

Iowa had called a timeout. The head coach had met the quarterback halfway out onto the field to berate him. The quarterback quietly passed him on the way to the sideline.

"Anything I can do, Dad?"

He pondered the question for several minutes, long enough for an incomplete pass and a pathetic fifteen-yard punt. "I think that's part of the puzzle, too, Mark. Education is your field, too. I'm not sure how we handle not talking about that."

I laughed. "Well, that's how it's been the last few days."

My dad smiled. "Don't think I haven't noticed. It's been strange. I keep waiting for you to talk more about the job, but you stay away from anything specific. I've been afraid to push you for details. Should I?"

It was my turn to ponder the question for a minute or two, long enough for Boston College to scamper for a 55-yard touchdown run. Upstairs I could hear my mom coughing again.

"It's been a rough couple of months, Dad. And then the last couple of weeks have really gotten to me. I'm not sure if I'm cut out for this highest level of administration."

"Why don't you think so?"

"Well, the attention to banalities, the obsession with the surface, the hesitancy to be transparent: I knew there'd be un-pleasantries with a provost position, but not to the extreme I'm seeing."

Mom coughed again. I changed the topic. "Is she alright? She's been coughing a lot."

"We're not sure, Mark. She's been to her regular doctor who has prescribed some drugs, but nothing's changed. She has an appointment with another doctor right after we get back. I do worry about your mother. She's slowed down a lot."

"As have you."

"Well, neither of us is aging well. She'll be seventy in March and I'll be sixty-nine in November, you know."

"Yes, I do. But, that's still young."

"Maybe for some, Mark?"

Meanwhile, Iowa threw an interception and Boston College took a knee. "Let's hit the hay, Dad. We both could use a good night's sleep."

"Sure thing, son. Let's talk more tomorrow."

I ended up unable to fall asleep, so while the rest of the house's occupants settled, I washed the bourbon glasses and some dishes scattered around the kitchen. It was pitch black outside, and I relived the conversation from just an hour earlier. It felt like a weight slowly being lifted off of my chest. I wondered if underneath that weight lay my own hairshirt.

Part Five:
Oral Exams

Chapter Eighteen

The Monday after New Year's, cabinet meetings returned to 7:30 AM start times. Due to the last minute change for the starting time, I had to reschedule a breakfast meeting with Charlotte Webb about the new plans for the library renovation, who then had to reschedule a meeting with CIO Alan Yost about access rights for the library's computers. Yost turned around, then, to reschedule a meeting with Bill Howell, Athletic Director, at which they were going to discuss wireless internet in the field house, forcing Howell to reschedule a meeting with Kiana King about student athletes in the allied health programs, which then caused King to contact Shelley about rescheduling our one-on-one later in the week. King sent me an e-mail complaining about the change to which all I could do was e-mail her back to say I shared her frustration. Such is the life of academia: time is a precious commodity to be hoarded, stolen, bartered and valued beyond any budgetary worth.

Berrian, for once, arrived last to cabinet that morning. He came into the room like a bronzed god, tanned to the point of leathery skin. My colleagues exchanged the expected banter about him spending too much time on the beach and about the rest of us envying him too much. For the most part, I stayed out of the repartee. Berrian cut it short anyway to launch into the meeting.

"Let's begin with the arrest in the Hartley case," he said. "Any updates?"

We all looked around the room at each other. Finally, I broke the silence. "I don't think any of us have talked to anyone since I called you in the Bahamas, Bob. I figured you'd be the one with the update."

"Not much to say. I talked to Marsh several times while on vacation, and provided my own 'no comment' to a couple of calls from the press."

"Did Marsh have more information?"

"Not really. The case looks like a slam dunk. The kid ... what's his name?"

"Karl Billingsley."

"Yeah, that guy. He's confessed. They found Hartley's IMET folder in his possession. I don't think they're worried about this one."

"Well, good, then," said Victor.

"Anybody know why Marsh keeps busting my butt about why we didn't give her a heads up about this Billingsley character?"

"What do you mean?" asked Hank.

"She keeps suggesting we covered this up. Billingsley's fingerprints were one of several unidentified fingerprints left at the scene, but since he has no record, his fingerprints weren't on file. Since we didn't tell them to check him out, they weren't able to get his fingerprints until they broke the IMET angle."

"How did you respond to that?" asked Howard.

"I kept telling her that I barely knew about Billingsley. I just don't get what she's harping about."

Others might have been nervous about telling the boss the obvious, but I was beyond caring. Still, I chose my words carefully. "Her question isn't just about you, Bob, I'm guessing. I think she's wondering how they could talk to so many people here and not have one person say, 'hey, maybe Hartley's student worker can be some help.' No one mentioned this because almost none of us knew about it. The police can't understand how a university could have such a top secret activity going on. They apparently don't believe us, and I can't say I blame them."

"What is the big deal? Hell, I barely remembered it."

"Are you listening to me, Bob? It isn't about whether you could remember it or not. It's about a whole university basically having no freaking clue about a major proposal being developed. It looks like we hid this. They're cops, you know. They look for suspicious activities."

"The kid's a nut job. Now that he's confessed, they should just wrap this up."

"I give up." I looked at my colleagues around the U-shaped table. "Anybody else want to take a shot?"

"I have to admit, Mark, that we shouldn't make a mountain out of a molehill here," said Howard. "Just let it die down."

I could feel the heat in my face increasing. How were the others handling this? Victor squirmed around in his chair, avoiding eye contact, but Caroline and Tim looked intent on interceding. Hank had leaned back in his chair, removing himself from my line of sight. "It won't die down, Howard. The media and the courts will keep it alive."

"Screw the media. I'm tired of this discussion. Let's move on!" ordered Berrian.

Tim finally spoke up. "Mark's right, Bob, in that the media may not let this just die. You can say 'screw them,' but that doesn't change the fact that they'll do what they do. Even with conveying the basic facts, this little-known activity at Boan will be made public. We better be ready to counter punch."

Berrian grimaced. "At the risk of allowing this discussion to go on longer, what do you suggest, Tim?"

"I suggest we release a statement that basically says we were unaware just how secretively Hartley carried on this work. We can even cite the 'unfortunate circumstances' surrounding the transition from Provost Palmer through Provost Carter that allowed Hartley to proceed without the normal checks and balances."

"That could work," suggested Victor. "The paperwork that went through on Billingsley was incredibly vague in its details. There's nothing in the documentation of that student worker position, I'm pretty sure, that would contradict that basic story."

Berrian stroked his chin. "Do you think this is necessary?"

"It's the right thing to do to protect Boan."

"What do the rest of you think?"

"Wait a minute," I exploded. "We're talking about lying here. What about our values statement: 'Act with Honor; Honor all Actions'?"

"Now, now, Mark," responded Tim. "There is no 'lying' going on here. Isn't it accurate to say that everyone here was unaware just how secretively Hartley pursued this project?"

"No! Victor and Bob knew."

"No," said Tim in a maddeningly soothing voice, "Victor and Bob have already admitted that they had pretty much forgotten what Hartley was doing. If they have 'forgotten,' is that not the same as saying they were 'unaware'?"

"You're kidding, right?"

"And, isn't it true that in the transition between Riley and you that this topic never came up?"

"That's because Riley didn't know about it! Jesus Christ!"

"Settle down, Mark. And Riley didn't know because Palmer didn't tell her. Isn't all this 'unfortunate'?"

I kept shaking my head in disbelief. "So, we throw Palmer under the bus again? He'll have more tread marks on him than Wile E. Coyote."

"When have we ever thrown Palmer under the bus?" asked Berrian.

"Never mind. Inside joke."

"Let me see if I have this straight," proclaimed Caroline. "We will spin this story to show us as clueless and dense as opposed to calculating and cagey? Is that right?" I stifled a laugh.

Tim laid his hand on Caroline's shoulder. "Don't characterize it that way, Caroline. We will show that a university is a very complex place and that pockets of people can sometimes operate outside of the knowledge of others."

"Then, that will be the truth," I muttered.

"I still don't know what the big deal is, but as of now, this discussion is over. Tim will work on the statement, and everybody else will shut up about it." Berrian looked at each of us, holding my gaze for the longest. "Understood?"

After a few seconds of silence, he resumed the meeting. "Next agenda item: 'Speaker—Women's History Month.' Caroline, what have you got?"

"As you all now know, Janet Reno has had to cancel her presentation during Women's History Month. We need to decide on her replacement. And we need to decide fast."

"Is that in February?" asked Hank.

"No, that's Black History Month. Women's is March." Caroline had pulled out her BlackBerry to search her calendar. "We're hoping for a speaker at the beginning of the month, but at this point, we can adjust to later given our tight deadline."

"Who's our speaker for Black History Month?"

"Condoleezza Rice."

"Well, couldn't we get Rice to speak for both months?" asked Howard.

"You're kidding, Howard, right? This is another of your jokes?"

"Actually, this time, it wasn't. Have her give one speech about both blacks and women."

"Forget about it. Do you want me to schedule it for 11:30 on February 28, so that she can speak for an hour and change topics dramatically at midnight?"

"I was only trying to help, Caroline."

Caroline had turned to face Berrian again. "The committee for organizing Women's History Month activities had recommended a few others in the fall when we chose Reno. Let me remind you of their recommendations: Sandra Day O'Connor, Maya Lin, Geraldine Ferraro, Maya Angelou, and Gloria Steinem."

Berrian's face looked as if he sucked on a lemon. "First off, no Steinem and no Ferraro. Who were the other ones?"

"Wait a second, Bob," I interrupted. "Why so quick on dismissing Ferraro and Steinem?"

"We don't need the kind of press they can bring."

I felt as if my head would explode. "We just finished talking about the press associated with the coverage of a spectacular murder investigation of one of our deans, and we're worried about the press that a feminist or a former politician might bring."

"Goodness, Mark, what bee's got into your bonnet today?" Berrian continued with his infuriating way of remaining calm in the face of my indignation. "Who were the other ones, Caroline?"

Caroline gave me a smirk and responded, "Sandra Day O'Connor, Maya Lin and Maya Angelou."

"Remind me again of these Mayas?" asked Berrian.

"Surely you know Maya Angelou, sir?" I asked. "The famous poet who read at Clinton's inauguration?"

"Oh, yeah, that woman."

"Yes, **that** woman," sneered Caroline.

"Oh, give me a break, Caroline. I probably hid my head in my hands all through Clinton's inauguration."

'As opposed to hiding it in the sand all through Obama's,' I thought.

"She's incredibly famous, Bob. I seriously doubt we could get her at this point. She doesn't lecture much and given this short notice...."

"And that leaves O'Connor and the other Maya. What's her last name again?"

"Lin."

"Dang, why can't I remember that? And what has she done?"

"She designed the Vietnam Vet War Memorial." Caroline had an amazing ability to maintain her composure with people when I know I would want to rip off their heads.

"The one in Washington D.C.?"

"No, Bob, the one in Calcutta, India," teased Howard.

"Yes, the one in D.C."

"Oh, shut up, Howard. I'd say O'Connor is my first choice, Lin's my second. What do others think?"

"Either's fine with me," said Tim.

"Same," grunted Hank.

"That's fine," responded Victor, "but we might need more names as backup. We are talking barely two months."

"I'll have the committee quickly recommend other names. Mark or Howard, any objections to Lin or O'Connor?"

I flicked my hand to show I was fine with it.

"I'm o.k.," said Howard, "but I do have a question."

"What, Howard?" asked Caroline tensely.

"When is Caucasian Male month?"

"That's an all-year recognition, Mr. Entitled," I responded.

"It better be November. About the time the average Caucasian male spends all his free time on the couch watching football. Then, at Thanksgiving, we eat turkey, the perfect symbol for Caucasian males." Caroline turned to face Bob again. "That's it for this topic, Bob."

"The next topic is town halls," said Berrian. "We have those starting in a couple of weeks. You can see the dates on the agenda. We'll do two with faculty and staff and then the following week have three town halls with students. Everyone has their calendars cleared for these, correct? I want all of the executive team at each one."

The rest of us mumbled that we understood.

"I'll give a brief 'state of the university' at the beginning of each town hall—something around five minutes. Nothing too long," continued Berrian. "I'll highlight success with enrollment, fund-raising, staffing, probably remind everyone of upcoming goal review in relation to the strategic plan, budget preparation for next fiscal year. What else should I mention?"

"How about the launch of the SturgeOne Card?" asked Hank. "Everyone needs to know we will be implementing those in fall for students, with faculty and staff getting them at the turn of the fiscal year."

"Is it too early to tell them this, Hank? Isn't this only going to cause the Chicken Littles to start freaking out?"

"Bob, we need to start training faculty and staff in March or April. That's not that far away," Caroline exclaimed.

"I don't know. Anytime we get into a specific initiative like that in front of the masses, we have the potential to get bogged down in the details. I prefer to keep the discussion at the thirty thousand foot level."

"You mean the level where no one can see anything and frankly has to trust the pilot?"

Caroline surprised me; for the first time since my arrival, I could see a slight chink in her armor. This was the closest she had ever come to direct defiance of Berrian.

"Don't be so damn cynical, Caroline," snapped Berrian. "It is unproductive to have town halls disintegrate into debates about the design of a debit card, which is exactly what would happen here."

"And I would argue, Bob, that if we manage the discussion, we can allow the information to be shared, the important concerns and observations to be heard, and the detail-peddling to be curbed by our direction."

I decided to add my two cents. "Besides, Bob, I have often seen the audience themselves police each other when it comes to this kind of unproductive nit-picking. Henry Van Wyck has done it several times at faculty meetings. I've been accused of planting her in meetings to tell people to shut up, but the truth of the matter is I don't have to. Trust all of us to manage the situation."

"Hmm, I don't know," responded Berrian. "Let me think about it. What else?"

"It's not so much another item, Bob, but a question," said a slightly shaking Victor.

"What, Victor?"

"When you said you would like to highlight 'success with staffing,' what do you mean?"

"Well, the executive team is set for the first time in a couple of years. I will point out that the university should be proud to finally have a full team, thanks to the addition of Mark and Tim. In addition, we have hired Lance Meeks as VP of Corporate Services and Sheila Tharp as VP of Training and Development. That reminds me, Veronica, schedule both of them to come to be introduced to cabinet at our next meeting. They started in early December, but we haven't had them come to one of our meetings, yet."

"Back to the main point, Bob. Do you think faculty and staff will, uh ..." Caroline searched for just the right word. "Do you think they will appreciate that message, Bob?"

"What do you mean, Caroline?"

"Well, staffing at the levels below us is a bit chaotic right now. Mark has the two open dean positions. Advising has had three key people let go and we have decided not to replace them right away. We still need call center staff. My colleagues can probably name key open positions in their areas. I'm just wondering if your message will be lost among all those open and uncertain staffing areas."

"That's kind of why I asked, Bob," commented Victor. "Especially in Caroline's area, there are a lot of morale issues because people are being asked to do more when positions are vacated and no one is hired."

"But, that will be my point," smiled Berrian. "That we have the executive team in place to now drive decision-making."

"Drive it down, you mean?" asked Caroline.

"What do you mean?" Berrian eyed Caroline cautiously.

"We promote a culture of decision-making at the lowest level, but we don't always exhibit that."

"Nonsense. What does that have to do with staffing?"

"Everything. We have staff all over the university unable to make decisions because they have no supervisor to direct them. They are not empowered to make any decisions themselves, so they make no decision. Even at the supervisory level, we have people ready to make a decision, even about whom to hire, and they can't because they wait for us to bless from above."

"What the hell is this? Is this 'let's make mountains out of molehills' day? Did all of you get soft on me over the holidays?" Berrian had stood up and begun his caged tiger pacing routine.

Caroline took a deep breath. "Allow me to go back to the primary issue: staffing. What kind of message do you think it sends when we tell our staff to applaud the hiring of two executive vice presidents for a total expense of, what Victor, probably $400,000?" Victor shrugged and Caroline carried on. "That $400,000 could probably hire seven front-line staff people, who work with students all the time."

"Salaries aren't public knowledge, are they, Victor?" Berrian asked with great concern.

"Of course, not, Bob," said Caroline. "That doesn't mean they aren't smart enough to guesstimate. Again, I think you're missing the bigger picture."

"Is that the thirty-thousand foot picture, Caroline?" asked Howard.

"All right, that's enough of all of this!" yelled Berrian. "What is it with you people today?"

As he paced, we sat eyes lowered. Eventually, he settled back into his seat to tackle the next agenda topic. Unfortunately, the reaction by the rest of the executive team resembled our reaction on the second day of the retreat. We offered little of substance to the discussions of complaint procedures or building projects or anything else. Caroline sat noticeably stewing, twirling her reading glasses with one hand and rubbing her eyes frequently with the other. Victor nervously took notes, making little eye contact with anyone else at the table. Howard cracked no jokes, never needled Berrian or the rest of us, keeping one eye on his BlackBerry and the other on Berrian. Tim listened the most attentively of all of us, but provided short, concise answers only when called upon. Veronica's laptop gave her something to hide behind. Hank, usually the most dependable member of cabinet, in terms of sustaining a normal modus operandi, showed perceptible signs of discomfort through a wide array of facial expressions. Beyond observing my colleagues, I simply tuned out, something I no longer fretted about.

Throughout the rest of the meeting, Berrian was either oblivious to the marked changes in his executive team or indifferent to them. As a result, when we finished early, we all excused ourselves and hurried out of the room. Since most headed back to the Administration Building, I decided to take a walk around the campus to get some fresh air. Snow lay on the ground, but the temperatures hovered around freezing with a bit of sun peeking through the clouds. I headed toward the field house, which represented the farthest point away from where I was. There and back should take twenty minutes to a half hour, enough time to collect my thoughts.

Along the way, I passed the expected bands of smokers standing the requisite twenty feet from the entrance to the closest building. Most huddled together, not bothering to put on coats for their three minutes of tobacco. Students mingled with faculty and staff, including several I never would have pegged as smokers until seeing them in that twenty-foot no smoking zone. You have to hand it to smokers. Despite all the barriers put up by society, they still find a way to get in a smoke.

Nearing the field house, I jogged inside to take advantage of the restrooms. Even though it was early afternoon, the place was surprisingly empty. Given the semester had only just begun, students still went to their classes as opposed to skipping classes to take advantage of the pool tables, exercise equipment, basketball courts, or racquetball courts. Walking the main level provided a great view of the racquetball courts from above. The first two courts stood empty, but in the third court, Dewayne Wilson played against someone I didn't recognize. I stopped to watch, waving at Dewayne at the first opportunity when he glanced up behind him. Occasionally, a long shot came up to hit the Plexiglas separating the court from me, causing me to flinch.

Watching Wilson fling himself around the racquetball court against a ruthless opponent, I mulled over his potential. While still a little green, as Jennifer Riley had told me initially, he showed quick learning ability, strong instincts, and a personality that could help him rise within the organization. His colleagues had responded favorably to his chairing the dean search committee. Give him another year and he could be a viable candidate for dean, which, because of his minority background, would serve university leadership well. As the only black leader at the dean or executive vice president level, Kiana King was not the ideal role model to attract more diversity in leadership. Riley and I had recently discussed the ways we could both mentor Wilson, but I had not had any opportunity to do my part since the dean search petered out a month earlier.

I leaned against the Plexiglas while enjoying the game. Wilson was getting slaughtered, despite the fact that he played well. His opponent, a short, balding black man with stubbly legs, was simply relentless, running Wilson all around the court. Wilson to his credit never gave up, diving for balls and crashing into wall after wall. After a couple of minutes, Wilson adjusted his playing strategy, and effectively used all four walls to force his opponent to be reactive as opposed to proactive. Finally, at one point, Wilson gave remarkable effort to dive forward to return the ball but ended up prostrate on the court. Meanwhile his opponent smashed his return so that the ball came off the front wall and banged off the back of Wilson's head. The game must have been over, because while Wilson stayed on the ground, rubbing his head, wondering what had hit him, his adversary strutted around the court, waving his racquet in the air.

I walked down the stairs to talk briefly to Wilson before he limped to the locker room, meeting him in the hallway outside the court's doorway. His Lincoln University t-shirt was completely soaked from sweat. His opponent remained on the court.

"Hey, Mark. Decided to watch a couple of hacks playing racquetball, eh?"

"You both are quite good. The only hacking may have come from blood in the mouth."

"Yes, it was intense. Lance always pushes me to the extreme." At that point, Lance had come through the doorway. He, too, wore a Lincoln University t-shirt.

"Is that a tiger?" I asked pointing at the emblem on Dewayne's shirt.

"A blue tiger."

"A blue tiger? What the heck? Was he the product of some mushroom-induced marketing meetings in the 60's?"

'Hey, don't be dissing the tiger," said Lance, stepping between me and Dewayne.

"He isn't dissing him, Lance. By the way, Mark, I assume you have met Lance Meeks, the new head of corporate services."

"Actually, I haven't." I held out my hand and received, not surprisingly, a death grip for a handshake. "Pleased to meet you. Mark Carter, Provost."

"Ah," smiled Meeks. "I wondered when I'd get around to meeting you."

"Well, you know, the holiday season is a difficult time to meet new colleagues."

"I was surprised you weren't part of the interviews."

"You weren't, Mark?" asked a surprised Dewayne.

"No, and I'm not sure why. Anyway, am I to assume you guys went to school together?"

"Yep, good old Lincoln University," answered Wilson. "We met our junior year and have been friends since. I encouraged Lance to apply to Boan."

"Have you always subjected poor Dewayne here to such physical abuse?"

"Absolutely. I try to toughen the lad up."

"How tough is that head?" I asked Dewayne. "That last shot really bounced off it."

Wilson rubbed the back of his head. "Ah, that's nothing. Lance can't hurt me."

Meeks slapped Wilson on the back. "I'm going to get started on a shower. Nice to meet you, Mark."

As Meeks walk away, I held Wilson's arm for a quick second. "Hey, Dewayne, I haven't had a chance yet to tell you how much I appreciated your leadership with the search committee. Just because we didn't find anybody doesn't mean you didn't do a good job."

He wiped his face with the only remaining square inch of dry shirt. "Thanks. It was an interesting experience. I really do appreciate the opportunity to step out of my normal duties."

"I think you have a great career ahead of you if you wish to do more than teach."

"That's what Lance keeps telling me," he said, pointing his racquet toward the locker room Meeks had disappeared in. "He says I have to be tougher, though. More aggressive with what I believe and all that. I'm not sure that's my style."

I pondered that for a moment. "I don't believe you have to adapt your personality that way, Dewayne. Just go with your natural talents and abilities."

"I'm special education, Mark. How do those skills translate to higher education?"

"Are you freaking kidding? Higher education administration is full of attention deficit disorders. Sit in one meeting and listen to unbelievable fuzzy math and you'll be convinced everyone has dyscalculia. And while there may not be cases of dyslexia, I would argue that most administrators suffer from dysliteracyia. They're not illiterate, they're anti-literate."

Wilson chortled. "You really shouldn't make light of people with learning disabilities, Mark."

"I know, Dewayne. It's an insult to compare them to a higher education administrator. Anyway, you need to hit the shower. That shirt is about ready to grow legs and walk away."

That night I sat on my porch and reflected on the start of the winter semester. As a teacher, a chair, even as a dean, the start of a new semester represented new hope. In my role now, the weeks simply blended together into a never-ending fourth dimension where time became irrelevant and immeasurable.

I watched a squirrel approach one of my bird feeders. Even enjoying my porch and yard had become a never-ending struggle, thanks to a family of squirrels. As winter came, we had put food and suet out for the birds, but the squirrels constantly stole both. At the beginning, Alyssa and I found it a bit of a game, trying to see which of us could bean a squirrel with tennis balls. Eventually, we invested in fancier birdfeeders purported to be squirrel-proof, but weren't. We sprinkled ground red hot pepper in with the bird food, which reportedly kept the squirrels away, but succeeded only slightly more than when we greased the poles the squirrels climbed. Every night, just like tonight, I was destined to scream the foulest profanities at the furry bastards as I watched them again and again beat me in a battle of wits between rodent and human.

The snow also started to pile up. We never received any record snowfalls, but each day dropped a few more inches on top of what already lay on the ground, and it added up. I have never minded the cold, but driving in snow wore on me. As a result of the trifecta of weather, work and rodent, I recognized that I must be a difficult husband and father to be around.

Chapter Nineteen

A few weeks later, when Caroline and I decided we wanted another faculty member for our retention committee I recommended Dewayne Wilson. He was an obvious choice because of his background in learning theories. He would complement Annie Langenstine, Department of English, the only other faculty member on the committee. Wilson joined us for the first time at our late January meeting.

That meeting's agenda was dominated by the discussion of data and metrics related to our course delivery systems. Tanya Tyler had provided Caroline and me a sneak preview of the data before the meeting, and we were both excited, although for slightly different reasons. Caroline believed she had solid evidence showing that average class size had absolutely nothing to do with student success, while I saw the foundation for an argument showing that accelerated deliveries related directly to retention problems.

Two members missed the January retention meeting leaving us with the stern, but suddenly optimistic, Caroline, the new, eager-to-please Dewayne Wilson, the prim and proper Annie Langenstine, the numbers-filled Tanya Tyler, and solid-as-a-rock Jennifer Riley. After months of speculation and discussion, all of us were genuinely pleased to finally have some data to examine. Tyler spent the fall semester setting up a number of processes to allow her to gather success rate information for students.

In the meeting room, Tyler brought handouts replete with numbers. All of it appeared completely unintelligible at first glance, and my initial reaction was to run screaming from what looked to be endless sudoku. However, Tyler quickly began explaining each handout via a computer and smartboard.

"This first sheet," she said, gesturing toward the screen, "shows the success for fifteen-week traditional in-seat classes. As you can see the numbers have been pretty consistent for the last two years." Sure enough, Tyler could point to mid 60% retention rates, mid 70% pass rates, and high 70% student satisfaction scores for the fifteen-week in-seat classes.

"Remind me how we define 'retention?'" asked Wilson.

"It's the number of students who are still with the university from fall semester to following fall semester," replied Tyler.

Wilson nodded his head in understanding. "The second sheet," Tyler continued, advancing her word document, "shows the success of seven-week online courses. As you can see, retention is in the low 60% range, pass rates in the mid 60% range with a low 80% for student satisfaction."

"That surprises me," divulged Wilson.

"Why?" asked Tyler.

"It just does. I suppose I'm merely admitting to my own perception about online."

I laughed. "Don't worry, Dewayne. Caroline, Tanya and I have heard that all before. It was the subject of a painful University Council meeting."

Wilson continued, "I thought online courses had absolutely no restrictions. And with no restrictions came chaos."

Tyler shook her head. "Online has an assessment instrument that students have to pass to get into the class; in addition, online faculty go through a rigid training and assessment themselves." Tyler waved her finger at me, exaggeratedly. "This is why you have to name a head for online academics, Mark. Your own people don't know the truth."

"You want to do it, Tanya?"

"Hell, no! What kind of idiot would want to oversee a function of the university that we can't even define?"

"That's the problem. No one wants to do it. And whether we go outside to find somebody is a decision hung up in HR hell."

"Anyway," said Tanya, getting us back on task, "here's where things start getting really interesting. The third page shows the seven-week basic accelerated format. Remember, for this and the last three deliveries we only can go back about a year: low 50% retention rates; high 50% pass rates; mid 60% student satisfaction scores. We see some significant differences from the first two."

"And remind me," asked Wilson, "is there an entrance assessment for students in these courses?"

"No. There is nothing."

"How comparable are the numbers?" asked Riley.

"You mean in terms of total students as compared to the other two deliveries?"

"Uh, yeah, that would be a better way to say it," replied Riley smiling.

"No significant difference. Frankly, we had a huge number of students in the seven-week basic accelerated, so I'm most comfortable with this comparison to the previous two deliveries."

"The mad rush for the 'need for speed'?" asked Riley.

"Oh, yeah." Tyler moved to the fourth sheet. "Here we have the honors accelerated. Not surprisingly, we had high 80% retention rates, mid 80% pass rates, but low satisfaction scores, in the high 50%."

"Isn't that fascinating?" said Caroline who had been quiet up until then. "So, the better students don't necessarily like the fast pace. Did you capture the satisfaction scores for honors students in the other delivery formats?"

"Certainly. That's buried near the bottom of these pages, where I show specific breakdown by demographics. Satisfaction rates are high among honors students in traditional and online, not so much for the standard accelerated."

"Interesting," I said, sucking on the end of my pen. "So, Caroline, which one of us gets to tell the boss that our best students prefer non-accelerated to accelerated?"

"Uh, I plan to be out of town that day. Perhaps you can take it?" Caroline winked at me and I smiled back.

"Don't get too excited, you two. The sample size in all the honors' cases is pretty small. After all, the average class size for honors' courses ranges from six in the accelerated to fourteen in the non-accelerated classes."

"Is it just me," asked Wilson, "or is everybody's head spinning right about now?"

"Oh, don't worry, Dewayne," spoke the usually quiet Langenstine. "A few meetings like this and not only will your head spin but you will be blaspheming a priest."

"So are we left with the other two accelerated deliveries, Tanya?" I asked.

"Yes, we are." She advanced the word document to the sheet proclaiming 'accelerated for professionals.' "Now, in this case, the adult working students prefer the accelerated. See, the low 80% satisfaction scores. However, retention in this format is in the mid 40% and pass rates are in the high 50%."

"Holy crap. Is that really mid 40% retention?" Wilson asked.

"Unfortunately, so. But keep in mind, another relatively low sample of the population."

"And how do they compare with the working adult numbers in the other formats?" I asked.

"Well, there's almost no sample size there. Almost all of them flooded to the accelerated options as soon as we offered them."

"That's true," confirmed Cruz. "We spent hours last year processing change of status forms."

"So, anyone want to speculate on the dramatically low retention? Is it obvious that they can't keep up?" asked Caroline.

"They like it; they just don't stick with it. Isn't that a remarkable phenomenon?" said Langenstine.

"It could be our new marketing campaign: 'so good that it's bad for you.' Can you see it on a bumper sticker?" asked Riley.

"This can be the one you discuss with Berrian, Caroline," I exclaimed.

"Oh, I can hear him now. 'If they like it, but they aren't being retained, then clearly it's the right thing to do, we just have to do it better.'"

"Let me get to the last one, everybody." Tanya displayed blended accelerated on the screen. "Retention rates are o.k. at mid 50%, but pass rates are only about 50%, and student satisfaction is only in the mid 60's."

We all leaned back in our chairs and contemplated everything we had seen. No one spoke for several minutes.

"Let me show you what I discovered," announced Tyler, switching the computer to a different screen and displaying a series of line graphs. "On these graphs, I removed the honors accelerated as it is an outlier. It doesn't take an honors student to see why that group is not representative of the rest of the university. However, taking the other five deliveries, there is a correlation between contact hours and retention rates. The more direct contact between student and teacher, the more likely the students are to be retained."

"You mean I've sat in these stupid meetings for almost two years and this is the obvious conclusion we come to," said Langenstine in a rare moment of spontaneity.

I laughed. "It appears so."

"But, I don't understand, Tanya," interrupted Wilson. "The five-week accelerated has a higher retention rate than the seven-week basic accelerated."

"That's because we tell students to expect an additional three hours each week using online as supplement to the twenty hours of actual face-to-face time. So, technically they have thirty-five 'contact' hours with faculty, while the regular accelerated has twenty-eight 'contact' hours."

"And that explains," stated Riley, standing up to get closer to the screen, "why the seven-week online has the higher retention rate. We also tell students there to expect five to six hours a week being online."

"Yeah, but it's not really constant contact with the faculty member," argued Langenstine.

"It's not really about the physical contact with the faculty member," started Tyler.

"Damn straight, it better not be about physical contact," I interjected.

Tyler smiled. "I stand corrected by the provost. Anyway, I think we argue that it's about structured engagement with the 'course.'"

"That's double talk," declared Langenstine. "That's hardly the same as the contact hours we have with students in the classroom."

"Be careful, there, Annie," I said, stepping in. "Don't generalize. Do you spend every hour in the classroom in complete engagement with the students?"

"Of course, I do. What are you insinuating? I never let a class out early."

"I've never met a faculty member who admits they do. But, that's not my point. What I mean is—do you assign group projects?"

"You know I do, Mark. They're part of the skills we teach."

"And do you let the students work in groups sometimes while you merely observe?"

Langenstine hesitated. She could feel the net falling around her. "Well, naturally."

"And do you devote class time to tests, quizzes, and presentations?"

"Yes," she replied quietly.

"This is what Tanya has hit upon. 'Contact hours' is a very loose way to describe the time students are 'forced' to work in some kind of structured manner. It seems to me, as I look at this data, that academics needs to go back and analyze the structure, or lack thereof, in these accelerated deliveries. We might need to add more hours of structured activity, or we might have to abandon them completely."

"By the way," spoke an observably glowing Tyler, "there is a similar trend with pass rates. It's just not as clean. For example, the pass rates are pretty much the same once you get below thirty-five contact hours."

"As for the satisfaction scores?" asked Riley.

"God, who knows? Can we convince the big guy that they are red herrings?"

"Yeah, sure, Tanya. Caroline and I will let you tell him that directly."

"And throughout all of these, the size of the class hasn't mattered, right, Tanya?" asked Caroline.

"Not significantly."

"Your issue, Caroline, is a corollary to the main one. If we can limit the options for delivery, based upon retention and pass rate data, then you will get larger classes as a general rule. Finance isn't going to agree to a different average class size based upon anything here."

"I know that, Mark, but that doesn't mean that Bob will understand. If he can be convinced there is a correlation, he'll twist Turing's arm, and we'll be good."

I laughed. "O.k., good luck with that one."

My one-on-one with Berrian followed Caroline's the next week, and she must not have had any luck. The two of them ran over the scheduled time, allowing me to see a noticeably troubled Caroline leave Berrian's office, while he scowled at her, holding the door. "Come on, Mark," he yapped, "let's get started."

Even before I could address my agenda items, the usual starting point for our meetings, he plunged into a discussion about retention.

"Caroline just showed me the latest data from the retention committee. She believes that the evidence suggests we need to alter some of our policies surrounding deliveries and class size. Is that how you see it?"

Would it be possible to buy time for the full hour and get out of here without answering that question directly? "That's hard to say, Bob, since I don't know exactly what she told you."

"She said you two had already discussed it."

"It depends what the 'it' is."

"Don't go Clinton on me."

"I'm not kidding, Bob. How can I tell you if I agree with Caroline when I don't know what she presented to you?" Outside, more snow fell.

Berrian rummaged around a pile of papers sitting on his desk. "Jesus Christ," he grumbled. "Where the hell is that... ?" Finally, in frustration, he pushed the pile of papers off the desk. "I can't find the specifics. It's basically the argument that retention declines with the accelerated offerings. How that relates to class size, I can't remember."

I figured that while Berrian thrashed around his office, trying to find Caroline's documentation, I could play the ignorant card as long as I needed. However, I wasn't about to let Caroline dangle.

"Here's a graph of the retention and pass rates for all the deliveries. I do have some thoughts about this."

"Damn it, that's it. That's exactly what she showed me."

"Good, then you're familiar with it. The data may not be ideal, as in some cases we only have one year of information, but it compares similarly to other patterns."

"Yes, yes. I'm remembering now." Bob hunched far over his desk reviewing the material.

"I don't know how Caroline expressed it to you, but the evidence is especially strong that the more contact hours increase, the more retention and pass rates increase."

"She said that the more we engage students, the more likely they are to succeed."

"That would be a way to put it."

"So, the issue is with faculty not engaging students enough?"

"It's not that simple, Bob."

"Why not? Isn't that exactly what this shows?"

I took a deep breath. How much time did I have left? Forty-five minutes to navigate this discussion? "I would talk about it in terms of structured learning. Leaving students to learn without structure inevitably puts them at risk. And if you think about it, it makes sense."

"Absolutely. Go on."

"Well, for instance, in a regular fifteen-week class, students get forty-five hours of structured learning activities. That may be direct learning from the instructor, through lecture or discussion, but that may also be quizzes, tests, group work, field projects, and so forth."

"Sure. When I taught I loved to use quizzes to see how much they were learning." Berrian beamed as if he had just described his role in storming Omaha Beach.

I ignored the comment and continued. "This is why I hesitate to say it's about the faculty not engaging them enough. In some of these scenarios, the instructor provides a general structure, such as group work, and then monitors the students to ensure they learn from each other."

Bob had leaned back in his chair. "This is great stuff. You've explained it well."

"So, reason follows that if we give students only twenty-eight hours of structured learning, then we're expecting them to figure out the other necessary seventeen hours of learning on their own."

"O.k., now you lost me."

"How?"

"How what?"

"How have I lost you?"

"What kind of question is that?"

"It's a reasonable question. If you're driving, and I'm in a car leading you, and you call my cell to say, 'you lost me,' that could have happened because all of a sudden, I went too fast. Or, maybe I made a green light but you got stopped at a red light. Maybe we entered a neighborhood you're not familiar with. Perhaps we hit a big traffic jam and you literally can't see me anymore. To ask, 'how did I lose you?' is a perfectly acceptable response."

"Damn it, Mark, you're giving me a headache." The vein on his forehead supported that.

"So, in what way did you not understand what I said?"

"You suggested that twenty-some hours of structured learning leaves about twenty hours of unstructured learning. Is that right?"

"Well, twenty-eight hours structured and seventeen unstructured, but, yes, you got the gist." I would need to navigate this discussion very carefully.

"Then why don't faculty structure seventeen other hours that students are expected to complete?"

"Well, if they do that, then they would have the traditional fifteen-week course."

"Can't we get them to do it in seven weeks or five weeks?"

I forced myself to continue smiling as if explaining the theory of relativity to an eager young freshman. "Students would be sitting in classrooms for incredibly long periods of time, five to six hours at a time. Attention spans and energy levels would be challenged."

"Then have the faculty create the structure outside of the classroom."

I watched the snow fall outside of Berrian's window. As Kenny Rogers sang, "you got to know when to fold them."

"I tell you what, Bob, let me compile some comparative information on the structures in each of these classes and I'll get back to you." This suggestion would buy me more time, allowing me to reconvene with Caroline to see exactly how her discussion went astray, and to strategize a plan of attack.

"Excellent. Now before you leave, I need you to look into this complaint."

He handed me a printout of an e-mail. Even before I looked at it, I pondered whether to point out that we still had a half hour and my agenda to discuss. But Kenny's voice echoed in my head, "know when to walk away."

"Will do, Bob. I'll get back to you." As I left his office, I conjured more lines from a second Kenny Rogers song, "Coward of The County": "walk away from trouble if you can." I didn't know which was worse, that I had backed down from Berrian or that Kenny Rogers had become the soundtrack of my life.

Between the snow and the moving target of my work life, I spent yet another evening sullen and restless. Natalie and Alyssa continued to respect that I needed room to be alone.

The next day when I looked at the complaint I saw it had also been addressed to Caroline. A student was on the warpath about textbooks again.

Dear President Berrian and Vice President Cruz:

I am an out-of-work parent which takes one class a semesster at your university in order to provide for my family. Your university already costs a lot of money and the textbooks are killing me. How can you allow a math textbook to cost $125? And on top of that, we have to go the books website to find the answers for working out the problems. My math teacher complains about the book all the time. Classmates have all ready told me that I'll get about $10 back for it. That's a disgrace. You really need to do something about this. Me and my classmates are so frustrated that we are starting a petishon to force you to lower the costs of your books. We will share it with channel 11 and then youll have to answer to a lot of people.

Noel Brown

I went looking for Caroline to compare notes on the complaint. I caught her leaving her office. "Hey, Caroline, I was going to see if you had a few minutes. I got forwarded that complaint about the textbooks."

"Which complaint?"

"The one from the math student. You know, the illiterate one?"

"Jesus. The one from Noel Brown? That came to me almost two weeks ago. You just now got it from Bob?" Had I come at a bad time? Caroline never used 'Jesus' in frustration.

"Just yesterday."

"That burns me. I told him I had everything under control."

"Oh, sorry to hear that. Can we at least discuss for a few minutes so that we can report the same response?"

Caroline looked to her left and her right. No one else was near. "I was going off campus to Mario's for lunch. Want to join me?"

I looked at my watch: barely 11:00. "It's a little early, but sure."

"Great. I just have to get away from this nuthouse every once in awhile. You want to ride with me or drive separately."

"I'll go with you if that's alright." Even though the snow had stopped falling the evening before, I still entertained no desire to drive in it any more than I had to.

In her car, while we drove through the snowy Indiana streets, I saw a book of *New York Times* Sunday Crosswords on the floor by my feet. "Hey, you a crossword fan, Caroline?" I asked, picking up the book.

"I am. I like to do them on my lunch break to relax my brain."

I burst out laughing. "What does it say about Boan University that someone goes to the most difficult crossword puzzles on the planet to 'relax' her brain?"

"I'm not sure it's helping. You'll see none of them are complete. I get stuck and move on to the next puzzle."

"Are you talking about the crosswords or Boan?" Caroline snickered and continued to drive; I opened the book at random, leafing through the pages. There wasn't a single completed crossword; the most complete ones were about three-quarters filled out. I stopped at one near the front of the book. "It doesn't look like you were doing too poorly on this one. Let me see if I can help. The clue is 'why you're not the brightest bulb in the pack?' Eight letters. Third letter, 'R.' Damn, if it was ten letters, it could be 'work at Boan.'"

Caroline pulled into a surface parking lot across from Mario's pizzeria, a favorite escape from cooking for Natalie and me. Mario's featured mouth-watering pizza and an eclectic jukebox filled with records from the 60's, 70's and 80's.

After we ordered, Caroline wasted no time jumpstarting the conversation. "You know, Mark, this thing with the complaint is typical of how frustrated I am right now."

"How so?" I asked, sipping diet Coke.

"Berrian and I got that stupid e-mail almost two weeks ago and I told him I'd take care of it. Why has he now passed it on to you?"

"I don't know, Caroline. He may just want me to look into the math professor to make sure he's using the book."

"Oh, he's using the book. We've already verified that with several students."

"Who is the instructor?" A young waiter, probably one of our students, had walked over to the jukebox. He placed a coin in the machine and I waited to hear his selection.

"Someone named Calhoun?"

I pursed my lips and tried to place a face to the name. "I don't think I know him. Maybe he is an adjunct?"

"I don't know," replied Caroline, cleaning the table with her napkin. She reached over to the table next to us and pulled a paper napkin off of it. "I really wasn't concerned about that. I'm just trying to manage the in-coming petition."

"You really worried this student can get others to rally around her?" From the jukebox came the unmistakable opening chords of "Sultans of Swing."

"It's a him, Mark. The name is pronounced 'Nool,' not 'No El.' Anyway, he's been able to rally a lot of students. He walks the halls and basically accosts students to sign."

"Can we stop him by saying he's harassing other people?"

"Probably, but that could actually make things worse. I've been trying to ride him out. Heck, he's a senior and won't be around that much longer."

"What?" I exclaimed. "A senior? How the hell did that happen, given his writing skills?"

"Oh yeah, we looked up his record. He's passed all his English sequence."

"How many classes does he have left?"

"Three. All in the math sequence."

"Unbelievable. How the hell did we allow that to happen?"

"You know it happens with students all the time. Self-scheduling is a separate issue I'm working on, Mark. Now you can see why I wanted to keep Berrian out of this until I had it all wrapped up."

"I'm not going to change that strategy. I came to you today in support."

Caroline stared at a young couple playing footsie in a nearby booth. Without taking her eyes off of them, she continued. "I really could use the support right now, Mark."

"What do you mean?"

"Bob's been hammering me about a lot of things. He's all over me about the GAP plans. Hates whatever I propose for a different complaint procedure. Blames me for letting the retention committee get too caught up in accelerated deliveries."

"That's one of the reasons I wanted to talk today. What happened at your last one-on-one?"

The couple Caroline watched now tried to be more clandestine with their flirting.

Caroline turned back to look at me. A tear in her eye surprised me. "He never let me explain anything about the data. He railed on and on about how I better represent student needs and let you worry about the academic concerns. My number one goal, he said, was to give the students what they want."

"Ugh." I didn't know what else to say. For a couple of minutes, Caroline didn't say anything either. In the meantime, Dire Straits gave way to John Cougar's "Authority Song," and footsie couple left making us the only customers in the restaurant. Of course, it was still only 11:35.

Finally, with a deep breath, she started up again. "I also think I have a snake in my department, Mark."

Flesh crawling, I stuttered, "what do you mean?"

"I think one of my own staff members is undermining me to Bob. Good lord, why am I even telling you this?"

"It's o.k., Caroline. I'm honored and what's said in Mario's stays in Mario's." She looked like my words had comforted her. "Why do you think this?"

She continued to hesitate before almost every response. I had a feeling this conversation came at a great emotional cost. "Mostly, it's just my gut and I've always valued my gut tremendously. It feels like my staff is acting differently around me, as are Veronica and Bob."

"Have you talked to Veronica? She's such a sweetheart that I can't believe she wouldn't tell you something." I could see our pizza coming out of the oven and realized that hunger had set in.

"No. You're the first person I've talked about this to."

"Do you have reasons to believe it's a specific staff member?"

Caroline pushed her drink away to give the waiter room to set down plates. After he had left to get the pizza, she leaned over to me and whispered, "Rochelle Wallace."

"Rochelle!" I exclaimed probably too loudly. Looking around, I could see the waiter cutting our pizza. Led Zeppelin's "Fool in the Rain" probably covered our voices anyway. "Why Rochelle?"

"She's not happy with me for how I keep online student services mixed in with the rest of the student services. I knew she was incredibly ambitious when we hired her; almost every day, though, I need to tell her to slow down and think about what's best for the university, not necessarily what's best for online."

"That's not much of a reason to suspect her of going to the president, though. Ah, thank you!" The waiter had left a gorgeous vegetarian pizza in the center of the table. "Let me serve you a piece."

"As I said, Mark, it's really just a gut feeling." I left a slice of pizza on her plate, cheese hanging over the side and stringing back to the pizza pan.

We ate in relative silence for several minutes. Three teenage boys came in, ordered and proceeded to start trash talking each other loudly, even over the jukebox. When Queen's "Another One Bites the Dust" came on, one of the boys screamed out, "who played this shit?" and proceeded to throw one of his tennis shoes at the jukebox, hitting it solidly enough to cause the record to skip and the machine to proceed to the next selection: David Bowie's "Let's Dance."

From behind the counter, one of the staff members yelled, "Damn it, Richie. Haven't we warned you?"

"Boy, don't you wish we could do that at a meeting? Take off a shoe and throw it at Bob or Howard to get them to shut up."

"It would take more than a shoe to get Shue to shut up."

"Very good, Dr. Cruz. You don't let that humor out of its cage very often."

"If you ask me, we spend too much time wallowing in good old boy yucks." She took a long drink and fought the stringy cheese on her pizza.

"I find it helps me. Otherwise, I would zone out way too often."

"I can see that. To each his own, right? So, what else did you want to talk about?"

I paused to think. "Well, we covered the complaint; I'm going to let you keep handling it and you'll keep me posted. We probably still need to determine our direction for the retention angle on accelerated deliveries." I finished my piece and reached for a second.

"I don't think I'll tackle that again with Bob for a few weeks. I left that meeting so confused and angry that I can't even remember his recommendations."

"That's o.k. I took the easy way out and bought myself some time to 'study' the situation more. Let me take the lead and fend off Bob until we're both ready to present to him."

As we finished our pizza, talking mostly about bits and pieces from work, I could see Caroline relaxing. Finally, before we left, I had to change the subject. "Quickly, Caroline, before we leave, let me ask you something. For the first time today, I learned something personal about you. You like crosswords. What else do you like to do?"

"Mark, please. Do you think this is speed dating?"

I looked around the restaurant to see the three yahoos on the other side of the room still razzing each other. Behind the counter, the two male staff members looked incredibly bored. One read a *USA Today* while the other tossed an onion up and down. "No, I don't think this is speed dating. I'm not sure which of us would have it worse after our time ran out." I got a slight smile. "So, tell me, what else does Caroline Cruz like to do?"

"Miguel and I enjoy board games: Backgammon, Chess, Scrabble, and so forth. We're pretty competitive."

"No kidding!"

"Oh, yeah," she answered, leaving her Boan credit card out for the waiter. "We have an on-going game of chess right now. Each one of us makes one move a day. He makes a move after I leave for work in the morning, and then I make a move before I go to bed."

"O.k.," I said with mock apprehension. "And why?"

"It's just a different way to play. Keeps us sharp. Makes it a little more fun. The worst part about playing chess normally is watching my husband take twenty minutes to make a move. It drives me absolutely crazy. So, this way, he can think about his move at night and in the early morning, then I can make mine within minutes of getting home at night."

"It does sound kind of fun." The bored waiter had come over to run Caroline's credit card.

"It should be. The down side is that I have had him running around the board for literally three weeks now. He's down to three pieces; I have six. I can't get him into checkmate and he won't concede. So each day we just keep prolonging the ultimate resolution: that his king is mine!" Caroline let out a good-natured fake evil laugh.

"My, my, you are competitive, aren't you? You'd fit right in with the Friday basketball games."

"Oh, please!" challenged Caroline, her mood changing instantaneously.

"The boys won't let a girl play. I'm actually not that bad, but it is a boys-only game."

"Have you ever asked?"

"I did a long time ago and got some patronizing response from Bob." The waiter had returned with the credit card slip, so while Caroline signed, I dashed to the rest room to wash my hands. "Ready?" asked Caroline when I returned.

"I sure am." I turned around to the waiter piling our plates up at the counter. "By the way, you have a burnt out bulb in the bathroom. Not the place you want your customers fumbling in the dark."

"Oh, thanks, bud," replied the slow-speaking kid.

"That's it!" I shouted, holding the door for Caroline. "That's the answer to the crossword clue from the car: 'you're *burnt out*.'"

"Speak for yourself, Mark. I haven't quite reached that stage yet."

"No, I meant that the answer to 'why you're not the brightest bulb in the pack?' is because you're 'burnt out.' **Burnt out** is the eight letter answer."

"Not bad, Carter," said Caroline as we got to the car. And as we drove back to campus, she admitted, "this was actually fun. Let's do it again."

Chapter Twenty

However, we didn't do it again. A week later Berrian informed the executive team that Caroline had left the university to pursue other opportunities. He told us nothing else, and from the reaction of most of her staff, the decision came completely unexpectedly. Garrett Jones organized the cleaning out of her office, and Rochelle Wallace was named interim Executive Vice President for Student Services. Angry and concerned, I felt the need to say something to somebody. Gun shy about going directly to Berrian, I started with Victor Woo.

Victor provided little information. All he would say was that Caroline resigned, that the separation was amicable, and that he and Bob reviewed all of Caroline's staff to determine that Wallace was the best person to serve as interim. When I told him Caroline had suggested Wallace might be undermining her, Victor's Adam's apple bounced up and down nervously, and he promised through chattering teeth that he would look into the charge.

As with many of my frustrations that winter, I turned more and more to my father. Our December chat opened a door for phone conversations that offered me a listener experienced in some of the aggravations associated with educational politics. I believed he received the same kind of sounding board in return, as he openly talked about the news and information he still received concerning secondary education. Natalie banned me to my upstairs office for all these impulsive calls to my father, as she tired of hearing the same bellyaching for the third or fourth time without hearing the other half of the conversation. My father ultimately recommended that I not confront the president about Caroline's departure.

"He's not going to tell you what really happened, anyway, Mark."

"I know that, Dad, but I still would like to see what he says. I could learn a lot from his reactions that might help me decide just how happy I can be in this role."

"And where will that put you? You'll either know the woman was outright fired, or, just as likely, got so fed up that she decided to resign. Even if there was no body language or anything to suggest that she didn't resign in a completely confrontational context, you'd never believe it, would you?"

I laughed. "I think you have me pegged there, Dad."

"See, that's the result of a closed environment in which many people work. Because of legal concerns, privacy issues, and positive messaging, the truth is no longer relevant. The prevailing perception is more important than the truth."

"Oh, god, whatever you say, don't say that perception is reality to the person who holds it! I hate that over-used banality."

I could hear my mother calling for my father. "One second, dear, I'm with Mark. You know where those armchair philosophers get that statement wrong, don't you, Mark?"

"Where?"

"For the life of an institution, it's not important if a single person holds a perception. But, if a majority of people hold that perception, then it's not simply reality, it's a dangerous cancer to what the institution could be."

I pondered what he said for a few seconds. "That's good, Dad. Anyway, Mom needs you, so we should hang up. Is she o.k., by the way?"

"We have another doctor's appointment next week. She's doing relatively o.k. Don't worry."

"O.k. Thanks, Dad. I'll think about what you said."

"Don't think just about what I said. Think about what everybody is saying there. What is the culture really like and what is your ability to impact it?"

After hanging up, I thought back to some of the earliest comments conveyed by faculty and staff upon my arrival. Repeatedly, faculty believed that things went on differently behind closed doors with the administration. Had I been able to change that? Was that the case of academics? My ego told me that the answer to the second question was "no" and "a little" to the first question. However, with Caroline abruptly gone, I wasn't sure. With town halls scheduled over the next two weeks, numerous future opportunities presented themselves to take the pulse of the institution.

The first town hall occurred on an early Monday evening, the best time to capture the faculty and staff who covered night classes and departmental hours. As with many universities, Boan's evening and night schedules were jam packed with students who worked during the day and then squeezed their courses in at night. Despite scheduling the town hall partially during a natural break between classes, the turnout was rather small. Berrian paced around the auditorium saying to anyone within hearing range, "this doesn't seem like many people. Does this seem like many people to you?"

A rather scant collection of finger foods had been brought in to feed the participants, not enough to replace anyone's dinner, and so a few attendees could be heard grumbling about being starved. Finally, about five minutes after the scheduled start time, with an audience of maybe forty faculty and staff spread across the vast auditorium, Berrian started. His opening remarks about the strength and direction of the university received animated enthusiasm by members of Howard's admissions staff who mostly sat in the middle section of the auditorium, while faculty and other staff members remained on the edges, both in terms of seats and appreciation for the president's message.

Berrian had the boldness to cite executive staffing stability despite the absence of Caroline. As he praised Rochelle Wallace for stepping into the interim position, she rose up from her seated position behind Berrian and gave a half wave to the audience. A few of the bright-faced admissions representatives applauded. My eyes focused on the margins where the real story could be found. Most faculty looked disinterested; a few other staff members appeared morose.

After his opening ten minute salvo, Berrian asked the audience for questions. One of the effervescent admissions reps raised her hand.

"Will we be doing more radio advertising?"

Berrian flashed the woman his best smile. "We're looking at our advertising dollars to determine the best way to use them. Radio is certainly one of the possible venues where we might spend more."

"The reason I ask," the vivacious blondie added, "is that I listen to WOWO, and I never hear an advertisement for us. It could be a huge market."

"We have to decide which radio market is the right one for us. Is it a station like WOWO?" A smattering of applause rose from the admissions cheer team. "Maybe it's a sports station?" A young man I didn't know from down in the front corner pumped his fist in the air. "Maybe it's National Public Radio?" The majority of the center aisle groaned, while a few faculty members relegated to the corners and the back smiled for the first time. "We'll analyze them all and decide. Great question. Next?"

No one raised their hands for several seconds. "Come on, I know there's more on your mind."

Finally, a grey-haired woman from the left aisle stood up and raised her hand.

"Mr. President, I'm Edith Ritenour, an adjunct in nursing. Until recently, I was credentialed to teach a number of nursing classes; now I'm being told that I can't teach basic courses that I really enjoy, such as 'Community Health Issues.' This is incredibly unfair, because the university is not consistently applying its own credentialing standards. I have no doubt the university would not apply these standards to Margaret Higgins Sanger."

Berrian turned and looked for me in the row of performing monkeys sitting behind him. "Perhaps Dr. Carter, our provost, can help you after this town hall, Ms. Ritenour? I really can't speak to the specifics. As most of you know, we are in a transition with nursing leadership. Nevertheless, Mark will meet with you afterwards and learn more about your concern. And, Mark, let's make sure we double check the credentials on this Margaret woman. What was her last name, again?"

While Berrian looked with all earnestness at Ritenour, a rumble of laughter started spreading around the sides and the corners of the auditorium. Berrian looked at various faculty members and Boan staff in partially-hidden moments of mirth and turned bright red. I jumped up to join Berrian at the lectern and covered the microphone with my hand. "She was alluding to the famous nurse Margaret Sanger, Bob. She's been dead forty years."

Bob looked at me, somehow turning an even deeper shade of crimson red. As I back-pedaled to my seat, Bob turned back to the audience and pronounced, "I appear to have misheard Ms. Ritenour. I thought she said 'Margaret Langer.' My mistake."

That was pretty much the highlight of the evening. Additional questions and comments were few and far between, coming mostly from the pep section in the middle. Berrian left almost immediately afterwards, so I had no chance to learn about his reaction to the whole town hall.

On Thursday morning, we lined up again behind Berrian as his rogues gallery. If turn-out disappointed earlier in the week, it was a little worse this time. About thirty-five Boan employees spread themselves throughout the auditorium. As far as I could tell, none of the participants came from Howard's area. Most, actually, came from my areas, with a significant representation from the libraries and from faculty.

This time, Berrian's incredibly quick reference to the SturgeOne card generated the first response, from Phil Hickey, history faculty member. "Excuse me," he said, interrupting Berrian before he got too far into his next point, "what are you talking about with the 'SturgeOne Card?'"

Berrian glanced behind himself at Hank and me with a look that said, 'this is why I didn't want to go here.' He spun back around, though, and immediately answered Hickey's question. "The SturgeOne Card is the one-card-does-all that students, faculty and staff will all get, starting with faculty and staff this summer. It will serve as your ID and your debit card for all things Boan."

"What if I don't want one?" asked Hickey. I groaned and buried my head in my hands.

"Well, it's not really a question of wanting one," said Berrian. "It's a requirement of being employed."

"Did we have any say in this?" asked Hickey.

"Of course." Berrian turned back around to face me and Hank. "Mark or Hank, weren't the faculty and staff involved in this?"

We both stood up. I looked at Hank to see if he would respond first. Luckily, he did. "This should be no surprise, Phil," Hank suggested. "There's been communication, surveys and information about the one card for several months."

"This is the first I've heard of it today."

Greg Friend, sitting next to Phil, slapped him on the back. "Where the hell you been, Phil? We were told about this. We weren't asked, but we were told a month or so ago."

"See, there you go," responded a pleased Berrian.

"Phil, let's talk afterwards, and I'll see where we've mis-communicated." I sat back down while Berrian resumed his canned 'off-the-cuff' opening remarks.

The question part of this town hall began on the dull side. Several faculty asked about the open dean positions, and I provided as much of a status update as possible. One staff member asked if we would start a football program, and Berrian rattled off a long, involved answer that culminated with an awkward figure of speech: "consider it fourth down, and we're taking a time out to decide if we want to punt or go for it."

Finally, just before the president prepared to say, "if there are no more questions, thank you for coming," Henry Van Wyck raised her hand. She had arrived late and had slipped into the back row. When she stood up, she was still a little difficult to see.

"Dr. Berrian, I'm not sure if this is really a question or just a comment that will reflect badly on me."

"Oh, hush," said Berrian. "I want people to be honest and open at these town halls."

"Well, thank you, for saying that. I'm not sure everyone always believes that, but that's not really my point. I want to know why administration has never publicly addressed the mess with Michael Hartley's secret proposal to IMET. Why did almost everyone in the university have to learn about that from the newspapers?"

I glanced at Hank to my right. "Uh-oh," I whispered, although I felt great pride for Van Wyck at that moment.

"That?" exclaimed Berrian. "Why do we want to rehash that? That's water under the bridge. The kid's been arrested and Boan moves forward."

"I'm not sure you understand, Dr. Berrian. I don't want an explanation as to why the student killed Hartley; I'm just wondering if the university deserves full disclosure on how that project got approved."

From around the auditorium, murmurs of agreement came from other faculty and staff. I had once seen a *Nature* program where a herd of water buffalo teamed up to attack a lion, and I could sense the same kind of predatory balancing act here.

"Dr. Van Wyck, there's not that much to say," spoke Berrian. "And, the project's dead in the water now."

"In that water under the bridge, you mean?"

Berrian was perceptibly puzzled. "Huh?"

"Nothing, sir. But, back to the point." Henry had moved from her seat to walk down one of the aisles to get closer to the stage. "I'm sure I speak for many here that while it's comforting to know that project is no longer moving forward, our apprehension is about the way it got started. Why can't your office, or the provost, or someone, speak to us about the nature of that project's genesis?"

Berrian glanced at his watch. "Look, Henrietta, it's getting late. Our scheduled time is done, and I'm sure most of the audience needs to get back to work. Maybe you and I can talk afterwards."

"I can stick around," said Phil Hickey. Others around the room buzzed in support.

"Look, everybody, trust me, this was a silly little side project of Hartley's. If any of us really knew what he intended, we would have put a stop to it."

"So, you're saying you had no knowledge of it?" asked Hickey, now also standing.

"What is this, a press conference? Let's drop this discussion. Trust me, it wasn't that big of a deal."

"Stop telling us to 'trust you,' sir. That's the whole point," exclaimed Van Wyck, her voice rising just a little.

"What the hell does that mean?" Berrian yelled. From around the room, weaker members of the herd chickened out and scrambled left and right to find exits. I stepped forward to the lectern to attempt to help Berrian, but he nearly shoved me off the stage. "Come on, Henry, explain that to me."

Van Wyck had lost some of her vigor. She had backed up several stairs of the aisle. "Dr. Berrian, I don't raise this issue to start a fight. I raise it for the good of the institution. People need to know what happened."

"Nothing happened. Christ, why is that so hard to understand?"

Hickey had not backed down. "Answer her question, President Berrian."

Berrian looked beside himself. "There's nothing to answer. Nothing happened!"

"In a way, you're probably right. 'Nothing' probably did happen, which is not much more solace to us." Van Wyck waved her arm around the room to include her comrades. As she looked, though, she realized that the numbers had dwindled substantially to six people.

"O.k., almost everyone has left. This town hall is over. Thanks for coming," said Berrian, attempting to preserve whatever good-will he believed existed. However, after the last of the few audience members had left, Berrian turned to us, standing around, confused and anxious behind him, and went ballistic.

"What the hell was that? Carter, I want Van Wyck fucking gone."

"Now, hold on, Bob. You told her that you wanted open discussion."

"That wasn't an open discussion. She had no intention of hearing me. She just wanted to rabble rouse. And she almost succeeded, getting that one idiot, what's his name again, to join in."

I ignored the reference to Hickey. "In all honesty, Bob, I think she did have the intention of hearing you. You just weren't answering her question."

"What more is there to answer? The project is dead like Hartley. We can live with his cold body rotting away, why can't we live with the project's cold body rotting away?"

I chuckled. "Interesting figure of speech, Bob, but still not the point. The point is that no one has ever explained how the university could let Hartley do this so secretively."

Berrian fidgeted. "I don't get this. Am I just stupid? What do the rest of you think?"

Initially, no one responded, until after a few seconds, Rochelle Wallace spoke. "I agree with you, Bob. People need to get over this and move on." While she looked smug, the rest of the executive team remained stoned-face.

"Well, I have had enough. We get a pretty decent turnout for the two town halls, and now this will be the lingering memory of them."

"Did you say 'decent turnout,' Bob? I disagree."

"What do you mean, Mark? Didn't we have about a hundred over the two days?"

"I don't think so. I figured maybe eighty over the two days. What did the rest of you think?" I asked.

"We had seventy-seven over the two days," proclaimed Victor.

"Did you actually count them, Victor?" asked Hank.

"Yes, I did."

"Wow, and you didn't even take off your shoes," said Howard.

"Seventy-seven is still pretty good," asserted Berrian.

"It's not even 20% of our full-time staff, and less than 15% if we count adjunct."

"Oh, yeah, that's right. Mark, find out why that adjunct got in here on Monday."

"Excuse me? These town halls were open to all faculty and staff, including adjunct."

"Is that right, Victor?"

I could see Victor's Adam's apple bouncing up and down. "Yes, it is."

"O.k., next year, no adjuncts."

"What? You've got to be kidding." It was all I could do not to scream at Berrian.

"No, I'm not, Mark, and I'm getting tired of your insubordination. Now, I'm getting the hell out of here. And I'm telling you, Mark, I want Van Wyck gone. I know she's faculty and there's all sorts of touchy-feely crap we have to deal with like covering her classes and tenure and crap. But, she's got to be out of here."

It didn't take long after this exchange, including heartrending conversations with Natalie and Alyssa, for me to decide to look elsewhere for a job. Given my concern—and let's face it, guilt—about my parents' health and well-being, I recommended we move to Arizona, an idea which Natalie supported. Because she had still not found a job and Alyssa had only been in the school system for a year, we had a rare window of opportunity to make one last move until Alyssa went off to college. Quickly, I applied to every academic job I could find in Arizona, figuring that even if we lived three hours from my parents, that was better than a four-hour plane ride.

I managed to stall Berrian on the firing of Van Wyck, confirming for him that all the (mostly non-existent) touchy-feely things had to be addressed. I said nothing to Van Wyck, who never asked me about the town hall incident. Life in the university went on, as it always does, driven by the clockwork routine of lectures, exams, and projects. No one at the university knew I sought a new position. I attended every meeting, task force, and university event, supportive and dependable. When Sandra Day O'Connor presented the key note address for our Women's History Month lecture series, the auditorium overflowed with students, faculty and staff. Disappointingly, I was the only executive administrator there, and when O'Connor talked about breaking I-rod supported concrete ceilings, Jennifer Riley, Gertrude Fulbright and I exchanged frustrated glances because they represented the highest ranking female officers of the university present. Somewhere Caroline Cruz must still have been recovering from having the entire ceiling collapse all around her.

By the first of April, my resignation letter arrived on Berrian's desk. In typical Berrian fashion, he accepted it without much ado. If I had submitted a request for five hundred dollars to purchase more testing for students in accelerated classes, I have no doubt he would have detonated. The news of my resignation, however, caused him as little consternation as a fly landing on the hood of his car. It took only seconds for both of us to agree I would stay through commencement before leaving for the Arizona desert.

Part Six:
Commencement

Chapter Twenty-One

My first commencement at Boan served as my last commencement. That would not have been what I envisioned back in August, when I expected to preside over many commencement ceremonies. Thus, I stood, with a heavy heart, watching the streams of red and blue regalia flow into the field house, students beaming, cameras flashing, fighting tears forming in my eyes. This would not be my last day at Boan (I had a week left to hand things back over to Jennifer 'Interim' Riley), but it would effectively be my last day to struggle with regret and anger for what had occurred and what could have been accomplished.

As the organist concluded the processional, I stepped to the lectern. For about a half a minute, the field house (we were in the process of dropping the "Taylor" name as more reports of Nazi connections came out) rattled with the applause of the graduates and their guests. Then, with a simple wave of the hand, I quieted the attendees.

"Please be seated. Graduates, Boan Trustees, faculty, staff and administrators, family and friends, welcome to Boan's one hundred and fifth commencement ceremony."

A new round of thunderous applause broke out, and I took a half-step back to wait out the cheering. Directly in front of and below me, the faculty sat, craning their necks upward to see the stage.

"I am Dr. Mark Carter, Provost for Boan University. Today's the day we've all waited for, the day each of you shed the clothing marking you as student and apprentice and instead cloak yourself in the regalia of wisdom and knowledge to go forth into the world."

More applause broke out, less thunderous than before. Some graduates almost certainly were already texting as opposed to listening.

"On stage are Board of Trustees and Boan administrators whose positions would not exist without you. I am honored to be the first of many on this stage to offer you congratulations."

I did the half-step back again as the cheering built to another crescendo.

"This is not the opportunity for me to share how the collective efforts of the people on this stage impacted your education, which is too bad, as it would be telling. Know that every student at Boan has always been at the heart of our interest."

I heard a few bursts of laughter from the faculty below me; half-turning to my right I could see President Berrian and Chairman Oliphant smiling blankly into the bright lights.

"Your education has not always come easily. No one knows that better than the faculty, staff and administrators who celebrate your success today. Your success is our success. We look to make your education memorable, and measure that success, as you do, by degrees."

I paused to allow a tiny smattering of applause to work its way through the audience. Down below me, Christina Llewellyn, squeezed in the middle of the first row of faculty, read a book she had tucked in her robe. She unquestionably wouldn't be the only one. I had brought a book to a Farrington commencement or two as a faculty member.

"Look around you at the various shapes, sizes, colors, and natures of your fellow classmates. You're part of one of the most diverse graduating classes in the history of Boan University. Some of you are twenty-one or twenty-two and ready to charge into the workplace. Others of you are forty-one or forty-two, ready to embrace your existing workplace, where things will now go more slowly because there are no more papers to write and tests to study for." A round of applause started up again.

"Many of you will return to your native countries, while others of you will seek permanent citizenship in America. Some of you will break through glass ceilings; others of you will form the foundations of new emerging industries. From today on, though, all of you will be Boan alumni."

A slight glance to my right revealed Berrian checking his watch. I had told him not to expect more than three or four minutes for my welcome speech. Despite my yearning to go well past that and to make him a little nervous, I stuck with my planned script.

"From this day forward, then, think of what really matters: How you carry yourself and how you treat others. All of your successes: your special projects, your achievement of goals, your adherence to a company's bottom line; will be less important than the way you've conducted yourself. This is what I hope Boan has shown you. You are judged by your honesty and your integrity. Remember the Boan motto: 'Act with Honor. Honor all Actions.'

Those aren't just empty words plastered on coffee mugs, stickers and t-shirts."
I turned to gesture to the large Boan emblem and motto affixed to the wall of
the field house. The stage party had been positioned so that our backs were
to the emblem and motto, but so that the graduates and audience could see
that backdrop.

"These words," I said, sweeping my hands upwards toward them, "are a
code of conduct, a way of life, a compass when lost, the cornerstone to your
education. They are the permanent fixture that is Boan University." As I
turned back around to fully face the audience again, I heard a slight creak
from behind me. I assumed that someone on the makeshift wooden stage
must have shifted in a chair. However, then I heard a louder creak, and a
scream came from the audience.

"Look out, it's going to fall!"

I whipped around the see the right hand side of the emblem and motto
swinging along the wall. On the wall where the right side had been affixed,
a huge chunk of stone was visibly missing. Down on the stage, Victor Woo
picked up a huge screw. Tim from Victor's left and Howard from his right
both abandoned their chairs and moved to the far left side, looking cautiously
up at the swinging emblem.

"Everyone stay calm," I announced into the microphone as a buzz of
disbelief and amusement circulated the field house, more so than panic.
"Please give us just a couple of minutes before we resume." Out among
the students, I could see hundreds of cell phones held up above students'
heads, capturing the moment on camera. 'Where is the hired videographer?'
I wondered. He had slowly moved to the edge of the stage to get a closer shot.
I turned to locate Berrian to determine how he wanted to proceed.

"What the hell?" whispered Berrian to Oliphant. At this point the heavy
plaque had stopped swinging, so that "Act with Honor; Honor all Actions"
was completely vertical to the ground. Footsteps could be heard racing in from
the right side, and in a moment a facilities man had leapt up on the stage with
a ladder. "Give me one quick minute to check it out," he said.

"What do you want me to say, Bob?" I asked, pointing back at an audience
completely lost in loud chatter and flashbulbs.

"Keep telling them to sit tight. Hopefully, they can get this fixed
quickly."

"I hate to point this out to you, Bob," spoke Oliphant. "But the only quick
way to fix is to drill a new anchor and screw into the wall. I'm pretty sure I've
never attended a commencement ceremony where power drills supplied the
background music."

"Damn it," whispered Berrian, walking back to the ladder which the
facilities man had already ascended. I decided to wait before announcing

anything more. "Can you at least rip the damn thing completely off the wall so that we can move on?" asked Berrian.

The facilities man tried to pry his fingers under the left side of the hanging sign. He would not be able to slide even a piece of paper under it. "Sorry, sir. No dice. I'd have to get a crowbar or something and it would still take awhile."

"Shit. Shit. Shit," whispered Bob. By now, six or seven members of the stage party had walked to the ladder to see what was happening.

"Now what do we do?" asked Victor, still possessing the largest screw I had ever seen in my life.

"I don't know. Any thoughts?"

"If you ask me, sir," the facilities guy declared, "this side is still securely affixed. I think you can proceed. I doubt this baby is going anywhere."

"Yeah, right! You probably would have said that about the right side."

"I can't speak to that sir. This has been up here for several years. But, this side ain't budging."

"Tell you what," I suggested. "Let's move the back two rows over to the sides so that if this thing falls, all it will do is scare the hell out of us, but won't hit anybody."

"You think that's a good idea?" asked Berrian.

"What are our other options?"

We all stared at each other for a few seconds. "O.k., let's do it. Victor, coordinate the moving of the people in the back rows. Mark, get this damn show on the road again."

I returned to the lectern. "Everyone, sorry for that little surprise. We have been assured by maintenance that the sign is still securely attached to the wall, but for ultimate precaution, we are moving the people in the back rows to a place out of the immediate danger if the sign fell. We will proceed with Commencement. Graduates, family and friends, there is no reason to fear for the graduates' safety. You will be crossing the front part of the stage, so none of you will come anywhere close to that wall. So, let's proceed to commence!"

There was a loud round of applause, and I turned around to see half the stage party, mostly the Board of Trustees' members, looking very nervously at the wall. "Don't worry," I whispered to Selma Wellington within hearing distance, "as long as they don't break into 'We Will Rock You,' I think it will hold."

As the applause died down, I introduced Berrian. I actually felt sorry for Bob, as he tried to introduce the stage party, because he could no longer rely on the list tied to seating order provided by the registrar. Because the order had been shifted, it must have looked like a whack-a-mole game as a name was read, a board member popped out of his or her chair, and then somewhere else on the stage, the next board member arose with the subsequent reading of his or her name.

The rest of the ceremony proceeded without incident. Berrian and I shook seven hundred and eighty-one hands, each one sweatier than the previous. The deans read the name of their college's graduates, which meant that Michael Stewart read nineteen names, all in a soft voice that couldn't have been heard much past the stage. Jennifer Riley, covering both business and education, read the most names and dealt with the most difficult pronunciations. In the end, everyone acted pleased, and the stage party mingled in the staging room, waiting for the crowd to clear out so that we could get to our cars.

"Well, Mark," said Oliphant coming up to me. "I guess this is it. Sorry that you are leaving us so soon. Berrian says you have parent care that will force you to move."

I struggled to hang my doctoral hood on my hanger. I finally folded it in half and hung it over the hanger. "Yea, that's part of it, Jim. But, that's not the only reason."

"Well, anyway, best of luck, Mark." Oliphant had turned to slap Trent Dejeerling on the back. "Trent, buddy, was that something or what? Just think: if that son-of-a-bitch had fallen completely off the wall, who the hell would you have sued?"

Dejeerling laughed, while Quincy Ashland wormed his way past me to join their conversation. As I walked over to where Howard stood, I could hear Oliphant needle Ashland. "And, Quincy, how long would it have taken your emergency room to see me if I had been rushed there with a piece of the Boan emblem sticking out of my ass?"

"It's scary, Howard," I said as I settled near him. "I've come to you for the high-brow humor today."

"As I always say, 'I've got a million jokes. Six of them are actually funny.'"

"Oh, so there's one left I haven't heard, yet, eh?"

"Yeah. What do you call it when a giant plaque falls around higher education administrators and one of them dies?"

"What?"

"An accident. What do you call it when the giant plaque falls and none of them die?"

"I don't know."

"A tragedy."

"Ouch, I should have seen that one coming."

Hank came shuffling over to us. "I just looked outside. The crowd's thinning out a little bit. I'd like to get home in time to see some of the Masters."

"You know, that's something we never did around here," I said. "Golfing. I love to golf but we never once had a golf outing. I would have preferred that to the punishment of the Friday basketball."

"We did try that a few times when Bob started," replied Hank. "Remember that, Howard?"

"Oh, yeah. He was brutal. Not that any of us play well, but Bob's downright dangerous. His shot could likely end up anywhere except for the green."

"Why did you guys stop?"

"Bob basically pulled the plug on it. He said something about life being too short to chase a god-damn ball around a golf course with barely a prayer of hitting it right." From over on the other side of the staging room, Berrian had joined Oliphant, Dejeerling, and Ashland. All laughed raucously.

"Well, guys, I think I'm going to try to get out of here," declared Hank. "See you all Monday. That will be your last cabinet meeting, Mark?"

"You bet!"

"Lucky bastard."

"Natalie and Alyssa will meet me here," I mentioned to Howard, mostly to make small talk. "That probably wasn't the best idea. They must be swimming upstream against the sturgeon graduates."

"Another good one, Mark. I will miss your sense of humor."

Eventually, Natalie and Alyssa made their way into the staging room. By that point, all of the Board of Trustees had left, and only Veronica and I were left in the room. "Shucks," said Natalie, "I hoped to meet a couple of those illustrious board members."

"So, what did you think?" I asked.

"The sign falling was cooooolllllll," exclaimed Alyssa gleefully.

"So, that was your favorite part?"

"Oh, yeah, the rest was boring."

"Even when I spoke?"

"Especially when you spoke, Daddy."

"Gee, thanks," I replied, hugging my daughter.

"I thought you did very well and displayed grace under fire," said Natalie.

"Grace under falling concrete, you mean? It helps that I was the farthest away."

"You should have seen the looks on the faces of some of your colleagues. Who's the really cute old board member?"

"Matilda Upton?"

"Yeah, her. I thought she would have a heart attack." She leaned over and whispered in my ear, "Victor looked like he crapped his pants!"

"Natalie! How mean!"

We worked our way home and enjoyed a quiet, peaceful weekend. Even though my last day was just a week away, we weren't planning to move until after Alyssa got out of school. So, the pressure of preparing to move had yet to descend upon us.

Riley joined me for my last cabinet meeting to help set up the transition to her in the interim role. She discussed how we had appointed Dewayne Wilson as the interim dean of education, thus freeing up Jennifer to wear only two hats. Turing and Berrian discussed the final stages of the budget process for the new fiscal year, and I happily tuned most of it out. Only when Howard brought up Sherman Head and naming opportunities did I re-engage.

"Anyway, as I promised, I told Sherman Head that the field house naming was now a possibility. He is still committed to donating four million dollars."

"Wow. Can you even imagine having so much money that you can make that donation?" said Veronica.

"Hell, it's a steal," blustered Berrian. "We should get closer to ten million for a field house."

"Well, we already made most of the money from Taylor, god bless his Nazi soul," Howard responded. "In essence, this is play money."

"In Head's case, it really is 'play money,'" I cracked.

"And he still wants naming rights?"

"Oh, yeah," said Howard with a glint in his eye and a tremolo in his throat.

"Great. Ladies and gentlemen, may I present you the Sherman Head Field House?" Berrian declared with a flourish.

"Well, there's a hitch, Bob." Howard was evidently dragging out something enjoyable for him. "He doesn't want it called the Sherman Head Field House."

"Just 'Head Field House?' That's o.k. We can live with that, right?"

"No. Apparently Sherman wants to pay homage to some ancient relative of his."

Berrian frowned. "Oh, lord, what ancient relative?"

"Well, he's very proud of his ancestry, even though, his, like most African-Americans in this country, is linked to slavery. He wants to name it after his great, great grandmother."

"Uh-huh. And what else do you have to tell me, Howard?"

"Like most slaves, she went by one name, and he wants that name on the building."

"God damn it, Howard, what's the name?"

"Sally."

"Sally? That isn't so bad. I thought you would tell us it was something old fashioned like Minerva." Berrian slapped Hank, who, as usual sat to his right, on the back. "Sally's fine."

I laughed. "Think about it, Bob. It will be the Sally Field House."

"I love it," laughed Stevens.

"You mean you like it, you really, really like it?" replied Howard in a pathetic attempt at a woman's voice.

"No way. No fucking way," exploded Berrian. "We'll be a laughing stock. Tell Head we aren't agreeing to that."

"He's the one with the big checkbook, Bob. Are you sure you want to turn him down? Again, I might add!"

"He's got to understand why we don't want this."

"I got to tell you, Bob," I interrupted. "If you did this, for once you might really have faculty support. There would be a powerful historical context. You have an opportunity to explain publicly how Sally was stripped of all her identity except a first name. You could erect a plaque."

"Maybe this one could hold to the wall?" added Howard.

"Good Lord. We have to take this to the board. They may hate it too."

"Don't assume that, Bob," said Howard. "They really only care about the bottom line."

Eventually Berrian recognized that the Sally Field House might actually be good publicity for a university still smarting from having a dean killed by one of its own students. I have no idea if they erected a plaque, and if they did how well it held to the wall.

Some of my direct reports had a low-key get-together for me on my last afternoon. The predictable white cake with chocolate frosting, soft drinks, plastic ware, paper plates and paper cups were set in the middle of the administrative conference room, and people came and went all afternoon. Natalie and Alyssa came for a little while, although as Alyssa got bored, they escaped to find something more interesting than her father's goodbye party. Many people struggled with what to say, given that for many of them, the last time they had seen me was when I had begun just nine months earlier.

Jennifer Riley, Gertrude Fulbright and Shelley Ford were the constants. We sat around late in the afternoon, my box of personal items packed and waiting on my desk, four pieces of leftover cake sitting on individual plates, icing losing its luster.

"So, what are going to be your famous last words, Mark?" asked Jennifer.

"I didn't know I needed any."

"Oh, absolutely. Mostly because we fully expect something."

I sat there a moment and reflected upon the last nine months. "You know," I finally said, "I started this position wondering about the state of higher education. The good news is that I no longer wonder."

"Yeah, right!" cracked Shelley.

"The bad news is that now I worry about the state of higher education."

Shelley flicked a piece of stray cake at Riley. "See, I knew he was messing with us."

"Do you really think it's that bad, Mark?" asked Trudy.

"I don't know, Trudy. The truth of the matter is that my perception has been dramatically altered by just this one place. Farrington could be a little loony, but who knows what happened at the level above me?"

"I think if you had stuck it out, Mark, you might have made an impact."

"Well, we can speculate all we want. Yes, maybe I could have reduced the deliveries to three, maybe four, well-defined models. Maybe I could have filled the open dean positions with more people like you and Jennifer so that we could truly have inter-disciplinary studies. And, maybe just maybe, I could have convinced my colleagues at the executive level to be completely transparent and to truly build a culture of trust and quality."

"You could have done that, Mark," Jennifer suggested.

"Maybe? More than likely, though, I would have taken one of these plastic forks and jammed it in my eye."

"Mark!" shrieked Shelley.

"Besides, I think it's time for Dr. Riley here to stop accepting the bridesmaid role and to be the bride. You need to stop doing this just interim, Jennifer."

"I know, but your fork-in-the-eye analogy is hardly the best sales job."

"And you're pretty sure you'll stick with the faculty position you got in Arizona? No more administration?" asked Trudy.

"More than likely. I do want to be able to take care of my parents. Heck, while provost, I couldn't even take care of my wife and kid."

"That is such a lie," snapped Jennifer.

"It may be an overstatement, but it's not a lie. I can't keep up with my daughter's constantly changing life. Hell, at one point she went from hitting a boy to kissing that same boy. I need to make sure that never happens again."

Shelley laughed. "Never again?"

"Well, at least until she's thirty. I'd at least like to get her to reverse the order."

We sat for several minutes in silence, drinking our warm soft drinks out of chintzy paper cups. More and more people could be heard exiting the

Administration Building for the weekend. After a moment, Shelley said, "it's mighty quiet out there by now."

"Bob left at 3:45 and there's a definite domino effect after that. Usually Howard is only five or ten minutes behind him, and then the rest of us escape, depending upon how quickly we can wrap up what we're working on."

"Are you getting ready to escape, Mark?" Shelley asked

"I took flight several weeks ago. This has just been my spirit hanging around."

I kept my eye on Boan for awhile after I settled in Arizona. Working for Boan is like dating a beautiful, yet insane girl. One tries and tries to make it work, but in the end, escape is the only solution. Still, like a stalker surfing FaceBook, I found myself checking up on Boan, wondering if the fragile underpinnings had somehow been stabilized.

The College of Fine Arts was eliminated almost immediately after my departure. The final graduate from the program was a painter extraordinaire, who specialized in impressionistic scenes of vanishing American farmland, posted them on his website, associated them with John Mellencamp songs, and wrote rambling essays about the rapid depletion of natural resources.

Charlotte Webb e-mailed me to tell me that the library renovations began in the third week of the fall semester, disrupting research and bibliographic instruction, leading to a student petition demanding the work be put off until the following summer. The petition was ignored as Michael Hartley's third wife had promised a huge donation to the university if the renovation would be completed before Hartley's step-son started at Boan University. Webb had no idea if the renovation would bear Hartley's name.

Within a year, Boan's website, still incredibly difficult to navigate, revealed that the university now offered eight delivery options to meet the needs of students. Apparently, an online self-paced independent study was developed to serve military personnel all over the world; in addition, high school students could now get a jump on their college education by enrolling in "Secondary Education Accelerated Placement" (SEAP) courses. They were being offered in a weekend format, ensuring almost entirely that parents didn't have to interact with their gifted children.

Boan did eventually start a football program. The University of Michigan scheduled them in their inaugural year, and the Sturgeons trip to the Big House resulted in a thorough 77-0 thrashing. The team won one game the first three years it fielded a football team.

Peter Taylor's daughter sued the university over the removal of his name from the field house. Sherman Head reportedly helped finance the university's legal costs, and eventually the case was settled out of court, with Boan allegedly paying Taylor's daughter over a million dollars in settlement costs.

As for Jennifer Riley, she did eventually get appointed as provost. I sent her a postcard with rattlesnakes on it, and a brief note written on the back: "Congratulations. Watch out for the snakes." I heard nothing from her for a year, until one day I found a postcard in my mailbox. Nothing had been written on the blank side, but the front showed a still from an old Three Stooges movie—Curly has a fork sticking out of his eye.

CPSIA information can be obtained
at www.ICGtesting.com
Printed in the USA
LVOW03s0506210717
542091LV00003B/217/P